BY THE LIGHT OF DEAD STARS

ANDREW VAN WEY

BY THE LIGHT OF DEAD STARS

BEYOND THE LOST COAST

BOOK ONE

ANDREW VAN WEY

By the Light of Dead Stars is a work of fiction. The characters, incidents, and dialogue are products of the author's warped imagination and should obviously not be construed as real. Any resemblance to actual events or persons, living or dead, is entirely coincidental. Furthermore, any resemblance to actual events should be documented for science.

Cover Design: Damonza | Damonza.com
Interior Images: Deposit Photo | Depositphoto.com
Editing: Bodie Dykstra | Bdediting.com
ISBN-13: 978-1-956050-06-6 (hardcover)
ISBN-13: 978-1-956050-07-3 (paperback)

V.12.17.22

Visit the author online: andrewvanwey.com

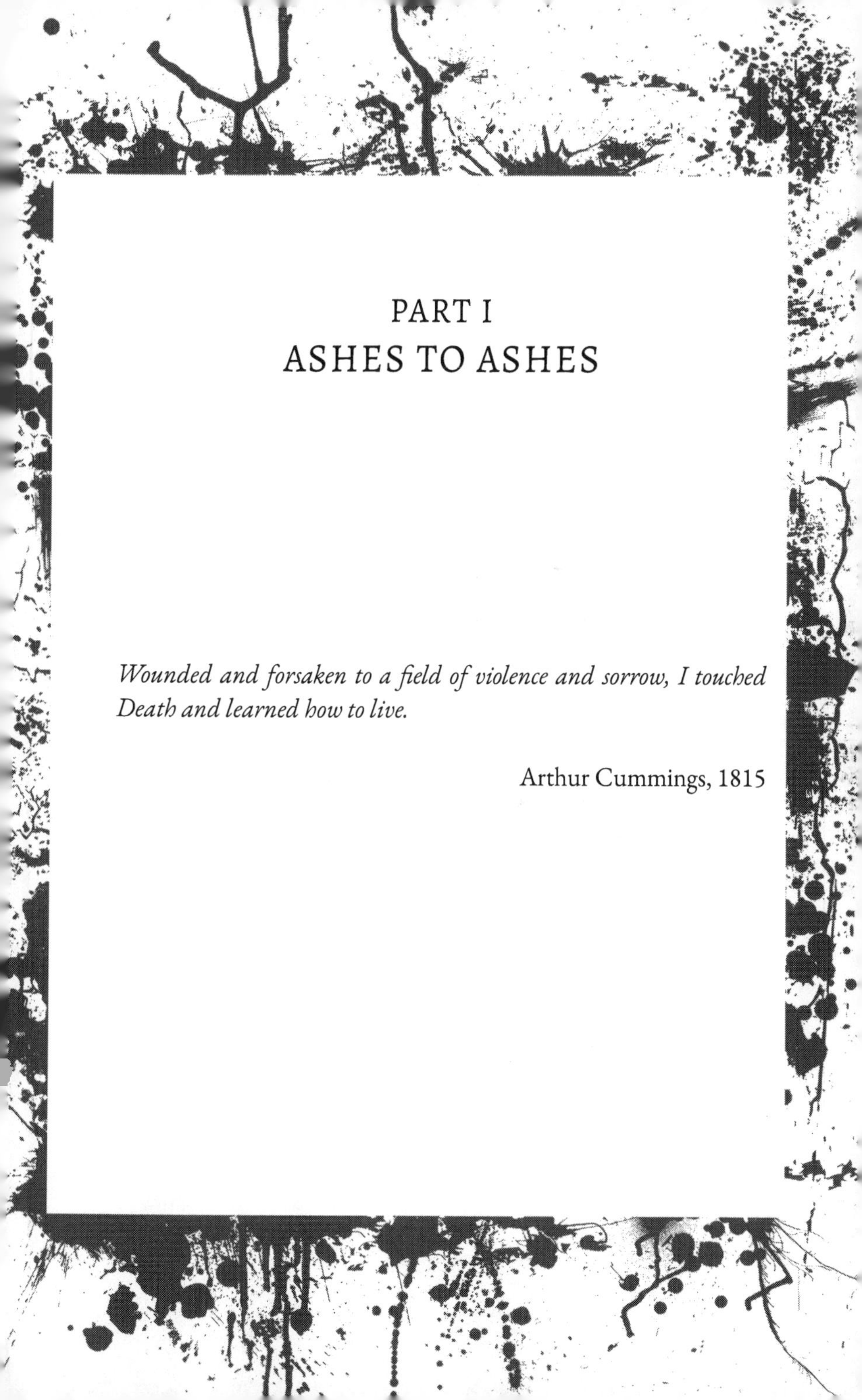

PART I
ASHES TO ASHES

Wounded and forsaken to a field of violence and sorrow, I touched Death and learned how to live.

Arthur Cummings, 1815

CHAPTER ONE

As she opened her eyes, the first thing thirteen-year-old Zelda Ruiz noticed was the blood running up her arm. Up, she realized, because she was hanging upside down.

Something long and flat chewed into the skin of her neck and compressed her chest. A seat belt. With numb focus, she traced the nylon shadow before her. A backpack. She shoved it aside.

Then she noticed the smoke.

Milky tendrils burped from the car's vents and fogged the air. An acrid tang of melting plastic coated her tongue. With a sharp tug and a quick press, she released the seat belt. She collapsed against the camping supplies lining the ceiling.

Ceiling. Seat belt. Upside down.

Something terrible had happened.

"Mom? Dad?" Crawling, Zelda pushed aside the folded tent and the pegs. Hadn't those been in the very back? She reached past a cooler dripping with frigid water. "Mom? Dad? What happened?"

Sharp teeth bit into her palm. That was glass mixed in with the water, she realized. She plucked the bloody shard from her skin as fresh memories assaulted her.

The squeal of the tires as she looked up from her phone.

The swerve of the car that rocked her body to the left.

Then the buckling crack as the guardrail gave way to a terrible weightlessness and a black splice in her mind.

Now here she was, crawling through the remnants of the family vacation. Pretzels bought for the drive home. Rubber fishing boots her dad wore in the river. Her mother's paperback novel, soaked and sitting in...

Blood. Oh, God. Blood speckled the pages.

"Zelda, honey, can you hear me?" her mother murmured from beyond a pile of sleeping bags.

"Yeah, Mom, are you okay?"

"I'm not sure. I... I think my legs are broken."

"Dad? Are you there? Dad? You need to help Mom."

Zelda could hear the desperate confusion in her own voice. One minute they'd been driving home, and the next they were...

Where?

A deep creak as metal moaned from below, followed by the clatter of rocks against the side of the car. The pooling water dripped to the left as everything shifted.

The car was starting to slide.

"Zelda, sweetie, can you hear me?" Her dad grunted from beyond a pile of pillows and duffel bags. "I need you to do something. Can you focus?"

"I'm... I can't get to you."

"Don't worry about me. I need you to climb out the window, to your right. Can you squeeze through?"

"I... I don't know. It's really tight."

"Try for me, honey."

Zelda inched her way to the side, untangling her leg from a blanket. She twisted and crawled through a dusty tunnel. Something scraped her knees. The ceiling, she realized. It was caved in here. A jagged ruin of rocks and glass. The whole window had collapsed.

"It's too small," she said. "I think I'm stuck."

The sharp angles of the buckled metal. The glass in the dim light. She could hear the fear in her voice, that childish squeak she hated and tried to suppress.

"Zelda, your right. Your *other* right." Her father's hand pushed a backpack aside, filling the rear with dappled light.

What she saw through the shattered windshield knotted her gut.

The family SUV lay wrecked and overturned against a bent copse of trees, trunks barely clutching the dry earth. Rocks and pebbles tumbled past scraggy weeds. Even the slope held a liquidity, as if it might all come loose and slide at any second.

A mountain. They were on the side of a fucking mountain.

"Guys, I don't think we should move. I think—"

The car groaned and shuddered. Sleeping bags battered her face and blocked her view. Somewhere, in the dark beyond, her mother cried out.

"Zelda, you need to listen to me," her father said. "Crawl to your right, okay? The window's broken. I can see it from here. You'll have to squeeze, but you can do it, okay? Go now."

"Dad—"

"Now, Zelda! Go!"

Zelda was scrawny for her age, all elbows and knees, and often gangly and awkward. But in this moment, her body moved swiftly, confidently, hands pushing aside camping gear and shoulders squeezing through the narrow gaps. Glass chewed her fingers, her arm. Something warm slid down her calf. She looked back to see her mother's hand touching her ankle. A beam of smoky light fell on her face, one eye swollen closed.

"You're the protector, Zelda," she whispered. "You need to stay strong for us."

A deep crunch and the car buckled and slid. The shaft of smoky light vanished as the pile collapsed and a new path opened up. The shattered window lay mere inches away.

"Go, sweetie," her mother called out. "Go fast!"

Twisting. Turning. Tunneling her way through the ruins. She squeezed out the window and fell onto the dusty slope of the mountain. High above, guardrails reached out in twisted fingers of metal and broken wood. Cars pulled to the side of the road and people looked over the edge. Someone was shouting and tying a rope. She could see thin waterfalls and drought-ridden trees and the bald, rocky peaks of the Sierra Nevada mountains.

She turned to the ruined SUV, where a tire still spun uselessly against the azure sky. Sliding on the rocks, Zelda stumbled back to her mother's side window. If she could break it... If she could just reach in and pull her out. Yes, then she could save them.

She found a sharp rock and raised it, remembering something a camp counselor once said: "To break a car window, you aim for the edges."

She swung.

And she missed.

Because the vehicle shifted.

It began as a slide and a turn, a thousand stones releasing their grip between the steep slope and the broken metal. Crunching, the rocks slid from the far side. With a shudder and a plume of dust, the SUV tilted. Her mother's hand pressed against the glass, and the car's darkness swallowed her face.

Then the dry trees and the parched earth could no longer hold it. The car rolled over and gained speed, tumbling down the cliff, end over end.

Zelda stared in numb horror as it all came apart: the windows and the doors, the chassis and the tires. With crackling echoes, all that she knew and loved lay scattered and burning, cruelly strewn across the jagged valley below.

She wasn't sure if she cried or if she screamed out their names. She only knew that her hand was still outstretched, still reaching for her mother when the first rescuers arrived.

CHAPTER TWO

There really was no place like Madrid in the late spring. The rain-scoured plazas. The narrow, cobbled streets all sleek and glistening. The drizzling water from the balconies and the grateful plants. Most of all, Mark Fitzsimmons loved the midnight walk home as the wine warmed his blood and softened his thoughts.

He did not love the four floors of creaky stairs he had to tiptoe up. Nor the old moaning door that betrayed his quiet entry to his apartment. Or the lock that he fumbled with, never sure whether he needed to turn it once or twice to the right.

He was almost inside when he heard the other door opening, and warm light fell upon his back. He smelled his neighbor's perfume and closed his eyes.

"Hey, you're getting home late."

Rosalía Bellano was a trilingual Spaniard with two master's degrees and a habit of switching careers every few years. Nearing forty, she exuded a calm poise that Mark found both attractive and intimidating; she knew what she wanted and rarely took no for an answer.

Tonight, he sensed, it would be a bottle of wine and a romp in the sack. Or perhaps just a conversation on the balcony, the wind tussling her hair as they watched the plaza below.

"It's midnight," he said. "Still early for Spain."

"Yes, this is true." Her soft gaze settled on his wine-flushed cheeks. "I thought you weren't drinking tonight."

He considered lying but doubted he could sell it. After eighteen months of this on-off relationship, she knew most of his tells. "Well, I didn't intend to," he said, "but Oleksi bought a few bottles and you know how it goes."

"Yes, a toast to everything. I think the only reason he hosts that book club is to hear himself talk."

"And to have people to drink with."

"You're kind to indulge him." She brushed something from his shoulder.

Despite being a few years older, he often felt like her junior. Sometimes they were friends, and sometimes they were lovers. Sometimes she got angry and didn't speak to him for a week.

Mostly, he sensed he was an emotional crutch. A face to complain to about her sexist boss, her spoiled sisters, and her parents when they asked why she hadn't gotten married, settled down, and given them grandkids.

"Have you eaten? I'm... *como se dice*? Trying some new *buñuelo* recipes." She motioned inside her apartment, where the scent of fried dough filled the air. "Maybe you could tell me which is your favorite."

She blinked those soft brown eyes. For a moment, he saw the rest of the night before him: the food and the wine, the tangled bedsheets. It'd be sunrise before they finally slept.

"I'm sorry," he said, "but I've got class in the morning."

She nodded. "*No te preocupes.* It's okay, *Professor*. I understand."

He winced. Despite the title on his shared office at the local university, he was far short of any chance at tenure. At forty-three, he was just a glorified ESL teacher with a focus on business English and a contract up for renewal in a few months.

Which was why he had to be sharp in the morning. His workshop was under observation.

"Ah, but here's an idea." A mischievous smirk tugged at her lips. "I'll bring you some *buñuelos*, one of each. *Mañana*, you tell me your favorite."

He could feel the wine softening his resolve.

"Yeah, sure. That sounds great."

"*Quince minutos*. I'll knock."

He closed the door, knowing that she would do more than knock. She'd arrive with two glasses and an alcohol she insisted paired well with the *buñuelos*. And he'd let her in because...

Because you're scared of being alone.

Because you can't remember the last time you fell asleep sober.

He brushed off the thoughts and tidied up his apartment. If this was to be their evening, he should present a good face. He dropped his phone on the charger and grabbed a beer from the fridge.

Then he saw the woman in his tub.

The bathroom lights were off, but her nude form was unmistakable. Bare shoulders lay beneath a curtain of dark hair. Her back curved as she leaned forward, shivering bumps where her spine met the steaming water.

Mark froze, unsure of who she was and what to do.

The Chinese dragon tattoo wound its way up the curve of her left shoulder, ending in a jagged mouth that had faded over nearly two decades. That tattoo... She was seventeen when she got it. Their mother had been furious.

That was his sister here in his bathtub.

And he was wrong about the water; it wasn't steaming.

She was.

"Maya?" He hesitated at the door, studying her form in the

dark water. Ash coated the surface, a whole murky blanket. "Maya, what are you doing here?"

She stared straight ahead, yet her eyes turned sidelong, zeroing in on him. Cinders glinted in her pupils, little smoldering coals of amber and orange.

"Mark, she needs you." Her voice was dry and gravelly, the words leaving her lips in dusty wisps. "She's alone. She needs a lighthouse for the storm that she's calling."

And her skin...

Pebbles of glass twinkled and mottled her flesh.

"Maya, it's okay. Whatever it is, I'll... Let me just get you a robe."

She stirred in the tub, knees sinking beneath the ash. "It's strange... how warm this sea is. But you listen to me, Mark. Please listen. I've seen it *all*. Her heart is an open wound, and they'll grow maggots inside. Don't let them put maggots in her heart."

"In whose?"

She opened her mouth, but no words came forth. Only the grinding moan of rocks and metal thrashing against each other.

Mark found himself stumbling five paces back, hands squeezed to his chest as an oily tinge burned his throat. He was sober, more sober than he'd been in months. And scared.

Scared for his sanity, yes, but mostly scared for his sister, Maya, whom he last saw two Christmases ago with her family, some eight thousand miles away.

"Don't let them grow maggots in her heart."

Then she dipped forward into the bathwater. Her head and hair disappeared, followed by her shoulders. Her back was the last to descend, the shivering bumps of her spine and gray skin slipping into the murky depths.

Mark stood, frozen, searching the tub for signs of movement. No ripples or bubbles. No emergence of hair. Just dark water and that layer of ash, now settling flat.

Had something happened back home that made her fly all the

way out to Spain? Was this some sort of mental breakdown? And what was that grinding moan that left her throat?

Like the crunching of metal and glass.

Whatever her reasons, this was his baby sister and she needed his help. He pushed past his fear and rolled up his sleeves. He reached into the water.

His fingers brushed against the bottom of the tub.

He tried again and again, feeling for her shoulders, her limbs, anything amid the dark waters. He only found the stopper. The drain burbled and slurped while the waterline sank.

A knock at the door boomed through the apartment. Rosalía, yes, she'd know what to do. In ten quick paces, he was at the door, Rosalía standing there with her tray of *buñuelos* and a half-empty bottle of Chinchón.

"Hey, something weird just happened. My sister, she was..."

Her mischievous smile faded when she saw his damp, dirty hands. "What is that?"

He pulled her to the bathroom so she could see the water level sinking, sinking, and then... nothing. Just a layer of muck at the bottom of the tub, speckled with torn plastic and pebbled glass.

"Mark, what's going on? Was that in your pipes?"

"I don't know how to explain it," he said. "But I need to call Maya."

He was halfway to his phone charger when it rang. He didn't recognize the number, but he knew the California area code. His mouth went pasty as he answered.

"Hello?"

"Mark? Is this Mark Fitzsimmons?"

"Speaking."

That voice. It held the same accent that sometimes came out when his brother-in-law spoke quickly.

No, he thought. No, not Maya and J.C.

"This is Alejandro, Juan Carlos's brother. We met at the wedding and a few Christmases ago."

Mark remembered Alejandro, a customs broker out of El Paso. They'd gotten drunk together and laughed about their accents. Him, a *norteño* with a Texas twang, and Mark, a gringo with a Castilian lisp. They'd rented a scary movie from the nineties, a real gory one, and had gotten in trouble for letting Zelda stay up and watch it with them.

But how did he get this number? And why was he calling?

A lighthouse for the storm.

Maggots in her heart.

"Mark, this is really hard for me to say." Alejandro's voice shook. "I'm so sorry to tell you this, but..."

But Mark knew. He knew what was coming.

He'd known it for ten minutes.

CHAPTER THREE

The funeral was tasteful, modest, and touching; it captured their spirits.

At least, that was what everyone kept telling Zelda.

There were rocks from the shore of Lake Merriam, where her parents met while camped at neighboring sites. There were the shoes from when they hiked the Inca Trail, pregnant with her. There was a notarized article of incorporation from when her dad founded Snowstorm Interactive. Beside it lay the contract when he hired employee number five: his wife.

A great many things lay here upon the stone altar at the front of the chapel. Postcards and letters her mom wrote in college. An old baseball mitt placed by a weeping man who coached her father in high school. A poem read by a woman with lavender hair. A pair of yellowed PlayStation controllers beside tickets to the Blue Man Group at the Astor Place Theatre, 1993.

Zelda did the math in her head. Juan Carlos would have been her age when he'd seen the performance.

It was odd to think of her father as a teenager.

She never had.

The only thing missing was their bodies.

Zelda shifted in the pew. She had a distant memory of the funeral director explaining her parents' will had stipulated cremation and no coffins. Just a companion urn with their ashes intermingled. The entire week had gone by in a blur.

"Hey, Zelda."

Uncle Mark sank into the empty pew in front of her. His shaggy hair hung to his shoulders and his suit was a little too loose, reminding her of a kid playing dress-up. He flashed a soft smile beneath kind, wounded eyes.

"So, how're you holding up? You doing okay?"

She hated that question. People expected her to break down, to carry tissues, to cry, which she hadn't and refused to do. She pulled up her hoodie and shifted in the pew, the groan of wood echoing through the quiet chapel.

"Yeah, I'm fine."

Uncle Mark glanced back at the next room. She hoped he would leave and rejoin the memorial reception out there. She just wanted to be left alone in here.

Alone with her parents.

"Sorry, that was a pretty stupid question, wasn't it? I'm really bad at these things."

She flicked her smartphone on and off, on and off.

"Do you remember my mom?" he asked. "Your grandmother?"

After a quiet beat, she said, "Barely."

"You would've been, what, three or four when she passed? She was wonderful. Real outgoing, life of the party, just... warm, you know? And then cancer. Boom, gone in a few weeks. Anyway, everyone kept asking if I was okay. It's like, how are you supposed to answer? You say yes, and no one believes you. You say no, and they try to comfort you like you're going to break, and that's just... weird."

She smelled alcohol on his breath, whiskey perhaps. She wondered where he got it. Her grandparents on her dad's side were

Mexican Catholic and they'd insisted the reception be dry, classy, and somber.

Which was why she was here, in the chapel, and not out there in the hall, listening to another story about her amazing father, who built a company, or her passionate mother, whose eyes she inherited.

She just wanted to put the whole day behind her.

She just wanted it all to be over.

She clenched her toes and swung her legs. Maybe the silence would drive Uncle Mark away. She liked him, but she liked solitude more.

"Anyway, at the memorial, your mom and I were sitting here. Not *here* here, but at a different funeral home, watching people sobbing their eyes out. Then it hit us. It wasn't how my mom wanted to be remembered, you know? Bunch of people crying into their Diet Cokes. So your mom and I, we took her ashes and we split. A year or so later, we had our own memorial. Scattered her ashes at the playground she took us to as a kid."

Zelda's eyes narrowed. "I can't just, like, ghost with their ashes."

"No, no no no, that's not what I meant. What I'm saying is..." She followed his gaze back to the door and the adjoining reception. "Zelda, you do you, okay? Whatever you need to get through this, your mom would understand. They both would."

Zelda swiped another text message of condolence off her phone and waited for Uncle Mark to get the hint. Why did adults linger too long?

"If you need anything... Well, I guess that's cliche too, right?"

He stood up and awkwardly shuffled away, then paused by the chapel door. Plucking something from his jacket, he returned and placed it upon the altar, among all the other tributes to a pair of lives now come to an end.

Then he left.

Zelda sat, listening to the distant hum of conversations, the clink of plates and glasses, the polite laughter and occasional tears. She wandered up to the front of the chapel.

It was a strange thing, this urn sitting here on the altar. It didn't seem right that her parents could be reduced to something that fit in a ceramic vase. It didn't seem final. A part of her was still at that canyon, wrapped in a blanket, waiting for the paramedics and rescue workers to ascend on their ropes and tell her it was okay, her parents were fine, they'd be coming up any moment.

She reached out and touched the lid of the urn. It was cold. So cold she recoiled. No, it wasn't right for her parents. They had always loved the warm sun, the outdoors, and whimsical objects. Two years ago, her mother had helped her build a Little Free Library for the front of their house. They had placed books and canned goods inside it, secretly watching as neighbors stopped by. They had speculated about the most popular books and wondered what snacks a passerby might enjoy.

And then the teenage years had started.

They talked less. Their tastes diverged. Zelda stopped enjoying her mother's constant presence, the volunteering at school, the nightly talks before bed. Why had everything that once felt warm and good taken on a sour taste?

Zelda traced the urn's lid. What did it look like inside? This couldn't be her parents, could it? She had to be sure. She held the base with her left hand and carefully tried lifting the top.

It didn't open.

She tried again, pulling harder. Still nothing. Perhaps it was meant to be closed, sealed forever. But that didn't make sense. How would they scatter ashes when she was ready?

"Not yet, sweetie..."

The whisper came from over her left shoulder, a warm breath caressing her ear and rustling her hair. She spun as a gasp flew past her lips. "Mom?"

There was just the empty reception hall.

Then she heard the clink of ceramic and stone.

She wasn't sure if she had bumped the urn as she turned or if her nervous fingers hadn't fully returned it to the altar. It didn't matter.

The urn teetered on the edge and then fell. She reached out a second too late.

A heavy *crunch* filled the quiet chapel. The urn didn't break on the first of the marbled steps, nor on the second.

On the third step, it simply shattered. A curl of amber dust rose as the shards rocked and spun and came to a stop amid a starburst of ash.

Zelda froze mid-step, one shoe at the altar, the other ash-spattered beside her parents' cracked urn. Her arms hung suspended outward. She didn't know what else to do with her hands.

And that was when her grandparents and her Uncle Alejandro looked in from the reception hall. Grandmother Ruiz—her *abuela* —with her black veil and tear-riddled cheeks.

Grandmother Ruiz, now shrieking.

CHAPTER FOUR

Mark had only met Mr. and Mrs. Ruiz a few times over the years. He sensed they never cared for him. They were formal and distant, their questions like cold fingers probing for status and wealth. Which university did he teach at and how was it ranked? Why wasn't he married? What was it that he really did out in Spain?

He was surprised to find Mr. and Mrs. Ruiz waiting outside the probate attorney's office on Tuesday. Along with their son, Alejandro, who could hardly meet his eyes.

Fifteen minutes later, Mark understood why.

The three attorneys sat inside a conference room with a view of the San Francisco Bay. Mr. Hoffman, the estate attorney, whom Mark had met at the memorial. Mr. Shariz, the probate attorney, whose name was one of several that formed the signage downstairs. Ms. Chou, who sat closest to the Ruizes and drilled Mark with a dark stare.

"Your sister- and brother-in-law are leaving behind a rather sizable estate," Mr. Shariz said, and slid a stack of papers across the polished black table. "I'm not sure how much they told you, but it's complicated, as these things often are."

Mark leafed through a few pages. He'd never seen a will before. He knew he should have one himself, now that he owned an apartment. And yet, he'd kept putting it off, reasoning he'd do it next year, next tax season, or whenever he moved back to the U.S.

If he ever would.

And besides, he was only forty-three. That was still young, wasn't it?

Yet here it sat, the last will and testament of Maya Fitzsimmons-Ruiz, thirty-nine, and Juan Carlos Ruiz, forty-two. They'd always had their act together.

"There's a lot to unpack," the probate attorney continued. "We can go over the broad strokes, but you'll want to have your counsel drill down to the specifics."

"My counsel?" Mark asked. "Isn't that what you are?"

The probate attorney cleared his throat and glanced at Mr. and Mrs. Ruiz. Alejandro muttered something, stood up, and left the room. There seemed to be a charge forming in the air, like the moments before a thunderstorm.

Or bad news.

"Mark, may I call you Mark?" This was Ms. Chou now, removing her glasses and leaning against the black table. "Zelda's grandparents have raised some... concerns with the will. Your sister, it seems, and Juan Carlos, they made some changes in the past year. Sizable changes."

"There's nothing irregular about updating a will, Cynthia," Mr. Hoffman said. His voice was deep and his eyes sharp. He reminded Mark of a guard dog in a window. Friendly yet always alert.

"Of course not, *Frank*," Ms. Chou said, with salt in her words. "Nevertheless, my clients would like to point out that certain decisions may not be in the best interest of the estate."

"Maya and Juan Carlos's estate," Mr. Hoffman said. "Not the Ruizes'. Your clients weren't even supposed to see the will until this reading."

Ms. Chou sighed. "This isn't the movies, Frank. There's no legal requirement for a reading. If you have a problem, take it up with the Superior Court. They provided the copy, as they were obligated to do."

"An *early* copy. Convenient, isn't it?"

"There's hardly anything convenient about this," Ms. Chou said. "Especially for my clients, who have flown thousands of miles on their granddaughter's behalf and are still mourning."

"Maya and Juan Carlos were quite generous to your clients—"

"They feel otherwise. Especially in regard to guardianship."

It was all happening so fast, and Mark didn't understand it. Four days ago, he'd just stepped off the plane. Hell, he was still jet-lagged and a little hung over. And now these people were speaking around him. That was the thing about living abroad for so long. Your mother tongue didn't vanish, but it sometimes slowed down.

"I'm sorry," Mark said. "I'm confused about what's going on."

"Of course he's confused. What else is new?" That was Mrs. Ruiz, her eyes on her lap and her words aimed somewhere under the table.

Mr. Ruiz gave her hand a squeeze and said, "He's a stranger to them—to our granddaughter—and we're supposed to accept that? No. No no no. This isn't fair."

Mark turned to them, actually seeing them now. The hardness in their eyes. Their distant demeanor all morning.

What the hell was going on?

"Fair is subjective, Mr. Ruiz." Mr. Hoffman leaned in. "And, with regard to the will, irrelevant. What is relevant are the wishes of the deceased."

"A will that was recently changed," Ms. Chou said. "There's precedent to contest it."

"And plenty to uphold it," Mr. Shariz said, adding, "When it comes to family custody."

"Precedent nonetheless. It's on this basis that my clients are contesting it, not on Mr. Fitzsimmons's relationship with the decedents and their daughter." She turned those cold eyes on Mark. "Or lack thereof."

Custody?

Relationships?

The chair squeaked as Mark leaned forward and rubbed his temples. He was twenty-three again, his company's legal team explaining that they were broke. That their office equipment needed to be liquidated to pay salaries. That the investors were furious and Mark might even be held responsible if he didn't step down.

And now, twenty years later, he was hearing an old song from new lips.

"All of you just... shut up for a moment," he said. "What's in the will?"

FIFTEEN MINUTES LATER, MARK TOOK A DEEP BREATH BY a koi pond among the back gardens of Hoffman, Shariz, and Bellingham, LLP. The bay breeze suffused the air, cool and salty. High above, crows circled.

"Your sister- and brother-in-law felt that Zelda had a strong bond with you," Mr. Hoffman said. "And that it would be in her best interests for you to have guardianship, should you wish."

Mark scoffed. "I don't know why they thought that. I've barely been a part of her life. Of any of theirs."

"Clearly, Mr. and Mrs. Ruiz agree. Which is why they're contesting the will. And why they are threatening to sue for custody, should you accept guardianship."

Mark shook his head. He'd had a dog once, a mutt some expat had abandoned. He'd kept her for three years until she passed away in her sleep. He was never quite sure if he was a good owner or not.

But his niece? A thirteen-year-old girl?

"Jesus." He watched the koi sliding through the dark waters. "What does Zelda want?"

"Zelda?" For a moment, it looked like Mr. Hoffman was on the verge of smiling. "I'm afraid what she wants is immaterial. California courts hold that a minor may express preference after fourteen, but there's no mandate. Certainly none a judge is obligated to follow."

"Okay, but has anyone asked her? I mean, if she wants to go to Texas with the Ruizes, why shouldn't she?"

"She very well may. However, Juan Carlos and Maya felt her best interests were elsewhere."

"Well, that's certainly not me. I don't..."

"You don't what, Mr. Fitzsimmons?"

I don't live here, he thought.

I don't know a thing about kids.

Most of all, *I don't have my shit together.* Even the Ruizes could see that.

"I don't know," he said. "I'll have to think about it. I mean... How would that even work? I live in Madrid. My apartment, my job, my whole life is in Spain."

"Until custody is determined, I'm afraid that life would have to wait. Ms. Chou is smart. She's already petitioned for travel restrictions. They feel that Zelda shouldn't travel until the matter is settled."

"Unless they're the ones that take her."

Mr. Hoffman nodded. "These disputes are rarely honorable. You have to understand, Zelda's inheritance is... sizable. Her parents anticipated such a struggle."

"But that's her money. She gets to choose where it goes."

"Yes, in a perfect world, that's how it works. But this is California. Half the child actors have empty bank accounts while their parents drive Bentleys. Heck, my daughter got her first job as a waitress, and the owner tried to pocket her tips. I had to send him a cease and desist."

Mark's head spun. From what he'd read of the will, he was to receive the deed to their house in Alder Glen, an affluent community near where he'd grown up. The thought of returning tightened his stomach and tensed his back. This was a landscape of failures and ghosts.

"I can't do this," he said. "My job's in Madrid. I have a girlfriend." Or whatever Rosalía was, he thought. "I don't even like the Bay Area."

"No one likes the Bay Area," Mr. Hoffman said. "Not anymore. But I understand your concerns. I'll see what I can do."

They shook hands, there at the edge of the koi pond. Then Mr. Hoffman reached into his jacket and pulled out an envelope.

"Almost forgot. Here's the key to the house. Just don't sell the furniture or list it on Zillow until the paperwork is done, okay? Mr. Shariz will be stopping by to keep an eye on things. I'm sure Ms. Chou will as well."

Mark studied the keys in the envelope. These should be Zelda's. It didn't feel right that they were in his hands now. "Aren't the Ruizes staying there?"

"I'm told that they are."

"So what do I do?"

"That's up to you, Mr. Fitzsimmons. But if someone was suing me, well... I'd probably dump their luggage on the curb."

And he gave Mark a wink.

CHAPTER FIVE

Zelda watched from her bedroom window as her grandparents climbed into the rental Mercedes and Uncle Alejandro drove them away. They didn't even look back at the house.

For the past half hour, she'd listened in on the argument downstairs. Whenever adults tried to whisper, they just ended up talking louder.

First, it was something about Uncle Mark, the house, and a hotel he offered to stay at. They accused him of being duplicitous and butting into their lives.

Next, it was about Zelda and Texas. They accused her of needing structure and discipline and God in her life.

Then it turned to her parents' wishes and vague threats of using the law to solve some disagreement. She'd never trusted her grandmother. She'd even caught her stealing silverware once.

Finally, her grandfather raised his voice, accusing Uncle Mark of being the problem, and then Alejandro insisted they only speak through an attorney. Next thing she knew, Uncle Mark was apologizing, her grandparents were packing, and no one seemed to be saying the same thing.

Was this how some families grieved? By tearing into each other?

Alone in the driveway now, Uncle Mark pulled an old backpack from the passenger seat of his rented sedan. He straightened a loose fencepost on his way in.

She sat back down at her desk and resumed her science homework. Her teachers had been understanding and their condolences plentiful. Still, she had work to catch up on, something to bury herself in and help her forget.

That her parents were no longer just down the hall.

That her mom wasn't jogging on the treadmill downstairs.

That her dad would never stop by her bedroom again, asking how her day was.

Ten minutes into a video explaining mitosis and meiosis, her phone chirped. She grabbed it, recognizing the alert. She swiped the notification, launching *Critical Mass*.

The game was the latest flagship title from her father's company, Snowstorm Interactive. She was one of the lucky thousands invited to the closed beta test before it released in another six months.

The game displayed a map of the neighborhood, rendered onscreen as a stylized, cell-shaded landscape. Instead of suburban houses, there were English cottages. Instead of lawns, there were fields full of cartoon crops and strange vegetables. Trees smiled and clouds glared with ominous eyes. Planes, UFOs, and the occasional tentacled dragon filled a lavender sky. The game's design was both whimsical and surreal, fantastical and futuristic, contemporary and retro.

It was already number one in the App Store.

A red light pulsed on the map, indicating an upcoming attack. She tapped the screen, scrolling past her neighborhood until the red darkened to deep plum and the pulse became a solid circle. There, at nearby Greer Park, was the site of the impending invasion.

A level 272 Cyber Minotaur named Hendrix was spawning.

She double-tapped the screen, locating other live players.

Blaze Crash, a level 44 Laser Paladin four blocks away.

HockeyMom420, a level 87 Sunwalker, a little closer.

And xXxMau'DibxXx, a level 141 Shadow Rogue, indicating that he was on the way to the park and Looking For Group.

It was going to be a slaughter.

Maybe they'd get lucky and wound the monster, but they'd lose more experience than they'd gain. Death wasn't permanent in *Critical Mass*, but it cost your character some gear and ten percent of their levels. These players simply didn't have the skills or loadout to take down a legendary rare spawn, let alone a Cyber Minotaur.

But maybe she did.

"Zelda?" There was a knock at her bedroom door. "Hey, hope I'm not bothering you."

She closed her laptop, stuffed her phone in her pocket, and opened the door. Uncle Mark stood there, awkwardly filling the hall. One hand found its way to the back of his neck. The other went into his pocket.

"Listen, I was hoping we could chat for a moment."

"Actually, I've got something I need to do," she said.

"Oh." He looked at his shoes as if disappointed. "Can it wait?"

"It's, like, pretty time sensitive. Urgent, really."

They both hesitated, him in the hallway and her at her door and wanting to get past.

"Oh, like... *female* things?"

"What?"

For a half blink, his eyes seemed to peel themselves until they were white as an onion. "Never mind, I didn't mean it," he stammered. "I mean, I didn't mean what you probably think that I meant."

He took a step back, clearing a way to the bathroom. But she wasn't headed there. She grabbed her skateboard, took a right at the stairs, and followed them down to the front door. She could feel the cringe coming off Uncle Mark. Maybe it was right what her grandmother said: he was a loser.

Or maybe some adults just never grew into their skin.

His phone vibrated. "Okay, well, maybe we can talk when you get back or—"

She shouted sure, that sounded good, but the wind slammed the front door and cut off her words. The sidewalk rattled beneath her feet as her skateboard hit concrete.

Zelda had lived in Alder Glen for all of her thirteen years, yet it never quite felt like home. Her neighbors were a rotating parade of strangers that bought houses and sold them a few years later for a profit. Her friends came and went. The town occupied a nexus of Silicon Valley startups and multinational companies, school busses competing with tech busses. Her classmates were stressed, overworked, their time managed down to the hour.

Last summer, one of her best friends moved to Reno. This spring, her other best friend returned to Ohio. Both their homes were now what her father called ghost houses, owned by an investment company in Singapore, kept empty and dark yet somehow making money. It was all confusing.

But Alder Glen was safe, its streets smooth and well maintained. This was important as she skateboarded down Washington Lane. A rough street wasn't a fun ride.

She tapped her phone and double-checked *Critical Mass*. There was her character, gliding down the colorful streets in real time. She activated a battle shield and swapped in a few consumables for the fight. She glanced up, swerving her skateboard around a blue Tesla that rolled through a stop sign and had the audacity to honk.

She gave the driver the middle finger.

Dragging her foot, she came to a stop at the park. She refreshed the app. Sure enough, the Cyber Minotaur was still here, a thing of horns and metal skin, a sickle and barbed chain in its hands, twin rocket launchers mounted to its back.

This fight called for some strategy.

She spotted a circle of redwoods at the edge of the park where a small group had gathered. They held their phones up to the empty grove. Some tapped on their screen as if taking photos. Others swiped and stepped back. A few boomers simply watched, eyes scrunched, wondering what these strangers were all looking at through the screens.

"Dude, somebody toss me a heal," said a bearded guy in his twenties. "I can't tank this demon much longer."

"You're not tanking him at all." A tattooed woman in her mid-thirties frantically tapped her phone. "You're taking hits like wet tissue. But okay, heal incoming. You get that?"

"Anyone able to disarm him?" asked an Asian man whose girlfriend looked on with yawning boredom. "That sickle has insane reach. I can't even get close."

"I got it," Zelda said.

She had to pan her phone up and down just to fit the Cyber Minotaur on the screen. Where the redwoods stood in real life, the game world rendered them into stylized spikes, branches twisted and dripping neon moss. The ground was a grid of pastel shading, something her dad had said would be fixed in the coming months.

Her dad...

This was the first time she'd played *Critical Mass* since that weekend. Since the argument and the fight. Since everything went to shit.

"Who's the level 250?" Bearded Guy asked, turning his phone toward Zelda. "Holy shit, you're Neo-Ronin. Are those the Twin Blades of Spite?"

Zelda knew what they were seeing on their phones. A female samurai, clad in upgraded scrap armor, two wings made of blue light unfurling behind her. A bow with a glowing string crossed her back, while two identical katanas hung at her sides, blades burning green.

Her father had helped her level up, playing cooperatively with her through the fall and the winter. He'd taught her a few tricks, even assisted as she tracked down the Twin Blades.

But the game felt different now, sour and awkward.

She hesitated, glancing at the screen where the Cyber Minotaur launched a volley of rockets. The other players were taking damage.

"So, are you going to help us kill this thing?" the tattooed woman asked. "'Cause we could really use an assist before the whole town starts showing up."

She was right. Other players were coming now, lured by the potential for a massive payday, a boatload of experience, and some rare items. Zelda could see NoobCrusher, level 181, a block away. Closer still, HarmonLine99 broadcast an in-game message that he'd be happy to heal others. And here came HieronymusPrado, a level 46 Technomancer, already summoning robotic wolves for the fight.

"If you're just here to grief us and soak up XP, you can fuck off," the Asian man said. His girlfriend glared at Zelda.

On-screen, the ragtag battle raged on. The Cyber Minotaur swung its sickle and stomped. The players countered with melee attacks and fired ranged weapons. Every now and then, a tendril of rejuvenating blue light shot out as the healer did her best to keep the players alive.

And yet Zelda stood frozen. *Fight*, she told herself. *You've killed a Cyber Minotaur before. You know the weak spot under its armor. Just raise your phone, charge your weapons, and aim.*

She raised her phone, tried to press the button on the screen, but missed.

Her finger shook. No, she realized, not her finger but her whole hand. The phone slipped from her grasp.

She wiped leaves off the screen and raised it. Now the Cyber Minotaur's eyes glowed red, its nostrils flared, and its metal mouth drew in a deep breath. It was going to burn the other players.

For a moment, that wasn't a Jet Paladin there, on-screen,

raising his nanotech shield and hiding. That was her father, Juan Carlos.

Nor was that a Sunwalker holding up her hands and sending out beams of healing light. That was her mother, Maya.

The squeal of brakes.

The crunch of metal.

The world tilting sideways.

Flames poured from its mouth as the creature reared back. Then came a violent shudder and the pixelated fire swallowed them all.

Zelda let out a cry and dropped her phone again. No, she tossed it away.

Because of the warmth. She could feel the heat on her hand.

"Jesus, kid," the bearded man said. "Did you just buy your account or what?"

"Welp, I'm dead," the Asian guy said. "There goes twenty-two levels and an epic ring."

"Yep, I'm toast." The tattooed woman glared at Zelda. "And here come the vultures."

"Did I miss it?" asked a familiar voice. Zelda brushed off her screen and glanced at the new arrivals. HieronymusPrado, the Technomancer, was the closest. "Did you already kill it?"

"We chipped off half its health," the bearded guy said. "No thanks to her."

That was when Zelda turned and saw Uncle Mark standing there, in real life.

Where HieronymusPrado stood in the game.

CHAPTER SIX

Mark wasn't bothered that they didn't defeat the Cyber Minotaur. Or that his Technomancer got lashed with a chain and killed in three hits. Or that he lost ten percent of his levels, his credits, and several rare items. It was just a game, after all, one he wasn't very good at.

What amused him most was Zelda's expression when she learned he played *Critical Mass*. It was like she saw him in a new light.

"I didn't, like, take you for a gamer and all," she said, carrying her skateboard under her arm. "And a Technomancer. That's a hard class to play."

They were on the way home now, the spring breeze rustling the leaves and the trees. A family walking a golden doodle nodded as they passed.

"I'm more old school," he said. "Super Nintendo, PlayStation, that was my peak. But your dad was proud of this game, and I wanted to help test it."

"Sorry about the fight. I must've lagged out."

He sensed there was more to it, but he didn't push. "I'm just happy to see a legendary spawn. Six months of playing, I think the best I found was a level 60 Water Worm."

"So is it, like, popular in Europe or whatever?"

He smiled. "You kidding? It's popular everywhere. I've got this German banker buddy who offered five thousand euros for my beta account."

"Is that a lot of money?"

"For a teacher? Fuc—" He cleared his throat. "Heck yes it is."

She smirked. They turned the corner at Romero Way. These quiet streets were odd to his senses, the houses hollow, everything a little too magazine perfect.

He missed his Madrid. The loud plazas, the smoothed stones, the old wooden doors that creaked when he entered. He missed the time-worn stairs up to his apartment and how they bowed in the center from a century of footsteps. Sometimes he closed his eyes and imagined the history soaked into the walls.

"Maggots. They'll put maggots in her heart."

Stiffening, he drew in a sharp breath. "Zelda, I have to ask you something."

She glanced up at him. Those eyes... No thirteen-year-old's eyes should look so battle-scarred and hardened. And yet they were an echo of his sister as well. Maya had always been an old soul.

"So listen. This is kind of awkward, but your grandparents—"

"They want me to go to Texas with them," she said. "Yeah, I know."

"Right." He swallowed. "Okay, cool. But the thing is, it's also like—"

"My parents didn't trust them."

"Oh." He scratched his neck. "So, um, did you talk to them? Your parents, I mean."

She shrugged. "I overheard them."

"See, I guess what I'm getting at—"

"Zelda! Zelda deary, is that you?"

The voice came from the other side of a blue picket fence and a row of burgundy roses. The woman was in her sixties, dyed yellow hair jutting out from beneath a gardening hat. She held dirty sheers and wore a practiced smile that spoke of lawn parties and gossip.

She wrapped Zelda in a tight hug that she didn't return.

"What a tragedy, dear. What an awful, awful tragedy. Your parents... so young. It just breaks my heart, deary, breaks it all into pieces."

She smoothed Zelda's hair and ran a hand over her shoulders, straightening the baggy shirt that hung to one side. It struck Mark that he was watching a woman he didn't even know put her hands on his niece. And judging by Zelda's posture, she didn't care for it.

He reached between them and offered her a handshake. "Mark Fitzsimmons. Zelda's uncle."

"Yes, Maya's older brother. Why I've heard so much about you. Annie Paxton, neighbor and friend."

Zelda stepped back and readjusted her shoulder so the T-shirt hung off it. Mark listened as Mrs. Paxton offered a second wave of condolences, then a third. She filled them on her own tragedies: two divorces, a dog with leukemia, and the recent suicide of her favorite celebrity chef. She offered the phone number of her therapist, a woman who specialized in past-life regression.

Mark smiled and nodded and took down the number. They excused themselves and walked on down the street.

"Do you want this number?" he asked Zelda. "It didn't seem like you did, but no judgment."

"Just kill me now."

He laughed. "Yeah, not really my thing, either."

After a moment, she said, "Isn't it weird how, like, your past life is always someone famous? Like, 'Oh, you were Joan of Arc!' or 'Surprise! You were Cleopatra!' It's never like, 'Yeah, you were just some nobody that popped out five crotch goblins and died of cholera at nineteen. Oh, and before that, you were a cow that made a nice pair of boots.'"

"I never thought of that. But I guess I've never explored my past lives."

"Sorry. I get sort of dark sometimes." She shifted the skateboard to her left shoulder.

They were only two blocks from her house now and he needed to have a talk, *the* talk, the one his lawyer said would determine all the other talks that followed. He could feel that pit in his throat.

"So, Zelda, you know I live in Spain, right?"

She nodded.

"And, well... I haven't lived in the States since my mid-twenties. That's longer than you've been alive."

She nodded again.

"I guess what I'm trying to say is—"

"You gotta head back. I know."

He did. He had to. And yet...

Why was this so hard? She was just a girl, just a thirteen-year-old child, and not even his. He had a life back in Madrid. A decent salary, good healthcare, and plenty of time for vacation. He had drinking friends, hiking friends, and friends who dragged him to Ibiza or Greece in the summer. He had an apartment he'd finally paid off.

"She needs a lighthouse for the storm."

He cleared his throat. "The thing is, like, I don't really know you that well. But if you wanted me to, I could. What I mean is, I could stay here, you know? For a while until... Well, just *until*. Or maybe until you got sick of me. Is that... Would that be something you'd like?"

He knew what she was going to say. *No. No thanks. I'll pass.* He couldn't blame her. He didn't know a thing about kids, only that he'd never wanted them. They were messy and noisy and caused all sorts of problems.

But he liked Zelda.

She'd always been clever, mischievous, and different. Still, what could he offer her? His own father had left before he could remember; his mom always worked two or three jobs. Christ, he'd fumble the whole thing.

And besides, Zelda wasn't a kid. She was a young woman, an adolescent, with rough waters ahead. He was no role model. Hell, he barely had ten grand in the bank. In fact, when he laid it all out now, he was the worst person in the world to be a guardian, a good influence, or to raise a young woman.

"Would you want me to stick around?" he repeated. "I mean, I'll screw everything up, but... if you need someone, I'm here."

Her eyes glistened in the twilight. She switched her skateboard to her right shoulder and looked away. Her chin rose and fell. Just a quick nod, so small he thought he might have imagined it.

"Yeah, Uncle Mark," she whispered, and he could hear her voice cracking. "I'd like that a lot."

PART II
YESTERDAY'S GHOSTS

I take my leave from the battlements of the east, the circumstances of War and its glory no more interest to this Voyager than the grapeshots and cannons and the wounds of the flesh. Begone, the follies of Men and their Nations!

To seek a new land and, perchance, a new life, is meaning enough to this turncoat.

To head West, and follow the good green road, and to dream of futures to come.

The Diary of Arthur Cummings

CHAPTER SEVEN

For a few weeks, a quiet routine settled over their lives. Mark needed a car, so he brought Zelda to a used dealership to help pick out a color. She found a forest-green Subaru Outback. They drove it off the lot.

Caught up on her classwork, she returned to school in late April. Her teachers pulled her aside, whispering that they were there for her, whatever she needed.

The school counselor visited, often lingering outside the classroom before the first bell. The adults treated her like she was made of old glass.

A few of the students asked to see the scar on her left arm, a pink worm-like thing that ran from her wrist to her mid-forearm. After a few days, the gossip turned to Tracy Thompson and Mikaela Patel, who supposedly lost their virginity to some high school guys in Miami over spring break.

Zelda was glad to be out of the spotlight.

Most days, she took her time skateboarding home. The house felt different, quiet, cold. Uncle Mark did his best, cooking Spanish breakfasts and ordering delivery for dinner. He asked lots of questions.

How was her day? What did she learn? What was her favorite teacher and subject?

She didn't have the energy for long answers.

Her day was good. She learned about the Mesopotamians. Her favorite teacher was Mr. Lee because he left her alone.

And then she went up to her room, night after night.

Sometimes she felt guilty. Uncle Mark reminded her of a puppy, friendly and well-meaning but clumsy and eager. She kept him at a distance. He could change his mind, after all. He could leave at any time and he probably would. No reason to get attached.

Her grandparents stopped by twice a week. So did a rotating group of social workers and attorneys. They called the sessions strange names, like "welfare checks" or "neutral intermissions" or "family health updates."

Sometimes, her grandmother whispered to Zelda, telling her she could speak freely. If she wasn't comfortable, she could make a sign or call the social worker's phone number. Sometimes, her grandmother whispered to the attorney as they left, looking back at Zelda with disappointment in her eyes.

She felt like taffy stretched between clumsy hands and sharp teeth.

She didn't want to spy on Uncle Mark but he made it easy. The house was quiet, and he paced nervously when he spoke on the phone, sometimes beneath her bedroom window.

On some nights and mornings, he talked with his friends in Spain, making arrangements to rent out his apartment. Or to his girlfriend—someone named Rosy—who wasn't happy. After a few weeks, Zelda could hear her yelling at him. Sometimes, she found him drinking alone in the kitchen and chewing his nails.

Every Monday and Thursday, a parade of attorneys visited. He spoke to them politely but was insistent and firm. Once, she heard him say that he just wanted what was best for his niece, and he'd fight for whatever that was. He used the word "fuck" several times, as in, "Fuck that. I'll spend every fucking penny I have, if that's what it fucking takes."

She smiled and tiptoed upstairs.

It was a Saturday, and they were at Whole Foods. Uncle Mark insisted they go shopping together. He said that in Spain, the food was fresh, and you didn't just raid Costco once a month like some sort of barbarian war party. If Zelda wanted more of her microwave burritos, she had to come.

"Besides," he said, "maybe you'll find something beyond the frozen food section."

Zelda sort of doubted it.

But basket in hand, she made a lap of the store while he still strolled the produce section. He inspected eggplants, turning them over before deciding on the right one. He touched a half dozen portobello mushrooms, shaking his head. When he noticed her watching, he called her over.

"You want to learn how you can tell a good avocado?"

"Not really."

"Too bad. You want those chocolate pretzels? You've got to endure some healthy nonsense."

"Isn't that, like, blackmail or child abuse?"

"For sure. Here, press your thumb against it. What do you feel?"

She did as instructed, the dimpled skin of the avocado sliding under the pad of her thumb. He pressed on her hand. It was the first time he'd touched her other than the awkward hug at the funeral.

"See? Not too soft, not too hard. Now try this other one. What do you feel?"

"It's... kind of mushy, right?"

"Right. Cut it open, it's probably brown in some places. Decent for guacamole, but—"

"Holy shit," boomed a voice by the potatoes. "Is that Mark fucking Fitzsimmons?"

The man with the basket wore weekend casual joggers and white running shoes, athleisure wear donned more for status than function. His near-perfect haircut looked refreshed weekly. When he saw Zelda, his hand rose to his mouth.

"Oh man, sorry about the F-bomb. Is this your daughter?"

"My niece," Mark said. "Zelda, this is Timothy Kwon. Timothy, this is—"

"Zelda, right." Timothy gave Mark a smack on his biceps and flashed a grin so white it almost looked painted. "So wow, this is a trip. You're back in the bay. Last I heard, you were off in Thailand like, ten years ago?"

"Malaysia," Mark said. Zelda noticed that his posture had changed; he seemed to have shrunk. "And that was closer to fifteen. I taught there for a year."

"Taught? You were a teacher?"

This seemed to amuse Timothy, who shifted and crossed his arms, getting closer to Mark. Mark, in turn, backed toward the garlic. Were some men just not aware of the space they filled and the volume of their voices?

"I mean, I'm still teaching," Mark said. "Actually, I'm at a university in Madrid. Or I was."

"Whoa, good for you. So you're not chasing investors or founding more startups?"

Again, with that shiny smile that brought a blush to Uncle Mark's cheeks. He gave a weak shake of his head. "No. That was a one-time thing."

"Oh, I see," Timothy said. "Yeah, it's a hustle."

Uncle Mark scooted into the aisle so a mother with a cart could gather garlic and onions. There was an odd dynamic unfolding, Zelda sensed. She wasn't sure if she was looking at two old friends or two rivals sizing each other up. Whatever it was, Timothy seemed amused by it all. He got close again, giving Mark another smack in the shoulder.

"That's too bad. My company could always use someone with diverse experience and a global perspective."

Mark blinked. "Your company?"

"ZenWare. I mean, it's not *my* company, not like Acidsplash was *your* company or anything. I'm just the CFO. Got in on the ground floor."

He was bragging, she realized. Her father always told her to be wary of job titles and jargon thrown casually about.

"Wow, CFO. Nice," Mark said. "I'm so happy for you."

"Yep. We're still in the growth phase but leveling off. This economy, right?"

She glanced at a crate of jalapeño peppers tucked up against a shelf. Something moved and shifted deep in the shadows. Was that... Was that a rat?

"Zara, your uncle here was the idea wizard." Timothy's eyes bounced between Mark and her. "What was that one after Acidsplash? With the scanner—"

"FridgeFriend," Mark said. "Yeah, it—"

"FridgeFriend." Timothy laughed. "Get this: it was this app that scanned the contents of your fridge. All the labels and stuff, right? Told you everything you could make with it. Oh man, whatever happened to that?"

Mark hesitated. "We lost the patent when Acidsplash went belly up, right?"

"Oh, right. Yeah, things got pretty messy at the end."

Mark glanced down at his feet. "Man, I really regret how that all turned out. I'm sorry we had to let you go."

"Let me go? Psh. More like cut me loose. At least I got my severance and comped for equity when it was worth something, right? All good."

Zelda's gaze drifted back to the jalapeño peppers, where that small thing had moved behind the cardboard. That wasn't fur, she realized, but a shimmer, like light off something wet. It wasn't a rat but a dirty finger, stretching out from the dark shelf and scratching the green skin of a pepper.

Timothy clapped his hands, startling Zelda. "Well, listen, I've got CrossFit in fifteen, so... Great catching up with you. Good luck teaching... or whatever."

He gave Zelda a wink and then strolled off, stealing a glance at a woman in yoga pants as she bent over the bin of cheese.

"Uncle Mark?" Zelda pointed to the jalapeños where the finger retreated into the shadows. And then, with a blink, it was gone. "Uncle Mark, look."

But his mind was elsewhere. He was flustered, more so than usual. "Oh? What is it?"

He glanced where she pointed into the dark shelving past the crate of jalapeños. Several of the peppers were blistered and damp, mold blooming from cracked skin. Glistening rot hung from the underside of the shelf.

"Ah, good eye, Zelda." He returned the jalapeños to the shelf. "See? You're a natural. Grab some serrano peppers instead."

While she bagged the peppers, he squeezed down the aisle to the checkout stand, where Timothy Kwon thumbed through a magazine. She couldn't hear what they were saying, but Timothy nodded vigorously while Mark shifted. Then Timothy reached into his wallet and pulled out a card. They shook hands, Mark nodding and studying the card as if it were precious.

CHAPTER EIGHT

Mark spent the weekend updating his resume. It had been seven or eight years and he wasn't even sure what the proper format was anymore. Five different websites had five different answers. But with some tinkering, he filled out his work history, hit *print*, and checked it over.

Here it was, the curated story of his last two decades of employment in reverse order. Visiting Associate Professor of Business English. Business Language Head Instructor. English Language Specialist. English Tutor.

And then, at the bottom, Founder and CEO, Acidsplash, Inc.

Christ, that really was seventeen years ago. Even the name knotted his gut and sent a shiver down his spine.

He carried the laptop into the kitchen, found a bottle of Talisker in the liquor cabinet, and poured himself two fingers. In four weeks, he'd nearly cleaned out half of Maya and Juan Carlos's shelf.

Yes, he knew he had a problem. Yes, he told himself he would solve it soon. But damn, he needed a drink to send out this resume . It wasn't every day you asked someone you once laid off to hire you for a job.

He stared at the job title: *Consultant*. His finger trembled.

He needed a second sip for courage, so he poured another.

The truth was, Mark had never been good with money. School had taught him about the Marshall Plan, Mendel's fruit fly experiment, and how to find the hypotenuse of a right angle. But no one taught him about credit cards, how student debt stacked up, or how to run a startup in your early twenties. He'd learned each of these lessons the same way: through catastrophic mistakes.

Even now, he still felt like he was pretending to be an adult. Had everyone learned a few lessons he'd somehow missed?

But Zelda...

Shit, he'd need to get things in order, and fast. He'd already chewed through a chunk of his savings. Most of his money was in Spain and the exchange rate was brutal.

Do it, he told himself. *Do it for her.*

He hit *send*, and off it went with a *whoosh*. Then he emptied the glass.

He spent an hour pleasantly buzzed, preparing a cauliflower crust pizza with fresh basil, ham, mushrooms, and homemade tomato sauce. He let the cheese melt in two layers as his Italian friend had taught him. He tasted a hot slice and groaned. Perfection.

He was at the base of the stairs, carrying a tray up for Zelda, when his laptop pinged in the kitchen. A new email. He doubled back.

There, on-screen, was a reply from Timothy Kwon's assistant.

Can you come in on Tuesday? We'd love to chat.

Yes, he replied, he certainly could. He hit *send* and knocked back another dram of scotch in celebration.

He picked up Zelda's tray and climbed the stairs, shouting out, "Dinner's ready! Cauliflower crust pizza, coming right up."

There was a distant, slamming door, then the tip-tap of footsteps at the far end of the second floor. The house wasn't old, but it still creaked in places. Another hurried shuffle down the hall.

"Zelda?"

"Leave it outside my door," she shouted. "I'm... busy."

As he reached the top of the stairs, a click at Zelda's bedroom door echoed out. A shadow passed by on the other side. The light darkened.

"Everything okay?"

"Fine."

But she didn't sound fine. Even with the door between them, he could sense something in her voice. A stutter, perhaps. A quiver. Or a crack.

He hesitated at her door, listening. They ate separately most nights. Him, usually between six and seven. Her, as late as nine or ten. He didn't want to force her to join him downstairs, but he hoped one day she might. Mostly, he hoped he wasn't intruding.

"Don't let the pizza get cold. I think you'll like it."

"Yep, totally will. For sure."

He left the tray on the end table outside.

Then he noticed the master bedroom door ajar and slowly closing. As if someone had left it in a hurry.

For the past several weeks, Mark slept in the guest bedroom downstairs. That was what he still felt like: a guest. Legally, the house was tied up in probate and he didn't want to change a thing. The only other rooms with beds were Zelda's and the master.

Maya and Juan Carlos had bought the house the year Zelda was born, planning to renovate and eventually resell it. After his company took off, they could have afforded a place five times the size. But they told him they liked the neighborhood and the easy commute to their jobs. Most days, Maya could bike.

Maya.

It still seemed impossible that his sister was gone. Sometimes it pierced him, a blade thrust from the shadows and cutting a deep part of his soul. In quiet moments, it felt like he couldn't get enough air.

And then other moments, nothing. Just a numb void.

He hesitated outside the master bedroom. The lights were off, the curtains closed. Some dirty laundry lay in a hamper and the bed was lazily made. It occurred to him that they must have left for the lakeside vacation in a hurry, telling themselves they'd clean up when they returned.

He ran his hand along the bed, straightening the sheets and smoothing the edges of the blanket. He folded the duvet back. He picked a hair off the pillowcase, a thick curl that he recognized as Juan Carlos's. Mark had always envied the man's rugged good looks and full head of hair.

He was about to leave when he smelled a faint smokey odor. He breathed in again. It was something burning or burnt and it came from the closet.

He hesitated there at the door, his mind returning to Madrid and what he'd seen in his bathtub. He hadn't told anyone besides Rosy, and she had dismissed it with a wave of her hand.

But he knew what he'd seen.

His sister, shivering and broken.

Still, he told himself he was an adult, a ward in charge of a thirteen-year-old girl. There were no such things as ghosts. And if there were, this house would only be haunted by the good ones.

So he opened the closet and turned on the light.

The first thing he saw was his sister's clothes. Shirts and jackets, hoodies and blouses, pants and dresses. Maya had a lot of closet space to work with. Next, he noticed the empty hangers.

A dozen or so of Maya's shirts and jackets lay in a pile on the closet floor. A sleeping bag had been unrolled, and a pillow was propped in the corner. One of Zelda's wireless earbuds lay nearby.

Beside them sat a plastic bag and a ceramic container within. The new urn.

So that was the noise, he realized. The fast-closing door, the stomping. Zelda had been resting in here with her parents, where the scent of her mother still clung to clothes she would never wear.

CHAPTER NINE

Zelda shifted in the hard plastic chair and let the ice pack slide from her face. She inspected her reflection off the glass of the principal's door. A decent shiner darkened her cheek. A scratch reddened her neck. And the collar of her shirt hung torn and loose. Not bad, considering how many punches were thrown.

"That was your uncle." The school secretary hung up the phone. "He'll be here shortly."

Zelda nodded and put the ice pack back on her cheek. "Thanks."

The secretary pursed her lips and sat down behind her desk, but not before spearing Zelda with another sad glance. The silence hung heavy in the office, so Zelda took out her phone to pass the time.

Then she remembered the screen.

Her fingers traced the edge of the broken case, the crushed metal corner, the cracked glass where it had landed on concrete during the fight. It was all sort of a blur. She held the power button, trying to reset it again and again.

Still nothing. The screen didn't light up.

Despite being the daughter of a video game designer and despite living in the heart of Silicon Valley, her parents weren't like most others. They limited her access to new technology. They didn't buy her the latest iPhone, the newest computer, the best wireless earbuds. This phone was over two years old, gifted at Christmas when she was eleven. It was one of her favorite possessions.

And now it was broken.

"You know, Zelda, I know a thing or two about losing a parent," the secretary said while stapling papers. "Cancer took my dad when I was nineteen."

Zelda studied her shoelaces. "Okay."

After another moment of silence, the secretary sighed and returned to whatever it was a school secretary did. Sometimes it felt like there were more administrators than actual teachers at this school. And besides, what the heck did she expect? Some meaningful one-on-one time, secretary to student? She was old enough to be Zelda's grandma.

Fifteen minutes later, the office door clicked and shoes squeaked on the linoleum. Uncle Mark entered the principal's office wearing a suit, a loose tie, and a nice shirt he'd been ironing this morning. Shit, the interview. Zelda hoped she hadn't cost him the job.

"Hey, you okay?"

She nodded. "Sorry if I ruined your interview, Uncle Mark."

"Ah, it wouldn't have worked out." He waved it off. "Okay, let's see your face, kiddo."

She lifted the ice pack. He put a soft knuckle to her chin, tilting her head and inspecting the bruise. She smelled his cologne and noticed how smooth his cheeks were. He looked ten years younger.

"You shaved off your beard."

"This? Well, it was time, wasn't it?" He touched her ripped shirt collar. "What's this?"

"Jerome tried to grab me, I think."

His eyes blazed and his jaw tightened. "So, tell me what happened?"

"It was nothing—"

"Actually, Zelda, it wasn't nothing." That was Principal Bhagmavan, his office door opening and his brow scrunching into that look of frustration he'd worn since the incident. "As we discussed, physical altercations are a serious matter, okay?"

She blinked and gave him a tiny, defiant nod. He sucked in air through his yellow teeth.

"Mr. Bagmaven," Uncle Mark said. "I'm her—"

"*Bhagmavan*," he corrected. "Dr. Bhagmavan. And yes, you must be her uncle, Mark. Please come in." He gestured to the office and the chair opposite that enormous desk that the middle school students all dreaded. "Zelda, wait outside."

Uncle Mark stopped at the door. "Actually, I'd like to hear her side as well. From what I gathered, some other kid started it."

"Side?" Principal Bhagmavan cleared his throat. "I'm afraid there aren't sides when violence occurs. We have a zero-tolerance policy here. Zelda will have plenty of time to tell you her impression of the day's events later."

She didn't like how he said "plenty of time." She knew the school took a dim view of fighting, but she didn't care. Jerome deserved it. Not just for what he did to her mother's shirt, but because he'd been a prick to everyone, all year.

"Zelda, is that okay with you?" Uncle Mark asked, still lingering at the door.

"Mr. Fitzsimmons, this isn't open for negotiation. Zelda can wait out here—"

"Hey, Bag Muffin," Uncle Mark snapped. "Pump the brakes on this bitter principal act, okay? She lost her parents. So take a deep breath and, I dunno, try being a human for a moment."

The ice pack slipped from Zelda's face and landed on the floor with a crunch. She'd never seen someone stand up to the principal, nor call him Bag Muffin, which seemed to cut him deeply. She wished a student had thought of that name long ago, instead of Dr. Baldie or the Bog Man.

For a moment, the entire office teetered on some weird precipice. The principal stammered. The secretary stood and stared at Uncle Mark, phone limp in her hand like she'd forgotten how to hold it.

"Zelda?" Uncle Mark asked. "Do you mind waiting out here?"

She gave a small nod. "Yeah. Fine."

"Okay." Then he turned to the principal, the man's eyes narrowing as the vein in his forehead pulsed. "All right, Doc, let's do this."

They closed the door and the principal shut the blinds from inside the office. Zelda looked down and started counting spots on the floor. She was in a world of trouble now. Still, a tiny smile pulled at her lips as she thought of the name Uncle Mark had given the man.

"Bag Muffin," she whispered, and the secretary scowled at the words. "Bag Muffin."

CHAPTER TEN

Certificates, citations, and diplomas crowded the beige walls of Dr. Bhagmavan's office. Mark tried to listen as the principal explained the situation with Zelda and Jerome. How the boy had been sitting behind her in class. How he'd drawn on her shirt when she told him not to, again and again. How she'd hit him when the ink didn't come out.

Yet beneath the principal's lecture, Mark's mind wandered back to the job interview an hour ago, replaying every awkward second.

He'd shown up to ZenWare early with five hard copies of his resume and a spring to his step. It was nice knowing a friendly face on the inside. He'd waited in the lobby, with several other candidates, trying to ignore their casual clothes and how much younger they were. He didn't know much about the gig, only that Timothy Kwon's assistant had said they'd find the perfect place for him here, at ZenWare, where he could put his talents to use.

Perhaps in-house education, he hoped. Or corporate communications.

Or perhaps he could liaise with international clients. He had experience writing copy for Swiss and German entrepreneurs.

Then came the interview.

"The important thing is never to let it ring more than two times before answering," the young woman said. "That's a big no-no."

Mark cleared his throat and scrunched his forehead. Timothy Kwon's receptionist sat before him, all precise smiles and a colorful blouse. She was taking a job at Apple in customer support in two weeks, she said. Her priority now was finding a suitable replacement.

"I'm sorry, receptionist?" Mark asked. "Like, answering the phones?"

"Actually, it's *way* more complicated than that." She switched her gum from one cheek to the other. "Timothy's got a script he likes depending on the day of the week. And there's a lot of scheduling too. Dry cleaning. Haircut. Yoga sessions. Oh, and he's super particular about what Uber he takes. No compact cars, no ride shares, no color blue."

Mark's eyes narrowed. "Wait, you're serious?"

"Mmhmm. So, like, how do you two know each other?"

Mark glanced past the bleach-haired receptionist to the corner office and the window, where Timothy Kwon looked back. He gave Mark a dark smile and a wink.

Mother fucker.

"Mr. Fitzsimmons, do you understand the severity of the situation?" That was Principal Bhagmavan now, tapping his pen on the desk between them. Mark blinked and refocused. The principal's office and Zelda, right. He was too scattered today, too angry. He was getting sloppy.

"I'm not sure," Mark said. "I mean, I get that she shouldn't have hit that Jerome kid, I really do—"

"We have a no-tolerance policy," the principal said.

"Right, you've said that. But that's her mother's shirt Jerome drew on, twice from what you've said. That's like, what do you call it? Provocation."

The principal clasped his hands and gave a slight bow of the head as if exhausted. "Jerome's actions are a separate matter that will be dealt with. I can't divulge any more, but be assured actions will be taken."

"Fair enough."

"What's concerning isn't just Zelda's response but her demeanor as a whole. Her grades are down this year, and so is her interest in her coursework. Her teachers tell me she hardly pays attention in class."

"Yeah, well, welcome to thirteen, Doc." It was meant as a joke, but Mark realized it came off as bitter.

"My thesis focused on adolescent educational development."

And my master's is in business administration, Mark thought. *But it doesn't make me a master of business.* Instead, he said, "I just meant that it's a difficult age, you know? Hormones flying, neurons changing—"

"Be that as it may, even if Zelda's grades miraculously rise, she's on track to fail eighth-grade math. That, coupled with her suspension and—"

The chair squeaked as Mark scooted forward. "Wait, suspension?"

"Suspension, yes." The principal nodded his shiny head. "As I've said, we have a zero-tolerance policy with regards to violence—"

"It's not violence. The sacking of Troy, that's violence. This is just..." Mark squeezed the bridge of his nose. "It was an altercation. Didn't you ever get into a disagreement in school?"

Those icy eyes narrowed. And Mark realized he wasn't talking with a man, or in some ways even a human, but an administrator. A creature who thrived among the rules and regulations of bureaucracy, not the nuance and imperfections of people.

"I'm afraid my hands are tied," the principal said. "Once a student strikes another—regardless of provocation, as you say—a series of protocols are activated. An investigation, a disciplinary hearing, and so on. With three weeks left until graduation—and in light of Zelda's recent trauma—we're permitting her to finish middle school remotely."

"You're permitting her?"

The principal nodded. "A case could be made for police involvement. Jerome's family would like to avoid that. We all would."

Police, great. He wasn't sure how that would affect the guardianship, but he knew it wouldn't help.

After a moment of silence, he pointed out the window to the baseball field at the edge of campus. "I went to Fairmont for middle school," he said. "Three towns over. See that fence just past the dugout? I got beat up there after the game by some kids from this school. Coach told me I took the hits like the man. It's sure not the nineties anymore, is it, Doc?"

"No, it isn't," the principal said. "And that's a good thing."

MARK FOUND ZELDA OUTSIDE, SITTING ON A BENCH IN the shadow of an elm tree by the bicycle cages. She had her backpack and a cardboard box filled with the contents of her locker. She rolled her skateboard underfoot, back and forth, back and forth.

"How you doing, slugger?" he asked.

Her eyes glistened and he held out his hands.

"I'm sorry. I didn't mean anything bad by that."

After a moment, she said, "I really messed up."

He glanced at her shirt. The collar stretched and torn on the left. The black ink where Jerome had filled in one of the plaid patches with his Sharpie. He remembered seeing Maya in that shirt once or twice in her late teens and early twenties. She had always been small, and it fit Zelda perfectly. Or it had, until...

"So, like, I'm expelled, aren't I?"

He sat on the bench beside her and considered his words. The wind was cool, the sun warm on their shoulders. They watched a PE class circle the field, the coach shouting encouragements.

"Suspended," he said. "You can't attend graduation. You can't walk. They'll mail the diploma in, like, six to eight weeks."

She gave a quick, sharp nod, lips trembling.

"Hey, listen, it's just middle school graduation, okay?" he said. "It really doesn't matter that much."

He regretted his words instantly. To her, it probably did matter. It was the highest grade she'd achieved, the furthest she'd gone. To her, it might be worthy of celebration. High school loomed on the other side of this summer.

"What I mean is, well, of course it's important," he stammered. "It's a major accomplishment—"

"I don't care about that. It's just..."

She hesitated and looked off while relief washed over him. God, he was awful at this. When he wasn't snapping at the principal, he was accidentally belittling her accomplishments. He should just sew his mouth shut before he messed the girl up.

She said, "If you need to go, I understand."

"Go?"

"Like, back to Spain. You know? *Go* go."

"You trying to get rid of me?"

She shook her head. Sometimes, when she spoke, it was so vibrant, so full of life. Other times, it was like her lungs were too weak and the wind died behind her lips.

"No."

"Good. 'Cause you're going to have to try harder than that, okay?"

She wiped her eyes. "Okay."

The school doors clanked to their right. A large woman and an even larger kid walked out, his shoulders slouched and his head hung low. With a swollen eye, he glanced at Zelda, then muttered something to his mother. She looked back at the two of them with contempt.

Then she smacked her son. Gave Jerome a solid thump in the back of his head.

And off they went.

"That kid's enormous," Mark said when they were out of earshot. "What's he, like a senior in high school?"

"He's in my grade. He's kind of a bully."

"And you fought him," he muttered. "Bad ass." He knew he shouldn't encourage her, but he couldn't help it.

A smirk tugged at the corners of her lips and then faded just as fast. "I'm sorry the interview didn't work out."

Mark removed his tie and folded it. "Sometimes old friends aren't that reliable. Or even that friendly. I probably deserved it."

"Deserved it?"

He leaned back against the bench and sighed. "After college, I helped Timothy Kwon and some others get a company off the ground. Then I sort of crashed it into a mountain. The whole thing was a mess."

And I ran away from it all, he thought.

Zelda rocked her skateboard back and forth. "My dad said people here treat relationships like transactions."

"Yeah, J.C.'s a smart guy." He realized he'd used the wrong tense. "Man, sometimes the whole area feels too small."

She stopped rolling her skateboard and glanced up at him. "So why don't we move?"

CHAPTER ELEVEN

Leaving the Bay Area turned out to be easier than they expected. Despite the challenges to Mark's guardianship and the mess that was probate, Maya and Juan Carlos had kept their finances in order, leaving behind a paid-off mortgage and minimal debt. He couldn't sell the house, but he learned there were other options.

The attorneys—Mr. Hoffman, Mr. Shariz, and Mrs. Phong, a no-nonsense Vietnamese woman who swore like a sailor—knew exactly who to call and what to say. By borrowing against the value of the house, Mark and Zelda could afford to put the Bay Area behind them. The only requirement per his attorneys was that they stay in the state. Courts looked nervously at guardians crossing jurisdictions.

It was on a sunny Tuesday that Mark and Zelda drove over Redwood Pass, where the coastal fog swept in from the northwest. The Subaru's stereo blared for most of the drive. He introduced her to Sublime and Guns N' Roses, but she quickly grew bored. She schooled him on synthwave and some musicians called Post Malone and the Weeknd. He wasn't sure if they were rappers or pop stars, but the autotune bothered his ears.

She turned the music down while reviewing their checklist.

"Beaches nearby. Mountains a plus. Walkable and bike-friendly. Movie theater. Lots of parks and trees and little crime." She twirled the pencil in her hand. "Okay, so what else?"

"Educated population," he said.

"Good schools?"

"I'm not sending you to the circus, if that's what you're asking."

She wrote it down in the notebook. As the car took a turn, Mark slowed to pass a pair of cyclists peddling hard up the hill.

"Bikes." She pointed and ticked off the box.

"And a good bookstore," he said. "Not one of those creepy ones that only sell bible comics and Kevin Sorbo documentaries."

"Who's Kevin Sorbo?"

"That you're asking that question proves you have good taste."

She tapped her pencil. "So... Literate and religiously diverse?"

"Bingo."

They passed a sign for West Pine, population 821. The car was nearing the summit now, the fog thickening. Peaks scraped the gray haze over vineyards tucked down willow-lined driveways. He could smell the ocean, salty and cool.

"What about you?" he asked. "What are Zelda's requirements for her perfect little town?"

She dug the pencil eraser into her chin. "Fast internet. A lighthouse. At least one old bridge. Maybe a Ferris wheel or, like, some sort of rides. Oh, and a skatepark. Gotta have a skatepark."

For a half mile, the fog thickened until the air was so wet it beaded the windshield. He turned on the wipers. Redwoods stretched into the mist, great columns of amber bark and shadows over glistening ferns.

Mark noticed that Zelda had stiffened and was clutching the armrest. He checked his speed, slowing down and taking the curves slow.

"First impressions aren't looking good for old Greywood Bay," he said. "If we can even see the place."

And then the fog parted.

Mark's eyes darted about as the landscape unfurled before them. His words failed. Soft hills rose to sharp mountains on the right. Redwoods and pines gave way to a wide valley where farms lay nestled among the hollows. Mist swaddled a river here and a lake there, delicate fingers resting among the folds of terrain.

"Wow, that's quite something," he said, turning the wheel as the road descended toward the ocean.

To their left, the Pacific carved a crescent out of towering cliffs where rivers merged into the city's namesake: Greywood Bay. There were docks and piers, a small regional airport at the south edge of the city. Wind-shaped cypresses topped sandy dunes where the occasional car laden with surfboards sat parked on the side of the road.

"There's your lighthouse." He pointed to a red and white structure looming on a rise of jagged rocks a mile or two off the coast. "But I doubt the internet connection is fast."

They drove for several miles, Mark eyeing the highway, pleased that the lanes were wide, the road smooth, and the drivers competent and safe. Every now and then, they passed cyclists in spandex and aerodynamic helmets. Sometimes one or two, or sometimes a dozen or more. He wondered what a group of cyclists was called. A flock? A peddle? A chain?

He was pleased to see Zelda turning her head frequently, taking in the curiosities as they passed. A run-down psychic parlor on the county outskirts. An ostrich farm. Something that looked like a track for ATVs or dirt bikes.

He'd been worried the suspension and the looming specter of summer school might break her already-frayed spirits, but the girl was resilient. After Bag Muffin's office, she'd started talking more, sometimes in complete sentences. She'd even joined the search for properties close enough to the Bay Area that they could visit when needed.

And he had to admit, she had a brilliant eye.

After all, she'd found Greywood Bay.

The town teased them in glimpses. There were wide sidewalks and shady parks with plenty of trees. A cute downtown that stretched on for a mile and ended at a wharf. Art boutiques displayed tasteful sculptures and paintings, while sports stores hawked kayaks and athletic wear. Artisanal bakeries sat beside coffee shops, the air perfumed with roasted beans. Zelda counted four bookstores before giving up.

"Nice place," he said as the GPS instructed them to turn right at the movie theater and then continue on Timberman Parkway for another two miles. "Organic grocery, fresh sushi, something called Tender Veggies. Check it out: comic book store."

"I don't like comics."

"Seriously? We'll change that. Your mom and I used to drive your grandmother crazy, spending our allowance on *Spawn*, *Cable*, *Death of Superman*..."

While he talked comics, she took out her repaired phone and checked the signal. Five bars. That was good. No use living in a nice place if she couldn't reach the rest of the world.

Or have a little fun.

She launched *Critical Mass* and watched her character synch up with the new location. It pleased her to discover there were hundreds of active players in the community. The leaderboard was competitive. She wasn't even the highest level, not by a long shot. That was someone named KanyeFishStick500, at a shocking level 721.

She spent a few minutes tapping the screen, scrolling around, and exploring Greywood Bay's virtual doppelgänger. There was a scrimmage at a nearby beach, a bunch of level 20s and 30s fighting for weekly control of a meteor that had crashed and would yield a hefty bounty of credits. So, there were people to play with and some rare spawns to hunt.

Yeah, she had a good feeling about this town.

"Here we are," Mark said.

The street threaded its way between a pair of stone arches recently built and a sign that read, *Raven's Valley: You're Finally Home.*

CHAPTER TWELVE

Edward Strathmore IV groaned as he stepped out of his Jaguar at 33 Manzanita Way. His back was killing him from a weekend of golf. He was already late for his lunch with some potential investors. This pit stop would cut into his business. But still, it had to be done.

He found Diana Betancourt waiting on the porch with the prospective buyers. There was a man in his forties, a bit soggy beneath a polo pullover. The teenage girl wore a Santa Cruz Skateboards T-shirt a little too long. His instinct was to tell Diana to make it a short showing; they probably couldn't afford the place. Yet he reminded himself that this was Northern California, after all. Money sometimes came dressed in a hoodie and shopped at the farmers market.

"Thanks for coming over, Ed," Diana said. "The app was acting phooey again and I couldn't unlock the front door." She introduced the clients, gesturing to Edward. "One of the many perks of having our grand visionary nearby, isn't that right?"

"Grand visionary, huh." Compliments never felt right to his ears, not with three generations of wealth behind him. He used the master key to open up the house.

Diana let out a polite chuckle as he shut off the alarm. There was something slightly desperate about her, he thought. Her laugh was too fast and practiced. Her demeanor twitchy. Even her business card felt a little forced.

Diana Betancourt

Raven's Valley Real Estate & Residential Expert

"I'm just down the street!"

The teenage girl turned the card over. "I don't get it."

Diana closed the front door. "Oh, it's just that I live in Raven's Valley as well. I believe I was the fifth buyer? Is that right, Ed?"

"Fourth, technically."

"You must really believe in the development," the man said. His name was Mark, and he seemed friendly enough.

"We prefer the term 'cultivated community,'" she said. "'Development' conjures up images of tract housing off the interstate, doesn't it? Cookie-cutter homes and car dealerships. Here, you'll find Strathmore & Daniels has created something truly special."

Edward let them wander ahead. He needed to troubleshoot the SmartHome app on his phone without stepping on Diana's sales pitch.

"So he's the architect?" Mark asked.

"Mr. Strathmore focuses on the business end," Diana said. "Although you can see his touches all around. The lovely restored wood and brickwork. The exposed beams. It takes a village to build one, doesn't it?"

Edward silently groaned. He found the problem with the app and adjusted Diana's permissions so she could unlock the front door. He showed it to her discretely while Mark and his niece continued the walkthrough.

Their gaze swept through the entryway and into the living room. Edward always enjoyed these little moments. He wasn't an architect or a designer, but he chose most of the materials. There was exposed brickwork on one side, giving it a tasteful, industrial feeling. On the other side, restored trim framed wide windows that looked out on a yard landscaped for gardening and play. Rustic beams ran down the center of the living room and joined a mantle of reclaimed redwood. Mark paused at the open riser stairs with the rod railing. He ran a hand down the antique banister that balanced out the modern and the timeless.

"So, this isn't a new house," Mark said. "I mean, it is, but it isn't."

Diana nodded. "All 222 homes in Raven's Valley have been built from the ground up with recycled materials. Upcycling, I believe the kids call it. We're one of the state's first certified eco-friendly communities, a model for decades to come. A home as unique as the families within."

"Whoa," Zelda said from the top of the stairs. "Check out the chandelier."

Mark looked up to see brushed pipes forming something like a triangle inside a cube, the bulbs tastefully recessed among brushed aluminum.

"Everything's connected to solar and smart-integrated. You can control each room with an app." She passed Mark her phone, where little icons represented zones and features that could be changed. Motion sensors. Heating. Light. He tapped the hallway upstairs and adjusted the lights.

"Uncle Mark, the lights just turned blue," she shouted. "Did you do that?"

"No idea what you're talking about."

Diana led him through the dining room and into the kitchen. Edward lingered in the rear in case something didn't work.

Like before, Mark noted the open floor space and granite countertops, the recessed stove and the twin sinks. When he ran a hand over the in-wall refrigerator, the door opened silently.

"Touch-friendly," Diana said. "Oh, and the electric stoves are pressure sensitive. No need to worry about whether you left them on."

Mark toggled a few buttons near the kitchen island, smiling as the thin TV rose from the counter. "In case I want to watch Netflix while prepping dinner."

"Or video chat over breakfast," Diana added. "We have a growing number of transplants who work from home. WFH, as they say."

"What are the internet speeds?" Zelda poked her head in from the dining room.

"Quite excellent."

"One hundred? Two fifty?"

"Gigabit," Edward said. "Technically closer to two and a half, but we can't call it that until the city finishes the connection."

"Whoa," Zelda muttered, and disappeared into the dining room.

"Every zone is home office ready," Diana said. "Set up a work-space down the hall and you can commute in your underwear."

She squeaked out a giggle and covered her mouth when Edward eyed her. She was jittery today. Perhaps it was that odd son stressing her out. Rumor was, he'd been through some sort of trauma in the winter. Or perhaps she'd hit a rough patch with her husband, Randall.

Whatever it was, he just wished she wouldn't bring it to work. He might have to find a different agent for the Hawk's Hollow venture once the funding came through and the rest of the land was acquired.

"How many houses have you sold?" Mark asked.

"Oh, well, that would be 222," she said. "This is the final unit."

Mark stopped at the back porch. "This is the last home?"

"The last unit in Raven's Valley."

"I thought the brochure said it just opened."

"Forty percent of the units were pre-sold before breaking ground. Officially, the community opened on March 1st. However, some residents are still settling in. You probably saw a few of the trucks."

"Forty percent," Mark said. "That must've been one hell of an investment."

He didn't know the half of it, Edward thought. All the greased hands and gifts just to cut an inch of red tape. All the campaign contributions, the kickbacks, the threats of litigation. Even with the Strathmore name, turning a valley of dead lumberyards and warehouses into a community had taken half a decade and most of his hairline. Some nights, he still woke up in a sweat, fearful a keystone deal had collapsed.

He followed them into the garage-workshop. The designs were all different, but at a minimum, they could fit two cars, four bicycles, a workbench and tools, with enough room left over for a pair of Peloton bikes. He took a moment to admire the space.

Frank Lloyd Wright.

Joseph Eichler.

And maybe someday Edward Strathmore IV. It was a good enough thought.

A clatter of wheels from the other side of the garage door ended his reverie. Diana opened it to find Zelda there, her skateboard making figure eights in the driveway.

"Cement's smooth," she said, turning sharply.

Diana winced at the squeak of the deck, the clack of the wheels. What was it about skateboards that bothered some people?

"You know, technically that's concrete," Edward said. "Well, concrete mixed with a rubber substrate. Cement is really just one ingredient in concrete."

"I always learn something new." Again, Diana chirped and smiled a little too widely. She reminded him of a meerkat. "And what do you do, Mr. Fitzsimmons?"

"Education," he said. "I was a professor in Madrid until… Well, I'm in transition."

"Ah, I see."

Edward could see her calculations. A single resident, a teacher's salary. Greywood Bay wasn't expensive, but she was still running the numbers.

"So, are you teaching at Bayview or Middlemarsh? Or maybe the university—"

"I'm not sure yet." Mark gave the side gate a jostle. Solid, well constructed. "We have a place in Alder Glen we'll be renting out. Maybe I'll substitute for a while."

There it was, Edward thought. Another Bay Area resident seeking a quiet life a few hours to the north. Hell, they might offer in cash. Sure, it wasn't as good as the commission his company made passing the financing off to the bank, but a sale was a sale. More importantly, he could tell the investors Raven's Valley had officially sold out.

"You know, we could probably—"

He was about to tell Mr. Fitzsimmons they could knock two and a half and percent off the price when Diana's eyes sparkled and her hand started waving. "Oh! I should introduce you to Ms. Layne. Excuse me a moment. Stacey. Stacey!"

The two men watched her shuffle to the front yard and wave at a jogger.

Stacey Layne was a friendly local in her late thirties with chestnut hair tied back in a ponytail. She had a sharp neckline and even sharper eyes. She'd moved back to Greywood Bay a decade ago, hired to rejuvenate the school district's floundering literacy rates. After her recent divorce, Edward had even invited her on a date. She declined, saying the country club wasn't her scene.

"Stacey, this is Mr. Fitzsimmons, Mr. Mark Fitzsimmons," Diana said. "He's a teacher—a professor, actually. He's considering 33 Manzanita."

"Ah, another body for the salt mines, eh? I'm a bit sweaty to shake hands, so fist bump." They touched knuckles and Stacey put her foot on the fencepost to stretch, skin glistening in the light. "All jokes aside, it's a pretty good place to live. So, what have they got you teaching at the university?"

"Oh, I'm not," Mark said. "I mean, I don't have anything lined up."

"Really? And you're just... moving here sans job? That's bold."

"Stacey raised nearly thirty grand for the library this spring," Diana said. "She even convinced the district to install a book vending machine at the high school. My son loved it."

"Lloyd's always been a bookworm." Then she hesitated, her brow furrowing. "Mark, you're not a Spanish teacher by any chance?"

His eyes sparkled. "I've lived in Spain for nearly a decade."

"Interesting. Any outstanding warrants, Interpol flags, orders to stay five hundred feet from a playground?"

Mark grinned. "Not that I'm aware of. Why?"

She bit her lower lip, giving Diana and Edward a quick glance. "Okay, so this stays between us, but Sophie Saperstein's health took a turn for the worse. She's taking the summer off. She hasn't announced it yet, but—"

"Oh, poor Sophie," Diana said. "I'll put her in my prayers."

"Yeah, she'd appreciate that," Stacey said.

Edward doubted the old bird would care. Sophie was widowed and flush with money. A regular attendee of town halls, she was a NIMBY who decried nearly every change to the city: not in *my* backyard.

Still, her years of teaching and church service had earned her pull in the community. Edward needed her. First for Raven's Valley, and now for the Hawk's Hollow expansion. He'd even knocked fifteen percent off that bungalow unit they sold her, eating the loss.

"I can't promise anything in the fall," Stacey said, "but her summer class is open. Might be a good way to get a foot in the door."

"That's actually pretty interesting," Mark said. "Is that at Bayview or Middlemarsh—"

"Oh, no no no," Diana said. "Ms. Layne teaches at Neumann

Prep. That's the private K through twelve. You probably passed it coming in."

Edward couldn't help but notice Stacey blushing at Diana's words. Not everyone knew the ins and outs of the town. The little cliques and the clans. The school rivalries and resentments. Edward's own son, Edward V, was a third-grader at Neumann. The tuition alone was the price of a nice car.

Stacey's smart watch vibrated. "Okay, I'm four miles short of my run," she said. "So if you're interested, shoot me your resume. Good luck."

And then she took off, her walk becoming a quick jog that made Edward tired just by watching.

Fifteen minutes later, he climbed back into his Jaguar, confident that Mr. Fitzsimmons would buy the place as long as Diana didn't push the sale. He turned on the engine and studied the house. Yeah, things weren't perfect and compromises had been made. Still, he was proud of what he'd played a part in building. Another monument to the Strathmore legacy, one that stretched back to his great-grandfather. And, if he played it right, one that would reach out to his great-grandchildren.

Something caught his eye in the home. Zelda and Mark and Diana were downstairs; he could see them all through the living room window.

But upstairs...

Was that water dripping down the bedroom window? Was that someone looking out from the shadows? Someone covered in wet dirt?

Edward squinted, and then it was gone. A glimmer off the glass, the reflection of a car, or a sunbeam at a strange angle.

At least, that was what he told himself.

CHAPTER THIRTEEN

Lloyd Betancourt's nineteen-year-old body tingled and twisted every time someone stared at him. He wanted to become vapor. And yet here he was, driving down from the mountains and across town, dozens of eyes turning upon him. Most people stared, mouths agape. Several waved or pointed at his vehicle, as if he didn't know what he'd done. A few even screamed as he drove past. Children, mostly. Plus that hippie who ran the vegan bakery.

Lloyd might've laughed if he wasn't so worried. His stepdad was going to flip out when he saw the dented pickup truck, the blood-stained hood, and the deer embedded in the grill.

Well, what was left of the deer.

He gunned it through the south entrance to Raven's Valley and stopped at 77 Palo Verde. He executed a three-point turn and reversed into the garage. He left the front of the pickup jutting out.

Then he got the hose.

He wasn't sure if the deer had died when he first struck it or in the panicked minutes that followed. But now, looking at the red mess in the grill, he knew nothing could have survived.

Not without its legs.

With a bucket, a mop, and a lot of coughing and gagging, Lloyd pried the broken limbs and antlers from the metal and plastic. He sprayed the truck down several times until the water was pink and foamy. He swept the remains into a pile at the edge of the driveway and started hosing again.

That was when he heard the rumble.

A classic Camaro's 454 Big Block engine sounded like no other car on the road. It burbled and purred, and—if you knew who was behind the wheel—it put a knot in your gut.

"Shit," Lloyd muttered. "Shit shit shit."

His muscles tensed. He had done most of his vertical growing and was filling out horizontally now. Pretzels and pizza and Hot Pockets over the past several months had given him a gut that he noticed when he slouched.

And he always slouched when Randall was around.

"Jesus Christ," Randall said, parking the jet-black '68 Camaro in the driveway and stepping out. "Jesus fuckin' Christ, Lloyd. I got three calls—three different phone calls—all telling me someone's driving the company truck through town like a damn serial killer."

"I didn't know what to do," Lloyd said. "The deer... it just—"

"Well, what you don't do is take Main Street with Bambi's broken ass sticking out of the grill. God almighty, just look at this mess."

Randall stood there a moment, hands on his hips, thumbs tucked into his duty belt. As a veteran, a former cop, and now a security guard, he kept his posture rigid, as if inspecting the world and finding it out of line. His uniform was crisp, the logo glistening in the late afternoon light: *Raven's Valley Community Safety*.

Lloyd never felt safe with his stepdad around.

"I'm sorry, Randall," he said. "It happened so fast I couldn't stop."

"Of course it happened fast. You think a deer'll throw itself in front of you all slow-like? And where the hell were you, anyway?"

Lloyd swallowed. He knew Randall didn't like him driving the pickup, especially now that it was a work vehicle. But he'd sent him to drop off that pool table he'd resold on Craigslist. He never said which way to come home. So Lloyd took his time, cranking up the music, getting lost on the mountain roads for fun and gunning it on the straightaways, laughing for the first time in months.

Until the deer stepped onto the asphalt.

"I was just driving back," Lloyd said.

"What took you so long? You weren't joyriding, were you?"

"They only had one person to take delivery. You know how heavy it is?"

"'Course I do. Bent my back just putting it in there."

Except he didn't, Lloyd thought. Lloyd hired those Guatemalans at the Home Depot, and they helped load it in. Randall just complained they were scratching the bed.

Randall and Lloyd stood there a moment and studied the ruined grill, two men who didn't know how to talk to each other. Then a gasp broke their silence.

"Heavens! What a horrible mess, my goodness!"

Lloyd turned to greet his mother, Diana. A grocery tote hung from her arm, a bottle of wine and some bread poking out. She was dressed in her realtor's best, that salmon-pink outfit from Neiman Marcus that Randall called a lesbian power suit but Lloyd kind of liked. When she dressed up nice, she looked confident and strong.

Perhaps one day she'd be strong on her own.

Lloyd told his mother what happened while Randall eyed him, no doubt searching for holes in the story. All the while, she just shook her head and said, "Awful. Just awful. That poor little thing." She noticed Lloyd's blood-spattered pants. "And how about you, sweetie? Are you doing all right?"

"Of course he's all right," Randall said. "That's six thousand pounds of American steel. It's my premiums that are fucked. A-gain."

Lloyd nodded. "Yeah, I'm fine. You look nice, Mom."

She smiled. "Thanks. And, good news: it looks like I just sold the last house in Raven's Valley."

"Grats."

"Grats?" Randall asked. "What, 'congratulations' is too hard to say?"

Lloyd ignored him for now. He knew his stepdad's moods, and they could be misdirected at best. He said, "We should celebrate. I'll help with dinner when I'm finished. Why don't you all head inside?"

"Well, aren't you a gentleman?" She gave him a kiss on the cheek and a pat on the shoulder.

After fifteen minutes of cleaning, Lloyd bagged the limbs and clumps of fur, the antlers and entrails. He put it in a second bag and dropped it in the garbage. The sun was setting, the fog rolling through the dry hills and settling over Raven's Valley. He listened to the chorus of crickets. Sometimes, he thought he could hear patterns in their songs.

Inside, he showered off, then helped his mom finish prepping dinner. Despite living here for several months now, they were still getting used to the new kitchen, the built-in appliances, and all the nooks for pots and pans and utensils. It was impressive, this thoughtful design.

The only thing he didn't like was Randall's massive salt-water fish tank. The aquarium took up the entire shelf between the kitchen and dining room. Lloyd could hear it burbling late at night, all the fish lit up by that purple glow that suffused the walls.

"Lloyd, make yourself useful and fetch me that six-pack of Fogwalker," Randall said. He was sitting at the kitchen table and reading the newspaper. He hadn't lifted a finger to help. "You know, that crap from the farmers market."

Lloyd glanced down at the cutting board and the knife. "I am being useful."

Randall lowered the paper and gave Lloyd a cold gaze. "Aww, hitting that deer make you cry? Don't get soft on us now. C'mon, chop-chop."

Lloyd wiped his eyes, surprised to see that, yes, they were watering. Stupid onion. His mom gave his hand an affectionate pat. "I'll finish up here, sweetie."

He washed his hands and went to the back porch, searching for the beers. "There's no Fogwalker, Randall. Just Coors."

"That's 'cause it's downstairs, genius."

Sighing, Lloyd went to the hall and opened the basement door. He could hear Randall speaking quietly. "That kid of yours... I swear, I give him chance after chance and he does nothing but fumble."

"He's had a rough couple of months," his mom whispered. "We need to be patient. Besides, he's not in the best headspace."

"Headspace, safe space. These kids and their trigger warnings. Babe, the world isn't Sesame Street. We're not doing the future any good by sanding down all the corners."

Lloyd lingered there at the top of the basement stairs. He could only hear the rustle of the newspaper, the sizzle of chopped onions and beef in the skillet. Then he descended.

The basements of Raven's Valley were ample and thoughtfully designed, built to be used as game rooms, home theaters, or second offices. For the Betancourt family, it served as storage. This was a place where the contents of their old house still lived in boxes and suitcases. Where paintings and family photos leaned against the walls, awaiting rehanging. To Lloyd, it was a reminder there was a life before Randall. A life where his dad slept next to his mom and her practiced laughs didn't scream of sadness.

Lloyd found the six-pack of Fogwalker Ale near the crawlspace. As he walked up the stairs, he read the label. He'd tried alcohol this past year in college and quite enjoyed it. He'd tried other things, too. Things that you chewed or placed on your tongue. Things that expanded your mind and cast your thoughts across the darkness of space.

He didn't like those things.

He was halfway up the stairs when he heard the whisper over his left shoulder.

"Death."

Pausing at the landing, Lloyd looked around. He knew he'd heard a voice, some effeminate whisper from the shadowy depths.

"Hello?"

"Death. Mmm... You wear it upon you."

A shiver wormed up Lloyd's back and curled under his shoulders. He heard it, yes; he heard that woman's voice near the bottom of the stairs.

And yet, all he found was a group of cardboard boxes, a crawlspace that descended into the depths of the foundation, and some dusty framed art prints that once hung on the walls of his old house.

Armando the Great.

The poster was an antique, a relic from the 1920s and printed in the Art Deco style of the time. Armando's pale skin and purple turban-wrapped head floated over faded text proclaiming:

SEE! THE GREATEST MENTALIST IN THE WEST!
HEAR! A PERSONAL READING OF YOUR AURA,
YOUR ESSENCE, YOUR LUCKY NUMBERS!
DISCOVER! PAST LIVES UNCOVERED AND
FUTURES TO CHOOSE!
ARMANDO THE GREAT AWAITS YOU AT THE
EMBRIDGE EXPO & FESTIVAL OF CURIOSITY! FORT
DARROW, CALIFORNIA, OCTOBER 5TH TO 13TH.

Lloyd knew every inch of the poster. He had stared at it as a child, frightened by the man's sharp jawline, his goat-like beard, and how the head hovered among the swirls of paint like it lived on its own.

But it was Armando's piercing eyes that always bothered Lloyd. Eyes that seemed to follow him as he walked past. It was those eyes that were wrong, Lloyd realized. Hadn't they always been open?

But now one was shut.

Carefully, slowly, he reached out and rubbed dust from the glass. Armando's left eye... did it just twitch?

"Death," a voice whispered. *"Mmm... I can smell it upon you. You walk at the edge of the Nether."*

"The Nether?" Lloyd realized he'd said it out loud. He could see his breath fogging the poster's glass. When had he gotten so close?

"You can mold a great key with your hands, Lloyd Betancourt. A key to stretch across the cosmos. A key to fray the veil. A key—"

A shadow crossed the basement door and fell over the poster. "Jesus, Lloyd, what's taking so long?" Randall asked. "Here, just gimme that."

With a sigh, he descended the stairs and took the beer. He paused to study his stepson for a moment, as if really seeing him for the first time in months.

"You doing okay?"

"I was..." Lloyd swallowed and looked at the poster, where Armando the Great's ever-tracking eyes stared back, both of them open.

"What, just playing with yourself? Damn, kid, we gotta get you a girlfriend. Or a boyfriend. Or... whatever." Randall gave Lloyd a double-pat on the shoulder, the closest thing to a hug he was capable of. "C'mon, dinner's ready."

Lloyd followed him up the stairs, pausing to look back at that poster sitting before the crawlspace. Armando the Great, his floating head, and those eyes. As Lloyd turned out the basement light, he was certain of one thing.

Armando the Great winked once again.

CHAPTER FOURTEEN

Annie Paxton brewed herself a cup of rosemary tea and savored the steamy aroma. Pine and charred wood, a hint of camphor perhaps. Pliny the Elder called it "the dew of the sea." To her, it was the scent of her husband's cooking. It made her smile.

Carrying the mug, she paused in the hallway and straightened their wedding photo on the wall. "Miss you, sweetie."

She kissed her finger and pressed it against the glass. Like always, Walter smiled back from that moment of framed youth. Goodness, how young they both looked.

And how in love.

Sipping the tea, she made her way through the house to the meditation room. She left her slippers by the door. Her tired feet brushed over the tatami mat. She retrieved her favorite meditation pillow.

Over the years, she had built this room into a sanctuary. There were the carved Buddhas from her trips to the orphanage in Cambodia that Walter had sponsored. The preserved branches from the Great Banyan Tree in Kolkata. The goatskin drum from the Buryat Shaman in Siberia.

But her favorite mementos were the colorful crystals Walter collected over the years and hung on strings to catch the light by the window. She didn't believe in all that hoopla about the healing power of gems. Nor about finding the right color for your chakras. As far as she was concerned, good vibrations was a song by the Beach Boys, not something given off by a crystal.

Mostly, she just liked the way they colored the room, a rainbow that reminded her of Walter.

Another sip of tea. Knees creaking, she crossed her legs and settled on the cushion. She let her eyes slowly close.

She started her meditation as she had for decades, listening to her thoughts as they raced by like speeding cars.

Here was one named Grandchildren, colored yellow and black like the school bus they rode. Had the kids gotten the new socks she'd mailed them? And if so, why hadn't they sent a thank-you note back?

Breathe in. Breathe out.

There went another thought, one she named the Future, rumbling past in a rusty cloud of fumes and chipped paint. Yes, the sea levels were rising, the air growing more tainted by the years. What was an old hippy to do? They'd betrayed the planet for low property taxes and a home that appreciated in value. They'd traded their beliefs for a pension.

Breathe in. Breathe out.

And then a new thought overtook her, one she envisioned not as a car or a fear but the crackling of a dark storm. The Ruizes and their poor daughter, Zelda.

She spent several breaths following that thought, watching her mind's storm cloud take shape. The turbulent edges formed of black-violet shadows. The roaring wind and the boiling air, hot and hazy and echoing with screams. Something like mud bloomed on her tongue.

Odd. It was the first time in years Annie Paxton opened her

eyes during meditation. She sipped the rosemary tea to clear the taste from her mouth.

The Ruizes. Zelda. Why had she thought of her poor neighbor down the street?

Because she had seen something on the girl the other week, Annie reminded herself. Something dark and sinuous she had tried to brush from her shoulder.

Annie blinked and let her eyes grow heavy again. She would send some good thoughts Zelda's way. Perhaps a healing chant. She would...

Her eyes snapped open. Her body tensed.

Because something had moved past the window and the crystals. A shadow now darkened the room.

Annie Paxton, who had trained her mind and nurtured her focus over decades, now found her attention wandering like a child full of sugar. Her eyes should be closed, her breath steady and slow. Instead, her gaze darted about the crystals. Her breath left her lips in a ragged gasp.

Because of the light.

The light through Walter's crystals was coming apart, like fraying threads in a loom. Reds and blues, greens and amber. The room spun with hues that speckled the walls. It was beautiful. She wondered if this was it. Perhaps a message from her late husband, one she'd hoped for after so many quiet years alone.

Then a new thought bloomed in her mind. It was morning, wasn't it? The sun would be on the eastern side of the house. The crystals, however, hung over the window that looked out to the west.

No, that wasn't sunlight pouring through the crystals, but something else. Something cold.

At this realization, one by one, the colors fled from the walls and floor, over the memento-filled shelves and across the warm tatami mats. Sparkling blues and verdant greens. Shimmering autumn crimson and gold. They all withdrew, leaving only a shadowy stain, black-violet at its edges, undulant and crawling.

That storm, she thought. The one that crackled in her mind. She'd given it form.

Because it wasn't a storm at all, but something ancient and waking.

No, Annie Paxton didn't believe in healing crystals, nor chakras, nor the power of stones. But she believed in her eyes and the dark light they saw. A shadow, now spilling across this room of calm thoughts and oozing toward her, inch by shivering inch.

CHAPTER FIFTEEN

Zelda had been worried she might cry as she boxed up her things. Instead, she felt something else: a lightness in her shoulders and a sense of relief.

It was a warm Friday in June, her last day in Alder Glen. Room by room, the house came apart. The movers stripped it of its furnishings and decorations until only bare walls and empty floor remained. She never realized how much space there was with everything gone.

She told herself this was a chance to start over. A fresh start. The movers weren't just stripping the house; they were giving her permission to let go and move on.

She wasn't sure she was ready.

"The urn," she said when she saw the empty spot by her bookshelf. "What did you do with it?"

A burly mover just looked at her blankly. Fear tightened her gut and turned the world crimson.

"My parents' urn," she snapped. "It's gray, about this big..." She checked every bedroom while another mover simply shrugged. "It's special, okay? You can't just mix it in with all the junk. Where did you put it?"

"It's okay, Zelda. It's okay." Uncle Mark emerged from the bathroom.

"No, it's not okay. They can't get lost—"

"I've got them right here." He retrieved a box full of framed photos. There it was, nestled among the family portraits.

She took the box.

"I just wanted to keep it safe," Uncle Mark said.

She nodded and muttered a quiet, "Thank you."

THAT AFTERNOON, SHE SKATEBOARDED DOWNTOWN AND got a boba tea with some classmates before they went their own ways for summer. One of them gave her a card, her last name spelled wrong. She realized she didn't really know anyone in her middle school all that well. So many friends had come and gone. She hoped high school would be different.

She spent a few hours at the local library, reading up on Greywood Bay, 250 miles to the north. It was part of an area known as the Lost Coast, an untamed section of California that ran for hundreds of miles.

Mostly, she was curious about the name and why gray was spelled with E and not an A. The librarian found a book in the regional history section that explained it.

> *When Arthur Cummings, a British poet and naturalist press-ganged into the War of 1812, fled west with frontiersmen and established a trading post, he remarked upon the abundance of driftwood scattered about the inlets and coves. There upon foggy shores lay redwood husks bleached by the sun, intermixed with the bones of dead whales, elephant seals, and all forms of wandering crustaceans who had the misfortune of getting lost upon those dry brambles.*
>
> *As an oarsman and navigator, he soon learned the currents*

were strong and the rocks treacherous. In the first five years of the post's fur trading and timber operation, eleven ships wrecked themselves upon the hidden reefs. Strong hulls and masts easily splintered by rocks joined the piles of wood, shell, and bone looming at the ankles of the great coastal cliffs.

Thus, he wrote to his partners in trade, warning their ship captains to be cautious of the temperamental tides and the sudden winds, the fog, and the lights at night that played tricks on the telescope, to be wary of Greywood Bay.

Zelda liked the sound of that. Yes, she liked it very much.

She checked the book out from the kiosk, telling herself she'd mail it back to the library in a month. Judging by the old binding and the cracked spine, she doubted they'd miss it.

That night they DoorDashed Indian food and ate it cross-legged on the floor of what had once been the living room. Uncle Mark's chewing echoed off the walls in the wide-open space. It was like chowing down in an empty dance studio.

"You excited?" he asked between a mouthful of samosa.

Zelda shrugged and soaked up some tikka masala with her naan. "I guess."

"I am," he said. "Excited, that is. And a little nervous, if I'm being honest. I ramble when I'm nervous. You like the masala? It's not too spicy?"

She shook her head. "It's fine."

"Good."

He ate for a while without speaking, chasing every few bites with a sip of Riesling. She noticed the bottle was nearly empty. She'd gotten drunk twice in her life. Once, when she was in Mexico on vacation and ordered a Long Island Iced Tea to see if she could. And a few months ago, in Lake Tahoe when...

No. She pushed that memory into the far darkness of her mind.

"How you feeling about summer school?" he asked. "Had a chance to check out the assignments?"

She nodded. She had. It was the usual stuff: using linear equations and applying the Pythagorean Theorem; finding distance, angles, and analyzing polygons; identifying *x*.

"If you need any help, I'll be just down the hall, okay?" He took an ample spoonful of chicken vindaloo and ate it. Zelda winced, knowing what was coming. "High school," he continued. "I haven't taught that age in a decade. So what do American high school kids do these days?"

"I don't know."

"I mean, is it like TikTok and selfies and Billie Eyelash or... Oh God." He waved a hand over his mouth. "That's *so* spicy. Can I please...?"

Eyes watering, he fumbled with her mango lassi and gulped down several sips.

"Oh, thank you."

Some days, it felt like Uncle Mark was just a big kid trying to act like a grown-up and fumbling. Sometimes, it made her smile. Other times, it gave her whiplash. Her parents had always been steady and quiet. But maybe that's all adults really were, just big kids with more responsibility and a lot of practice covering it up.

SHE ROLLED OUT HER SLEEPING BAG, USED A YOGA MAT as a cushion, and bunched pillows against the bare wall of her bedroom. She tried to sleep but kept focusing on the house and how empty and forlorn it sounded.

She could hear Uncle Mark mumbling on the phone downstairs, talking to his girlfriend. Or his ex-girlfriend, from the sound of the conversation. Rosy wasn't happy.

She wanted to tell him that he could go back to Spain if he wanted. That maybe living with her grandparents wouldn't be that bad. Yet that was a lie. She didn't like the way they grilled her during their weekly check-ins.

What was this about a fight you got into at school?

Do you feel uncomfortable around Uncle Mark?

Does he hug you or touch you in ways you don't like?

No, he didn't, but she was uncomfortable around them. They had spite in their eyes and their questions were hungry.

Zelda was almost asleep when she heard the crackling outside. Uncle Mark, probably pacing as Rosy gave him an earful long distance.

The crackling grew.

A branch snapped near the window and something ripped, like fabric. She sensed the presence, first as a shuffling, then as a shadow that crossed between the streetlight and her bedroom window. Wrapped in the sleeping bag, she shuffled over to the blinds. Quietly, she spread the metal slats and peered out.

Only shadows looked back. Just the old hawthorn tree looming outside her window, its leaves thick and its branches nettled with thorns.

Then something moved.

A hand stretched out from the leaves and passed through the moonlight. Glistening rubies spotted raw, wrinkled skin. No, Zelda realized, not rubies but blood. The leaves parted, and a face followed, a shivering mask crowned in gray hair, scratched cheeks beneath eyes wide and insane.

Zelda screamed and fell backward, the sleeping bag tangling her feet. The house shuddered as she came down hard on her bony ass. The slats snapped shut.

For a beat, nothing happened. Just a quiet night in the suburbs. And a faint scratching, as if the branches were tapping the glass.

Then the window shattered.

The old woman pushed herself through the glass, desperately stretching from the tree branch and grabbing the blinds. Her fingers spread them apart, splitting the metal slats, slicing her hand as her face pressed through the gap.

"She sees you! The Last Refugee, she sees into your heart. Run from her, child. Listen to me, Zelda. Please listen."

The woman's lips quivered, both maddening and familiar. Through the wet crimson mask, Zelda recognized her neighbor from down the street, Annie Paxton.

She was nearly naked.

Her limbs had been scourged and her nightgown torn on the thorny tree. As she pulled herself through the blinds, Zelda noticed her sagging breasts and one nipple nearly sliced off.

"Run, Zelda. Run! The Last Refugee stirs. She'll cinder the winds and blister your skin. Your tongue will be ash." Mrs. Paxton collapsed onto the floor, bringing the tangled blinds with her. "She dreams and schemes from beyond the dead stars. What hope do you have?"

Glass crackled beneath her knees as she rose from the floor, wearing the blinds like shattered armor. And her eyes....

A black-violet light rimmed the whites of her eyes, smoldering and vaporous. Her eyes stretched so wide Zelda thought they might just burst from her face.

"Please, deary, please, while your sanity lasts... Run... Run far from her glare!"

She stretched a trembling red hand toward Zelda. Closer, closer and—

Then a light filled the room and Uncle Mark grabbed Zelda, pulling her out through the bedroom door, and slamming it shut. Even in his pajamas, he moved fast, carrying her down the stairs, out the front door, and into the night.

CHAPTER SIXTEEN

Sipping warm tea and shivering, Mark watched the paramedics take the old woman away. Zelda sat on the porch nearby, her hoodie over her head as a policewoman wrote down her statement. Digital cameras clicked, white light capturing photos of the broken window and tree. Along the street, neighbors watched from behind fences and windows.

"And that's all you saw. You're sure of it?" the officer asked Mark. He was a young guy, late twenties and friendly.

"I heard a scream. I opened the bedroom door. And she was there, on the floor and coming at my niece."

The young officer scribbled it down. "And you didn't strike her, fight back, anything?"

Mark considered it, the adrenaline still coursing through his veins and drying his tongue. "No, we shut her in and called you. That's it."

"Did she say anything?"

"Yeah, she said a bunch of stuff, none of which made any sense." Mark rubbed his eyes. "Look, is she going to be all right?"

The officer shrugged. "I'm sure they'll get her some help. Did you and Ms. Paxton have any history of conflict or...?"

"No, of course not. She's just a sweet old hippie that lives down the street. I met her once, that's all. I don't understand why she'd do this."

The officer closed his notebook. "Personality change, confusion, out after ten. It's possible she's sundowning and thought she was home."

Mark glanced up at the tree, where scraps of nightgown still hung from the thorny branches. "Do sundowning seniors usually climb trees?"

The officer considered it. "Not that I've seen."

Mark finished giving his statement, fear tightening his shoulders as the cops jotted down his ID. This might make its way back to the lawyers, the counselor, and Judge Fulghum. The Ruiz family might find a way to spin it.

One by one, the cops drove off, leaving him and Zelda to the quiet, dark night.

"God, what a clusterfu—" He stopped himself. "How you hanging in there?"

Zelda closed the front door and locked them in the house. "Okay."

"Okay? Really?"

She shrugged.

"Zelda, an old woman just tore herself to shreds breaking in through your window. It's okay *not* to be okay. Hell, look at me." He held out his shaking hands. "I couldn't draw a straight line if I tried."

She lingered in the entryway, a girl with eyes too old for her thirteen years on this earth. She was going to retreat inward again. He could sense it with her stiffening posture. Where was that laughing child that once put an ice cream cone on his head? Where was that kid who had cheered when she hit a winning home run in Little League just a few years ago?

Her fingers picked at a notch in the doorframe. He had to squint just to see what it was.

A dozen little dates were penciled in the molding, markings where Zelda had grown. He recognized his sister's handwriting and how she crossed her sevens.

Zelda's lip trembled as she smeared one of the numbers. "I just..."

She teetered there for a moment, closing her eyes and consuming the silence. He wanted to hug her, to tell her none of this was her fault. That she was a good kid. And that the world always hurt those with good hearts most of all.

But she knew that already.

When her eyes opened, something had hardened within. "I just really want to leave this place," she said. "Too many memories."

Mark nodded. "Okay. Let's go right now."

A puff of air fled from her nose. "It's almost midnight."

"So? There's no rule saying we can't take off. I'll grab some coffee. We'll make the drive. We can catch the sunrise or you can snooze on the way."

"I don't think I could sleep."

"Okay, it's settled then. You're navigating."

Thirty minutes later, their bags were in the back of the Subaru as the headlights filled the driveway. While Zelda queued up some songs, Mark turned off the house lights, locked the door, and set the alarm.

"Here we go," he said, and put the car in drive.

She didn't look back.

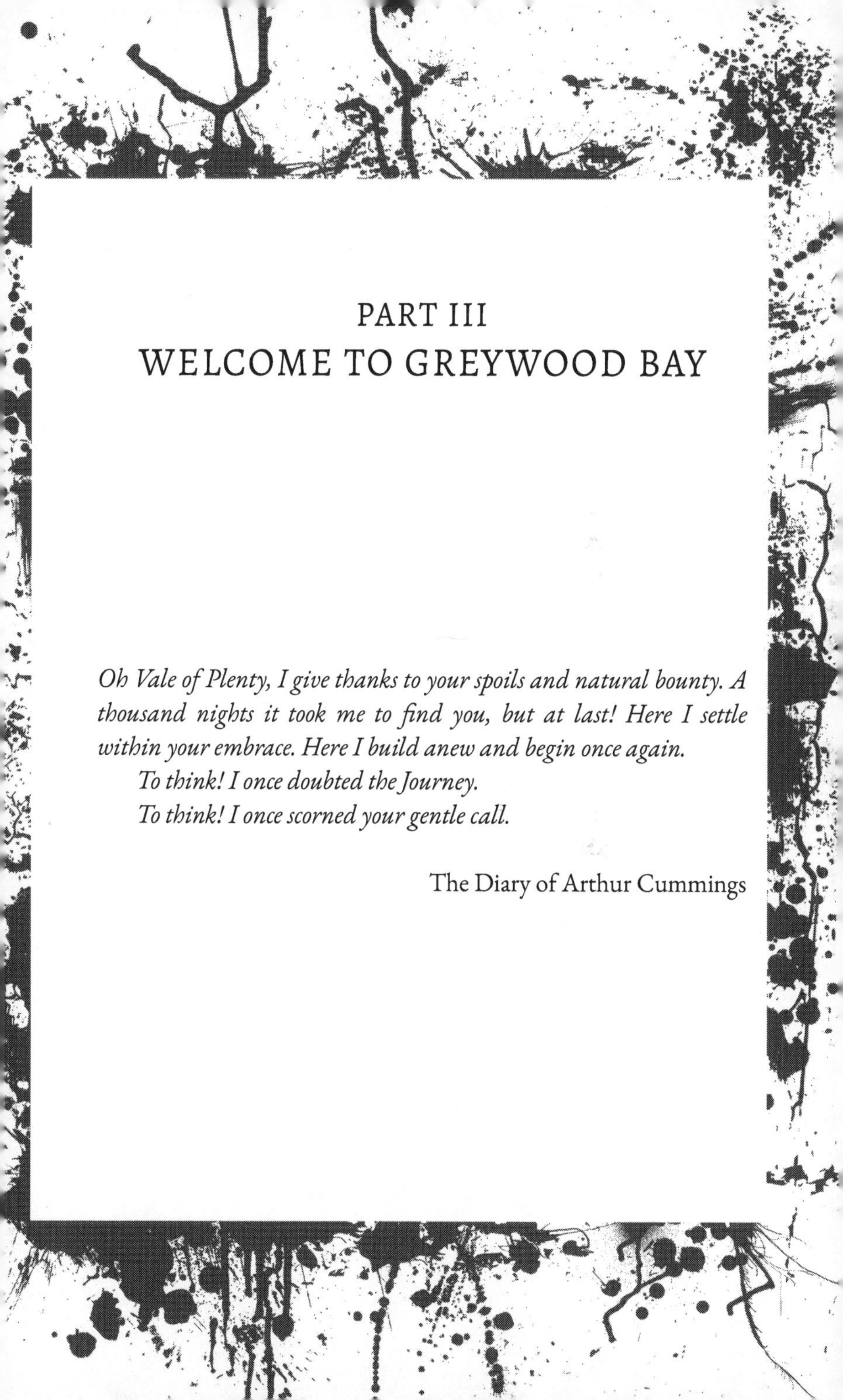

PART III
WELCOME TO GREYWOOD BAY

Oh Vale of Plenty, I give thanks to your spoils and natural bounty. A thousand nights it took me to find you, but at last! Here I settle within your embrace. Here I build anew and begin once again.

To think! I once doubted the Journey.

To think! I once scorned your gentle call.

The Diary of Arthur Cummings

CHAPTER SEVENTEEN

With a dramatic twist of his wrist and a sharp tug, Edward Strathmore IV pulled the cloth from the model and stepped back. Here at Raven's Peak, with the setting sun and the cool coastal breeze, he could let the landscape speak for itself. The golden slopes of the hills, the trails and the trees. Raven's Valley below, all 222 houses sold and sparkling.

Now the future lay before them.

"Well, look at that," said Ron Figueroa. He placed his mojito on the edge of the model and leaned in. "You really cut out five hundred little houses, my goodness."

Someone whistled and stepped closer. "Only thing missing is one of them model trains going around it." That was Bob Haverford, his spray-on tan a little too bright in the setting sunlight. "You could have it go through the center, right there."

Edward winced inside as Bob jabbed a greasy finger at the model of Hawk's Hollow. He should have waited until after the pitch to have the caterers bring out the hors d'oeuvres.

He let the investors pace the table, inspecting the little streets, the neighborhoods, the parks and playgrounds, all rendered at

1:240 scale. He was proud of the model. It had taken months and tens of thousands of dollars.

And yeah, it frustrated him to see the money men circling it like some science fair presentation. Poking at the little trees and spilling drinks on the streets. But hell, if it loosened their checkbooks, he could put on his best salesman's smile.

"Gentleman, ladies, future investors of Greywood Bay. I present Hawk's Hollow reimagined. A new community where contemporary comfort and rustic styling converge to meet the needs of the modern homeowner. Five hundred units for every price point, from the first-time buyer to the family looking for maximum amenities and square footage. We're taking everything we learned from Raven's Valley and doubling down. More parks and open spaces for the kids. Faster fiber connections to keep everyone online. Smart homes and a smart grid and all the charming, eco-friendly touches you've come to expect from Strathmore & Daniels. Each home as unique as the families inside, and—"

"Question for you, Ed." State Assemblyman Tai Vuong plucked a sautéed mushroom from a caterer's plate as it passed. "If all the houses are unique, how come these little models look the same?"

A murmur and a series of nods drifted through the pack of investors. A few leaned close to the model, towering godlike over the rubber streets and the trees made of painted fibers and foam.

Because it's a presentation, not a battle plan, you big idiot, Edward thought. *Because there's not enough time in the world to model it out all exact.*

Fortunately, his business partner Melissa read his look and intercepted.

"We felt your money was best spent on the actual units," she said. "Not in creating five hundred unique models. I suggested *Monopoly* pieces, but Eddie here overruled me."

Laughter filled the air and carried across the hills. She gave Edward a wink.

God, he hated this part of the job. The potential investors, all pacing like hyenas. The politicians, poking for angles and roadblocks. The old money and the new, all mixed in together and judging each other. Begging always felt distasteful, but he knew that's what this was: just a fancy dinner party in the foothills that he hoped would pay off.

Edward had never wanted to go into real estate development, but the Strathmore name had decided for him. So, here he stood, nine hundred feet above sea level. Raven's Valley to his right and the wasteland that could be Hawk's Hollow to his left.

"And you think you can fill every one of them?" asked Oleksandar Zaluzhnyi, one of the new money families who'd been snapping up property for a firm in Kyiv.

Edward nodded. "Interest rates are low and demand is through the roof. There's never been a better time to invest in the American dream. Now, if the law didn't stop me, I'd put every last penny in this myself. Or maybe our esteemed assemblyman here can legislate me a loophole."

Edward raised his martini as Assemblyman Vuong put his fingers in his ears. Another round of polite chuckles from the investors.

While they circled the model and perused the pamphlets, Edward backed off. He found a plate of smoked salmon on toast and dug in. He'd been so nervous he'd hardly eaten since lunch. Now, he was ravenous.

Wine in hand, Melissa found him and whispered, "I didn't know there were laws preventing us from owning." She gave him a coy smile and sipped her merlot.

"As my father always said, 'Never shit where you sleep.'" Edward chewed another hors d'oeuvre before his mouth got him in trouble.

Melissa raised a playful eyebrow. "Any other wise words from the great man?"

Edward swallowed. "'Ed, my boy, our family made its fortune

on timber and land, so if you join those tree-hugging park rangers, I'll tie you to a redwood and saw it down myself.'"

"Eww, stop. It's like he's right here." She gave him a playful nudge.

Edward liked Melissa. She came from the same place of status and understood the weight of legacy. Hell, neither of their marriages had worked out for similar reasons. Their partners saw endless checkbooks but didn't understand the upkeep wealth required. The donations given, the philanthropies founded. The endless social obligations. These were champagne problems, sure, and he knew he was whining. Still, that didn't mean he was wrong.

Then a new thought occurred: was she flirting with him? She stood a bit closer than usual, alcohol-flushed and chatty. Was he so focused on the pitch he'd missed her signals?

A hand patted his shoulder and ended his musing. "Ed, what a wonderful soiree." He knew who it was without turning.

Like Edward and Melissa, Larry Larchmont came from Greywood Bay gentry. Yet a cloud of misfortune clung to him, his eyes always a little too hungry. Edward reminded himself that all the rich families were just a few scandals away from collapse.

"Listen, Ed, I don't mean to sully your fun, but we still haven't gotten a deposit on materials. Is everything okay? You happy with the lumber?" Larry gave him a squeeze on the shoulder.

"Sorry, Larry, I'll get the accountants on that ASAP. But do me a favor: work on that swing of yours, okay? Gonna need you on the green in a few weeks."

Edward finished his martini and grabbed another from a tray. He had to get out of Larry's sad miasma. He could feel it oozing into his skin.

He spotted Vice Mayor Lydia Barton by the scenic lookout and made his way over. God help him, Larry was still on his tail.

"Quite the vision you've got for Hawk's Hollow," Lydia said. "I remember when this whole valley was on life support. South

River. The Old Mill. Didn't we used to buy dime bags from that day laborer, Juan, in Raven's Valley?"

With the flick of a diamond-ringed finger, she gestured to the houses and streets glowing in the evening's long light.

"It was Jorge," Edward said. "Juan bought us beer at Whiskey Gulch."

Larry asked, "Didn't you get robbed there one night?"

Edward forced a smile to his face. "Twice, actually."

Lydia smiled. "Well, cheers to gentrification."

"I'll drink to that."

"But there's still one problem with your plan, as I see it."

She pointed out to the west side of Raven's Valley, her finger tracing its way past the tennis courts and the dry Eel River, then stopping over a rusty wasteland of metal. Damn, he had hoped this wouldn't come up.

"Tell me, Ed. Just how on earth are you going to connect Raven's Valley to Hawk's Hollow without old Halgrove's patch of land?"

He took a long gulp of his martini. "We're still working on that."

CHAPTER EIGHTEEN

Down a cul-de-sac riddled in potholes and cracked pavement there loomed an old house, one bent and depressed and perpetually shrouded in dust. The ramshackle Victorian at the end of Ponderosa Court incubated sharp nails and moaned in the breeze. Its once-noble angles now conflicted, a tired ruin on the edge of collapse. Inside, shadows clawed at meandering halls, the walls broken and spotty. Logic and laughter no longer lived here. Only a scabrous form, one who emerged from the basement, tugging a tattered linen sack full of dirt.

Chester Halgrove was no friend to the light. With a wheeze from his tired lungs, he gave the sack a yank, dragging it up the rickety steps. He set it at the top of the stairs, the dark basement yawning below. He caught his breath.

Where was he going and where had he been? What was he doing now? He lingered for a moment, gripping the flimsy banister as he checked his old watch. Nearly noon.

Time slipped often these days. It played tricks on his mind and skipped around through the years. It muddied past and present.

Noon. Basement. Bag full of dirt. He studied his blistered palms and the shovel. Yes, he'd been burying something, hadn't he?

"No," he muttered. "You been diggin' it up."

The dirty sack, right. It needed to go *outside*, not in.

With a grunt, he gave the linen sack a sharp tug. Another pull, and it slid across the old floor. He dug his hands into the bag's ropes and braced his feet on the wood. His tired knees wobbled as he heaved.

Foot by miserable foot, he tugged the lumpy sack across the house. He could see the back porch, the windows papered over. Thirty feet. Twenty feet. Fifteen.

He did not see the loose rusty nail as it passed underfoot. His feet were calloused and black, his boots too thick to notice. He felt the bite of the nail only as it sliced into the linen.

And then tore.

"No," he muttered. "No, no, no no no."

Hands trembling, he fumbled with the old sack, clamping the seam as it split. Dry dirt spilled between his blistered fingers, first in a stream, then several. With a *scrich*, the old sack came apart.

Twigs and worms and loose fragments of brick, it all poured out. No matter how hard he tried, how fast he pushed the soil back into the sack, it continued to spill.

"Please," Chester moaned. "Please... Just a little longer. It's... almost... time."

One of the twigs wriggled and stroked his palm.

Chester gasped and fell backward, his arthritic bones jittering as sparks bloomed in his vision. Had he really just seen that?

He blinked away the dust and leaned forward. Sure enough, that wasn't a twig trying to poke its way out of the dirt.

It was a finger.

A damn finger wriggled and curled between the frayed linen seam.

Then another finger, and another, and a whole wretched hand.

Wheezing, Chester watched as two sickly gray hands clawed their way out from the seam.

"No, no, no, please..." Chester wiped his dusty eyes, seeing but not believing. The dry dirt moistened and the linen grew damp. Then it emerged.

A head—a fucking *head*—thrust out from the earth. It wasn't dry dirt but mud, glistening and wet. Dark lumps tumbled as the rotting face crowned its way out through the ripped linen.

A face that he knew.

"You." Mud dripped from the man's moldy green lips. "You did this to us. Coward."

Those eyes. Those cold milky eyes... They bore into Chester, spiteful and judging.

"I'm sorry," Chester moaned. "I'm sorry."

With a shivering twitch, the dead man stretched out a wet hand. Black fingers snatched a handful of Chester's tangled beard.

"Cow-ard," the dead man sputtered. "Cow-ard! COW-ARD!"

His grip was tight and his fingers unbreakable. He tugged Chester close, closer to the splitting sack with its dirt full of fingers. Closer to his gnashing, mud-spattered teeth.

And then Chester's hands moved on instinct. His index finger found a lump of mud and drew a circle on the floor. With a broad swipe, he traced a dark line across it. A third furious motion and he painted a dirty arc and added spattered dots.

A symbol they both knew.

The dead man's eyes flashed and his teeth gnashed.

And then... nothing.

The torn bag lay on its side, the seam unraveling as dry dirt spilled forth. There was no water or mud. The fingers, the hands, and that horrible face were all gone. Chester shuddered and wiped the symbol from the floor. Its job was finished.

But he still had so much to do.

Sighing, he tightened the sack. He was nearly at the back door when he saw the shadow pass the front porch. The doorbell buzzed.

No. Not now. This was a bad time for visitors.

"Mmm... It's always a bad time when your mind's filled with worms. Why not end it, old man? You—"

"Quiet." Chester raised a hand. He wasn't in the mood to argue, not with *her*. Not while strangers stood on his porch doing God-knew-what.

Cautiously, he lumbered over to the door and peeled a strip of newspaper from the window. The first thing he saw was the woman in the lavender suit. Diadra or Daniella or something. She carried a clipboard and had the stiff posture of someone peddling door-to-door bibles. Chester thought he might just bark at her, scare her off his damn porch.

But he was tired. So damn tired of it all.

Then he saw the man in the gray blazer. He paced the weedy garden, reaching up to touch one of the metal effigies. Chester threw open the door.

"Hands off it," he shouted. "Get away from Jerry Jenkins."

The woman let out a gasp while the man in the gray blazer blinked dimly at Chester. His hand fell from the seven-foot-tall metal sculpture to a briefcase he'd set on the ground. In the momentary quiet, Chester was aware that these two were the first people he'd talked to all month.

"Mmm... The first living people, old man."

"Good afternoon, Mr. Halgrove." The woman forced a smile to her face. She reminded him of a lemur, her smile shaky and her eyes a little too wide. "We wanted to touch base, to follow up on our discussion."

Chester squinted. "Discussion?"

The woman and the man in the blazer converged on the porch. A briefcase was hoisted and opened. Chester didn't like the snap of the clasps and the crinkling paper. The noon light was getting funny once again. How long had he been standing here? Minutes? Days?

"The offer, Mr. Halgrove, sir," the man said. "We dropped off the revised offer last month. On the twelfth, I believe." He consulted his phone, one of those smart ones with the whole internet inside. Chester didn't like those phones. Too much radiation and the auras kept shifting.

Just like this man and the woman.

Their auras fumed a saddle-leather brown, greedy and covetous.

"Have you given thought to the offer?" the man asked. "Strathmore & Daniels, they're willing to work through any concerns you might have. It's quite generous, this offer."

"More than generous." The woman ran a finger along the porch railing and wrinkled her nose.

"Sir, we're authorized to offer up to ten percent more," the man said, teeth sparkling white. "That's the best and final offer. But we'd need to get your preliminary signature today."

"My signature?" Chester rubbed his eyes. They were hurting something fierce now, the light all sharp and jagged. "What's my signature for?"

The man let out something of a derisive snort. The woman's eyes flashed with frustration.

She said, "For your property, Mr. Halgrove. We've been over this several times. Strathmore & Daniels want to purchase the entire lot. And given its condition, well, it's quite the offer."

He studied the pen in his blistered fingers, the pages with the little red arrows for his signature. They were all sitting now, together, around the old porch table. The woman held some sort of stamp. Had there been another splice of time?

"Wait... Just wait," Chester said. "I don't understand."

"Diana's a notary, sir," the man said. "It'll save us some time. Just... sign here. There you go..."

The house. The valley. He could be done with it all.

"And we could be done with each other."

But the effigies. And the damn basement. They'd find out what he'd done in the deep shadows below.

"No," he muttered. "No, no, no, the timing's all wrong. It doesn't happen like this."

He rose, letting the pen fall from his hand. The Diana woman and the charcoal-blazer fellow, they both stood with him, auras spiking violet and their eyes filling with greed. He scurried back to his door and slammed it shut.

"Mr. Halgrove, sir! Mr. Halgrove!"

He stuffed his fingers into his ears and collapsed to the floor. The house moaned and sighed. He watched the dust drifting through the sun-speared shadows and ruins of this once-opulent house.

Eventually, their voices faded. He was alone.

And yet, he sensed another. A new presence now, one beyond the broken walls.

A dark spark, bright for a moment, then gone.

Emergence.

His attention returned to the sack of dirt he'd left by the back porch.

It was crawling once again.

CHAPTER NINETEEN

As the movers delivered the last of the furnishings and the walls and rooms of 33 Manzanita Way grew crowded, Mark and Zelda fell back into old routines and embraced a few new ones.

They explored the community of Raven's Valley, smitten with the tree-lined streets, the jogging paths around the lake, the hiking trails that zigzagged through the foothills to the north, east, and west.

In the mornings, neighbors waved and introduced themselves. After fifteen years abroad, Mark found American friendliness uncanny. He'd lived below a German family in Madrid for years. They'd been one of his nicest neighbors and they hardly spoke.

Now, the Weilands across the street were offering to let him use their leaf blower or lawn mower while listing off the best restaurants in town. He'd known them all of five minutes.

In the evenings, the families walked dogs while crickets chirped and filled the sidewalks with song. It wasn't until Mark was unloading groceries one night that Zelda traced the crickets to a speaker at the base of a lamppost.

"It's just a recording," she said, listening as the song looped. "That's kind of creepy."

"I believe the French call it 'ambiance.'" He passed her a bag of groceries. "And yeah, it's pretty weird."

THE NEW TV ARRIVED A FEW DAYS LATER, CARRIED BY two burly men with a dozen tools on their belts. Mark knew just the place to install it: the living room mantle, with its gorgeous reclaimed wood. It was the centerpiece of the room and a natural point of focus. Yet when the installers put the TV down and unboxed it, Mark found the mantle already crowded.

Maya and Juan Carlos's urn sat beside a collection of framed photos Zelda had set up.

"Never mind," he told the installers. "We'll find somewhere else."

MARK TOOK THE BEDROOM AT THE TOP OF THE STAIRS and Zelda chose the one at the end of the hall. They made plans to turn the room between them into a study.

It pleased Zelda to discover that her bedroom window opened onto the top of the garage. With some careful climbing, she could push off against the chimney, shimmy alongside the solar panels, and hoist herself up onto the roof. There, she could see Raven's Valley all spread out around her, hundreds of homes and hundreds of families. And beyond, the lights of Greywood Bay blinked and the trees swayed in the ocean's breeze.

She wondered if she'd ever fit in.

At night, she often lay there, back against the warm shingles and the cool sky above. She watched stars emerge between fast-flowing currents of fog. She reminded herself that some of those stars might even be dead, and the light now hitting her eyes was only a memory of warmth.

CHAPTER TWENTY

The bell interrupted Mr. Barker's closing remarks and launched twenty-odd students from their desks. In seconds, books were gathered, pencils packed away, and backpacks slung over shoulders, all before the bell finished ringing. It was remarkable how fast kids moved when class was over.

"Now, what I was saying"—Mr. Barker tapped the whiteboard —"is that your first assignment... No no, don't groan. We're only just beginning this mathematical odyssey. Your homework is to find an object to triangulate."

The students raised their phones and took pictures as he scribbled on the board.

"This object could be anything. A mountain, a chimney, a lighthouse—"

"Dibs on the lighthouse," shouted a Middle Eastern boy named Ali. "Done!"

"And you need to go there and take a picture of it."

"Aww," Ali groaned. "It's so far."

"Yes, far. Distance. This week we'll be calculating the distance and height of your object, just like our Egyptian friends did thousands of years ago. Now go. Scram."

The students hurried out of the classroom, their footsteps filling the halls of Neumann Prep. Lockers slammed as books were swapped out or stowed. A large kid squeezed past Zelda, licked his finger, and jammed it in another student's ear. He took off laughing as the wet-eared student chased behind.

Zelda had never been to a private school before, let alone one that went from kindergarten all the way to twelfth grade. It was different from her old middle school, with its sad, sagging benches, crowded fields, and chain-link fences protecting bicycles.

Here, there were organic gardens and swimming pools, and the fields were wide and ample. A lacrosse team practiced while several students flew drones through an obstacle course. By the upper-level wing—what Zelda realized was high school—one group of students disassembled a car while another group recorded the procedure with cameras.

It all felt surreal.

Walking west across campus, she even found some ramps, rails, and a funbox set up in the parking lot. A banner proclaimed, *Greywood Bay Summer Skate Camp. Enroll now!* Counselors offered encouragement while nervous elementary students wobbled and tried turning on their skateboards.

Zelda put her own board down, skated past them, and ollied off the curb. A couple of girls went wide-eyed and pointed. She smiled and skated on.

At an intersection, someone shouted, "Hey! Hey you!"

She glanced back to see Ali struggling to peddle a bike that was too big. On the back rack sat a husky girl with red hair and a camouflage cast on her forearm.

Panting and wobbling, Ali pulled up to the curb. "Zelda, right?"

"Yeah."

"You left an earbud in the classroom," he said. "Fortunately, I'm both handsome and honest. Here you go, m'lady."

He gave a little bow and opened his hand, revealing her wireless earbud. She turned out her pocket. He was right; there was only one inside.

"Wow, thank you." She took the earbud. "I always lose these things."

"I have the eyes of an eagle," Ali said. "See that sign down there? I can read it from here. No right... turn when... children are... present."

"And you have the mouth of a monkey," said the girl on the rack. She jumped off, and the suspension rose an inch. "I'm Maura. This is Ali. He talks a lot, but he's okay."

"I process the world verbally," Ali said, and rang the bike's bell. "Also, FYI, but your shoes are mismatched."

He pointed to Zelda's sneakers, a blue Vans Authentic on her left foot, a green one on her right.

"It's called fashion." Maura gave Zelda a friendly wink. "So, are you here for summer school or the full year?"

It had been a week since they'd arrived, and Zelda realized this was the first time she was talking to someone her own age. She didn't quite know what to do with her body, her hands. She thumbed a skateboard wheel.

"Summer school, for sure. I failed math so—"

"No way!" Ali said. "I failed it too."

"Ali, we *all* failed math," Maura said. "That's why we're here."

"Well, I got an A in media studies and I'm retaking it."

"Because you're a glutton for punishment."

"Says the girl on the football team," Ali said. "Not that there's anything wrong with that. Oh, how's the arm, Tom Brady? Still broken? Buuuurn."

Maura gave Ali's leg a quick kick with her sandals. He scampered back, rubbing his shin and trying to keep the bike from falling over. "Ah, my bones are so tender. Why?"

Zelda couldn't help but smile at these two. In class, she'd been focused on the workshop and the first lesson, trying to keep up.

But now, she had the whole afternoon ahead of her and she didn't know a soul.

"So, where are you from?" Maura asked.

"She's from Raven's Valley," Ali said, still wincing and holding the bike. "I saw them moving in last week."

"Dude, could you mansplain for her any more?"

"I can mansplain for *hours*."

"Alder Glen," Zelda said. "But yeah, he's right. We moved in last week."

"Raven's Valley crew represent." Ali limped and pushed the bike forward.

Zelda wasn't sure why, but she walked alongside them. Maybe it was because they hadn't treated her like she was fragile, asking if she needed anything, if she was okay. Or maybe it was just because they were friendly.

"So, do you really play football?" she asked.

Maura nodded. "Ever since fourth grade."

"Cool." Zelda tried to imagine Maura in pads. The girl was big, not fat but strong and solid. There was a confidence in her walk that she envied.

"She also does jiujitsu and wrestles," Ali said. "She came third in the state championship."

"Seriously?"

Maura gave another nod and a smile, proud yet humble.

Ali said, "My girlfriend's a champ, yo."

"I'm not your girlfriend, Ali."

"Not yet," he said. "But technically, you are a girl who is my friend. So deny it all you want, but the evidence says otherwise. Oh! A rare spawn! BRB."

Ali fumbled with his phone, passing his bike off to Maura, who caught it a moment before it fell from the curb. "Ali, geez."

"Thanks, babe!"

He raced off down the sidewalk, hoisting his phone's screen to his face and almost colliding with a fence. Then he turned down a leafy side street and was gone.

"He loves that game," Maura said. "He got into the beta last week and it's all he's been talking about."

Zelda knew exactly what game she meant. She'd felt her phone vibrate as well, the little notification telling her they were nearing the location of a rare enemy. She had considered checking it out but decided against it.

"Alder Glen, huh?" Maura said. "We had a match there this spring. Coach bought us Zippy Burgers on the way back."

"Zippy Burger is the best," Zelda said. "Tell me you got the Cheesy Shock fries?"

"Hell yeah. That's the only way to go."

Then she did something that surprised Zelda. She reached out a fist. Zelda made her own, and they tapped knuckles.

They walked for another minute or so in silence. Zelda was still getting used to the sounds of Greywood Bay: the distant hum of the ocean and the cry of the gulls; the occasional buzz of a small plane taking off from the local airport; the wind that whipped down over the hills and rustled the trees, strong in the afternoon and evening.

"So, what do people do around here?" Zelda asked, adding, "Like, for fun and stuff."

Maura considered it. "Downtown's okay. The Marquee shows horror movies on Saturday night, so we sometimes sneak in. I saw *Re-Animator* a few weeks ago. You ever see that?"

Zelda shook her head.

"And there's a game store that sells, like, board games and tanks you can paint or Dungeons and Dragons stuff, if you're into that."

"My dad was."

Was. It still felt weird to say that.

"Oh! And there's a new park in Raven's Valley with a climbing wall. I want to try it but my doc says I have to wait until six months after the cast comes off. Something about stressing my bone before it fully heals."

"I've never rock-climbed."

"Lots of people come here for the rock-climbing and the hiking. My brother has to rescue them when they get stuck, which is, like, every month."

"He's a rock-climber?"

"Search and rescue with the Forest Service. But the park's got some good areas for skateboarding. Like, stairs and rails and stuff. Ali likes to fly his drone there."

"Cool."

"So... maybe we should check it out sometime?"

It took Zelda a beat to realize that was an invitation. "Yeah, that'd be fun."

Maura smiled. "Cool."

The street joined a bridge that spanned a dry river. Zelda noticed rusty barrels and shopping carts among the sand and rocks far below. Old grates and outlets lined the eroded banks. Maura followed her gaze.

"Drought's pretty bad, so Eel River's super dry. Otherwise, we could go tubing. But when it gets super hot, we've still got the beach. The waves are good, but the water's rough."

"Whoa," Zelda said. "What's that?"

Beyond the bridge and a block down, where the dry river ran up against a reedy footpath, stood a corrugated fence. From street level, it might have looked like any derelict part of town beyond Raven's Valley.

But from the bridge, they could see over the fence. Rusty cars teetered in stacks. Tangled wires and girders lay in scattered mounds. Refrigerators and washers, dented ovens and steel basins, entire rows of scrap all formed a labyrinth of decaying metal.

"That," Maura said, "is the heap."

"The heap?"

"Scrap heap. Some old guy named Chester owns it." She

stretched out her broken arm and pointed. "See all those sculptures and that totally haunted house?"

Zelda nodded. The Victorian house must've been gorgeous a hundred years ago. Now, the pine-green paint and navy trim were chipped away by years of neglect. Spotty shingles barely clung to a sagging roof.

It took her eyes a moment to find the sculptures. When she did, a chill ran up her spine.

They were hideous.

Dark metal forms of vague human suggestion posed about the scrap heap, on the brown lawn, across the reedy property. Some held shields, while others stretched out three or four arms. Some were barely human at all, just an amalgamation of limbs connected to a torso and featureless faces. Even from this distance, Zelda could see that the sculptures looked tormented.

"He's been here since, like, before the dinosaurs," Maura said. "Supposedly, his home is, like, historical or something."

"So, is he an artist or…?"

Maura shrugged. "My dad says he's just a big jerk. 'Stay off my darn lawn,' you know?"

They were on the downslope of the bridge now, the scrap heap and the decrepit house no longer visible. A couple of blocks ahead, the street met the eastern entrance to Raven's Valley.

Panting, Ali came running up behind them.

"Oh man, you totally missed it. The rare spawn? It was a level 30 blood hunter. I almost had it too. Then it used a gravity cannon in phase two and stun-locked me once I ran out of anti-grav potions."

"Dude, you're speaking in tongues," Maura said.

He held up a hand, still panting. "Ali fight. Ali die. Now Ali sad. Is that clear enough, or should I draw a picture with crayons?"

Maura tried to give him a punch, but he rolled just out of reach.

“Were there any others there?” Zelda asked. “Anyone else get a tap on the blood hunter?”

“Nah, I was solo. He even drops the plasma knife I need —*wait*. Do you play?”

Maura raised an eyebrow as Ali cocked his head. Zelda tried to hide her smirk.

She asked, “He was only level 30, you say?”

CHAPTER TWENTY-ONE

With a squeak of steel against linoleum, Mark pushed the last desk into place. He preferred grouping his students in fours as opposed to rows. It facilitated discussion, built camaraderie, and made group work easier. Still, he was sharing the classroom with other teachers, some who felt different. Best to not rock the boat.

With a knock, Stacy Layne poked her head in the classroom. She wore the same blazer and dark pleated pants he'd seen her in this morning, greeting the students and parents for the first day of summer school. He had wanted to talk, to say thanks, but she'd been busy.

"So, how'd it go?" she asked. "Not fleeing into the hills yet?"

"No, not yet. I wasn't sure which direction the hills were."

She flashed a friendly smile. "Give me a warning if you do so we can unleash the hounds."

"Honestly? The kids were great. The frosh and sophomores are pretty advanced. The juniors... well, they're a bit rough at the edges, but I only had two fall asleep."

"Only two? That's probably a record for this classroom."

They glanced around the room. Sophie Saperstein—Mrs. Saperstein to the students—favored framed posters with kitschy platitudes and saccharine images.

A group of kids frozen mid-jump and cheering below the text *TEAM: Together Everyone Achieves More.*

A man pulling a boulder by a chain with several others behind him. *Leadership starts from the front.*

A smiling dog racing after a car. *Chase your dreams.*

The only thing missing, Mark thought, was a cursive sign that read, *Live, Laugh, Love.*

"Yeah," he said. "It does have a sort of early-nineties vibe to it."

"I was thinking more of a Dramamine theme."

They stood there for a moment, her at the door and Mark zipping up his supplies. This wasn't his relaxed college in Madrid, but it felt nice to be back in the classroom. The past few months had knocked him off balance.

She asked, "So, how're you all settling into Raven's Valley?"

"Good. Great, actually. We keep finding something new in the house. Last night, Zelda set up the motion sensors and the video doorbell. I can scare the mailman with an app."

"Yeah, it's the first house I've had that comes with a tutorial on YouTube. Half the time, I can't get it working."

"You need a thirteen-year-old around. It's free tech support."

A loud click echoed out and the lights dimmed in the hall. Stacy said, "Well, that's the sign. They chase us out at 4:50. Anyway, if you need anything..." She motioned down the hall to her office and then left.

Mark shut down his computer, zipped up his bags, and turned off the lights. It was almost five and his nerves craved a glass of wine or perhaps a nice bourbon.

He knew he needed to be professional around Stacy. She wasn't only his boss, but she was in charge of the whole summer school program. A lot rode on a good enrollment. He was just seasonal, able to be fired faster than he'd been hired. But if he could get a foot in the door, he might get an appointment and then a faculty discount for Zelda in the fall.

And yet, he couldn't help himself.

He locked the classroom and found her outside her office. "Ms. Layne?"

She closed up while he hurried over.

"So, I don't really know anyone here yet," he said, "but I was wondering if you'd like to go grab a drink?"

She considered it for a moment. Had he overstepped some boundary? A decade and a half of living abroad had left him out of touch with contemporary America, a fact he'd realized while watching training videos all week. Trigger warnings, safe spaces, preferred pronouns, and more. Was it even appropriate to ask a colleague out for drinks? Probably not.

"I'll have to pass," Stacey said. "But how about a coffee instead?"

THE BREAKWATER CAFE WAS A MILE AND A HALF FROM Neumann Prep, a pleasant walk down a hill where the streets offered a sparkling view of the coast. Bicycles and motorcycles filled up the bulk of the cafe's parking lot. Sequoias loomed in the back. A redwood patio sat packed with picnic tables where leathernecks and cyclists, hippies and tech workers all ate and intermingled. There was a bohemian air to the grove, little dream catchers dangling from branches and wicker figurines hanging off the walls.

Coffees in hand, they squeezed between the tables, Stacey pausing to chat with a few locals, always remembering to introduce Mark as the Spanish teacher who was saving her ass. They found a quiet part of the patio and sat.

"How's the chicory coffee?" she asked as Mark took his first cool sip. "It's something different, right?"

"Yeah, it's tasty." It wasn't a lie. But a Moscow mule would have been better. Dampness was already dappling his neck.

"So, fair warning: this might be awkward." Stacey looked down at her cup. "And if it is, we don't have to talk about it."

"Okay, now I'm intrigued."

He sensed she was choosing her words. "You know we have to check backgrounds and everything, right? The district usually handles it, but since you were an eleventh-hour hire, I did some of it myself."

"Ah, so you're the reason I woke up in a cold sweat." He took another sip of coffee.

"The thing is, I noticed that you founded a company, but you left it off your resume. I thought maybe it was someone different, but then I saw a few photos."

He fought the urge to stiffen. Yeah, he had a good idea which photos she'd seen. They had been arranged by the Acidsplash PR team. Mark, Timothy Kwon, and a few of the other early founders all standing with their arms crossed beneath a row of smashed servers. Brooding stares, leather jackets, and someone even holding a sledgehammer. The caption: *Are These Silicon Valley Bad Boys the Pioneers of Tomorrow?*

No. It turned out they weren't.

"I was just wondering... why?" she continued. "I mean, we encourage innovation and entrepreneurship in our students. It's a cornerstone of our teaching philosophy. What you did, it's pretty neat."

"Neat, huh?" Mark repeated.

"And if I'm being honest, it's kind of intimidating."

He drummed his fingers on the table and glanced around. To their right, a young man pecked away on his laptop, fingers moving so fast he could've been playing piano. Mark knew that look. He was plugged in and focused. It was like looking back in time.

"The truth is, it wasn't that neat," he said. "I got lucky in grad school, met the right people and pitched an idea. We got funding and I got in way over my head. Worse, I got arrogant. For about two years, I honestly believed I was going to be the next Steve Jobs."

Stacey nodded, really listening and giving him space to talk. His friends in Spain, his colleagues, they only knew he came from the Bay Area and that he once worked in tech. None of them had ever bothered to look deeper.

He liked it that way.

"See, we hear all these myths, right? Jeff Bezos setting up Amazon in a garage. Elon Musk betting it all on Tesla. But that's all they are: myths. Sure, Bezos took a risk, but he was a senior VP at a hedge fund. Musk's family owned a sapphire mine. My point is, it's easy to fall into these echo chambers and lose sight of the truth. I did. I got cocky and it cost me the company."

"You were young," she said. "And failure's part of the process, right? I mean, I didn't even finish my first marathon. I got so nervous I kept stopping at the bathrooms and timed out."

"No, you're not wrong. But if you don't cross a finish line, it only affects you. I cost a hundred people their jobs. They don't teach you how to deal with that in business school. How to tell employees who worked eighty-hour weeks that their equity is worthless. That collection agencies are coming for the desks and the chairs and computers. Oh, and please don't talk to the press."

For a moment, Stacey didn't say anything. Damn, his spine was tense and his skin damp. It wasn't the sun or the alcohol his body craved.

It was that he'd held this all in for over a decade and a half. Locked it away in a box in his mind and ran away from it all. Told himself it belonged to a different Mark, someone who once wore his skin and spoke in his voice yet lacked the scars and shame of deep failure.

"You're right," Stacey said. "I don't know what that's like, but I appreciate you sharing it. Thank you."

He shrugged. "I like teaching. Education's my penance."

"Ah, now you're being too hard on yourself. Even Dante wasn't that cruel. I believe failed entrepreneurs are only sent to the third circle of hell. Us educators, we're much closer to the sixth."

CHAPTER TWENTY-TWO

Hell, Lloyd thought. This was some sort of hell.

He was clutching his chest, shivering on that frozen lake once again. The fraternity brothers stood on the far shore, waving their banners and laughing. A bitter wind howled in his face. He took three tenuous steps forward, bare toes sliding over the snow-dusted ice. His teeth chattered.

Because of the spoon, he realized. The spoon he held in his mouth.

Hell. Yes, this egg race was a Hell Week tradition. His pledge brothers scampered about, feet sliding across a hundred feet of Lake Shauvason's ice. Their near-naked bodies twisted, turned, and struggled to stay upright. The diapers did little to keep them warm, but they amused the brothers, who shouted from the far shore, "C'mon, Lloyd, pass off the egg! Mouth to mouth! There you go!"

Lloyd turned to see his pledge brother T.J. shivering and carrying the egg with the spoon in his mouth. He mumbled something to Lloyd, something like, "Take it."

Lloyd craned his neck, spoon trembling as T.J. passed the egg. Then it fell and cracked on the ice.

"Dammit, Lloyd," one of the pledge brothers said, removing the spoon and shaking his head. "We're gonna f-f-f-fucking freeze to d-d-d-death here."

There was a squawk from the megaphone on shore. Sir Mister Dawson Sir, their trainer, shouted, "Pledges! This is without a doubt the most pathetic egg relay I've seen in my entire career. You should be ashamed. Brotherhood is built on a foundation of teamwork, so work... AS A FUCKING TEAM!"

"Yes, sir, Mister Dawson sir," the pledges replied. After five weeks, it was a reflex.

Lloyd said, "S-s-sorry, guys. I'll s-s-start this n-n-next one."

Crossing his arms over his bare skin, he shuffled back to the bucket of eggs. As his pledge brothers reset to their positions every ten yards, a curious thought stopped Lloyd's hand: had he been here before?

Yes, he had. He was standing right here when—

A sound like a gunshot echoed across the frozen lake. All the laughing brothers on the shore and the grumbling pledges fell silent, beer cans lowering. The world held its breath.

Because something *shifted*. A crack raced out beneath Lloyd, spreading web-like in all directions. In the space of a single heartbeat, the flat ice underfoot became a field of shards.

"Lloyd! Run!" Sir Mr. Dawson Sir screamed through the bullhorn. "Pledges! On shore, now!"

Lloyd never ran.

The ice simply fell out beneath him. The frigid water knocked the breath from his lungs. Lloyd felt like a tube of toothpaste, all his warmth squeezed from his toes, up his body and out through his mouth.

And then he was under, splashing and thrashing, reaching for anything but finding only pieces of sharp ice. The dark blue abyss tilted him, turned him sideways. He rolled, scratching out desperately. He had never felt such cold.

It suffused him.

No, this wasn't how it should end. He was a freshman in college. He had his whole life ahead. He wasn't supposed to die here, drunk on some February morning, beneath a lake whose name he could hardly pronounce. Some cautionary tale to be spread across campus.

He pounded the ice, fingers searching for the hole. He tried to scream, but his lungs were two flat sacks without wind. His mouth opened and the cold water rushed in, filling his chest.

And then he saw it.

Her.

It wasn't a woman. It wasn't anything his mind could understand. Rather, he perceived her in fractured glimpses among panicked blinks.

A shape and a texture: unctuous black violet lit with iridescent pearl. An eye amidst a halo of dead stars. Crystalline bones unfolding, like the geodes and kaleidoscopes he peered into as a child. Wondrous, yes. Within those black-violet prisms pulsed colors beyond his knowing, skin of twisted roots and dark tumors, and a voice—*her* voice—that reached across the vast cosmos.

Crossed it for *him*.

She pressed herself up against the ice above. Her unblinking eye focused in on him, seeing him, and filled him with warmth.

She whispered, *"Lloyd, it's time to wake up."*

So that's what he did.

The cold ice at his fingertips became the cool sheets of his bed. The wet pressure inside his body burst as a gasp left his lips. He rose, not through the frozen lake but into the midnight shadows of his bedroom.

And the eye. Her eye. It no longer stared through the ice but faded behind the ceiling of his house. He felt a great presence retreating, up through the attic, up into the sky, into the cold reaches above Earth, and into the deepest recesses beyond space and time.

Whoa. Lloyd steadied himself.

This wasn't his first nightmare after the accident on the lake. Nor his fifth. He'd lost count after a dozen. The important thing was that he was safe now; he was at home, in his bed. Here, he could rebuild. Here, nothing could hurt him.

But that's not quite true, he thought. Randall. Randall always found a way.

Scratching himself, Lloyd crossed his bedroom, went to the bathroom, and urinated. He fished into his medicine cabinet, finding his anti-anxiety pills. Dr. Prescott had said she might up the dosage as needed.

He turned off the light and returned to his bed.

Then he saw the shadow.

Beneath the door, something loomed in the hallway outside his bedroom. Something that caught the light like a diamond and shimmered black violet. Something that coiled and undulated.

"Hello?"

Lloyd turned his phone's flashlight on. The thing beyond the door moved.

No. It *drifted*.

Perhaps it was Randall or his mother, checking in on him. Perhaps they had heard him screaming in his sleep yet again. Perhaps.

But if so, why hadn't they knocked? And now that he thought of it, hadn't that shape been there since the moment he woke up? Yes, he knew that it had.

With a nervous twist of the knob, Lloyd opened his bedroom door. The dark emptiness greeted him.

No, it wasn't Randall. He could hear his stepfather snoring down the hall.

Nor was it his mother.

That unctuous shadow oozed down the stairs.

Cell phone in hand, Lloyd followed it, vaguely aware that he was in his tighty-whities like that cold day on the lake. Yet tonight he was warm, confident, bathed in a black-violet glow. It was summer, and he had always preferred the heat to the cold.

Downstairs, Randall's fish tank shimmered blue upon the kitchen and living room walls. A starfish clung to the glass. In the hall, Lloyd caught a flicker as that dark ribbon turned and slid through the wall.

No, he realized. Through the basement door.

At this midnight hour, Lloyd was aware of two things. First, that he had been hurt, broken, and within him, a deep wound now festered. A wound he ignored with each breath. And second, he was aware he should be scared. Nothing good would come from following that black-violet light down these stairs.

He ignored that, too.

He turned on the basement lights. There, at the landing, where the stairs met the crawlspace, sat his stepdad's new toolbox, a fresh bag of charcoal briquettes, and a Costco-sized pack of toilet paper.

The black violet shimmered beyond.

He knew why.

"Lloyd," the voice whispered. *"It's time to awaken."*

He moved the toilet paper to one side, the bag of charcoal to the other. He slid the toolbox back.

It was the poster. Armando the Great's piercing eyes and his head floating over those swirls of a bygone era. What it must have been like to go to a carnival then. To see sword swallowers and freaks. To find out his fortune.

Armando's eyes, Lloyd realized. Had they always been that iridescent black violet?

"Wake up."

"I am awake," Lloyd muttered.

Armando's lips never moved, and yet Lloyd heard the voice all the same. A dusty whisper behind his ears. A wind circling his head.

"Yes, your eyes are open, but you're still slumbering through life.

Mmm... You can be more, Lloyd Betancourt. You should be so much more. You need to wake up."

Lloyd looked over his shoulder, half expecting Randall to come down. Yes, he knew this was weird; it was midnight, and he was talking to an old poster. And yet, he didn't quite care. Perhaps he was losing his mind at nineteen, but he didn't think so.

Perhaps it was the opposite.

"Who are you? And what do you want?"

"A friend who heard you cry out from the ice. Yes, a friend who wants to help you... ascend."

"Ascend? What, like fly? You're going to give me some wings, Armando? That your trick?" He smirked, studying that old mentalist on the cracked poster. He could feel those eyes boring into him as he wiped a scuff from the glass.

Then a bug landed on his hand.

It was a horsefly, big and nasty. Lloyd killed it with a quick slap.

Armando didn't move, at least not that Lloyd saw. And yet, there was a shift within the poster, as if the man's lips had risen into something like a smirk. That black-violet shimmer traced the edges. Lloyd tasted a momentary charge, like a battery on his tongue.

Fly. He had said "fly" and mocked Armando. Then a fly landed on his hand.

"Yes, you see. We can work together, Lloyd; we can help one another. Seek death in my name and I'll pay you with great strength."

Lloyd took a deep breath. Yeah, he had to admit, he felt kind of good. Like he'd stepped out of the shower and his day was just starting. Like Randall hadn't yelled at him yet.

"What do you mean... seek death?"

"Mmm, the Nether is endless and vast, yet it still has boundaries. Some of these edges are more frayed than others. Be my emis-

sary, Lloyd; be my right hand of torment. Help me open your door from beyond."

Nether? Door? Lloyd didn't like the archaic way Armando spoke. But if the poster was almost a century old, he supposed its speech might be outdated.

"But first: a secret, yes. That is my gift. Mmm... A gesture of good faith to use as you see fit."

"What kind of secret?"

Armando just stared, the poster taking on a dim luster. Had it ever been talking? An odd fog hung over the past several minutes, like Lloyd had been watching someone else walking around in his skin.

He repeated, "What kind of secret?"

There was no answer. No, of course not. Heck, he'd probably sleepwalked all the way down here.

Then he heard a distant clink.

It came from upstairs; Lloyd was sure of it. He'd left the basement door open and he could pinpoint exactly where the sound echoed from.

Randall's office at the end of the hall.

When his mother first said they were moving into Raven's Valley, she'd promised Lloyd a room he could use for his hobbies. He had looked forward to putting his painted tanks and airplanes on the shelves. He even drew up a plan for the displays.

Yet when they moved in, Randall claimed it as his office. He was an entrepreneur, he said. He wasn't just the head of Community Safety at Raven's Valley, but a businessman too. Every businessman needed an office.

But to Lloyd, he was just a hustler who bought and resold things he made Lloyd deliver. Every week he chased some new get-rich scheme.

Now, Lloyd stood in Randall's office, eyes sweeping the messy shelves crowded with coupons and boxes. The sound he had heard was unlike any other: a clink of metal falling against wood. And there it was, glimmering in the moonlight.

A key.

It must've fallen from the desk.

A gesture of good faith, Lloyd thought. A gift.

He thumbed the key, turning it over and studying the logo. Craftsman.

Back in the basement, he found Randall's tool chest near the pile of toilet paper. The key fit perfectly. With a quick turn, the lock opened and Lloyd peered inside.

His eyes took in the contents of that tool chest and a smirk rose to his lips. There were no tools stored inside.

But there were DVDs and a few magazines.

CHAPTER TWENTY-THREE

Randy's day was turning out to be a real doozy, and it wasn't even noon.

His back killed him something fierce, that old injury from Iraq flaring up each time he twisted. The piano he'd bought on Craigslist and moved to his storage locker was more busted up than he thought. Three different tuners couldn't fix it, and he was in the hole.

And now his marble starfish was missing.

He paced the length of the saltwater aquarium, breath steaming the glass. He tapped, scaring a school of clownfish. Where the hell was that damn starfish? Had something eaten it?

That didn't make sense.

"Mom, the upstairs bathroom's out of TP," Lloyd said as he passed through the kitchen.

"Well, get some yourself," Randy snapped.

"I'm late for work."

Lloyd gave Diana a kiss on the cheek, something that always creeped Randy out. At nineteen, the kid was a little too old for affection. Besides, his good cheer this morning put a burr in Randy's boot. He was smiling too much.

"Have a good day, everyone," Lloyd said, and hurried out.

Randy offered a grunt and circled the aquarium, searching for that damn starfish. He used the tongs to tilt a rocky cave, teasing out a few blennies. Still nothing.

After a moment, he asked, "You haven't seen Lloyd messing around in here, have you?"

Diana didn't answer.

He turned to find himself alone in the kitchen, his wife nowhere to be seen. For another few minutes, he scoured the fish tank, muttering and peeking behind rocks.

Then his phone chirped.

As chief of Community Safety and a registered security guard for Strathmore Properties, LLC, Randy had to be on call. Two hundred and twenty-two homes in Raven's Valley meant at least as many problems.

Sometimes, it was just a cat stuck in a tree. Or a missing package.

Sometimes, it was a malfunctioning gate.

Every now and then, it was something a little more exciting, fireworks or spray paint, a loud argument or a fight. Randy liked such moments. It made him feel like the law officer he used to be.

"Yep, talk to me, Dispatch."

This call wasn't one of them.

It seemed Sophie Saperstein wasn't happy again. Nothing new. She had a litany of complaints going back to March 3rd, the day she'd moved in and discovered her neighbor could see into her bedroom. She'd called it a public safety issue and pinged the security office three times before noon.

Today wasn't shaping up to be any different.

"Yep, three kids, a drone, Pickford Park, by the climbing wall. Copy that."

He hung up and checked the tank once more, but the marble starfish was still a no-show. Had it gotten stuck behind a rock? He'd have to check later.

He retrieved his duty belt from his office and made sure his Taser was charged. He couldn't carry a gun; this was California, after all. And besides, the spineless Edward Strathmore was always going on about optics and appearances. He even ordered Randy to remove the *Blue Lives Matter* bumper sticker from the pickup, insisting that security guards needed to stay politically neutral.

Randy was almost out the front door when he noticed the basement was still open. He poked his head in.

There, at the bottom of the stairs, sat Diana, a few rolls of toilet paper and some magazines spread out on the steps.

And his toolbox. It was open.

No fuckin' way.

His heart thrummed and his throat turned bitter. He was about to step back when she turned her watery eyes on him.

"What is this?" she asked. "Randy, is this all yours?"

Randy swallowed. He could see the magazines all scattered about like a crime scene. Tia Kinx and the curvy Alexa Rockets reclining poolside while Guy Harding's swimsuit barely contained his erection. And that was one of the tamer photos.

"I'm... Well, it's not *all* mine," he sputtered. "I'm just holding it for a friend."

"A friend? Who?"

He was no longer in his late forties but fifteen again, his mom pulling the Penthouses and Hustlers from under his bed. She had been furious, her face plum red as she called him all sorts of things. But Diana, she just studied the magazines, confusion and sadness sheening her eyes. He wasn't sure what was worse.

"I'm not angry," she said. "I know you have needs. I'm just... There's just so many. And so... *specific.*"

Yeah, he had an idea what she was talking about. Perhaps *Hot Chocolate Booties Volume 5* or *One Night in Hong Kong*. Maybe *Spring Break Sluts*. It didn't matter now. She had it all, the full catalog of his kinks and vices.

Which meant he had to deflect and put her on the back foot.

He said, "Wait, what were you doing snooping in my stuff?"

"Your stuff? Randy, I bought you this toolbox. And I wasn't snooping. I just came to get toilet paper. I saw a page poking out, so I opened it."

"You opened it?"

"There was a woman's..." She lowered her voice. "You could see a vagina on the page, sticking right out. Of course I opened it."

"Where'd you get the key?"

"Key? I... It wasn't locked."

Shit, had he left it unlocked after his last viewing? Damn, what a fuck-up.

A curious thought flicked through his mind: had Lloyd set this all up?

No, it was absurd. The key was unlabeled, left on Randy's desk with so many others. Lloyd was too dumb to pull anything off.

"If you need to talk about this," Diana said, swallowing, "I think we should discuss this with a professional—"

"No, this is private," he snapped. "There's nothing to discuss. Absolutely nothing. Here."

He marched down those stairs and rounded up the magazines. He dumped them into the toolbox. Jesus, he really was a teenager again, moving the nudie mags to the treehouse. Only it wasn't his mom or his dad he was afraid of, but his wife.

Hell, she deserved it, he told himself. Maybe if she initiated more. If she didn't just lie there. If she did some of the things he saw on those pages...

"I'm late to work." He shoved the magazines inside and slammed the lid.

"Randy, please, I'm not angry. I'm just—"

"Yeah yeah yeah, I know. You're just disappointed."

"No, that's not it at all." Something sad sparkled in her eyes. "I just think we should talk about this."

He studied her. Diana. His Diana. Here, in the basement of the house she'd mostly bought for them both. He caught a flash of the woman he'd met at the small business owner's luncheon six years ago. That woman he'd fallen in love with. The woman whose hand he'd asked for, even though both of them had gone and screwed up their first marriages.

Yet something had grown between them over the years, hadn't it? He'd lost his job on the force and some of his mojo. They'd stopped telling each other their needs.

Yet here he was, his box of shame in his hand, as she told him it was okay, that it was normal and healthy, but he just needed to open up.

His body tensed and rejected it like a poison. "I said I'm late to work."

"Randy, wait—"

He left her there in the basement, hurrying out to the pickup with its busted grill. He threw the toolbox in the passenger seat and drove off.

CHAPTER TWENTY-FOUR

"Okay, Z-bird, try hanging with one hand," Ali shouted over the buzz of his DJI drone. "Aaaand, there we go."

Zelda held the pose for another ten seconds, clutching the climbing wall's shaped grip. She dangled from the midpoint of the structure. From here, she could see the roofs of the nearby houses, the fences, even into a few backyards. Raven's Valley looked like a train set, tree-lined streets all perfect and green. If she climbed higher, she might see her house.

"All right, you can stop showing off now," Ali said. "Come peep the footage."

Zelda swung around and climbed down the structure while Ali's drone auto-parked on the grass. For the last twenty minutes, Maura had been practicing her left-handed football passes through a Y-branch of a young magnolia. She meandered over now.

With a few swipes on his tablet, Ali dragged the final video clip to the editing software. Here it was, his little movie. First, a wide establishing shot sweeping in over the park. Then, a winding medium shot of the thirty-foot climbing wall. Next came a close-up of Zelda's hands as she reached for the grip. A slow-motion shot followed as she took the leap from one handhold, grabbed another, and swung around the climbing wall's angled corner.

"That's pretty cool, right? I cranked the frames to two forty, added a bokeh effect, and used a shallow focus."

"Is that why it looks so high up?" Zelda asked.

Maura said, "You were like twenty feet off the ground, at least."

"Really? It didn't seem that high." She studied the video, the drone's POV moving around her dynamically as she neared the top of the structure. Her long arms and skinny frame. Did all kids look so goofy at this age?

Ali said, "I wasn't gonna say anything 'cause I wanted to get the shots. But truthfully? My ass cheeks were clenched."

Maura nudged him. "That's disgusting."

"What? It's natural. Look it up. It's called acute stress response when your sphincter constricts."

"Eww, I don't want to know about your butthole."

"Okay, first off, a sphincter is *not* a butthole. And second..."

Zelda tuned them out and studied the video. There was something odd about it, about her and the view near the top of the climbing wall. It took her a moment to figure it out.

From the highest point of the structure, it was a long drop onto the all-weather rubber matting below. She'd almost fallen. But she'd been alone up there, the climbing wall empty all morning.

Yet on the video, she could see something else. She paused and scrubbed it back a few seconds.

There, perched like a gargoyle at the top, loomed a blurry shadow. A sinuous black arm stretched out, three fingers reaching down toward Zelda.

Like it wanted to grab her.

She pressed *play*. On the video, her fingers slipped from the green handhold and she almost fell. Even twenty minutes later, she could still taste the tang of adrenaline from the near miss. Then her hand snatched out, latching onto an adjacent blue grip. With a quick adjustment, she brought her left leg up and out and into a three-point hold. She swayed a moment, breathing hard as the drone buzzed past.

There it was on-screen again, that shadowed *thing* crouching at the top of the wall. It quivered and twisted.

"Whoa, what's that?" Maura said, ending the debate about butts and sphincters and leaning close to the tablet.

"I don't know," Zelda said. "But you see it, right?"

"Uh, yeah I see it. Looks like it's reaching for you."

Zelda turned back to the climbing wall behind them. Just thirty-odd feet of angled wood and support beams at the edge of the park. The morning light shimmered off it.

She asked, "You guys sure no one else was up there?"

"Not unless they've been hiding since we started filming," Ali said. "It's probably a shadow."

"A shadow?" Maura laughed. "Dude, that thing's, like, crawling down the side."

"Yeah, which is why it's a shadow."

"It's not a shadow."

"Then what is it?"

Maura glanced at Zelda for a second. It was the first time she had seen something like hesitation on the big girl's face. She said, "Maybe it's a ghost."

Zelda felt the air blow past her nose. She didn't mean to scoff, but she had.

Maura shrugged. "What? Creepy shadow-things crawling down a wall? What else is it?"

"Okay, first off, there's no such thing as ghosts," Ali said. "And second, what's it the ghost of? Spiderman? No one died in this park. That's not even high enough to kill you."

"Maybe they fell on their head."

"Yeah, or maybe you fell on yours. It's a climbing wall, not a haunted house. Besides, that thing was probably built at Home

Depot. There's, like, a million reasons why it's not a ghost. Light refraction, lens flares, an effect or a filter—"

"An effect, really?"

Ali tapped and swiped on the tablet. On-screen, Zelda's skin turned blue as her face became a zombie. Another swipe, another couple of taps, and she had a halo as the dramatic music turned to soothing harps. "See? I turned my mom into a cat on her Zoom meeting last week. It doesn't mean she's got nine lives."

Scrubbing back through the video, Zelda wasn't quite sure what she thought. Yes, there it was again, hazy and dark. A thin, glistening body with an arm stretched out toward her. And yet, maybe Ali was right. Perhaps it was a shadow because it didn't have legs.

Unless...

Unless it was emerging from the structure itself.

"Look, it's simple science," Ali said. "If it can be recorded, it can reflect light. If it can reflect light, it can be measured and understood. A ghost is supernatural. Thus, it can't be a ghost."

"Yeah, well, you can be measured but no one understands you."

"That's because I read at a college level and—"

A siren squawked and a voice hissed over a speaker, "Hey! You kids, over here."

Zelda turned to see a white pickup with a busted grill pulling up to the edge of the park and flashing its lights. The sign on the side read, *Raven's Valley Safety & Security*.

"Ah, not him again," Ali muttered.

"Is he a cop?" Zelda asked.

"Used to be," Maura muttered. "Dude's a total prick."

"C'mon over here," the security officer barked over the PA. "All three of you. Big Red, yeah, there we go. And you too, Ali Baba. Scoot your brown butt over, chop-chop."

Zelda blinked. Had she really heard that? The way Ali and

Maura were moving seemed like this wasn't their first run-in with this man.

"That means you too, Scarecrow. Get your rear in gear, all of you."

Scarecrow? Was he talking about her? Zelda seethed and started skateboarding over, her jaw already clenched. She wanted to see this man, see his face and tell him where to put his microphone.

As she skated close to the pickup, he barked out, "Whoa there, Wheels. That's close enough. Stay there, by the curb." Then he climbed out.

He wore a dark uniform, crisp and cared for. She could tell he worked out when he was younger, but the paunch of middle age now gripped his waist. He hoisted his duty belt, hand lingering by his Taser just long enough to draw her eye.

"I thought I told you not to fly your drone over houses," the security guard said. "We've been over this."

"I wasn't flying it over houses," Ali said. "I stayed in the park."

"I got a report that says otherwise. Someone complained you were flying it high enough to see over fences. You're not peeping into bedrooms, are you?"

"What? No, we weren't." Ali was short, but now he seemed to be shrinking even more. "Who complained?"

"That's confidential, so don't worry about that. I also got a complaint there were kids screwing around on the structure."

"We weren't screwing around," Maura said. "It's a climbing wall. It's meant to be climbed."

"Yeah, maybe so, but that's for adult recreation. With gear and—"

"There's no sign that says that," Zelda said. She had checked the park's rules the other day when she first practiced skateboarding. All it said was that the park was open from sunrise to sunset, dog owners needed to pick up their poop, and all fireworks were forbidden during the drought.

The security guard's gaze swung to her. He reminded her of a pigeon, eyes a little too beady and busy.

"There doesn't need to be a sign when it's common sense. Kids not permitted." His lazy gaze drifted back to Ali. "Next time I get word of you flying your drone where you shouldn't, I'm going to impound it. Copy me, Aladdin?"

"His name is Ali," Zelda snapped. "Not Aladdin or Ali Baba. And speaking of names, what's yours, Officer?"

It was just a twitch, but Zelda saw her question landing like a bee sting. His eyes sparkled and his mustache quivered. Here was a man who didn't like to be questioned. A man used to giving orders and having them followed.

"Don't worry about my name, String Bean. Just worry about listening to my orders—"

"No, I think I do want your name," Zelda said. "You just used racial slurs on my friend. It's not the fifties, Captain Pornstache. In fact..."

Her shaking hands found their way to her pocket. In a flick, she had her phone out and the camera app opened. She raised it so she was in-frame with the officer behind her.

"Why don't you tell the internet what you just called him? It was Aladdin, right? I think they'd like to listen."

Zelda was distantly aware that she was talking. But these weren't her words leaving her lips. They were her mother's. Maya, who had always been quiet and kind yet fierce when provoked. For a moment, she felt more connected than she had been in years.

A sour glare spread across the security guard's face, quickly subsumed by something else: fear. His tongue circled his lips, and he sucked air between his teeth. He gave the camera a nervous glance.

"So, uh, you kids stay safe," he said. "And y'all keep out of trouble, hear me?"

They heard him but they didn't answer. He shuffled back to

his white pickup. He gave them a long stare that said everything: he'd remember this.

Then he put the car in drive, turned the flashing lights off, and reversed out of the parking lot.

A moment of total silence passed while Zelda's heart fluttered. Lightheaded, she gripped her skateboard. "Sorry. I didn't really record anything."

"Dude," Maura said. "That was the most badass thing I've ever seen."

CHAPTER TWENTY-FIVE

Mark tried to drive and listen to Rosalía but found himself quickly failing at both. As she chewed his ear off, he rolled through a stop sign at the eastern edge of Raven's Valley. A group of cyclists glared. He waved and apologized, switching Rosalía to the car's speaker as they pedaled on.

"I just don't understand how you can be so... What's the word? Wishy-washy. How you can't give me an answer?"

It was a Friday afternoon in Greywood Bay, which meant it was late Friday night in Madrid. He could hear the alcohol slurring Rosalía's words and lighting a fire in her voice.

"I don't know what you want me to say, Rosy." He rubbed his eyes. "I'm doing the best I can."

"Everyone does the best that they can. But you've been out there for months. Are you even coming back? Or am I just managing your Airbnb for you now?"

He sighed. "No, you're not just managing it. You're helping me out, really. Thank you. You're—"

"Helping? Oh, I'm so glad I'm *helping*." Sarcasm oozed through the line. "It's so wonderful to be such a *help* while you do whatever it is that you're doing."

Toes curling, he headed west along a street between that junkyard on the left and the dry river on the right.

"What I'm doing is taking care of my niece. I've got a video hearing in a half hour and I need to brush up. Christ, I don't even know if I'm helping. Maybe I'm just messing her up."

"You're not her father, okay? Honestly, I don't even know why you're doing this."

Because of his sister, he thought.

Because of her desperate words on that hazy night when she appeared in his bathtub.

And because, for the first time in years, he felt like he was a part of something more than himself.

"No, you're right," he said. "I'm not her dad. But I am family."

"Family, huh?" He could hear the clink of the bottle, the pouring liquid. She was having a nightcap in her kitchen. God, he missed the tall ceilings of the apartment, the music, the murmurs off the plaza that formed the soothing hum to his life in Madrid. "So what about us?" she continued. "Am I just some last Spanish fling before you head home?"

And there it was.

He'd known for a while that Rosalía saw their relationship differently. This was his fault, he supposed. He'd never drawn boundaries. Never wanted to hurt her. He'd just assumed they were on the same page.

And he'd been wrong.

At their age, most of their friends were married or years into raising a family. He'd never wanted that. He'd just wanted someone to drink with, to go on vacation with, someone to sleep next to because on some nights that was better than sleeping alone.

"I'm so sorry, Rosy," he said. "I don't know what else to say. Maybe I can visit after my summer classes, but it's complicated."

"Is it? Is it *complicated*, Mark?"

He turned at the east entrance to Raven's Valley, giving the attendant a wave. He was pleased that after a few weeks he was getting the lay of the land and the people. The houses might be different, but the streets were so similar it still felt like a labyrinth.

Glacier Point Drive becoming Yosemite Road.

Mayacamas Way merging with Muir Lane and then dumping him onto Tulare Street.

Where was he now? Spruce Street, right. He saw some kids up ahead.

"Rosy, hold on a second."

He muted the call and pulled up to the far curb, rolling down the window. "Hey there."

Zelda walked with her friends, Ali and Maura. He'd met them the other day when they stopped by after class. He liked them. He envied how easy it was for kids to make friends at school. All they seemed to need was one thing in common.

"Hey, Uncle Mark." Zelda gave him one of her patented nods: the slightest rise of her chin and a flat smile.

"How'd that video turn out?"

She shrugged. "Okay."

Grinning, Ali leaned against the hood. "No no no, it wasn't just okay. Zelda... was... AMAZING! In fact, you might want to consider acting lessons because—dare I say it?—you have a budding action star in the making."

Mark smiled. This Ali kid was a firecracker. "That's great. I hope the video turns out well."

"I'm gonna drop in some dubstep, CG in a few drones shooting lasers at her. It's gonna be tiiiight." Then he gasped. "Snap! A rare spawn. BRB."

Ali took off running, leaving his bike to tip over into a coyote bush. Maura scrambled to grab it. "You're welcome!" She turned to Mark. "He's really into that game."

"Him and half the world."

Zelda stood there, carrying her skateboard over the shoulder by the trucks and rocking her ankles. Her whole posture screamed, *When are you leaving?* And yet, Mark couldn't help himself.

He asked, "So, where you off to?"

"Downtown," Zelda said.

He sensed that was as much as she was going to give him.

"Do you need any money or a ride?"

She shook her head.

"Well, let me know what you all decide on for dinner. I can order out, or if you want to watch a movie or something..."

"Yeah, I'll text you."

"Right."

"Be good."

"Bye, Mr. Fitzsimmons," Maura said with a flirtatious smile.

And then they were off, Zelda carrying her skateboard, Maura pushing the bike. For a moment, Mark envied them. The summer always seemed endless when you were that age. When a bike and some friends were all that you needed. When so much could happen in a month.

But then he remembered his own teenage years as well. All those clumsy fumblings, the confusion and emotions. Life had started feeling raw and sharp, hadn't it?

He pushed the thought away, put the car in drive, and unmuted the phone.

"Sorry about that, Rosy. I..." He glanced at the screen. The call was over. He redialed her number, but it went straight to voicemail.

She'd turned off her phone.

CHAPTER TWENTY-SIX

Getting the whole legal team on one video call was like herding cats. Mark set his laptop up in the kitchen, making sure the background was pleasant: the yard from the open kitchen, summer squash he'd planted with Zelda, the fence and the trees. He wore a navy hopsack blazer and a soft, earthy tie that complemented his eyes. He sat straight as his lawyers joined the screen, one by one.

"Mark, before we bring the judge and the Ruizes on the line, I just wanted to check in, make sure nothing blindsides us." That was Ms. Phong in the top-right box, straightening her papers before her. "How's Zelda? Anything we need to know about?"

"No. Nothing I can think of. Summer school's going well. She likes her classes. She—"

"How're her grades?" Mr. Hoffman asked.

"Good, so far."

"And you've seen them?" Ms. Phong asked.

"What, like her test scores?"

"Test scores or report cards. Talked to her teacher?"

"She said she got a B+ on the first major test. Her teacher's just down the hall and we've talked a few times. He'd tell me if anything was off, I think."

"Be sure to double-check," Mr. Shariz said. "It's impressive what my fourteen-year-old can whip up on Photoshop."

"I'll get on that." Mark had never considered that. One more fear to add to the list.

Then the sink turned on.

He glanced at the faucet, the hiss of water spilling into the stainless-steel basin. "Sorry, one second."

He hurried to the sink. Odd. The handle was in the off position, but the little sensor was blinking. He waved his palm over the laser. After another ten seconds, it finally shut off. He hurried back to the laptop.

"Tactically, we need to present a unified front, Mr. Fitzsimmons," Ms. Phong said. "The Ruizes are going to bring up that incident at the school. They're going to poke for holes and dig into your past."

"What about it?"

"That company you ran," Mr. Hoffman said. "They'll spin it as a negative, something like, 'If he ignored his fiduciary duties, how can we entrust him with a child?' Of course, it's not relevant. Still, it wouldn't surprise me if the Ruizes have hired a private eye to poke around."

"You're serious?" Somehow his tongue had dried out and his foot was bouncing so hard it rattled the table.

"These things often get messy," Ms. Phong said. "But the most important thing to remember is that—"

The computer chimed as three more boxes appeared on the screen. The Ruizes, their attorney, and the judge. Mark's heart beat so heavy he felt it in his jaw.

Judge Fulghum was an unreadable woman with a sharp nose and eyebrows like twin caterpillars. A high bookshelf loomed behind her. In the rare moments her eyes rose from her papers and her desk to the camera, they flickered sharp behind wireframe glasses.

Mark was no longer forty-three but fourteen, called before his teacher to explain why his science quiz matched his best friend's. Had he cheated? No, of course not. But his friend had probably copied his answers. How could he explain without throwing his buddy under the bus?

Which was how he felt now as Judge Fulghum grilled him again and again.

Did he intend to stay in the U.S.?

Had Zelda expressed an interest in therapy?

What kind of environment was he providing at home and what were their routines?

After thirty minutes, he could no longer ignore the moisture pooling in his armpits and the sweat on his brow. Even his on-screen reflection glistened.

Thankfully, the judge called for a five-minute break. He stole a glance at the SmartHome app on his phone. No wonder he was hot. The temperature in Zone 7, the kitchen, was at *Max Heat*. He set it to *Low* and opened a window.

Then he noticed the motion sensors.

He'd configured the SmartHome app to ping him with movement when no one was home. They were blinking green now. Zone 7, the kitchen, and Zone 11, the hallway upstairs.

"Zelda?" He double-checked the screen to make sure he was muted. Two minutes left until Judge Fulghum returned. "Zelda, you home?"

A pang of fear. If she was, had she heard them talking about her? The Ruiz's had made insinuations about her mental health, insinuations he didn't agree with. Ms. Phong was right: this was messy. Their sharp questioning was the last thing she should hear and get in her head.

Then he heard it again, water pouring. Not into stainless steel this time, but a ceramic basin.

The bathroom upstairs.

One minute left.

He raced up the stairs while checking the app. Sure enough, Zone 12, the bathroom, was green and the water indicator blinked. He checked Zelda's dark bedroom. The piles of dirty clothes, the skateboards leaning against her desk, the music posters already pinned to the walls. God, it was humid up here.

But no, she wasn't home.

"Okay, folks, let's dig back into this. Mr. Fitzsimmons, will you be rejoining us?"

That was the judge in Mark's earbud, the Bluetooth connection warbling and hissing.

"Yes, sorry. I just had to step away for a moment."

"Go on and step back. We'd like to hear from your side and the clock's ticking."

"Yep. I'll be right there."

The bathroom lights were off, but water poured from the sink. Like the kitchen, motion sensors blinked red beneath the faucet. With a twist of the spring-loaded handle, he shut the sink off.

"Mr. Fitzsimmons?"

"I'm sorry. I'm coming."

Then the shower started up.

"Your honor, I'll present while my client returns." That was Ms. Phong, thank God. Mark fumbled with the bathtub while she got into their side of the hearing, beginning with the recent changes Maya and Juan Carlos had made to their will, including their wishes for Zelda's custody.

Mark tapped the waterproof touch pad at the edge of the tub again and again until the water pressure dropped and the faucet finally shut off. All the clever technology in this house—all its energy-saving features, smart sensors, eco-friendly recycled construction—and the place had more bugs than an anthill. He missed the sturdy old pipes of his Spanish apartment that had survived revolutions and wars.

Ms. Phong said, "And because the Ruizes are contesting several amendments in the will, it's vital to be clear why these articles were amended. Mr. Shariz can testify to that."

"Right. Thanks, Elena." Mark could hear Mr. Shariz clearing his throat and shuffling papers. "Considering the tragedy of the past couple months, I had hoped to afford my clients some posthumous privacy. Maya and Juan Carlos understood they had a considerable estate. More so, they understood that certain parties would be drawn to it. They amended their will not out of duplicity as the Ruiz's claim, but for one simple reason: they were finalizing an amicable separation."

Mark found the words simply jumping from his mouth. "Wait, they were getting divorced?"

He was leaning over the tub when it happened. A rumble from above. Then the shower sprayed him. Cold water streamed down his neck, his back, and knocked out an earbud.

"Folks, I'm hearing a lot of noise on my end," Judge Fulghum said. "Mr. Fitzsimmons, are you flushing a toilet or something? Are—"

Then the other earbud died out.

Horrified, Mark scrambled out from under the cold water. He was done with this bathroom and its buggy features. He found the access panel in the tiles by the toilet, opened it, and shut the water off directly at the pipe.

Toweling off and still reeling, he rushed downstairs. Maya and J.C., were they really getting divorced? But their marriage had been perfect.

He slid into his seat in the kitchen. He didn't realize how horrible he looked until he saw his lawyers' faces on-screen, eyes widening at his picture, hair messy and soaked from his head to his chest.

CHAPTER TWENTY-SEVEN

With the ocean breeze in her hair and the sun on her shoulder, Zelda spent the afternoon roaming downtown with Ali and Maura. She liked Greywood Bay. It was old-school cool, a surf-side mountain-town vibe with just enough of the modern to feel convenient.

There was an upscale organic grocery store and a local farmers market. There was a Vietnamese restaurant that made a killer bánh mì and a Ferris wheel at the end of Coogan's Wharf. There was a Tibetan goods store hawking crystals, incense, and carved figures. The Marquee was putting up posters for a nineties horror marathon starting next week with *Jacob's Ladder*.

Ali insisted they visit the Last Castle, a tabletop gaming and miniature store that smelled of cut plastic and paint. Scouring video game collectibles, he raised a twelve-inch figurine. "Hey, Z to the E-L-D-A. Check it out: it's you."

She glanced past a table full of model tanks. What he held made her scowl. "Lame."

Ali adjusted the unpainted Princess Zelda figure. "Whaaaat? Zelda's not lame, Zelda. Zelda's awesome. You apologize to Zelda, Zelda."

"Dude, stop saying her name like that," Maura said. "It's giving me a headache."

"You hurt Zelda's feelings." He placed the figure back on the table. She was detailed, her elven ears long and her crown sharp. Ali was right; she would look nice with the right paints.

Yet Zelda always squirmed when she saw the character she was named after. Like hearing her own voice recorded and played back.

"Question for the real Zelda," Ali said, moving on to the model airplanes. "What *Legend of Zelda* game was your favorite and why was it *Breath of the Wild*?"

"I never played them."

Ali spun on his heels. "What? Your namesake and you never played a Zelda game?"

"No, and I never will. It's a stupid game with a stupid name. Besides, she's not even the main character."

"Blasphemy." Ali ran his fingers over the boxes. "*The Skyward Sword. A Link to the Past.* A lot of people think the series peaked with *Ocarina of Time*, but I contend—*whoa!*" He lifted a box featuring a model cybernetic drone with lasers and missiles on the cover. He squinted and turned it over. "A Skynet Hunter-Killer. I wonder if this is the mark seven or the mark eight."

Maura asked, "How do you have room for all this stuff in your brain?"

"It's 'cause I don't bang my head in football."

"That's the mark seven," said a young man behind the counter. He lowered a book on Operation Desert Storm. His hair was oily, his frame soggy, and he had eyes that made Zelda sad. His name tag read *Lloyd*. "We had a few mark eights, but they never sold."

"Yeah, 'cause they're abominations," Ali said. "OG Terminator HK mark seven limited edition. How much is it? There's no price."

Lloyd gestured to the counter. "Let me scan it." A beep and a couple of taps on the keyboard. "Fifty-nine, plus tax."

"Awww," Ali groaned. "I've got, like, twelve bucks on my cash card."

Lloyd shrugged and pointed to the back, where a bunch of old boxes sat stacked in a heap. "Maybe try one of the returns. Sorry."

Zelda tried not to stare at the young man, but there was something off about him. Wispy shadows clung to the edge of his skin. Something like a dark starfish flickered on his neck and then faded.

And those sad eyes... When they rose from his book to meet Zelda's, it was like looking at two pairs. One, a young man bored at his job. And another pair, black-violet and seething. Zelda broke off her gaze.

"Ready?" Maura opened the door.

Ali returned the box to the table of tanks and airplanes. "Z-dog, let's biz-ounce."

Zelda hesitated by the table of models. She'd only known these two kids for a few weeks, but she liked them. Maura, always encouraging and congratulating her when she tried a new skateboard trick. Ali, helping her with her math. Even when he made fun of her, she knew it came from a place of affection.

"Hey," she asked him. "You really like that Hunter-Killer thing?"

"You kidding? *Terminator 2* is unquestionably an American masterpiece. My dad showed it to me when I was six and I've been ob-*sessed*."

She wanted to see Ali smile, sure, so her hand went for her wallet. But she also wanted another look at that dark *thing* within that young man. She grabbed the box and returned to the counter. She studied Lloyd as he rang up the purchase.

Whatever had been lurking behind his eyes was now gone.

CHAPTER TWENTY-EIGHT

Ali didn't stop grinning all afternoon. He turned the box over again and again, reading off the different armaments and explaining how the Hunter-Killers were the original variant of Skynet's line of terminators. After twenty minutes of facts, both Maura and Zelda had to ask him to chill.

"I'm just so excited," he said. "But okay, new subject. Our topic: how awesome is Zelda?"

A blush warmed her cheeks.

"Pretty awesome," Maura said. "What you did with that security guard? I was, like, frozen. How'd you'd even think that fast?"

For a moment, Zelda said nothing. The answer felt a little too raw. They followed the sidewalk back toward Raven's Valley, sticking to side streets until it brought them to the dry river path.

Then she said, "My mom taught me."

She wanted to leave it at that but sensed they were waiting for more.

"She was like an environmental activist and stuff. You remember that oil spill that killed all those seals? She took me to protest the company's shareholder meeting. The cops showed up, started shoving people, covering their badges and just being total dicks. She pulled out her camera, did that, and some of them backed off." Her jaw clenched. "I *hate* bullies."

Ali said, "Your parents must've been awesome."

"Ali..." Maura whispered.

"What? I'm just addressing the elephant in the room."

"You. You're the elephant in the room."

Of course, Ali and Maura knew about her parents. Ali said he'd googled her the night after they met, curious how a thirteen-year-old girl had such a high-level character in *Critical Mass*. He'd found an obituary and a dozen articles about the death of Juan Carlos Ruiz, video game director. There was even talk of memorializing her father by naming an in-game character after him.

Zelda wasn't sure how she felt about that.

"Yeah," she said. "They were pretty awesome."

"But your uncle seems cool too," Ali said.

"And kind of hot," Maura added.

Ali put his fingers in his ears. "La la la, not listening."

They were a half mile from home when they noticed the traffic. A line of cars sat backed up to the Raven's Valley south gate, where a construction worker waved them back. Drivers grumbled, backing their cars up and making U-turns.

As they neared the gate, they understood why. The entire street was being dug up.

"Sorry, kids, you'll need to go around," one of the construction workers said.

"That's, like, so far away," Ali whined.

"Yeah, well, it's that or your internet doesn't get upgraded."

"We'll go around."

They followed a footpath along the tall walls of Raven's Valley until the concrete grew spotty and the weeds tall. Empty industrial parks and desolate lots loomed across the dry river. A sign read:

Coming Soon: Hawk's Hollow!
A Home as Unique as Your Family!
Starting at Just $749,000
Strathmore & Daniels, Inc.

They were a quarter mile from their streets, just outside a reedy wall, when Maura's eyes twinkled and a grin tugged at her lip. "You guys want to cut through?"

Zelda asked, "Cut through?"

"The scrap heap," Maura said. "Chester's junkyard."

"Chester the Molester," Ali said.

"Nah, he's more like a serial killer. I swear he's burying bodies in there."

"You also swear you saw a ghost."

"Think about it: it's the perfect place to get rid of dead bodies. You've got old cars. You could put 'em in trunks, in the back seats—"

"Do you know how much a decomposing body smells? There'd be seagulls, rats, crows, dogs, cats, flies. I left a half-eaten giant Hershey Kiss on my desk and the ants were as thick as a carpet. My mom almost killed me."

"Okay then." Maura stopped at a gap in the old concrete wall where a chain-link fence had been cut and a *No Trespassing* sign hung loose. "No bodies, right? What are you waiting for?"

Ali studied the gap. It was now twice in one day that Zelda had seen fear on his face. First, with the security guard. Now here, before this rusty hole at the edge of the junkyard.

He said, "It's probably a dead end."

Maura shook her head. "It'll take us out, by the tennis courts and the rec center. My brother showed me."

Ali thumbed the model drone box. "My tetanus vaccine is, like, waaaay out of date—"

"Screw it," Zelda said. She ducked down, climbing through

the hole in the chain link and squeezing between the concrete walls.

For a moment, she thought Ali might be right: perhaps it was a dead end. The concrete was ancient, rusty rebar jutting out. Then one wall ended, leaving a gap wide enough to squeeze through.

Here she was, in some far corner of a junkyard where dented cars loomed in towers and old pipes formed rusty pyres. In dry mounds, wires and chains lay forever tangled. The whole place creaked in the breeze.

"Grab the front wheel," Maura said, pushing Ali's bike through the gap.

Zelda pulled it from the front. Then came Ali, doing his best to avoid the sharp edges of rebar. His foot bumped into a beer bottle, sent it spinning and cracking against the wall.

"Nice," Maura said. "Can you broadcast the rest of our movements?"

Ali let out a whistle as he emerged. "Whoa."

They followed the narrow rows between the stacks and piles, Maura pointing to turn left here or right there. Dry dirt and curls of rogue metal crunched underfoot. Rats scampered under wires and raced through the guts of forlorn appliances.

Zelda felt something odd as they walked here, a certain peace. Calm suffused this labyrinth of sharp edges and scraps, as if it existed outside of Greywood Bay, outside of time itself. She thought of Maura's words about her parents. Yes, they were pretty awesome.

Were.

And for the first time in months, her mind didn't push them away.

A flash of her father, J.C., and how he laughed as he showed her the beta of the game his company was creating. A laugh that always seemed like it was only for her.

And her mother, Maya, and how fierce she could be when the world was unjust. Telling Zelda's grandmother that her daughter could skateboard and paint her nails black if she wanted. Not every girl had to wear pink.

And the three of them sailing out onto the lake, where the sky matched the sapphire waters, the shorebirds cried out, and the waves lulled her senses.

And then, after lunch, when her parents said they needed to have a family discussion, to talk about something serious, and Zelda noticed they were sitting apart.

"Whoa," Ali said, ending her reverie. "That's a lot of dirt."

They passed mound after mound of dry earth and roots and the occasional rock or brick intermixed. A shovel rested against a stump.

"Told you he's burying bodies out here." Maura gave Ali an ominous glance.

"Psh, right." Ali laughed, a little too loud.

The path widened to a courtyard, an open metal shed, and a series of tarps strung overhead to block out the sun. Tired, twisted trees leaned in the breeze. But it was the cracked concrete patio that drew their attention.

This was some sort of workshop or welder's space. Gas tanks lay scattered about, rusty and chipped. Zelda recognized a few symbols from science class. Argon. Helium. Oxygen. And more.

"I bet it's where he makes those creepy sculptures," Maura said. "A workshop of the damned."

Sure enough, at the center of the work area, three twisted metal legs rose to a deformed torso. A single arm stretched out. Atop it, nearly seven feet above them, a near-featureless head looked down, three eyes and a mouth frozen in a scream.

Ali muttered, "This is some serial killer artwork."

A pile of half-forged arms lay near the sculpture, like the artist was trying out different configurations. Inside the open shed, dozens of scraps of butcher paper hung from the walls and flapped in the breeze.

"It's like his blueprints or something," Zelda said.

"Yeah," Ali said. "How to make a couch out of skin in five easy steps. Step one: find a dumb kid. Step two..."

Zelda entered the shed, mindful of the clumped slag and metal filings underfoot. She studied the pieces of butcher paper fluttering along the wall.

These were diagrams, she realized. Welding spots and materials all sketched in quick charcoal strokes. A name was scrawled at the bottom: *Gretchen Swann*.

Scribbled in red ink over the black diagrams were dozens of symbols. Bizarre things of long curves or sharp, jagged turns. Things of dots and dashes or spirals.

Things of no human language.

"Hey," Zelda said. "Check that sculpture. Is there anything written on it?"

"What do you mean—*ooooh*," Ali said. "Yeah, there's these crazy hieroglyphs."

Ali laid his model box at the foot of the half-finished sculpture. He and Maura traced the body, the long arm. Sure enough, those mad symbols were scratched into the rugged metal in deep grooves and ruts.

"Sharp." Maura winced as a loose curl of metal cut her finger. "Damn, that's really bleeding."

"And that's tetanus for you," Ali said. "Seriously, get your shot ASAP. I saw this movie where—"

He was stretching to inspect the arm when the whole sculpture shuddered. The metal head squeaked in the socket, and the head lolled to the right. Three empty eyes and a frozen, cavernous scream turned to Ali.

Ali shrieked and stumbled back, his hand wrenching the arm.

With a low groan, the whole sculpture teetered. Because it wasn't one piece, they realized, but dozens all loosely connected. A clatter of gears and a stretching of springs as the joints shifted. The arm fell from its socket.

"Oh God, it's heavy," Ali gasped and spilled over.

In a clang of metal upon concrete, the sculpture collapsed. Hidden bolts and old springs, rusty wires and chains, it all came apart, echoing across the junkyard in a thunderous boom, heavy enough to crush bones.

But not Ali.

Maura had him in her arms, having just yanked him away. They lay entangled, looking upon the mess that had nearly flattened him.

"Ali, you idiot," Maura seethed.

"No," Ali moaned. "My Hunter-Killer."

The box lay beneath a wide metal leg and the bulk of the torso. Ali tried to pull it out, but the cardboard tore and the pile shifted. It was stuck.

"Guys," Zelda whispered. "Look."

Fear widened their eyes and stiffened their backs.

They couldn't see the entire man stumbling down the row of scrapped refrigerators and ovens, just part of him. Just enough. He was disheveled, clad in dirty rags and some sort of leather apron. A welder's mask barely contained an explosion of ratty gray hair and an ash-speckled beard. What little of his skin they could see was pockmarked, bumpy, and red.

"J'harr, is that you?" the man shouted, voice raspy and rattling. "The fire ready? I don't feel it yet."

Chester, Zelda thought. The man's name was Chester.

"J'harr, I'm done playing door master, you hear? If you've brung your devils, then get ready for mine. My body's old, but there's still fight in my bones."

They stood frozen as Chester clattered and clanged down the narrow aisle, bumping against something that caused a pile of hubcaps to shift.

Maura mouthed, *Run.*

So that's what they did.

The two girls grabbed the bike, and Ali snatched his backpack. They squeezed past the open shed, racing away from the row

Chester shambled down. They took a left at an old tree, where three more sculptures stood frozen in a dance of agony.

"Go faster," Ali said. "I don't want to become a skin couch."

Maura pointed to a gap between old refrigerators and Ali scrambled over. She went next, hoisting the bike from the front while Zelda pushed the rear wheel. It fit, but only just.

Metal clattered behind them, and then a raggedy shape stumbled around the corner. Chester was closer than Zelda thought possible—and so much faster. He raised the welding mask, his face a scabbed visage of confusion and anger. Mad eyes sparkled behind cracked glasses.

Eyes that locked onto Zelda and narrowed.

"You..." he said. "You wear her scar, but you're not her thrall. You're too early... or too late." He stretched out a gloved hand, frayed and blackened. "Tell me, child, are you here to relieve me?"

Zelda was in mid-crawl through the gap when his hand snatched her ankle. She could smell his hot breath, his sour sweat. He reeked of insanity.

"No, this is wrong," he said. "The wrong time and wrong place."

His fingers gripped her leg, tugging her back. This was it, she thought. Age thirteen and killed by a psychopath in his junkyard. All those warnings they had laughed at were right.

Then Maura clambered over Zelda, pivoted, and kicked. A metallic *thunk* echoed, and Zelda felt the gloved hand release her leg. She slid through the gap as Ali tugged her forward.

They tumbled between refrigerators. Then Zelda was on her feet, heart racing. Maura pulled the bike onward while Ali scrambled ahead. "Did you see his face? Oh geez, he's definitely going to skin us."

"Shut up, Ali," Maura hissed.

They raced through a confusion of containers and scrap, then across a dead lawn overtaken by weeds. They found themselves in a parched garden blanketed in dry ivy and deadfall.

Ahead, even more sculptures loomed. Some were vine-choked and dirty, as if they'd been waiting for decades. Others were newer, their twisted features a mockery of the human form. Some had two heads or three legs or four arms. Others were hunched, an amalgamation of limbs and torsos and mouths stretched in frozen gasps. A few hands clutched weapons, swords and spears, clubs and shields.

"Shit, we went the wrong way," Maura said. "Shit shit shit."

"Wrong way?" Ali whispered. "You took us right to his torture porn garden."

Zelda studied their surroundings. The dry plants. The rickety Victorian house she'd seen from the bridge. She could make out the windows, all covered in newspaper from the inside. Paint flaked from the walls and loose shutters. Beyond, there was a porch with a lean to it.

A front porch.

Which meant there was a way out.

"C'mon." She pushed through the reeds and climbed over a thin hedge. Branches scratched at her ankles, reminding her that crazy old man had actually touched her, actually laid hands on her body.

And Maura had punted him in the head.

"Do you know where we're going?" Ali asked.

"If there's a porch," Zelda said, "there has to be a driveway, right? A mailbox and a way out."

"Yeah," Ali said. "Unless it's fenced and guarded by hellhounds."

They rounded a large, scraggily hedge and reached a dry fountain where a gravel driveway merged with the dirt. Ali was right; it was fenced. But not very high. The only hellhounds were a pair of garden gnomes half swallowed by ivy.

And the sculptures...

If the labyrinthian scrapyard was a workshop, the front yard was some sort of museum of madness. Twisted sculptures stood in various poses, some hoisting spears or shields made of hubcaps and covered with weird markings. Others simply slouched in rusty exhaustion, limp marionettes.

"Go," Maura said. "Go, go, go."

The fence had a gate that they threw open. Another hundred feet on the gravel driveway, and there it was: the mailbox and the street beyond.

Feet pounding, hearts drumming, they emerged onto Ponderosa Court. They were just past the eastern edge of Raven's Valley, the furthest finger of the development. The evening echoed with the *tock* of tennis balls against rackets and the squeak of shoes on the courts.

And still they ran, bodies aching, lungs burning, fighting for breath, and then, as they collapsed on the grass by the rec center, their husky gasps slowly gave way to laughter.

CHAPTER TWENTY-NINE

Mark sometimes wondered if all kids thought adults were stupid. Or was it just Zelda?

She came home, her legs scratched and her hoodie smeared with dirt and grime. She had a sort of manic energy about her, as if she'd guzzled a bunch of Red Bulls. She'd moved quickly, trying to avoid him and hurrying upstairs to her bedroom, saying she had to go to the bathroom and start in on her homework.

Confused, Mark lingered at the bottom of the stairs, working up the courage to knock on her door. He didn't dare enter her bedroom without permission. A thirteen-year-old girl was enough of a minefield to navigate.

And yet...

Had something bad happened to her?

"Zelda, if there's anything we need to talk about," he said, "I just want you to know that I'm always here, okay?"

"Thanks, Uncle Mark." He could hear water running. And yet, she called out from far closer than the bathroom.

He lingered in the hall for a moment, unsure of what to do.

Nothing, he realized. Sometimes that seemed like all she wanted. And if so, he could at least be there if she changed her mind.

He returned to the kitchen, to his pile of quizzes that needed grading and his third glass of scotch. The hearing today had changed little, just bought them some time. Still, he was reeling from the news. He thought of Zelda and her parents' crumbling marriage.

Had she known about the divorce?

Had her parents told her?

It just seemed to keep getting worse for the poor girl.

He had no idea how much worse it would get.

PART IV
THE OLD WOMAN IN RED

The Cahto carve totems and erect great effigies in a mockery of man's design, endeavoring perhaps to scare us settlers away. I pushed over one totem and took the axe to another, and no Great Spirit of Bears or Elk has struck me down.

Have I found Paradise here, amongst the westernmost wilds where the sun sets in gold and the stars speak in black-violet? Perchance that I have. Or perchance Paradise has slipped through the veil to bless us with a glimpse of its Glory, lest our ships stray into the depths.

The Diary of Arthur Cummings

CHAPTER THIRTY

It was a Tuesday when Lloyd found the squirrel on the side of the road. He felt sad for the thing, its little paws curled into its chest and its eyes shut as if peacefully sleeping. He gave it a nudge to make sure. No, it was too stiff to be resting.

He glanced around the neighborhood. There was some sort of BBQ in the air and a group of seniors doing tai chi at the park. Stacey Layne stretched at a fence, getting ready for an afternoon jog. Lloyd stole a glance at her ass and wondered if what Randall said was true: had her husband really left her 'cause she wouldn't put out?

He waited until she jogged off before pulling a bag from his backpack. He put his hand inside it, picked up the squirrel, and flipped the bag inside out. Then he put the bag inside another. He was getting good at this. He'd had plenty of practice.

Whistling to himself, Lloyd wondered what secret Armando might reveal next. He'd been coy lately, demanding larger... *contributions*. Lloyd could no longer barter with a feeder mouse or a stray cat. He doubted roadkill would earn him even a whisper. Still, he had to try.

There was so much he wanted to learn.

Three blocks later, he returned home, happy that neither Randall's Camaro nor the pickup was in the driveway. He had the house to himself.

Downstairs in the basement, he pushed aside the stacked toilet paper, an old cooler, and a twelve-pack of beer by the crawlspace.

Here he was, Armando the Great, that disembodied head floating over hypnotic swirls of old paint. A dim luster lived in those eyes. All Lloyd saw was an old poster. Odd.

"Got something for you," he said.

He moved the poster frame aside and placed the bags in an old cooler inside the crawlspace. There were other things within. Canning jars and little Tupperware boxes, each containing contributions Lloyd preferred to forget. *Offer but don't see*, he told himself. *Think but don't feel.*

"I know it's not much, but it's the best I could do." Lloyd scooted the poster back in front of the crawlspace.

Armando stared silently. Was there something in his eyes? A scowl of disapproval?

"Our discourse exacts a great toll, Lloyd Betancourt. The Nether is not easily frayed. Do you think this dry husk worthy of barter?"

"It's all I could find," Lloyd whispered.

"Mmm... I've traded knowledge for pelts before, sallow one. It's not flesh my pups crave, but the fresh souls within. Take your wretched offering and chew it yourself. There's no nourishment in it for us."

It was a curious feeling. First, a damp breath exhaled from the crawl space, reeking of death and decay. Then a tickle scratched deep in Lloyd's throat. He coughed as the air thickened.

With a dry gag, Lloyd clawed at his mouth. He was choking. He reached past his teeth and his tongue, grasped the blockage, and tugged. Something bushy bristled past his lips, and then it was out.

A black squirrel's tail fell into his lap.

"Lloyd?"

Randall's voice boomed upstairs, drifting from his office. A door opened and the floorboards creaked. Lloyd stuffed the squirrel's tail in his pocket as the shadow appeared at the basement door.

"The hell are you doing down here?" Randall wore his blazer and a tie, hair combed and his face clean-shaven. "Why do I always find you in weird places?"

"I was getting some sparkling water," Lloyd said. "We're out upstairs."

"Fine, whatever. Just... c'mon up. I need you to do something."

A favor, Lloyd realized. That was the only reason Randall was ever nice.

He grabbed the sparkling waters and headed up, licking his lips as that horrible taste clung to his tongue. He caught a flicker from Armando's smirk before Randall turned off the lights.

"Why are both the cars gone?" Lloyd asked.

"Insurance finally gave it the all-clear to get the Ford fixed. Your mom's got the sixty-eight."

Lloyd brought the cans to the kitchen and opened the fridge. "You dressed up to get the car repaired?"

"Hell no. But that asshat banker at Wells Fargo is making me come in to sign some forms. They let you do everything over the internet except run a small business. That's bureaucracy for you."

Lloyd braced himself for one of Randall's tirades. How the government always fucked him. First the military and then the VA. Next it was the spineless administrators on the police force who made him resign after the complaint of excessive force. It was the same song sung on a different day; Lloyd knew the tune. He also knew to listen and nod along.

"Anyway, Saperstein's been blowing up my phone. Something about a cookout at the park and their music. I'd go check on it, but that banker has me by the short and curlies. I need you to swing by, unofficially. Just see if you can't calm her."

"You want me to stop by Mrs. Saperstein's?"

Randall rested a hairy arm on the refrigerator. "'Calm her' is the operative word. Placation. She's just old and lonely. Probably wants a pair of ears to chew off. Take some notes if you need. That always makes her feel heard. Tell her you're my deputy today."

"Deputy, right. So, do I get to drive your Camaro?"

"Yeah, that's a funny one." Randall chuckled and gave Lloyd's neck a squeeze, a little too hard. "Go on, jog over. Fresh air'll do you some good."

Lloyd didn't bother to tell him that he'd already had hours' worth of fresh air while scouting for dead things. He still tasted them on his lips.

CHAPTER THIRTY-ONE

Zelda ignored the rumbling in her stomach and the odd pain in her side. Today was officially the midpoint of summer school and mid-term exams. She turned the page. With Ali's study tips, she'd become more confident in her methods and answers. She made good time through the test.

Behind her, Elliot gave her chair a light nudge. Zelda turned to see his eyes flick to her exam. She shook her head and ignored the kick that came to her chair. He could cheat off someone else.

After forty-five minutes, Mr. Barker called the exam and the pencils stopped moving. The students passed their papers forward. Maura glanced back at Zelda, whispering, "How'd it go?"

Zelda gave her a thumbs up. Despite the curious flutter in her gut, she was happy. She'd probably get a B, or an A− if she got lucky. Which meant she could coast by on C's the second half of the term.

Mr. Barker finished stacking the tests, then lowered the projector screen. "So, because the school district mandates that you spend the remaining two hours in the classroom, we're going to watch a movie—"

"Sweet!" Ali pumped his fist.

"—about the power of math."

"Aww," Ali groaned.

"That's right, math and baseball. I present... *Moneyball*. Show of hands: who's seen this masterpiece already?"

Twenty sets of eyes blinked back at the teacher. Not a single student raised their hand.

"Well then, you, my numerical adventurers, are in for a treat. This is the true story of how sharp minds and statistics—not home runs—saved the Oakland A's."

"Wait, isn't Brad Pitt in this?" someone asked.

"Ah, yes he is."

Maura straightened up and winked back at Zelda, mouthing, *D-I-L-F.*

"Gross," Ali muttered.

Zelda spent the first hour of the movie doodling until her eyelids grew heavy and her blinks grew longer and longer. The dark classroom. The warm seat. She was falling asleep. The dialogue-heavy movie didn't help.

Why did teachers always have to choose movies with lessons or connections to the subject? Why couldn't they just put on something scary, or funny, or at least entertaining? Not everything needed a connecting theme or a deeper meaning or...

Zelda felt her gaze bob, rise, and then bob again. Her cheek slid through her palm and her head lolled to the right. She caught her pencil just before it fell off her desk.

Her gaze returned to...

Her notebook and doodles. There was something different about them.

Odd scribbles and wide arcs crossed jagged lines. She'd filled the whole page with those symbols found on Chester's sculptures.

"Hey, check this out." She went to nudge Maura, but Maura's desk was empty.

No. The whole classroom was empty.

Where were her classmates? Why were the desks vacant? Had she slept through the bell?

The movie still played from the projector. But the movie was all *wrong*.

A low-angle shot filled the screen, the perspective from a shower or a bathroom perhaps. The picture was hazy, like the projector was unfocused or the lens was oily. Something red and wet lingered at the edge of the shot.

"Hello?" Zelda asked. "Mr. Barker? Maura? Ali?"

Her voice echoed through the dark classroom. Mr. Barker's chair was empty.

They were playing a prank on her; that had to be it. They were probably hiding.

She walked to the front, hoping to see Mr. Barker crouching behind his desk, grinning his dopey grin. But he wasn't there.

And that screen.

Zelda studied the movie a moment longer, the perspective still low and fuzzy, the white tiles bathed in bright light. She was right; it was a bathroom. There was the base of a toilet at the edge of the screen. Squinting, she could make out red tendrils on the porcelain base.

They were glistening and wet.

She didn't like this prank. It was weird and cruel. That Ali and Maura would go along with this made her angry. Were they going to be waiting out in the hall, phones raised as they laughed?

She was going to give them all sorts of hell.

She opened the door, telling herself not to give in to the anger. Not to give them satisfaction.

She found no classmates or teacher. No laughing students. No one shuffling between classes. Dark halls stood before her.

She could see another dim classroom across the way. Had she slept through the end of the day? Was she alone and locked in the school?

No. Not totally alone. Someone shuffled at the far end of the hall.

A woman—an *old* woman—limped past distant lockers and doors. Something dark and wet matted one side of her hair. A slipper clung to her left foot, going *swish, swish, swish* on the floor. Her right foot was bare.

But it was the trail of blood she left behind that tightened Zelda's spine. Little red gems dripped and painted a crimson smear on the floor.

The old woman raised a hand to her blouse, adjusting it before pushing a distant door open. There was something weak about her movements, something confused. Was it like Ms. Paxton back in Alder Glen? Was this woman sundowning too?

No, Zelda sensed it was something far worse.

Every ounce of her screamed, *Turn away!* She pushed that fear to a small corner of her mind. The old woman was wounded and needed help.

"Ma'am," Zelda called out. "Are you injured? Do you need someone?"

Her words echoed down the hall, so small and timid. The door did not open.

Fifty paces, and she passed the smeared blood and loose slipper. A blue rectangle hung on the door. *Women's Restroom.*

"Ma'am, you're bleeding. You... You really should get some help. Ma'am?"

Zelda hesitated at the bathroom door. Nothing good would come from going inside. She knew it in her bones. And yet, there was no one else to call, no one else who could help this old woman. Without Zelda, she was alone and bleeding...

Broken.

Zelda choked back her fears and opened the door.

"Ma'am? I think you're hurt."

Her wavering voice echoed off the bathroom walls and stalls.

Her reflection shivered in a mirror: just a scared girl, thirteen and always trying to act older, indifferent, and numb.

But the blood...

Something moved in the furthest stall. Something *sloshed.*

Carefully, slowly, Zelda followed the droplets to the stalls. She gave them a wide berth. If the door was closed or locked, she didn't know what to do. Crawl under or look over, or perhaps just leave the confused lady for someone else to assist.

The stall was open, thank God.

And it was empty.

The trail of blood ended right at the base of the toilet in a smear and a handful of specks. A single crimson droplet floated in the clear water, dissipating like smoke in the wind.

Then the toilet rumbled.

A massive bubble burped from the pipes. It hit the surface and expanded, bloody tendrils reddening the water. Another burp and up came a second red bubble. Then another, and another, and soon the water was churning, darkening, and rising. With a final burp, the water hit the edge of the toilet and poured onto the floor.

Zelda stepped back, but not fast enough. The blood hit her sandals, her toes, sent her stumbling backward. The bathroom teetered as the walls collapsed and—

And then the white bathroom was subsumed with brightness. Mr. Barker stood at the door, his finger toggling the light switch. The mirrors stretched into windows; the stalls became desks. Where there was only emptiness, students now zipped up their backpacks and stood as the bell chimed.

Zelda rose, wiping sleep from her eyes when a curious pain fluttered deep inside her abdomen. She was damp.

And it wasn't her toes.

"Dude, did you just get your period?" asked Elliot from the desk behind her. "Holy shit, someone get a mop."

Her hands went to the back of her shorts and her bare thighs. She felt it. *No, not here. Please not here.*

"Elliot," Mr. Barker snapped. "Go to the principal's office. Now."

"But... class is over."

"I don't care if it's Sunday. Go. Now."

Zelda's world spun. Red spotted her fingertips, and a wet imprint marred her beige chair. Something dripped down her right thigh. She knew that this was a thing that happened; she'd had a few talks with her mom.

And yet, nothing had prepared her for this moment. The dream, the toilet, and her light khaki shorts. Worst of all were the eyes of her classmates. The sidelong glances cast by students as they filed from the classroom and pretended not to giggle.

CHAPTER THIRTY-TWO

Wiping sweat from his forehead, Lloyd crossed the park. One day he'd learn to say no, he told himself. One day, he'd stand up to Randall and his endless tasks. The deliveries of those stupid items he bought. Helping him move barrels and boxes, used furniture and appliances.

For a while, Randall had gotten into some weird MLM that specialized in vitamins and weight-loss supplements. Now they sat in a storage locker, like half the other crap he hoarded, sure bets that never paid off.

But today, Lloyd was happy he did Randall's job for him.

Fortunate, really.

He'd visited Mrs. Saperstein's and listened while she complained about the park, the smell of the barbecue, and the noise from the party. They were playing their music too loud, she said. They looked suspicious. And did they have a permit to grill?

He'd said he'd take a look and get back.

Now, he checked the park's sign and found nothing about a permit.

But he did see the party.

They were Tongans, the Taumalolo family from a few blocks

over. Birthday balloons fluttered over picnic tables. There were twenty relatives at least, the older ones seated at the benches and tables, the young ones playing rugby or chasing each other. They were chatty and happy and, yes, perhaps a little loud, but so what? Mostly, Lloyd suspected Mrs. Saperstein didn't like the fact that their music was hip-hop, and it wasn't in English.

"You're that security guy's kid, yeah?" asked Mr. Taumalolo, a barrel-chested man with tattoos down one arm and eyes like warm honey. "Larry or Leonard or—"

"Lloyd. And he's my stepdad." After a beat, Lloyd's hands found their way into his pockets. "So, this is kind of awkward, but we got a noise complaint. And—"

"Yeah, Sophie Saperstein, right?" Mr. Taumalolo smirked.

"I can't really say, sir."

"No, of course not." He caught a stray rugby pass and flung the ball back to the kids. "It's my nephew's sixteenth birthday. They drove down from Oregon so we're not stopping the festivities. But I'll tell you what, we'll turn down the music, and maybe I can send you over with a peace offering for old Sophie."

Lloyd watched as Mr. Taumalolo whispered to his wife. She laughed and began filling a large paper plate with an assortment of meats and fruits. There was grilled pineapple and mango, glistening sausages and piles of barbecued ribs. Chicken wings covered in garlic, lemon, and pepper. There was lamb sliced so thin it was almost transparent until Mrs. Taumalolo rolled it up and stacked it upon a bed of yellow rice.

While she filled the plate, Mr. Taumalolo studied Lloyd. "You know, my daughter goes to your college." He gestured to a tall girl playing frisbee with a group of athletic young men. "Irma, she's a sophomore."

"She's at Trinity State?"

"And majoring in art, God help me." He laughed, yet his eyes darkened. "Listen, I heard what happened. That fraternity and the lake. That... *accident*."

Lloyd shrugged. So, word really had traveled. He didn't remember much, and what he did was just a fractured blur of senses.

The chill of the ice as they gave him mouth-to-mouth.

The crack of his ribs as they compressed his chest.

The whir of the helicopter as the state forest passed underneath.

"It was nothing," he said.

Mr. Taumalolo wasn't buying it. "Maybe, but it wasn't fair what you went through. I'm an attorney, you know. Accidents, injuries, those kinds of things. If it turns out it wasn't nothing, well... can I give you my card?"

Lloyd didn't want anything to do with that university, the fraternity, or that time of his life. He'd put it in a box, locked it, and shoved it to the far recesses of his wounded mind.

Still, he took Mr. Taumalolo's card and pretended to read it.

With a crinkling tear, Mrs. Taumalolo wrapped the plate of food in aluminum foil and handed it to him. It probably weighed five pounds.

"There's some extra plates underneath," Mr. Taumalolo said. "If it doesn't all end up at Sophie's doorstep, well, our secret." He winked and gave Lloyd's shoulder a soft pat. "And do keep in mind that some injuries take a while to be noticed. You've got my card."

Lloyd thanked him and walked off, the scent of barbecue dancing beneath his nose and rumbling his gut. He hadn't realized how hungry he was.

Sophie Saperstein lived at the end of Maple Way in what the Raven's Valley brochure called a "garden bungalow unit," a single-story two-bedroom, two-bath ideal for first-time homeowners or retirees. Like all the houses, it was unique. Thick, recycled beams met the sloping roof and eaves. An attic vent styled like a dormer window loomed over the front door. Lloyd glanced up at the glass, certain that someone had been watching him approach.

But the window was empty.

He rang the bell and waited. From the porch, he could see inside, where Sophie's collectible plates crowded the walls. Opera hummed from the speakers, perhaps an attempt to drown out the hip-hop of the party. Lloyd wondered why a woman who hated noise had bought a house adjacent to the largest park in Raven's Valley.

Then he heard the raspy moan.

It came during a gap in the music, when the female opera singer had finished her sharp note and the male had yet to let loose his pipes. It sounded like a cry of—

"Help..."

Had he really heard that? He told himself it must've just been an echo. A musical distortion off the walls and windows.

"Help..."

A tingle crawled up his body. No, he definitely heard that. The cry drifted through the house from the back. It was Mrs. Saperstein's voice, the same voice that scolded him years ago over his Spanish conjugation and pronunciation.

"Mrs. Saperstein, I'm coming in."

He opened the screen door and entered. A dozen little crystal cats sat in a display case, their gemstone eyes sparkling and watching him enter. He smelled burned toast and spotted the makings of a sandwich in the kitchen.

"Mrs. Saperstein?"

Nothing. He walked deeper into the house.

He saw the broken pot first, the soil and the plant. Next came the fallen stool, just outside the bathroom. Then he saw the body.

She had fallen in the bathroom, and judging by the blood, she'd hit her head twice. First on the marble sink by the window. Then again on the tiled floor. Her broken glasses lay nearby.

Lloyd had read that head wounds bled, but nothing prepared

him for this. The old lady lay upon a mirror of shimmering crimson.

A mirror in which he saw himself standing and staring.

But not moving.

"Help..." Mrs. Saperstein muttered. She lay near the toilet, hair matted on one side. Her lips made little puckering motions, like a tired fish blowing red bubbles. Her toes curled near a fallen slipper.

With unblinking eyes, Lloyd stared at the red lake that nearly spanned the whole bathroom. He felt... What did he feel? Powerful, yes. In this moment, he had the power to save a life and become a hero.

Or...

His thoughts drifted to Armando the Great. What had he whispered?

"It's not flesh my pups crave, but the fresh souls within."

Lloyd tilted his head. "I'm here, Mrs. Saperstein."

"Help..."

"That's right, Mrs. Saperstein. Help is on the way. Don't you worry."

His back slid down the doorframe and his legs crossed underneath. He watched the old woman spasm as the little red bubbles by her lips grew weaker and smaller.

He placed the warm plate in his lap and peeled back the tinfoil. A deep breath. Barbecue sauce and grilled pineapple, rice and so much more to enjoy. He was lucky. Yes, he had this meal to himself.

He sensed he wasn't the only one getting ready to eat.

In the red reflection, something crawled down the walls. A skittering shadow of claw and tail. A thing of bony spine, inky skin, and six crooked legs.

Pups, Lloyd thought.

Rings and chains hung from tumorous dark skin. Tendrils unfolded from its tormented form, thin umbilicals stretching skyward and connecting to something *beyond.* Even a reflected glimpse was too much and his mind recoiled. No, he couldn't see them or their master; he didn't want to. Yet he felt every hair rise as they passed by.

"Help..."

The pups would have to be patient. He sensed their meal wasn't ready, not quite.

But his lunch was cooling.

He studied the plate and the choices before him. A chicken wing, perhaps. Or some of those ribs. He sunk his teeth into a sausage and moaned as he chewed. Yes, it was delicious, more flavorful than he imagined, each bite better than the last.

CHAPTER THIRTY-THREE

Mark put the Subaru in park and left the stereo running. "I'll be right back."

Zelda sat in the passenger seat wearing the basketball shorts he kept in his gym bag at Neumann. When he'd heard from Steve Barker what happened at the end of math class, he'd hurried across campus. He'd found Zelda cleaning the chair, her hoodie around her waist and a meek look in her eyes.

Poor girl.

He closed the car door, hesitating and drumming his fingers along the open window. *Say something*, he told himself. *Anything.*

"Look, this is totally normal, okay? You didn't do anything wrong."

She gave her usual quick nod and returned to her phone.

"Want me to grab some Aspirin or Midol? Anything else you want?"

"Just quiet, thanks." She turned up the car stereo.

Sighing, he crossed the parking lot and entered Target. He grabbed a red basket and hurried to the section for feminine products. When he found the row, his stomach dropped.

So many choices.

There were pads and tampons, and of course, he knew the difference. But what brand would be best? Zelda was physically active and Playtex had something called Sport. But there were lights, regulars, and supers. Another box promised leak-guard protection. Did that mean the others weren't absorbent? Some lacked applicators. Others were made of organic cotton. And what about lightly scented or unscented? Odor shield or gentle glide? It was all overwhelming.

He lingered, watching a woman in her twenties select a box of Tampax Pearl. She gave him a sidelong scowl as she placed it in her basket. Christ, he realized, he was being the worst thing a middle-aged guy could be: a creep.

He grabbed several boxes, put them in his basket, and shuffled off before someone called security. Near the counter, he realized all he had were feminine products, so he bought a bottle of wine, the latest issue of *Scientific American*, and a twin pack of dish soap. He added a Slim Jim by the checkout.

He cued for the self-service checkout but discovered it wouldn't sell alcohol. The cashier waved him over. "Sir, I'll take you right here."

Sir? When the hell had he become a sir?

He put down the Slim Jim and dish soap first. Then came the stack of tampons and pads.

Halfway through the purchase, a voice behind him said, "Hey, stranger."

He knew her voice. Stacey Layne, wearing a Neumann Prep hoodie with a red basket of her own. Her eyes flicked to the pile of feminine products. He wasn't sure why this was awkward. It was natural, of course, and nothing to be ashamed of.

And yet, it didn't feel right that he was the one to coach Zelda through it. He was just a tourist trying to be something he could never be: her parent.

"Wow, really covering all the bases there," Stacey said, and clocked the situation immediately. "First time it happened, I sent my big brother into Kroger's. He came back with a box of Depends, so you're ahead of the curve."

Mark swiped his credit card and took the bag. "How'd you know?"

"Awkward man, slight blush, every single tampon box possible. Plus, I had a disciplinary chat with a student who owes me an essay on good manners."

"Well, it's not every box." He stepped away from the register. "Fun times, right?"

"You've got an evening ahead."

"And a surly teenager to connect with. She'd probably rather eat glass than have 'the Talk.'"

Stacy smiled. "You're pretty green at this, aren't you?"

"Last winter, I spent a week listing the pros and cons of adopting another dog. I got an Xbox instead. I love my niece, but I'm the last person she probably wants to have this chat with. I can hear her raising the drawbridge from here."

After coffee the other week, he hadn't had another chance to connect with Stacey. He thought maybe she didn't care for him or his company. She was armored, as most teachers were after years in the classroom. Plus, she was probably out of his league.

But something softened on her face. An idea was forming. "So... Would she want another woman to talk to? Maybe go over the basics?"

Mark exhaled. "Oh thank God yes. Yes, we would."

CHAPTER THIRTY-FOUR

It turned out that Zelda liked Stacey. Or at least she appreciated her feminine guidance. What started as a quick chat by the car became a ride to their house, and then the two women took a trip to Zelda's bedroom upstairs.

Scotch in hand, Mark sat in the kitchen, reviewing the conversation on their drive home. Stacey had told Zelda that as coordinator for the summer school program, she had to talk to all the girls about such issues. It was a lie, but one she sold well. Zelda had given her standard single nod and a mumbled, "Okay."

He knocked the rest of the scotch back and poured another two fingers into the glass. Something crinkled and clinked. For a moment, he thought it was the ball of ice in his glass.

But no, it was the window above the sink.

A crack formed in the double-paned glass.

Like much of the house, the window frame was reclaimed wood, aged and tasteful, a piece of gorgeous history that fit right in with the natural surfaces and styling. The glass within bore a single white line as long as his finger.

A faint squeak and crunch. A second line appeared in the glass.

With a crinkle and a pop, it traced its way to the bottom of the frame.

A third curve left a milky crescent in the glass. Then a fourth crossed the others.

“Great,” Mark muttered. “Brand-new house and it’s falling apart.”

He licked his thumb and rubbed the double-paned glass. Odd, he didn’t feel the cracks. He leaned in over the sink, pressed his face close to the window.

With a faint crunch, a fifth line stretched across the glass, bisecting the other four at sharp angles.

Like some sort of weird symbol.

He took out his phone, opened the SmartHome app, and dimmed the kitchen lights. He pressed the phone’s flashlight against the glass.

No wonder he couldn’t feel the crack, he realized. The marks weren’t on the surface of the double-paned glass.

They were inside it.

“Nice mood lighting,” Stacey said, entering the kitchen.

Mark returned the lights to a warm color and full brightness. “How’d it go? Is she... okay?”

“My clinical diagnosis is she has what the kids call ‘cringe.’ Or at least I think that’s the word they use. Maybe that’s cringe, too.” Stacy leaned against the counter. “Yeah, she’s just embarrassed. She shouldn’t be, but that’s life at thirteen.”

“Thank you, really. You saved us both a lot of awkwardness.”

“Nah, I just kicked it down the road. She’s a smart girl. Plus that pretty face, those long legs. I don’t envy you and all the suitors you’ll be fending off in a few years.”

Her words hit him like a gut punch. A few years? Jesus, was he even going to be around that long? He wanted to be, of course, if that’s what Zelda wanted. And yet a few years felt impossibly far off. He’d only been around for a few months.

"What are you drinking?" he asked. "I'm partial to scotch, but there's beer, wine—"

"I'm good," she said, eyes lingering on the bottle of Cragganmore.

"Right, the marathon."

"Yeah, the marathon," she said. "I'll take a water though."

He filled her glass at the fridge and passed it to her. He sensed there was something else, a stiffening in her posture. Had he crossed some sort of boundary?

"So, I'm curious," he said, "but is your house sort of... buggy?"

"Buggy? Well, the SmartLock locked me in my attic last week. The motion lights go off on their own. Oh, and you know those heated tiles in our bathrooms? Yeah, every couple of weeks, they turn the place into a sauna. Frankly, I've given up on half the features. I'm just glad the walls aren't bleeding."

Mark grinned. "Raven's Valley isn't built on an Indian burial ground, is it?"

"Go back long enough and everything was a burial ground. But no, this was just part of the old lumber yards and mills. Kids used to sneak in, have keg parties, and climb around the equipment. Now, I'm not saying I did that, but... I might have a few scars."

He sipped his scotch, feeling warm and good. For a moment, work tomorrow didn't exist. Nor did the hearing next month. There was just Stacey and him, the only friend he really had in this town.

He said, "You've seen it change a lot, I bet. Do you miss the old Greywood Bay?"

She considered it. "Some people get nostalgic and want to preserve things, like the town is some fossil or a bug stuck in amber. What they forget is that things weren't perfect. We were just more ignorant. Unemployment was in the double digits through the nineties. There was crime and brain drain and the university almost closed. When I graduated high school, the choices were to get pregnant or get away. If you weren't a Larchmont or Strathmore or any of those rich families with their mansions on the bluffs, you were a townie. And townies didn't go to Neumann Prep."

"Did you?"

"No. But I'm on the inside now, and that's how I can change it." She finished her water. "Anyway, I should get going."

He walked her to the front door as Zelda's music thumped from the bedroom upstairs. Outside, the late afternoon was cool, the wind strong through the valley. Rivers of fog wormed their way down the hills. The recorded crickets were just starting to chirp. It struck Mark that he was no longer creeped out but now found their song oddly comforting.

Then they saw the cars down the street.

The emergency lights blinked pastel off the branches and trees. Two blocks down, where Manzanita met Maple Way, an ambulance, a fire truck, and a police cruiser filled the street. Neighbors gathered on their lawns.

Stacey said, "So, I don't want to rubberneck, but..."

"Yeah, me neither," Mark agreed, already walking beside her.

They came to a stop near the jogging path and the park, where a large family ate an early dinner by the grill. A few tossed frisbees, but most stared at the scene and the house.

There, on a bungalow's porch, a young man talked to a cop. His hands nervously clutched a foil-wrapped plate. Every now and then, his fingers drifted to his hair, brushing a lock from his eyes.

"That's Lloyd, Diana's son," Stacey said. "I taught him for two years. Nice boy, quiet." She gave a wave to a neighbor. "Pavarti, what's going on?"

Pavarti offered Mark the same friendly smile that she'd given him when she dropped off a welcome-to-the-neighborhood basket. Now, she placed a gentle hand on Stacy's forearm, whispering, "It's some sort of accident, I think. They've been in Sophie's place for a half hour now. First they took pictures, and then the paramedics went in through the side, and—*oh no...*" Pavarti squeezed Stacey's arm, pulling her close.

An audible gasp drifted through the crowd, beginning with those closest to the driveway and making its way back. Someone turned away.

Because of the gurney, Mark realized. And the shape underneath. The unmistakable shape of a body.

With a click, the paramedics guided the gurney down the steps, down the driveway, and to the back of the ambulance. A man removed his hat as it passed. Mark spotted disposable covers over the paramedics' shoes.

"Poor Sophie," Stacey said.

Mark had never met Sophie Saperstein. She was just a distant name and a face in the faculty photos he passed in the halls. And yet he felt her gravity all summer. Her classroom with its kitschy posters. His last-minute job because of her cancer's resurgence. Worst of all, the guilt that a small and dark part of him had hoped she would truly retire.

No, he thought, not a small part at all.

Because if she did, he might have a shot at her job. Because then Zelda could attend at a reduced rate. And because the attorneys and the judge would see what he was doing. Wouldn't they be pleased?

Yet now, watching the paramedics load the late Mrs. Saperstein into the ambulance, Mark felt only shame. What he'd hoped for had just come to pass.

CHAPTER THIRTY-FIVE

There were few words for what he was feeling right now. At least, few words that Lloyd knew. Ebullient perhaps. Galvanized. Or maybe percipient. He remembered it from a spelling quiz in AP English.

The interviewing officer clicked his pen and tucked it into his pocket. The notepad followed. With a sigh, he looked at the front yard of the bungalow house. The firemen were packing up as the ambulance departed.

He asked, “You sure you don’t want me to call your parents?”

“No,” Lloyd said. He could hardly feel his toes and he didn’t want to share this moment with anyone.

“Can I give you a ride?”

“I’m fine. It’s just a short walk.”

The officer glanced at the small crowd still lingering on the sidewalk and street. “Look, you did the right thing calling us, okay? But that doesn’t mean what you saw will feel good. We’ve got a grief counselor we can put you in touch with if—”

“I’m okay.” Lloyd wiped hair from his face. “Like you said, it was probably peaceful, wasn’t it?”

The cop gave Lloyd a pat on his shoulder and rose. "Yeah, kid, I'm sure it was."

The police escorted him as far as the front porch. Lloyd would have to make his way past the crowd to get home. There were a dozen or so, all these delicate people made of flesh and bone so easily broken. Today reminded him of that: how soft they all were.

And how hard he could become.

The Hallermans were the first to ask what happened. Squeezing past, he just said there'd been an accident and he'd found Sophie in the bathroom. By the time the paramedics arrived, she'd succumbed.

"Mmm... Consumed."

His thumbs circled the aluminum foil at the edge of the plate. He looked down at his shoes to really sell the performance.

After that, it was Ms. Singh and Ms. Layne and some middle-aged guy Lloyd didn't recognize. He gave a repeat performance and added a little shake of his head. "I wish I knew CPR or something... Maybe that would've helped."

"No, no, there's nothing you could do," Ms. Layne said. "She was lucky you found her. Lucky to have someone there with her, at the end."

He smiled inwardly. Yes, perhaps she was lucky. But they weren't alone. There had been others in that bathroom.

Things of scales and claws he could only perceive in that wet red reflection.

Things that had feasted on something like her soul.

"I should get going."

Both Ms. Singh and Ms. Layne said that if he needed anyone to talk to, they'd be happy to listen. Yet again, Lloyd stifled a grin.

Oh, he had someone to talk to, indeed. Someone who was waiting for him in the basement.

He could already hear the whispers from several blocks away.

"—yes, a great thing you've done. The veil is fraying. Come, Lloyd. Come and collect your reward."

Fifteen minutes later, Lloyd placed the leftover barbecue in the refrigerator. He checked Randall's office, the garage, all the usual spots, pleased to discover he was truly alone. He considered showering, yet he knew Armando the Great liked the fresh scent of death. He had to admit, he was developing a nose for it, too. It *cloaked* him, salty and sweet. For a moment, he stood there at the door to the basement, breathing in his own reek.

"Hurry, Lloyd. Hurry. It costs much to span the cosmos between us."

"Yeah, hold your horses."

In twelve steps, he was at the bottom of the basement, sliding aside folding chairs so he could see Armando's full splendor. Here it was, twenty-four by thirty-six inches of aged poster behind glass. That floating head, those piercing eyes. Had the painted swirls always held little tentacles and hands at their edges? Had Armando's face always been so clear you could see every pore?

A cool wind picked up in the basement as the lights flickered and dimmed.

"My pups are nourished, yes, and through them, I am fed. Mmm... But there's more work to be done, Lloyd, so much more to consume and to learn. Next, we must—"

"What about my reward?" Lloyd asked.

The lights flickered, colors shifting from warm yellow to dark violet. Was that annoyance he sensed? Yes, something was changing inside him, too. He could feel something *peeling.* The shedding of layers within things, behind things, above and below. If he focused, some walls and beams of the house now shivered and breathed.

And a few even murmured and screamed.

"Your reward, yes. Do you feel it now? You are becoming more. Mmm... This is a taste of the All Knowledge, a hint of my splendor. Be my emissary. Bring death in my name and—"

"No," Lloyd said. "I want more."

The poster didn't blink, and yet Lloyd sensed a great hesitation from within it, from beyond. The entire house held its breath.

"Your appetite, yes... but your body is weak, your mind still unready."

Lloyd's jaw tensed. Weak? Mrs. Saperstein had bled out for thirty minutes; he'd watched the whole thing. He'd felt the pups brush past and caught their feasting reflections.

No, he wasn't weak. He was ready. He was getting stronger and changing.

"If you want me to be your emissary, Armando, I want to see what I'm representing. Otherwise..."

He stood up and stepped back. The lights flickered as darkness bled out from the walls. The house groaned.

"Mmm... Very well. Look upon me for as long as you can."

Lloyd returned to the space before the poster. Calmly, he sat and stared at that old-time mentalist and those eyes like twin pools of darkness.

"But my name is not Armando."

It began somewhere behind the poster, somewhere *beyond*. Oily violet roots scratched at the edges of the frame. There was a low shuddering within the very house, as if something burped and woke from a deep slumber. Board by board, beam by beam, the walls simply fell away.

Lloyd found himself teetering upon a vast precipice, a cosmic maelstrom swirling on all sides. Towering clouds of crackling green and blue consumed shattered planets. Angry flames roared, leaving trails of gases and screaming tendrils of dust.

Lloyd gripped the banister as his body leaned back. But there was no back, no direction, and no stairs beneath him. He felt himself stretching, pulled taut and long, zooming now through the furious dust.

Lightning flashed, casting strobe-lit glimpses of the impossible.

Ruins spun among this interstellar tempest. A great civilization crushed to loose stones and rusty metal. Monuments and cathedrals and once-opulent towers, all tumbling and coming apart brick by brick, beam by beam. Statues of inhuman form limbed in arachnid configuration. Serpentine braids of crumbling metal formed impossible knots. Time-lost effigies spun in the dust, frozen shadows of life, but none that Lloyd's mind could assemble or perceive.

No, he thought. *Make it stop.*

But it did not.

There were several civilizations now, dozens, each rising and collapsing into fiery ruins and chaos. Lloyd's mind fumbled at it all, pawing desperate and dumb. He was an infant peering at a vast library and grasping for knowledge. He was a slug oozing across the greatest computer ever built. He was deaf and blind and begging someone to explain every spectrum of light.

No. Too much. His mind crumbled, crumbled, crumbled.

Then the ruins parted and he saw the center of it all: a single black star of undulating flesh. A sea of limbs and teeth swelled and collapsed beneath waves of tentacles and tongues. Valleys of mouths stretched into desperate screams. Mountains of hands scratched at each other, peeling dark skin from bone and tearing itself apart, again and again. Wings beating, claws scraping, great forests of jagged bone all crackling and infected and—

No. No more. I can't take it.

But it was the eyes that finally broke him.

The eyes were infinite.

The eyes were unblinking.

Cold light burst from each pupil, a black-violet beam lashing out across the vast coldness of space and time.

Those eyes. That light and that color. That *lack* of color. Lloyd knew that endless black violet, but only by abstraction. Because to know the beam's true hue, his mind desperately warned, would simply obliterate him.

He tried to close his eyes, but he no longer had eyelids. He tried to scream with no tongue.

Nothing.

Yes, he was nothing now. Just a mote in that beam's furious

current, screaming out from a hungry dead star beyond the edge of existence. Screaming with lips he no longer possessed.

Then the black-violet beam thinned and frayed, narrowing as it threaded the cosmos. Stars blinked past, warm and filled with light.

The beam pierced something new: the atmosphere of a blue-green planet. It pierced the clouds, rushing toward a house Lloyd recognized only from a memory of millennia past.

Home. This was his home. Yes, he remembered it. Here, the black-violet beam was just a single fiber, so wispy and delicate it humbled his scarred heart.

He felt something beneath him and the word bloomed in his mind.

Floor.

And something moving toward him.

Stairs.

And then an idea, a concept, something he'd studied in school.

Gravity.

Lloyd fell upon the stairs, his soft body bouncing and his hands flailing out. He was here, home, in his basement. His bones ached and his balance was off.

But he was alive.

The thing that wore Armando's face was right: Lloyd's mind wasn't ready.

Not ready yet.

CHAPTER THIRTY-SIX

Diana Betancourt took the keys from the valet and slipped in behind the wheel of Randy's obnoxious '68 Camaro. With a push of the accelerator, she put the country club behind her, the coastal highway in front.

She was a busy businesswoman, but she liked it that way. She crammed her mornings with meetings and home showings. Her afternoons were for social affairs that fed back into her real estate ventures. She saved the evenings for tennis, bible study, and volunteer work at the Woman's Club of Greywood Bay.

On weekends, she coached girls from marginalized communities around the county: the Central Americans that harvested grapes or vegetables or marijuana from the farms, the Filipinos that worked hospitality during the spring and summer, and the Eastern European nannies that were becoming more common with the town's growing population of dual-income parents.

Those were her favorite clients. They bought houses in cash and asked the fewest questions. They wanted a good school, clean air, and access to nature.

Yeah, some locals grumbled about the shifting demographics,

the influx of new money, the diversity. But to her, it was all good business. And these days, business was good.

She tuned the radio to the classics and hummed along to Amy Grant's "Baby, Baby." She was still buzzing after lunch at the clubhouse, where an old friend called her the epitome of success. She smiled for miles. Yes, she had been fortunate lately. She wasn't a Strathmore, a Daniels, or a Larchmont...

But maybe someday.

Wouldn't that show that bastard Donald for leaving her to raise Lloyd on her own? She imagined her ex-husband's trailer park life in Missoula, his tobacco-stained fingers tapping a crumb-spattered keyboard, googling her name and seeing *Greywood Bay's Premier Real Estate Broker*.

Now, to land the contract for Hawk's Hollow.

Randy texted, and she promised to pick him up at the bank after stopping for groceries. Driving along the coast, she envisioned a long line of billboards leading the way to that soon-to-be-developed valley. Coral pink, perhaps, and her in that black and silver suit that was powerful and pretty.

Yes, wouldn't that be nice?

She was at Whole Foods, trying to park the absurd muscle car, when her phone buzzed. It was Carol, a business acquaintance, always on the hunt for another property to add to her rental portfolio. This could be good news.

She fiddled with the Bluetooth receiver awkwardly installed in the classic dashboard. Why did men fall for such silly cars?

She had a Range Rover on pre-order, a fiftieth birthday present to herself for selling the last house in Raven's Valley. She hadn't told Randy because she knew he'd complain. But heck, she deserved it.

She gave up on the Bluetooth and simply put the phone to her ear. "Carol, what's new? I've been meaning to call you. Listen..."

She never got into her sales pitch.

What Carol told her didn't make an ounce of sense. Something about her son, about Sophie Saperstein, and a bunch of police. There'd been some sort of accident. And how was Lloyd handling all this?

When she had the whole story, she hung up and immediately dialed Lloyd. He didn't answer. She tried again until some asshole in a Prius honked and said Randy's car took up too much space.

She sped home to Raven's Valley, the engine rumbling down the crosstown expressway while Carol's words rattled about her mind.

"They said she had fallen in the bathroom that there was so much blood they needed a mop."

"Could you imagine what would have happened if nobody found her for weeks?"

"Poor Lloyd; he looked shaken, like he'd done something wrong."

Yes, poor Lloyd, she thought, and merged over a lane.

Her son wasn't well; she knew this. He'd always been different, sensitive, and fragile. Especially after that bastard Donald ran out on them both. And lately...

No. She pushed her worries aside. Placed them in a box and locked them away.

Yes, it was just a phase.

Yes, things would improve.

And yes, if she smiled and closed some more deals, didn't that mean everything else was all right? It had to. It must.

She pulled into the driveway at a quarter after seven, worried she'd forgotten something important. "Lloyd?" she called from the entryway. "Lloyd? Are you home?"

Home. Yes, there was something here in her home. Something festering and growing. She felt a presence, as if the walls were made of one-way mirrors and muddy forms watched from beyond.

"Lloyd? Sweetie? I heard the strangest thing..."

His bedroom was dark, empty. She spent a moment studying his space. The posters of airplanes and great naval battles. The models of tanks and the books of war. Randy had been so frustrated when Lloyd moved back after a semester and a half at college. He'd wanted to turn this bedroom into a man cave.

And she realized now, as she looked upon Lloyd's stuff, that she didn't really know her son all that well. She swore he'd grown out of those models years ago.

"Lloyd?"

Then she heard it, a faint muttering that came from downstairs.

From the basement.

The years had tempered her motherly instinct, but a fear gripped her and brought speed to her feet. Was that a voice from below? Was that several? She hurried downstairs, to the open basement door where—

Oh God, please...

Lloyd lay in a heap near the bottom of the stairs. One arm was tucked beneath his back, while the other clutched his face, splayed fingers concealing his eyes. He was motionless.

"No, no, no." She rushed down the stairs. She was dimly aware that the basement felt stretched as if pulled from its corners. And her footsteps... Why did they seem to echo across a cavernous void?

"Lloyd, honey, what happened?"

Then, just like that, the distant glaze left his eyes. He stirred and sat up. "Sorry, Mom. I must've fallen asleep."

"Fallen..." she stammered. "You were on the stairs, on the floor—"

"Yeah, I was really tired. Long day."

He stood up. Her boy, he stood up just like it was nothing and stifled a yawn. She smelled cooked meat on his breath.

"There's ribs in the fridge," he said. "Sausages, some chicken wings. You know, I think I'll grab some more."

He was halfway up the stairs when she found her voice.

"Lloyd, honey? I heard the strangest thing."

He paused and blinked. And in that blink, he knew what she meant. Had his eyes always been that sharp? That... *percipient*?

"Oh. That. Yeah, I was going to tell you, but I fell asleep."

"You... fell asleep," she repeated, "in the basement?"

"I was getting some paper towels and dozed off." He took a roll of 2-ply sheets from a shelf. "Don't worry, Mom. I'm just a bit rattled, that's all. We can talk about it later, if you want. But why don't you tell me about your day? Boy, am I hungry."

He hurried up the final steps and disappeared down the hall. A moment later, she could hear the refrigerator clicking open. *He's wounded*, she thought. Or something worse. This was only a shadow of her son. A husk wrapped in his skin.

No, silly thought, she told herself. If he wanted to talk about it, that's what he would do. And if he needed her help, wouldn't he ask?

Yes, she told herself all this and more.

The phone rang, startling her in that cool, cavernous basement. She glanced at the screen and remembered what she'd forgotten. It was Randy, still at the bank and waiting to be picked up.

CHAPTER THIRTY-SEVEN

Stifling a yawn, Zelda twirled the pencil and turned the page. She was on the third section of her math worksheets, the questions blurring together. She knew the solution but hated showing her work. Sometimes the answers just came to her.

The perimeter of a rectangle is 52 cm. If its width is 2 cm more than one-third of its length, find the dimensions of the rectangle.

The answer was obvious: *18 cm × 8 cm.*

And yet, working her way back and describing the steps took so much longer. Why couldn't they just check her answer and trust her?

By the time she was done detailing the steps, it was after eleven. Silence had replaced Uncle Mark's news on the downstairs TV. The house was asleep.

She took a break and found her phone, launching *Critical Mass.* She swiped to the friends list and saw Ali there, his character in stasis and recovering from a battle at the library. He was level 50 now, so she could craft him some better armor. After a few minutes of tapping, she created a kevlar surcoat and some nano-chain mail. She used a rare artifact, tinting it green to match his new plasma sword. She loaded the package into the game's dimensional transporter and sent it off across the galaxy.

Hopefully, Ali would be too excited about his new loot to bring up what happened in class.

Hopefully.

Her stomach fluttered as the cramps shifted. She picked up her pencil and resumed her math solutions. Odd. She didn't remember filling up half the worksheet.

Curious symbols covered half the page before her. Little loops twisted their way across sharp lines. Jagged zigs and zags intersected broad curves. It looked oddly astronomical, she thought. Maybe that's what Chester was, some sort of space geek.

Or maybe he was just crazy and his madness was contagious.

She crumpled up the worksheet and threw it away.

She freshened up and brushed her teeth. Several boxes of pads and tampons sat on the counter, remnants from the Talk with Ms. Layne. She had patiently explained the differences and her own preference. They were talking, she had said, woman to woman.

Zelda's science class had covered anatomy, reproduction, and sexual education as quickly as possible. The boys had cringed and groaned; the girls stayed silent. They were distant facts, answers on assignments and forgotten quizzes. They hadn't felt real until this afternoon.

Sticky-fingered boys could fumble at school dances, bragging about French kisses and trying to act cool. But when a girl bled, it was like they were some alien species.

It wasn't fair.

She should have been having the Talk with her mom, not her uncle's coworker. Sometimes, when she realized all they would miss, the world grew heavy and her breath caught in her chest. They would never see her first day of high school. Her graduation. Her first serious boyfriend. Or girlfriend. She wasn't really sure.

Yes, she was changing.

But her parents never would. They would remain ashes in an urn she couldn't bring herself to spread.

She spat in the sink, washed her mouth, and then climbed into bed. She sent Ali a message.

Sent some loot. Look 4 package in game.

Three little dots popped up in the bubble. Then the response.

No way. Ur 2 nice. Imma b ur math tutor 4ever.

Just help me pass summer school & we good, K?

Girl we gonna get u into it all. Stats. Calc. Probability. Ur gonna be MIT bound.

Gnite Ali.

Nite Z-dog.

She rolled over. For a moment, she wasn't sure what she was staring at on the wall. A scuff? No, a blister beneath the eggshell paint near the corner of the room where the rustic wood beam ran down from the ceiling.

She reached out and rubbed the paint blister.

It smoothed, leaving the wall flat and damp.

And the beam... had there always been something etched in the old wood? She turned her phone's flashlight on and leaned close. It was so faint it barely existed. Yet here they were, eight letters and a number.

ITAL FLO R 2

She ran her fingertips over the beam. The marks had been

branded deep but eroded by time. What had the real estate agent called it? Tasteful and timeless.

Then Zelda saw the light flickering outside.

The pulse drew her eye to the window and Manzanita Way beyond. Coastal fog bathed young magnolias in a gray soup. On most nights, Zelda liked it when the summer turned cold and the winds picked up.

But tonight, the fog unsettled her. There was a shape down on the street.

Someone looking up at her window.

A woman stood beneath the flickering streetlight, her posture rigid and stiff. Something dark glistened on the side of her head, and Zelda thought of crushed plums. The woman raised a hand in a twisted claw, rotating back and forth, back and forth.

She was trying to wave.

She couldn't see into this bedroom; Zelda told herself this. The lights were off and it was dark inside.

But why was she staring? Why did her eyes twinkle between each blink?

Because it was the woman from her dream, Zelda realized. Because that's what this was: another slumbering delusion.

She pinched the skin on her wrist. She felt that.

She pinched again, really digging her nail in. No, she definitely felt that.

Then her desk lamp flickered.

A low sucking noise echoed out, and a sense of displacement as the air pressure changed. The woman was no longer outside.

She now sat at the desk.

Dry, milky eyes locked onto Zelda's as the woman's droopy face turned. Her left cheek was flat, as if she'd slept for hours and her skin had yet to reset. Above her ear, that plum discoloration matted her hair and stained her skin. The rest was as gray as the fog.

Zelda reeled. She was beyond screaming, beyond reacting, her numb mind struggling to catch up. Only a squeak left her throat.

"Wait, please," the woman rasped. "I mean... no harm."

Her words came out dry and forced. Zelda sensed it took her a great effort to work her vocal cords.

Because she's dead, she thought. *Because she's a ghost.*

"No, not a ghost," the woman whispered. "A memory... that once burned... with life... And now... just an echo."

From a deep well of fortitude within her young mind, Zelda found her voice. "How did you—"

"Know what you were thinking?" the woman rasped. "It's all the same now. Yesterday... Tomorrow... Every moment intermixed... like the notes of a song played all at once. I think... I was once a young girl too, just like you. I think... I smiled for a time before... life stiffened... my heart."

As she spoke, her skin stretched against rigid joints and tendons. It wasn't like the movies or TV shows, Zelda thought. Zombies and white walkers shuffling and sprinting. This was a deep rigor, death's final form, and every inch resisted life's movement.

"Don't... let life stiffen... your heart."

Zelda swallowed. "I won't."

The woman tried to smile, pale lips stretching against dry teeth, forming something like a sneer. "That's what... I said... but I still died... without love... by my side."

Snakelike, her hand lashed out, seizing Zelda by the wrist. It was cold. Skin should never feel so cold and firm.

"You reached out to me... In my last moments... you tried... to help."

"It was just a dream; it wasn't anything." Zelda tried to pull away, but the dead grip was impossibly tight.

"It was everything... to me."

Amber liquid seeped from the woman's eye and slid down her pale cheek. She was crying.

And there was something else. Fresh wounds mottled her arms, her throat, and her chest. Gashes where teeth had sunk in and fangs had pierced skin. How hadn't Zelda noticed?

"A gift... My last gift... and a warning."

Then she squeezed Zelda's wrist and the world fell apart.

CHAPTER THIRTY-EIGHT

Sharp winds whirled around Zelda as a deep sucking noise filled her ears. The walls of the house shifted and fell. No, she realized. She had been pulled *through* them. Tugged across several hundred feet in a blur.

She now stood on the street, the dead woman's hand latched firm to her wrist. The light above blinked and buzzed in the fog. Recorded crickets sang from the speaker, each note slower than the last.

Chirp.

Chirp...

Chiiiiirrrrr...

The hairs on her arm rose as the mist dimpled her skin. Her stomach rumbled. No, this wasn't a dream.

"How did you do that?"

The old woman smiled that stiff grimace. "Not me... *We*. Through each other... the dead... and the living."

Another sucking noise, another whirl of wind, and motion rattled Zelda's stomach. Every muscle clenched. And then came a great drop, a rollercoaster plummeting down, down.

They stood beneath another sputtering streetlight now, a few blocks away from her home. The house looming before them was small, a two-bedroom single-floor home. Police tape threaded its porch.

"My stomach." Zelda clutched her sides as the motion sickened her. "Wait, just a moment—"

"No time. I've escaped her prison... but only for a moment. Her pups... still have my scent. And soon... they'll have others."

The old woman squeezed Zelda's wrist. The world pivoted and spun. Bushes and walls, bricks and fences, it all rushed past her in a whirl of cool wind.

Then another light blinked and buzzed above them.

Zelda bent over and vomited. For a moment, all she could do was stare down and fight to keep her balance. The concrete was different here, the sidewalk cracked and weedy. She wiped her eyes.

This wasn't Raven's Valley.

Or rather, it was just past the edge, where the tennis courts met the dry river on one side and unruly hedges joined old walls and wrought iron fences.

They stood beneath the tired glow of a rusty street light, that ramshackle house from before. Chester's squalid manor. Chester the Molester, who had chased them through his junkyard and dead gardens of madness.

"I do not know how... it will end... But I know this: there will be suffering and flames. Her pups... will feast and grow fat. And through them, she will strengthen... until her endless gaze spans the Nether... and unravels our veil."

Head spinning, stomach churning, Zelda choked down her dizziness and confusion.

"Veil? What's a veil? And why can't you just speak—"

The woman pressed a stiff finger to Zelda's lips. "Even now... she scours. Once her dark gaze is fixed, it never... relents."

"Hold on, hold on, please—"

"Two... There are two forces in motion... One, who will bring suffering... And the other, who can bring souls to the light."

Another squeeze on her wrist, and Zelda felt something new. They no longer rushed through space, but space itself now swung around them. Stars danced through the sky. The fog thickened and boiled away. The haze grew acrid and choking.

They stood in the same spot, but the hedges and bushes burned around them. Fences glowed orange as heat simmered off the sidewalk and cinders rained down. The street lay so blanketed with ash it hardly existed.

Zelda heaved and doubled over, worried her stomach might just twist itself apart. Entire blocks of houses burned within walls of smoke. Someone ran past them, their clothes smoldering and their head a screaming wreath of flames.

Then came the shadows.

Pups, the old lady called them. They were anything but playful and cute. Six limbs lined a lizard-like body where horns and scales mixed with mangy, braided hair. Rusty rings pierced tormented flesh and pinched shaking tentacles. Quills collared thin necks rising to faces so alien, so impossible, Zelda could think only of creatures from the ocean's deep trenches.

When the flames fully engulfed the runner, when their wheezing screams gave out and their body collapsed, that's when it happened.

The pups pounced.

Zelda, who had long thought herself strong, cynical, and hardened by life, found that nothing had prepared her for this frenzied consumption.

Because it wasn't flesh being torn. No, she sensed it was much worse.

It was something like a soul—a *memory*—being devoured.

As they fed on that smoldering runner, Zelda's eyes rose skyward. Thin tendrils of black violet stretched from the pups, glistening cords that pulsed with each swallow.

High. Higher. Her eyes traced the tendrils until the black-violet cords pierced the rising ash and the falling cinders, until the gray haze parted, and there she saw something that did not belong in the sky.

A dark star, black and undulating, crested the fiery haze. There was no light upon that oily orb, and yet somehow light fled from its surface, from its skin. The pups and the dead star, they were feeding together. That dead star, it lived and it hungered.

"They've found me."

Heads turning, the pups shuddered and rose. Their cruel eyes saw Zelda and the old woman. One by one, they slouched toward them, inky grins splitting horned faces.

"Go," the old woman said. "I've kept you... too long."

"You can't stay here," Zelda said. "You need to leave."

The old woman's neck cracked as she tilted her head. Something like a smile stretched her lips as the pups drew closer and closer. "Funny," she said. "I think I've always... been here."

Then she let go of Zelda's wrist.

There wasn't a whirl or a rush of ashy wind. There wasn't a blur of bushes and fences zooming past. There was just the faint sucking noise and a sudden tear deep within. Zelda found herself standing by her desk, the lamp blinking twice before shutting off.

For a moment, she stood still, clutching the back of her chair and willing herself not to vomit. Pain wracked her abdomen, two knives sliding at upward angles. She rubbed her sore wrist.

This was a dream, she told herself. A waking dream. Was this what happened when girls became women? That had to be it. Yes, a dream.

She wanted to believe that more than anything.

But her wobbly gaze fell to her desk, where an amber tear that had slid down a pale cheek now dampened her homework.

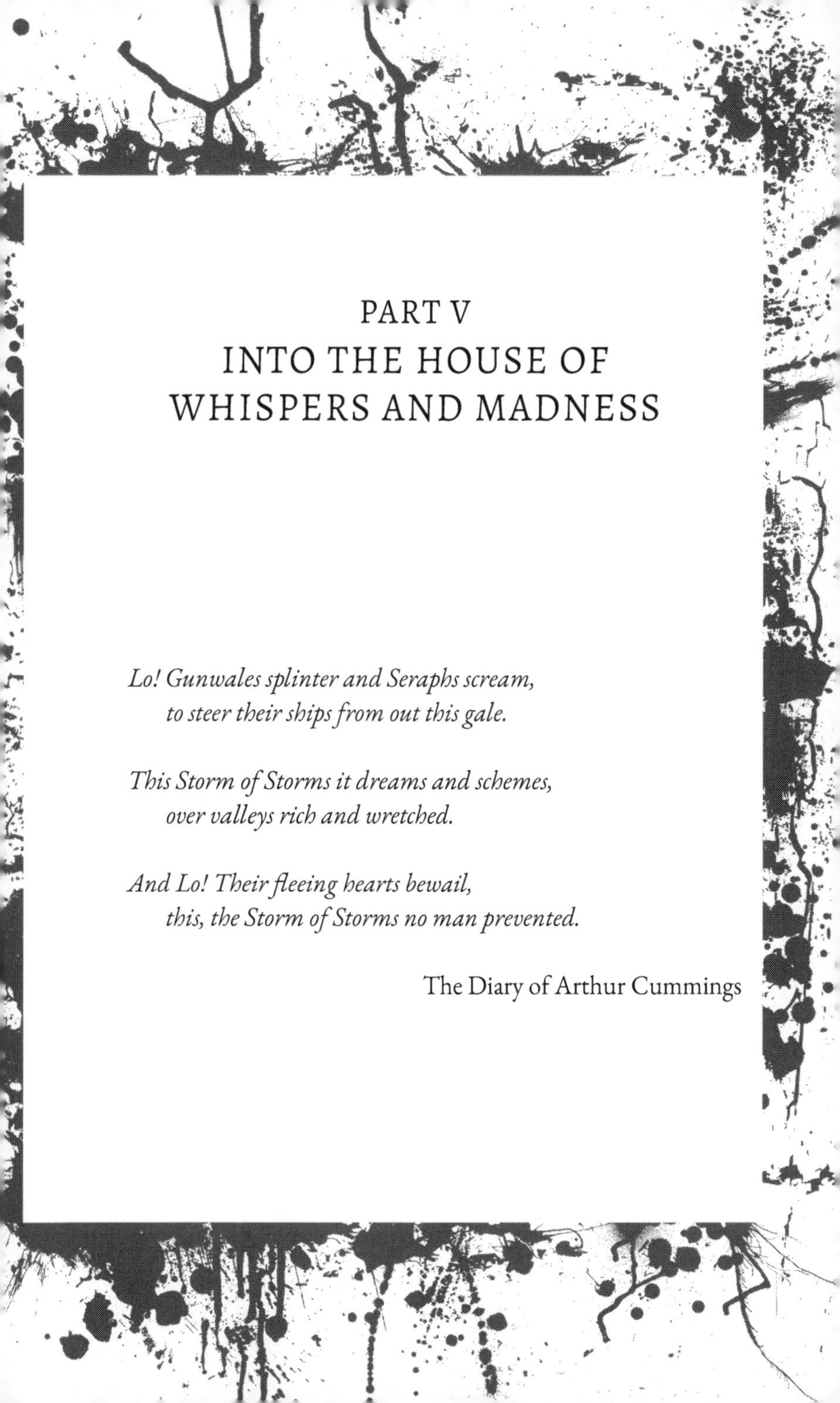

PART V

INTO THE HOUSE OF WHISPERS AND MADNESS

Lo! Gunwales splinter and Seraphs scream,
to steer their ships from out this gale.

This Storm of Storms it dreams and schemes,
over valleys rich and wretched.

And Lo! Their fleeing hearts bewail,
this, the Storm of Storms no man prevented.

The Diary of Arthur Cummings

CHAPTER THIRTY-NINE

Mark was halfway through his stack of midterms when Zelda's footfalls echoed through the house, bounding down the stairs three at a time. It made him smile, knowing that youth ran freely through the house. Even if it rattled his hungover skull.

"Morning, Zelda."

"Morning."

He watched her dig two frozen burritos from the freezer, bury them under shredded cheese, bacon bits, and sour cream, then slide it all into the microwave.

"I envy your metabolism. I could put away a whole pizza at your age. Now I just gain weight when I look at it."

She offered him her patented flat smile and quick nod, which was about as much as he expected this morning. He wasn't sure he was making much sense.

"How're you feeling? Need anything?"

A shake of her head. She drummed her fingers on the counter, waiting for the microwave.

"Well, if you do—"

"Did anything strange ever happen to you?" she asked.

He put his red pen down. "What do you mean?"

"Like, you know... At this time in your life. Adolescence and stuff."

"Puberty?"

She shuddered. "I hate that word."

"Yeah, it's pretty gross, right? They should call it something better. Puberty sounds raunchy. Is that a word people still use? Raunchy?"

"I don't know."

The microwave beeped and Zelda opened it, folded the paper plates in half so that they cocooned the cheese, bacon, and sour cream-covered burritos. She dropped them into her Tupperware and sealed it.

"But yeah," he said. "To answer your question, a lot of weird things happened. My sleep schedule pretty much flipped. I could never wind down at night 'cause my mind always raced. I almost failed tenth grade 'cause of that. Is that what you mean?"

"Yeah, I guess."

It felt like his answers displeased her. Some days, they could have full conversations and it left him smiling and happy, like they'd connected. Other days, they hardly spoke the same language.

She glanced at her phone. "I've gotta get to class."

"Need a lift?"

She shook her head, grabbed her skateboard, and slung her messenger bag over her shoulder. He knew she wasn't his daughter and that he'd never be her parent. And yet, there was something about the way the light sparkled in her eyes and caught her hair. She looked both fierce and so totally vulnerable. Kind yet armored. Innocent and an old soul. At moments like this, he was grateful to be a part of her life. A small part, but a part nonetheless.

He needed to be better for her. He needed to be present. He needed to drink less.

She said, "This is weird, but... did something happen last night?"

He thought back. Another fight with Rosy. A phone call with Ms. Phong and the Ruizes.

"Down the street," she added.

"Oh!" He had meant to tell her but wasn't sure she'd even care. "Yeah, Mrs. Saperstein passed away."

Zelda blinked. "Passed away?"

"She had an accident, fell, and hit her head. She was pretty old, so..." He shrugged as if to say that was expected.

Something changed in her eyes. That sparkle narrowed and she glanced at her shoes. "And they're sure of it?"

"Sure of what?"

"Like, they're sure it was an accident?"

"I'm not on the CSI squad, but why do you ask?" He could sense her teetering on the edge of some decision. "Zelda, what is it?"

She gave her usual flat smile and a shake of the head. Her phone chirped. "They're waiting for me. Gotta go."

And like that, she was gone, just a pair of mismatched sneakers pivoting, a ponytail swinging, and a few seconds later, the front door slammed shut. He could hear her skateboard hit the sidewalk, wheels clattering as she sped off to meet her friends, head to class, and pursue whatever it was teenage girls pursued as the long days of summer began to shorten.

CHAPTER FORTY

Zelda took a deep breath of salty air and just came out and said it. "So, I think I saw a ghost."

They sat at the edge of the bluffs overlooking Sandpiper Cove, the ocean breeze a relief in the midsummer heat. Maura watched the surfers carve waves while Ali edited his latest video homework assignment. Zelda pretended to review her latest math quiz, a C+.

The idea had been festering for days, growing in form and scratching around at her thoughts. The G-word: ghost. It took every ounce of her courage to say it. Yet now it hung there, clumsy and childish in the windy quiet between them.

What the hell had she done?

They'd never let her live this down. Even if they were her friends now, word would slip out and spread. She'd be that odd girl at Neumann in the fall. The one with weird superstitions who ate alone, mumbling to herself and always a little too desperate for conversation.

"You serious?" Maura said.

Zelda nodded.

"So, what did it look like? I mean, was it like the Babadook? Or, like, that nun from *The Conjuring*? Or—"

"If it was a clown in your drainpipe," Ali said, "I am never coming over to your house again. I hate clowns."

"Ali, you don't even believe in ghosts," Maura said.

"Yeah, but I believe in clowns and drainpipes. Mix the two and someone's losing an arm. Not gonna be me, Zeldarooni."

"Forget it," Zelda said.

"Uh-uh, no way." Maura lowered her binoculars, her stare shifting from the distant surfers to Zelda beside her. "You can't just drop that bomb and walk away. C'mon, what did it look like?"

After a moment, Zelda flicked her phone open to a photo she'd pulled from the school directory.

"Mrs. Saperstein?" Maura asked. "From Neumann?"

"Only, she said she wasn't a ghost. More like a memory." Zelda brushed a strand of hair from her face. "She was in my bedroom. She..."

Zelda stopped there. The rest was too strange, too unbelievable. The streetlights. The ash. And the pups. Days later, the memory was as foggy as the night that it had happened. She had tried her hardest to convince herself it was all just a dream.

But the amber tear on the homework...

The lingering scent of ash on her fingers...

And her wrist. It was tender and bruised all week.

"She was nice," Zelda said. "But she was really sad, too."

"Are ghosts ever happy?" Ali asked. "No, seriously. If I was a ghost—not saying they're real—but if I was, I'd be, like, singing songs and checking out the cheerleaders' locker room, you know? Not creeping in rando bedrooms."

"The first ghost with a restraining order," Maura said. "That's totally you."

"All that power and they just hang out in the shadows, rattling chains? Total waste."

"She didn't have chains," Zelda said. "And I don't think she had much power, either. Her skin was all... stiff and—"

"Wait, you touched her?" Maura scooted closer and poked Zelda's knee with her finger. "Like, *touch* touched her?"

Zelda's thumb brushed her wrist. "She was cold. Like room temperature cold and stiff—"

"That's algor mortis," Ali said. "Algor means 'cold' in Latin and mortis means 'death.'"

"Cool fact, Wikipedia," Maura said. "Okay, so did Ms. Saperstein say anything or what?"

Zelda gave a weak nod. "She kind of showed me something. Like, a fire or..."

That thing. That vast *thing* in the sky. The dark star of eyes and its hungering pups. How they savaged that poor flaming man.

"A fire?" Maura repeated.

"I think it was the future. What's the word? A premonition."

"So Mrs. Saperstein became a time-traveling ghost," Ali said. "That actually makes sense 'cause she was stuck in the past. Did you see her classroom?"

"Ali, do you have an off switch?" Maura asked.

"It's called being a skeptic and it's the foundation of good science."

"Okay, Einstein, so how do you explain it?"

Ali put his phone down. "Simple. Subconscious suggestion."

Maura raised an eyebrow. Zelda had an idea where Ali was going. They'd studied the brain in science this winter with a brief stop on psychology. Was it Freud or Jung who talked about the subconscious? Or was that the guy with those drooling dogs?

"If Zelda saw old lady Saperstein after she bit the dust," Ali continued, "it's probably a subconscious suggestion. I saw this hypnotist on YouTube trick a guy into thinking an ice cube was really a burning coal."

"On YouTube?" Maura asked.

Ali nodded.

"Well then, it has to be true."

"No, but the electrodes they hooked up to his brain were," Ali said. "And when they put the ice cube on the dude's hand, he screamed. They even measured his pain response. Boom. Subconscious suggestion. Like when you think your phone buzzed in your pocket, but it didn't."

Maura fidgeted with the binoculars. "After my dog died, I kept hearing her collar jingling and her nails clicking down the hall. Sometimes, I'd even reach down to scratch her."

Zelda studied the horizon, the sun on its downward arc over the Pacific and the waves glistening. In the far distance, that old lighthouse flickered. She'd been here six weeks and yet she still felt like a stranger. Would that ever go away?

"I want to believe that's true," she said. "Like, I really do. But the thing is, it happened last Tuesday night. I didn't know Mrs. Saperstein died until Wednesday."

Maura nodded. "Huh."

For once, Ali was out of explanations.

"Sometimes I think there's something wrong with me," Zelda said. "Like I'm crazy or cursed, or just a magnet for all the shit in the world. The night we moved away, this neighbor went nuts. And my parents..."

She hesitated. Because despite all her efforts to contain them, to ignore them, to deny them or bury them deep in her heart, the words were now fleeing past her lips on their own.

After a moment, Maura asked, "What about your parents?"

Zelda's gaze drifted to the shore, where a toddler chased seagulls while his father captured it on camera. She said, "I'm the reason that they're dead."

For the longest time, they sat there in silence. Three friends, caressed by the cool breeze, soaking the distant laughter of the beachgoers down the bluff.

"What do you mean?" Maura asked.

Zelda closed her eyes and breathed in that crisp ocean air. Her thumb traced the scar on her arm. If she focused, she could see it all: the actions and their effects, the invisible chain that led from a lakeside vacation to a canyon disaster.

She said, "My dad called it a business retreat. Just us and some other high-level people from the company and their families. We rented these houses at the lake all together. One night, I snuck out to a party and had a couple of drinks. I met this cute guy."

She licked her lips.

The smoky scent of the bonfire and the cool wind off the lake.

The sand underfoot, still warm from the sun when she dug in her toes.

And the crinkle of the red cup in her hand, the sour bite of margarita mix, and the burn of tequila. It kindled a fire in her gut. Like this moment was theirs, hers, and belonged only to the youth. Like life was just beginning. Like everything was warm and all right.

Then came the lights and the sirens.

"The cops raided the party," she said. "I got caught with a drink. My parents were super embarrassed 'cause, like, everyone saw the cops drop me off. We had this big fight 'cause they were getting divorced. Everyone heard that, too. That was the fourth day. The next morning, my dad packed up the car. My mom just wanted to leave, so we drove home three days early. And then..."

Something itched near her eye. She wiped her face, surprised to find that her cheeks were wet. Odd. She'd almost forgotten what it felt like. She hadn't shed any tears before.

Not at the memorial.

Nor those nights she'd slept in her mother's closet just to smell the scent of her clothes.

And not even when she looked back at the house she grew up in, fading in the midnight as Uncle Mark drove away.

Why was she crying here, on these bluffs, with these two kids she'd only known for the summer?

Because maybe that's how grief worked, she supposed. Maybe

grief was a thing that lived and grew and took form on its own. Maybe it followed its own rhythm and tempo. And maybe Ali was right, that something beneath her conscious thoughts was still wounded and healing.

She wiped her cheeks. "Sorry."

"That sucks," Maura said. "But it wasn't your fault. It's just shitty luck. And hey, maybe that's why Saperstein's ghost liked you."

"Yeah," Zelda said. "Or maybe I'm just going crazy."

"Well, I believe you." Maura glanced at Ali, who had gone curiously quiet. It was as if he simply didn't know how to find humor in this moment and settled for silence.

"Yeah, of course, Z-dog," he said. "I believe you too."

CHAPTER FORTY-ONE

Ali did not believe her.

He liked Zelda a lot. She was pretty and smart and said friendly things. She never teased him about his height or his geeky hobbies. She rarely laughed, but she did smile at his jokes, and somehow that felt more generous than anything.

But ghosts?

No. No way. This wasn't a movie or a video game or these silly books his sister read with her flashlight.

The Phantom of Andover.

Unholy Sacrament.

They Hunger.

This was real life, and in real life, things could be measured and tested. Even that shadow-thing on his video had a dozen explanations. Stupid filters or effects that hadn't been scrubbed. Buggy post-processing or a glitchy sensor. Heck, with a deepfake, he could turn the president into a dog. With Midjourney AI, he could generate surreal images that defied logic. Why couldn't his video-editing app add a creepy shadow by accident?

But Zelda had looked so sad and he didn't know what else to

say. "Tough break about the parents, Zeldarino, but I call bullshit on the ghosts?"

No.

"I believe you, too," was the kindest of lies.

It was 5:30 when they said goodbye. Zelda came first; her house was the closest to the gate of Raven's Valley. Ali waved to her uncle, who was fixing a light on their porch.

A few minutes later, Maura punched his arm, the signal to stop bicycling. She hopped off the rack, said she'd see him tomorrow, and sprinted off to her house. Rubbing his biceps, Ali recalled his mom's words: "That's her way of showing affection."

He just wished she'd find a way that didn't leave bruises.

He pedaled down Sycamore Way and swerved around a group of kids playing street hockey. He took a right onto Palm Place, past the seniors doing tai chi outside the sunken amphitheater. He waved at Mr. Kim and his daughter, both taping a flyer for their missing cat to a lamppost.

Ali liked Greywood Bay and Raven's Valley. It felt like one town nestled inside another. He liked the diversity, too. Most people didn't care about the color of his skin or the sound of his name. There was even a small mosque for his parents, as well as several other Iraqi families. When they came over for lunch, his mom reverted to her Arabic tongue with the other mothers, and he realized how eloquent and educated she truly was. It must be hard to be taken seriously in broken English.

Algebra, he thought, came from the Arabic word *al-jabr*, a reunion of broken parts. He should tell Zelda about that. Maybe Mr. Barker would give her extra credit. Maybe that'd cheer her up.

Then his phone chirped and buzzed and the thought vanished. He knew that sound and the pattern of vibrations.

It was *Critical Mass*, a rare spawn nearby.

Wheels squeaking on the asphalt, he came to a sliding stop at the intersection of Cottonwood and Vine. He swiped his phone and fumbled with the game's menu.

Here was his character, a level 53 Quantum Pirate, outfitted in the epic armor Zelda had sent. There was the in-game map, a cyberpunk version of east Raven's Valley and beyond. The dry river was rendered as empty cement canals. The parks were forests of sentient trees. And the streets were neon-lit paths between houses, stylized as squat outposts and edge-of-the-galaxy speakeasies.

Most important was the pulse four blocks away. A rare spawn.

No, a level 50 *legendary* rare spawn, Xooloocotiq'r, the Last Refugee.

Ali had memorized most of the game's rare creatures, but this one was new. Still, the game was in beta, and they were adding new content all the time. A legendary rare spawn dropped the best gear when defeated. *Always.*

He might have a shot.

He pedaled fast, left hand on the handlebar, right hand on his phone. He swiped and loaded up the gear for a fight. It would be a tough one. If someone else got there first, they'd have a better chance. But then they'd all have to share the spoils of battle: the credits and experience, the legendary weapons and armor. Ali didn't like that idea.

The longer Xooloocotiq'r remained undefeated, the larger the alert radius would grow. Soon, he'd be competing against every player in Raven's Valley. Or, God help him, every player in Greywood Bay.

He pedaled even faster.

Panting, he slid off his bike by the tennis courts and let it coast riderless into a bush. He took a right at the water fountain, raising his screen and activating AR mode. He panned back and forth, back and forth.

There, a flash at the far side of the tennis courts and past the playground. He hurried across the dry grass and kept his phone centered. He crossed a path and spun at the last second, narrowly avoiding a jogger.

"Hey, kid, watch out!"

Ali shouted an apology that was lost under the tock of tennis rackets and the squeak of sneakers on the courts. He was close. The map showed Xooloocotiq'r, the Last Refugee, some fifty feet away.

And then it didn't.

The screen crackled and the pixels shifted. Something like static hissed from the speakers. The rare spawn just moved.

It was now behind the tennis courts, between some hedges and a tall concrete fence three hundred feet away. Cursing, Ali hurried after it. There were still plenty of bugs to be squashed. And besides, rare spawns didn't stick around long before despawning. Perhaps this one was so rare its timer was measured in minutes and not hours.

Pushing aside the bushes and fronds, Ali found the narrow path beyond the courts. To his right stood an old cement wall covered with graffiti and reeking of piss. Ali groaned and tried to hold his breath.

He raised the phone. There it was, Xooloocotiq'r, another fifty feet and closing in. The thing wasn't large like a Cyber Minotaur or a Steam Golem. Nor was it broad and tanky, like the Iron Beetles or the Great Worm of Orlock. Rather, it was small and vaporous, a cloud of shifting oils and dark purples. It jittered and pulsed and didn't linger in one spot. Perhaps the art department was testing a new creature design.

No matter. It would drop loot all the same.

He swiped his screen, activating his anti-matter blaster and priming a tether grenade. He pressed hard for three seconds, winding up the throw.

He hit *release*.

And Xooloocotiq'r moved yet again.

On-screen, the grenade detonated without inflicting damage. So, the creature could teleport. It wasn't unheard of, but he'd never seen it without some visual warning. Now, there was only the empty row between the bushes and the smelly wall.

Where the hell had it gone?

He pinched the screen, switching to an overhead view. There, a few hundred feet to his right, that damn creature. It was on the far side of the wall. The nearest street was several blocks to the south, where the bridge met the dry river and the walking path. He lowered his phone.

That's when he saw the broken cinderblocks.

They lay in a pile just past where Xooloocotiq'r had appeared, a dusty mound covered in a season of dried leaves. Ali tested the pile, nudging it with his foot, pleased that it was firm and steady.

But he wasn't pleased with what he saw.

"Aww, serious?" He'd gotten such tunnel vision that he hadn't realized where he was.

This narrow hole in the wall stood at the western edge of the scrapyard.

CHAPTER FORTY-TWO

Ali spent several precious minutes considering his options. The hole in the wall was wide enough to squeeze through. He could track down the legendary rare spawn beyond. He could get all that experience and loot for his character. He could do all of these things.

Or he could turn back.

His fear put up a good fight but greed won out in the end. Turning sideways and ducking, he squeezed through the hole and emerged at the edge of the scrapyard. It was sunset, a time of long shadows and crows circling in the last rays of light. Far off, a tennis racket went *tock* in the wind.

The good news was that there weren't towers of old cars or piles of sharp wires to give him diseases. There were only a few shipping containers and dry tires stacked up in piles. If Chester the Molester was around, Ali would see him coming.

The bad news: he was trespassing again. The good news: if the fight was fast, it wouldn't matter. The armor Zelda had crafted upped his defenses and his chances of winning. Now, he just needed to engage.

Dirt crunching underfoot, Ali raised his phone and scanned to his right. Black violet pulsed on his screen. He could see Xooloocotiq'r's form for just a moment. Tentacles and arms intertwined in a tangle of oily dark skin.

Eyes.

So many eyes.

Ali readied his character's weapons. He'd need to tap and swipe fast. He centered the viewfinder on Xooloocotiq'r. He charged his plasma sword in one hand and primed his tether grenade. He counted down from three.

Then he attacked.

His screen registered the explosion and the strike. Pixels stretched and distorted. There was an odd crunch and a rumble, like chicken bones in the garbage disposal. Ali didn't see any hit points deducted, yet he sensed he'd aimed well and struck true. A critical ambush, if he was lucky, which meant he'd get another attack in a few seconds.

Then Xooloocotiq'r oozed backward.

Back into an open shipping container.

"Seriously?" Ali muttered. "Worst fight ever."

His shoe clanked upon the metal floor. It was dark inside. He didn't like the dark. And he definitely didn't like tight places. He hesitated. Why was he hesitating?

Because this isn't right, the logical part of his mind whispered. The part he always listened to. The part that felt oddly muted these past twenty minutes.

Tunnel vision, right.

He swiped down on the screen and activated the phone's flashlight. Sterile light scoured the container. He saw dirt and rags and dry leaves. He saw metal fenders stacked in a pile. He saw an old bathtub tipped on its side.

And there, in the corner, he saw Xooloocotiq'r, crouching and shivering and glaring with inky black eyes.

Ali's tongue went dry and his stomach tensed. His phone was

lowered and the screen wasn't before him. His app was on the flashlight setting.

There was Xooloocotiq'r.

Not on the screen or rendered in pixels.

But in real life.

"Yeah, fuuuuck that." Ali backed away from the shipping container. In three steps, Xooloocotiq'r simply winked out of existence. Had he really seen that? No, of course not. It was impossible. It didn't make sense. It was a subconscious suggestion, just Zelda's ghost rattling chains in his mind.

Still, he wasn't sticking around.

Ali turned and started to run. He would sprint back to the hole in the wall, back to his bike, back to his home where things were safe and sane and foul creatures from games didn't break the fourth wall. He would tell Zelda he might even believe her. There was something wrong in Raven's Valley.

He only made it three steps.

His ankle caught an old chain and yanked it taut. With a rattling clink, the links slid from the top of the shipping container. Ten feet of dusty metal lashed out and struck the ground next to Ali, spraying dirt and broken glass. He shielded his eyes as the dust settled, muttering, "That was close. That was way too close."

He didn't hear the board jostling loose atop the container, near silent upon a bed of dust. He only sensed the shadow and turned in time to see it: eight feet of falling hickory hardwood, weathered for a decade.

The two-by-four struck him in the temple and reduced his world to sparkling darkness. Warmth and wetness spread down his face. Wet rust bloomed on his tongue. His other cheek was dusty, dirtied, and now sliding against the dry earth.

Because he was being dragged, he realized.

Dragged by his legs.

He blinked away the haze and the blood. He was concussed or

worse, his brain murmured from a deep well of confusion. He needed medical attention.

"Think I... hit head..." Ali muttered. "Call Mom."

But the thing that pulled him by the leg didn't have ears to hear him or a mouth to reply. It had only a long, muddy arm with too many joints. It had wet fingers that bent the wrong way. It wrapped those fingers around his ankle and dragged him into the container, into the darkness.

And it had teeth.

So many teeth.

CHAPTER FORTY-THREE

Mark fired off his fourth job application and celebrated by pouring a fourth glass of scotch. One for one was what he promised himself. If he was going to get drunk tonight, he'd at least be productive.

The alternative was to give in to the fear.

Stacey Layne had broken the news this morning: he had a good chance of taking over the vacancy for Mrs. Saperstein's position. But regulations still meant the job had to be posted and all candidates considered, both inside and out. He didn't know who else had applied, only that by noon, the vacancy had surfaced on several education job boards.

One commenter wrote:

It's a no brainer. Greywood Bay is a gem and that school is top tier. I'm applying right away. Fifteen years exp. NYC+Texas, MA Linguistics, TESOL+CELTA & several journal publications. Good luck everybody!

So here he sat, making fallback plans and sending off resumes well after ten. Trying not to think about Zelda's tuition at

Neumann if he couldn't get the faculty rate. He took a deep sip and started in on the fifth application.

Outside, flashing lights grew brighter before stopping at the house. Reds and blues, never good news.

He peeked out the window to find a cop in a cruiser and a radio to her mouth. His fears turned to Zelda. Had the Ruizes won some surprise injunction or emergency hearing? Was this how it ended? A warrant and a police visit on a weeknight to ensure a smooth transfer of custody?

A woman stepped out of the back seat of the cruiser, her skin a beautiful shade of almond and a colorful scarf over her hair. He recognized her from the community center meeting two weeks ago, where she sat quietly in the back and took notes. He stuffed gum in his mouth on his way to the porch.

Officer Grafton was in her early thirties, with a friendly smile and a nervous gleam in her eyes. She introduced the woman as Yanar Hadid.

"Right, Ali's mom," Mark said. "We chatted at the HOA meeting."

"Yes, I remembering you," Yanar said. "This is, uh, how do you say? Forgive me, English is not good when nervous."

Officer Grafton opened her notepad. "Mr. Fitzsimmons, I—"

"Mark, please."

"Mark, right. Mrs. Hadid's son, Ali, he hasn't come home tonight. She thought he was still at school or maybe with his friends. However, we checked the school, the library he sometimes hangs out at, and nothing. We just spoke with a friend of his, Maura—"

"Is very nice girl," Mrs. Hadid said, nodding. "You know?"

"Red hair, broken arm," Mark said. "She's a wrestler, right?"

Mrs. Hadid nodded while the officer checked her notepad. "That's her. The thing is, she said that Ali dropped her off around six, on his bike. Before that, the only other person to see him was—"

"Zelda," he said. "Yeah, she said they were at the beach."

"Sandpiper Cove?" Officer Grafton asked.

"I think so. Why don't you come in and I'll see if she's awake." The officer looked at Yanar, who seemed confused. "Come in. It's cold."

Inside, they waited in the dining room while he went up to Zelda's room. He was about to knock on the door when it opened. Zelda wiped the sleep from her eyes. "What's with the cops?"

He told her about Ali and her eyes widened. She grabbed her hoodie and hurried down the stairs.

Mark listened to Zelda and Mrs. Yanar while he heated up water and made tea. It gave him something to do besides hover, which probably made his niece nervous. Officer Grafton let the mug of green tea sit, but Yanar thanked him and clutched it in her shaking hands. This poor woman was doing everything to keep it together.

"And he didn't come back again?" Officer Grafton asked. "You guys didn't meet up tonight? Sneak out?"

"No, of course not," Zelda said.

"It's okay if you did," Mark said. "You're not in trouble."

"I didn't," Zelda said, with an edge to her voice.

He gave her some space while she retraced their day: the afternoon at the beach after school, class time together, Ali arriving at campus with Maura on the back of his bike in the morning. All the while, Yanar sipped the tea and listened, fear creasing her forehead. Mark wasn't a parent, but he was starting to share a few fears. A missing child after ten was a nightmare.

"And you've tried his phone, right?" he asked.

"It just ring," Yanar said. "No answer."

"Can't the phone companies triangulate it? I thought they'd done that in..." He caught himself before the word *murder* left his lips. No, he didn't want to throw that out there. Instead, he said, "Like in true crime shows and stuff."

Officer Grafton sighed. "It's a slow process, and it doesn't quite work like that. But yeah, we already checked his Find My Friends. He must've switched it off a while ago. Kids don't like being tracked."

"I thought that wasn't possible."

Zelda let out a near-silent chuckle.

"What?"

"Seriously?" She looked at him with amusement. "Just switch it to airplane mode, then shut off location services, reboot, put your phone in lost mode, then reenable locations app by app. Every kid knows how to do it."

Mark scoffed. "Did you?"

She said nothing.

"Zelda, seriously?"

"The important thing here," Officer Grafton said, "is that we've confirmed timelines and they match. If Ali contacts you, you send him our way, okay? He's not in trouble."

"No trouble," Yanar repeated. "Is good boy, my son."

Her eyes were on Zelda, who shifted inside in that Red Sox hoodie. It was her father's, Mark realized. Juan Carlos had bought it when they'd all met up in Boston five years ago. Zelda would have been eight. Their biggest worry had been getting good tickets to the playoffs.

Now, it was a boy who never came home.

They excused themselves, the officer leading the way and Yanar at her side. Zelda stuck by the porch while Mark saw them off. Then Yanar turned and looked back at her.

"Ali have many good speaking about you. You are... wonderful friend. Thank you."

Officer Grafton put a gentle hand on Yanar's arm. She glanced back at Mark. "These things usually resolve themselves," she said. "Good night, Mr. Fitzsimmons. Night, Zelda."

Mark's sleep was fitful that night, Yanar's nervous eyes cutting through the warm blanket of scotch. He briefly dreamed of his sister and her words.

They'll grow maggots in her heart.

The next morning, the message blared out on his phone and tore him from sleep:

Emergency Alert
MISSING CHILD // HADID, ALI // 13, MALE //
LAST SEEN: RAVEN's VALLEY // CONTACT
POLICE IF LOCATED // THIS IS NOT A TEST

CHAPTER FORTY-FOUR

Without Ali to bike her to school, Maura's mom dropped her off near the flagpole. Zelda watched from her desk in Mr. Barker's room as she hurried across the lawn, through the school doors, and into the classroom before the first bell.

"Dude." She slid into her desk. "What the hell is going on?"

Zelda shook her head. "I don't know. Did you talk to the cop last night?"

"Hell yeah. And I told them everything. Ali dropped me off and that was that. Did he have another fight with his parents or something?"

"No. And his bike's missing too."

"Fuck..."

"Language, ladies," Mr. Barker said. "I know we still have a few minutes, but let's try to be civil."

"Sorry," Maura said, and leaned in. "Geez, this is super weird."

"You don't think he was mad at me or something?" Zelda asked.

Maura blinked. "Why would he be mad?"

"Yesterday, that ghost thing. I don't know. I just... He seemed kind of off after I said that stuff about my parents."

"Okay, first, you are way too self-critical, sister. Most of the time, his brain is on some other planet. And second, he's a guy. Emotions are uncomfortable. Plus, I've seen him pissed, trust me. His mom took his phone away 'cause he kept playing that game. He didn't know what to do with his hands all week."

Zelda's arm shot out and grabbed Maura's wrist. "Holy shit."

"Language again."

The second bell rang. As the students unpacked their backpacks, Mr. Barker took attendance. "Lucy? There you are. Douglas? Okay..."

Zelda leaned in, whispered, "His phone. Critical Mass."

Maura's eyes narrowed. "What about it?"

"Ali and I are friends in-game. I can see his location. Hold on."

She felt like an idiot. Of course the game had a friend locater. Taking down enemies together was a core feature. But she hadn't thought of that because her level was so much higher than Ali's. Every time they teamed up, it reduced his experience to near nothing. So she'd simply sent him items he could use.

But she could still see him.

Or, at the least, his last active location.

"Phones away, Zelda."

"One sec."

She swiped down until her friends list filled the screen. There he was: *Darth_Reaper99*. Last active encounter: *Unknown level ???* Last active location: *Raven's Valley, 3.2 miles*.

She zoomed in on the map and the word flew from her lips.

"Fuck."

"Zelda!" Mr. Barker snapped. His hands rose to his hips and his affable smile turned sour. "What's going on today?"

"I'm sorry." Before she knew it, she had grabbed her backpack and skateboard. "I've gotta go." She slid out of her desk and hurried to the door in six quick strides.

"Seriously?" Mr. Barker called out, but the door swung behind her and she was in the hall now, racing toward the school's entrance.

Maura caught up to her outside, huffing and breathing heavy. "Okay, hold up... You can't just like... walk out of school."

Zelda held her phone up and Maura squinted at the screen. It was *Critical Mass*'s in-game map, the retro-futuristic landscape projected over Greywood Bay. Zelda's character hovered in the center, where the school had been rendered into an abandoned space port.

She swiped three miles northeast until she was over Ali's last known location. She pinched and zoomed in.

"Okay, pretend I don't understand the game." Then Maura's eyes narrowed. "Wait, is that Raven's Valley?"

"Yeah, and the heap just beyond it," Zelda said. "But look where his character was last active."

Maura swiped and pinched the screen, moving the map around and zooming in. The game had rendered the dry river into a neon canal. The heap was an old factory burping green smoke.

But it was the house that held her attention. Even in-game, the old house had a desolate quality to it, lifeless and barren.

Zelda swiped to the same location in her maps application.

It was the house with the statues and the workshop at the edge of the junkyard.

It was Chester's creepy mansion.

CHAPTER FORTY-FIVE

Lloyd dreamed he was in the bathroom, thick rubber gloves protecting his hands as he drowned another cat in the tub. It thrashed and scratched and hissed between bubbles. With tears in his eyes, Lloyd turned away.

But there were others here in this bathroom, other *things* he'd collected.

Feeder mice and a few squirrels. A starfish and a handful of hermit crabs plucked from the saltwater aquarium. There were so many bugs that they clicked on the floor and crawled up the leg of Mrs. Saperstein, who sat on the toilet and simply glared through curdled eyes.

By the sink, a deer ambled in confused circles. Lloyd wondered, had he really swerved to avoid it that day? Or had he pressed the accelerator? Yes, both possibilities merged in his mind.

The deer stopped pacing and turned its hollow gaze upon him. Its eyes were two sets of black lips.

"Lloyd," it whispered. *"It's time to wake up."*

That was all it took to peel the dream layer back and reveal the morning world before him. Posters of airplanes and tanks lined his walls. An SR-71 Blackbird, wings tilted as it broke the sound barrier. An M1 Abrams with desert camouflage and its turret aimed at the viewer. A C-130 Hercules on takeoff.

But the most important poster wasn't here in his bedroom. It was everywhere. In the walls and the studs. In the very fabric of his dreams. It put dark lips on the eyes of that deer that now roused him from sleep.

Armando the Great.

"Mmm... You keep calling me that," he whispered. *"Now hurry down; we have much to discuss."*

Climbing out of bed, Lloyd's erection felt pressed against his tighty-whities. He slid into sweatpants and tucked his shame under the drawstring. He was tired of the way these dreams aroused him. He'd need to take care of himself soon.

"Later," he whispered. *"Now hurry. An old spider of mine has caught a fly, but there's still a fight in its wings."*

Lloyd tiptoed down the stairs, past the burbling aquarium and past Randall's office. He could hear his stepdad in there, listening to crappy eighties rock. He quietly closed the basement door and left the light off. He could see better in the darkness these days.

Yeah, he was changing, all right.

"There is a young one," the poster whispered. *"A boy ensnared in my emissary's trap."*

Lloyd said, "You said I was your emissary."

"I never said there was only one."

Lloyd didn't like the way Armando was playing his cards close to his chest.

"Mmm, the other... Time has brittled his bones and softened his teeth. The boy, he is wounded, yes, so you must finish the job."

"Finish?" Lloyd repeated. "Like... kill?"

The word was so lumpy he had to squeeze it from his throat. He wasn't sure that he could. In fact, no, he didn't think that he wanted to.

"Mmm... Tenderize the flesh so my pups can devour his soul."

"If you're so powerful, why do I have to keep doing your stuff?"

The dark basement shimmered and the walls flexed. Something growled deep in the foundation of the house. *"My reach is long, but even a god has its limits."*

"Is that what you are?"

Like oil under moonlight, eyes glinted in the shadows. He could feel their glare caressing his flesh. And that's all Lloyd was, he supposed. Just a small spec of flesh on a spinning rock in the infinite chaos of the cosmos.

"A god, yes," the darkness whispered. *"And in time, an echo of what you can become."*

Then the shadows receded and daylight poured through that long crawlspace beyond the poster. A dusty sunbeam fell on a metal box in a far corner, one Lloyd had never noticed. Like it was meant just for him.

He thumbed the box's curious latch. He peered inside. It was just some dented military box of Randall's. A few bullets and some old, folded maps sat loose. A white license plate with the word *IRAQ* leaned on the left side.

There, at the bottom, sat a Ka-Bar knife. Lloyd lifted it, sliding the seven-inch blade from its leather scabbard. He thumbed the clip point and winced.

Sharp. So very sharp.

"Soon, you will ascend," the voice said, *"and all the failings of flesh will no longer burden your soul. I will make you my emissary. Mmm... But first, we must fray this veil further. My pups hunger. Go, Lloyd. I will show you the way. Go, and see that they're fed."*

Lloyd sensed he stood at a great crossroads, a choice before him he'd yet to fully embrace. Yes, he had done things—done terrible things—but he told himself he had little choice.

The deer would have gotten hit anyway.

The cat shouldn't have been out of its house.

And old Sophie Saperstein, well, he hadn't killed her. No, no, of course not.

He just hadn't saved her.

Outside, it was just a warm summer morning in Raven's Valley. An Amazon delivery truck was already doing the rounds. A lanky girl skateboarded by while her friend jogged beside her. And despite the drought warning, the Parnells across the street were setting up a Slip 'N Slide on their dry lawn.

But to Lloyd, the world was *different*.

He could see beams and bricks and windows glowing in each house. He could sense that glorious dark star in the sky with its infinite eyes. Most of all, he could feel something to the northwest. A compass in his mind, black violet and shimmering, pointed him to a place of dark metal and something scared and trapped.

Something that needed to be... what was the word?

Tenderized, yes.

He was about to step off the porch when Randall shouted, "Hey, give me a hand here."

His stepdad carried an office chair, one of a dozen he'd been offloading last night. Another side hustle. Lloyd knew what that meant.

"C'mon, Lloyd, I've gotta deliver them by nine."

"I'm sort of busy."

"Yeah, busy playing pocket pool and doing fuck all. Grab a chair and be useful."

"Maybe another time—"

"Listen, I ain't asking. You live under this roof, you help carry some weight."

"It's not your roof, Randall. It's my mom's."

For a moment, Lloyd couldn't believe what he'd said. The words had surged forth, like someone else was moving his lips and giving breath to his voice. Even Randall blinked before narrowing his eyes.

"Well, it's a team effort, ain't it? So be a team player and help out. Chop-chop."

Sighing, Lloyd helped load the office chairs into the pickup, one after another, until they filled up the bed and jutted out. Randall used rope and bungee cords to tie them in but soon ran out.

"Climb back there and hold the others," Randall said. "Can't have them falling out on the crosstown expressway, can we?"

"Wait, you want me to come with you?" Lloyd wasn't sure why it was funny, but once again, Randall was grinning.

"How the hell else are we gonna offload 'em? Hop in. We'll make her a quick one."

Lloyd could feel the knife in his pocket, seven inches of 1095 carbon steel, sharp and hungering. His mind's compass spun, pointing to his great mission in the northwest. To that place of dark metal, where a boy waited inside.

Tenderize.

Lloyd could hear Armando whispering, *"What are you waiting for? We're running out of—"*

"Time's ticking," Randall said, tapping his wristwatch. "So, Lloyd, what's it gonna be?"

CHAPTER FORTY-SIX

The girls came to a stop near the edge of the park. Zelda's left knee wobbled and her right foot burned from kicking the skateboard for nearly three miles. Panting, Maura stumbled over to a water fountain by the tennis courts and took several gulps. For a moment, they said nothing as the adrenaline surged through their bodies and their lungs fought for air.

"I can't... believe we... just ran out of class," Maura said. "Aren't they going to call the cops or something?"

"I don't know," Zelda said. "I don't think it works like that. And it doesn't matter. Ali's in there."

She checked her phone once again. The game's map was far from accurate, but it showed Ali's character roughly five hundred feet away. Between them lay that rusty gate, the leaning fence, and the dry hedges. Chester's Victorian house loomed beyond, a thing of dark windows and crooked angles. She could almost smell the rot and the ruin.

This house. Sophie Saperstein had brought her to the edge of this very house. She had shown her a vision of fire and ash and torment.

This had to be the place.

"He's in there?" Maura swallowed as Zelda showed her the screen. Sure enough, that was the character's last active location, deep inside the old mansion.

Poor Ali, Zelda thought. He must be so scared.

If he's even alive.

No. She ignored that dark thought.

"So, what do we do now?" Maura asked. "What if he's home?"

Zelda had considered these questions while skateboarding over. "We'll need a distraction. But the thing is, I don't want to get you in trouble."

"Too late for that. We're playing hooky from class so I'm already in deep shit."

"Maybe. But if Ali's in there and we get him, none of that matters. So, I'm going to sneak around the side to the back door. You go bang on the porch, make some noise, try to draw old Chester out."

"I have to talk to him?"

"Stay on the porch or the walkway. Make him come outside to you. Tell him... Tell him you're missing a dog."

For a girl who threw touchdown passes and had a bedroom full of wrestling trophies, Maura actually seemed rattled. Her eyes darted about as she repeated the plan. "Porch, missing dog, make him come outside. Got it."

"Let's set timers. Wait five minutes, then knock. Sound good?"

"Okay, timer's set. Zelda, do you really think this is going to work?"

Zelda studied the old house, fear fluttering inside her ribs like a thousand butterflies. No, she wasn't sure it was going to work. She had enough doubts to fill a whole notebook. She was operating on momentum.

And yet, if he was in there, every second was precious.

She had to try something.

"It'll work," she said. "It has to."

While Maura lingered at the front, Zelda crept past a vine-threaded sculpture of a three-armed figure holding a shield. She stepped softly, using the balls of her feet to dampen the crackling dry grass. She followed the paint-chipped house along the side yard, crouching beneath the newspapered windows. All she heard was the creaking of distant metal in the scrapyard and a low mumble of a TV.

She checked her phone. Two and a half minutes.

As she passed huge piles of dirt, it occurred to her that some of the soil was freshly dug. She stopped to peek inside the house. Thick symbols adorned aged newspaper and dusty glass.

She found the back porch and tested the knob. The bolt turned with a click. A low creak, and she pushed the door inward.

Two minutes now.

Inside, she studied something like a pantry, glass so grimy it bronzed the morning light. Canned food lined drooping shelves. A fly buzzed against the window, forever trapped in these crooked walls.

The pantry connected to an open kitchen. Or at least, that's what Zelda guessed it had once been. Whatever this was now, it was no longer a room but a broken cavern.

Where walls once stood, there loomed only studs and slats and loose lath and plaster. A brickwork chimney leaned like a tired spine. Shattered stairs wound their way up to floors scattered with holes. Doors had been removed or rearranged, some leading to adjoining rooms while others simply opened to nothing but wall. The entire house was simultaneously undergoing excavation and collapsing in on itself. It made Zelda's head spin.

One minute.

Most concerning of all was the center of the house. Where stairs once wound their way down to a foyer, there was simply a gutted hole in the floor. Rickety stairs descended into darkness. A few work lights hung on bulbs, turning the halls into a lattice of shadows.

Zelda understood it now. This house might have been warm

and filled with laughter, but those days were long gone. Something festered within.

Something mad that had their friend in its grasp.

She checked her phone. Sure enough, Ali's character's last location was some fifty feet straight ahead. She peered across the exposed beams and broken walls to a distant door cracked ajar. Yes, something was in there. A sunbeam illuminated a rusty chain and a mattress with a shape curled upon it.

Like a boy tied to a bed.

Oh God, please be okay, Ali, please...

Then someone lumbered down the hall.

Chester wasn't in the next room, not quite, because there weren't really rooms here but dirt and half-dismantled spaces. She caught a glimpse of a raggedy form meandering past. It coughed and wheezed. A hand fell on an end table where old books towered and teetered. The fingernails were black and chewed to the quick.

Then her timer went off.

The vibration in Zelda's pocket was nearly silent, but not entirely. The buzz echoed across the dusty kitchen and through the splayed halls. The hand on the end table retracted.

Then came the face, an explosion of matted gray beard beneath feral eyes. Chester's head wasn't concealed beneath a welder's mask today, yet she now wished that it was.

His face was a canvas of symbols. Pockmarks covered his cheeks and forehead, his ears and neck. It was like he'd scribbled in black ink each morning and never washed it at night.

And now his mad eyes searched for the errant vibration. His dry lips twitched as a raspy cough left his lungs. "J'harr... you sneaking again?"

Please, Maura. Please, Zelda thought. *Just ring the doorbell and step off the porch. What's taking so long?*

A clang as an old buzzer echoed through the house. In a fast turn, Chester stomped off down the twisted halls.

This was it. She had to check that room with the bed.

She thumbed her phone and confirmed Ali's location. Fifty feet straight ahead. She scurried down a hall, past a tower of books. She took a right at a tired clock clicking away. A left at a chair half buried beneath sculptural blueprints. With each confusing new hall or gutted room, she could feel her sanity slipping.

From the far end of the house, light spread through the dust and the holes. She stole a glance and saw Chester standing at the front door, muttering in a low baritone rumble. She could hear Maura's distant voice.

Just a little longer. Please... Please...

There, at the end of a hall with its papered windows, the door stood ajar. Ali had to be in there.

Dodging a stack of paints and old shoes, Zelda threw the door open, expecting to see Ali tied to the bed or chained or—

It wasn't a bed, she realized, but old lumber beneath dusty tarps. Nor was this a body tied upon it. The canvas sacks lay under a loose chain, bundled like a young boy might sleep.

No, no no no.

Zelda pushed it, confirming that nothing and no body lay within. A trick of shadows and light.

Then she saw Ali's phone.

It sat on a table, the screen dirty and cracked. She thumbed the power button. For a moment, nothing happened. Then a red low-battery icon flashed before it shut off.

No. Ali had to be here. He *had* been here.

Zelda glanced back down the long hall to the front of the house.

Maura stood near the front door, her silhouette nearing the crack. Zelda could see Chester's back, not thirty feet off. And his trembling hand.

It was drifting to something hidden behind a stack of boxes.

His hand... Why was he reaching for something?

Zelda sprang into action, her feet carrying her in a silent sprint toward the front of the house.

Silent, until her foot kicked a stack of magazines.

She was ten feet away from Chester when he turned and his mad eyes widened. Here was another girl, someone coming from inside his house. His creeping hand retracted. "What the hell—"

Zelda wasn't muscular like Maura, but she was quick and had momentum on her side. In a shuddering gasp, she pushed Chester into the old wall and sent him crashing over a moth-eaten chair. His legs pinwheeled and splayed. A guttural cry left his throat as a hand lashed out, scraping newspaper from the window.

For one moment, he looked defenseless and pitiful. Just a scarecrow on his back, daylight beaming in as he tried to right himself with old bones and sore muscles.

That moment was soon over.

Zelda threw the front door open, where Maura backed away. "Oh my God. What'd you do?"

"His hand... He was going for something." She held up Ali's phone. "Look."

Maura's face twisted. She understood. If he had Ali's phone but not Ali...

A clatter behind them as Chester rose. "You... You again. You're too late... or too early."

"Go," Zelda shouted. "Run."

So that's what they did.

Their feet left the rickety porch and raced past the dry bushes. There was a distant noise beyond the front gate, something like a siren whooping. Then came a flash of lights.

"Please don't be pissed at me," Maura said between breaths. "But I totally freaked out and called the cops."

CHAPTER FORTY-SEVEN

It was just after nine when they stacked the last of the office chairs for delivery, no thanks to his knucklehead stepson who complained he had better places to be. Randy wasn't sure where those places were, only that Lloyd had been shifty lately. More shifty than usual.

His gut told him Lloyd had something to do with the missing fish. And the porno mags, too.

Mostly, he detested being near the young man. In the car, he'd noticed a patch of gray hairs coming in around Lloyd's right temple. Sometimes, the boy mumbled to himself. At an instinctual level, Randy smelled something rotten, even if he couldn't put it into words.

But the damn chairs wouldn't deliver themselves, and he was thin on time as it was.

Side hustling. Wasn't that what the kids called it these days?

So when he got the call that there was something going down near the tennis courts of Raven's Valley, he figured they'd swing by and have a look. He was the closest, after all, and technically still on the clock. Plus, he liked a bit of action. Pumping blood was good for the heart.

But the call was odd. Some girl claiming she found the location of that missing kid, Ali Baba or whatever. Randy whistled to Lloyd and shifted the pickup into drive. They made good time when he flashed his lights.

Yeah, Randy didn't care for that Iraqi boy or his family. He'd fought against their kind two decades ago, helped liberate that whole sullen country. All he had to show for his duty was a shitty back and a few knickknacks he'd plundered. That kid and his family, they were supposed to be refugees. So how'd they wind up with a house bigger than his?

Randy pulled up to the curb by the tennis courts. He squawked the siren and told Lloyd, "Just wait here a moment. It won't kill you."

That's when he saw them.

That stringy girl from the park, the one that had given him lip. And that bullish one, probably a lesbian who didn't know it yet. They raced down a reedy path, away from that old, rickety house.

Then he saw the man shambling after them, coming in fast in a manner that made Randy nervous.

And his face...

Jesus, the man's face was covered in some sort of scribble. Angry light burned in his eyes.

"What the fuck?"

Randy held a hand out to the girls as they rushed his pickup. His heart drummed in his chest. "Hold up, you two. C'mon over here and tell me what's going on."

The muscular one pointed to the ugly house. "He's got... our friend... He's got... Ali."

The stringy girl held up a phone. "This was inside."

Randy was distantly aware that a few tennis players had wandered over to the fence to watch the commotion. His head spun. "Hold up, ladies. Just settle down for a moment—"

"Why aren't you doing something?" the strong one said.

"Aren't you listening? He had a missing kid's phone in his house. It's like a fucking horror movie in there."

Randy glanced at the distant house with its dead lawn and sculptures. Yeah, he knew the place. Technically, this whole scratch of land was outside his patrol, but he told himself he had a duty to protect. It looked like a place people entered but never left. But that didn't mean it was what they said, right? Some people were just bad at upkeep.

And yet, the man lumbered toward them, a mad gleam in his eyes that sent Randy's right hand to his duty belt. "Just hold it right there, sir."

"Her! She's the one!" The man's rasp echoed of disease and carcinoma. His eyes flared with infection. "She was in my house. All of you were... but not *you*. Mabel? Can she see it too?"

"Officer, look at this," the stringy girl said. "It's Ali's phone. He's in there. You have to help him."

"Lloyd, take the girls over..." Randy glanced back at his pickup. The passenger door was open and his damn stepson was nowhere to be seen.

The *tock* of the tennis balls and the squeak of shoes died down. Onlookers gathered at the court fences. With his left hand, Randy shielded the girls from this man as his mind fought for balance. It was all happening too fast.

"Dispatch, I'm here at the tennis courts," he said, thumbing his radio. "You better have the cops assist. It looks like—sir! Sir! Step away from her!"

The man with the scribbled cheeks lashed an arm out, snatching onto that skinny girl's wrist. He turned it over, placing two fingers on it. "You're deathtouched," he coughed out. "But you're not her thrall. No, it's somebody else, somebody close." He pulled the skinny girl toward him. "This is all wrong—"

That's when Randy's instincts finally took over.

The Taser's barbed prongs struck the man in the chest and the neck. For a moment, Randy wasn't even sure that he'd fired. Then he heard the clicking as the taser discharged fifty thousand volts.

The man simply collapsed.

There were screams now, not from the girls or the man, but from someone at the tennis courts. One of the Raven's Valley regulars had her hands to her mouth. Randy was distantly aware that he was being recorded. Where had those cell phones all come from?

No, he thought. Not this. Not again.

His world slowed to a crawl.

The man, lying on the ground as his body convulsed.

The two girls, now stepping back.

And Randy's fingers on the trigger of his Taser, the battery going *tickity-tick-tick.*

Tongue dry and hands trembling, he let the taser fall from his grip. The man on the ground arched his legs as scabby hands curled to his chest and thumped his own ribs. His lips were turning blue.

"Hey... Hey, mister," Randy said. "Just stay there, okay?"

But he sensed his words weren't registering. Those mad eyes had lost focus, gone distant and glazed.

"I tried..." the man rasped. His dim eyes drifted to the skinny girl. "I tried to keep her glare... from turning... to you."

CHAPTER FORTY-EIGHT

It was the deep darkness, the deepest Ali had ever known. Time no longer existed, not in a measurable sense. He knew he was wounded; yes, he felt dried blood on his face. He thumbed the gash made by that thing that had struck him.

A chain?

A board?

Or something else?

Flashes in his mind: a muddy arm stretching out. A hand like branches. Fingers with dull teeth that gnawed at his skin, always in the seconds before he drifted to sleep.

He forced himself to stay awake, counting the seconds in his mind—one Mississippi, two Mississippi, three—until he stopped around a thousand and nodded off once again.

Then it returned: little teeth nibbling at his fingers, his elbow, his knees. Pinching and grinding and tugging at his skin.

Screaming, he kicked the shadows away. He was awake here, awake in this cavern of shadows, where time didn't matter. He banged on the metal walls and shouted for help. His raspy voice echoed back, a hollow mockery. He collapsed on the floor.

How long had it been? An hour? A day? A week or a lifetime? *Think*, Ali. *Think.*

He reviewed the hazy facts. He had urinated four times already. He knew he could usually hold his bladder for several hours at least. Four times three equaled twelve. So, twelve hours perhaps?

But he also knew he was getting dehydrated. His tongue clung to his mouth and his stomach constantly rumbled. Pain subsumed him as he lapsed into blurry patterns.

Sometimes, he banged on the metal walls and screamed. Sometimes, he prayed. Mostly, he wandered around, hands feeling blindly at the endless black void.

Where was he? Another vague memory of some metal container echoed in his mind. But this couldn't be it, could it? It was too... big. Too... vast.

He found something like a railing and stairs in the darkness. He descended, following them for minutes until he realized he should count each step. He stopped at 138. Was this some sort of bunker, or...

The darkness rumbled beside him. A low moan, wet and old, like stones among mud.

"Ah, you're quite the explorer," murmured a male voice to his left.

There was something wrong with the way the stranger spoke. Like his lips had caved in and his tongue was too loose.

"I gave her my teeth, but I can still chew. Come closer... *There.*"

Something wet suckled on Ali's ankle.

Empty gums.

Screaming, Ali ran back up the stairs, only to discover there were fewer than five steps to the top. The railing ended. He was back in the room he'd come from.

It didn't make any sense.

Okay, be logical. Get oriented.

He fumbled at the railing and the first step. He turned 180

degrees and marked the new direction in his mind. He took several steps forward, hands scouring the oily shadows.

There was something to his right. A wooden crate? His fingers slid past it and he continued.

To his left, his knee bumped an object soft and lumpy. His grandmother's agarwood perfume filled his nostrils as spindly fingers stroked his wrist.

"Ali… Why you rouse me from my nap?"

Gasping, he raced back to the stairs and the rail. Yet he sensed he was ascending now, somehow scrambling up a steep hill. The metal floor became angled. Little pebbles went *clickity-click* and crunched underfoot.

He stumbled on, chased by his dead grandmother's whispers and the toothless smacking of gums. He walked for minutes or hours or perhaps his whole life. Was he old now? Had he been here for decades and slowly gone mad?

Wobbling, he collapsed to his knees, where brittle twigs scraped his shins. He was climbing now, scrambling up some impossible hill. Grasping for traction on…

No, not twigs and rocks, his mind whispered. *Those are bones and teeth. Don't deny what your fingers know.*

Ali flung them away and crawled on, upward, clutching at the steep, jagged mountain. Infinite darkness stretched out in every direction, lightless and consuming.

And yet, he *perceived* something among it. Yes, a black-violet beam worming across the universe and now focused on him.

It hungered and thirsted.

That beam, it washed over him now, bathing every inch of his body in its ravenous glare. Something was coming for him. Something cosmic and ancient. A thing he could no longer hide from, no matter how deep he buried himself beneath this mountain of bones and teeth and—

And then, light.

A single luminous thread bloomed vertically and cleaved the shadows.

Ali crouched among the bones, watching the line grow taller and wider. It chased the darkness, the brightest thing he'd ever seen. Holding his hands to his face, he cried out as the light expanded into a rectangle.

A shape stood in the light. A shape so washed out he could hardly see more than a tall, thin smear. A shape he once knew.

Yes, that was a person there, in the expanding rectangle of light.

A person holding something sharp in their hand.

And he recognized that too, the curl of metal that made up a crowbar. And a second person, this one husky and wide at the waist. A third and fourth joined them, shouting words that Ali understood from a place of memory. These were people, his people, the people of Raven's Valley.

"It's him!" someone shouted. "We found him. Hold on there, kid. We're coming in."

Ali was laughing now, stretching out to the light as these hands reached into the darkness—to *his* darkness—this place he knew so well for so long. A place tinted by dream logic and already fading.

That was how they found the missing boy. Ali, sitting atop a small mound of dirt and leaves in the back of the container, laughing and reaching out with chewed, bloody fingers.

CHAPTER FORTY-NINE

Lloyd was in trouble, real trouble, the kind one couldn't get away from or shrug off. He'd helped Randall all morning while Armando chanted in his mind, nagging him to hurry, to follow the compass, to find what had been caught for the pups.

To tenderize.

But he'd fumbled that, hadn't he?

Ducking through a hole in an old concrete wall, Lloyd assumed he'd have the scrapyard to himself. Instead, there were a half dozen gathered by a rusty shipping container.

Where his mind's compass had pointed.

Someone had a crowbar and someone else hoisted a portable saw. A fireman hurried over with a Halligan bar. In the end, the Halligan and a hammer won out, bending the latch on the fifth strike. The metal door swung open.

Crouching, Lloyd watched from behind a stack of old tires as they helped a boy from the container. It was the same boy he'd seen at the Last Castle a few weeks ago.

Why would Armando want to hurt this kid? It didn't make sense.

"It doesn't have to make sense. All you needed to do was follow my command."

No. Lloyd wouldn't do it. And besides, he couldn't do it now. There were too many people.

"Idiot!"

The headache struck him from nowhere, rendering the metal piles into a mountain of bright blades. The wind shrieked through the rusty scrap. The world tilted.

Lloyd stumbled, fell to the dirt, and vomited. He'd never felt such a blazing sensation before. No, not since those lost minutes beneath the ice.

But the squeal of rending metal, the shimmer off the scrap... it was too much. If he could just retreat from the junkyard, it might go away. Lloyd clambered back and crawled through the hole in the wall. His stomach twisted and wrung itself empty.

And yet the sound pursued him. A static warble. A scraping of glass and metal. A billion dull teeth grinding on bone.

"Failure! Fool! I've had countless emissaries and none have been so clumsy and slow!"

Lloyd batted and slapped at the air, but the voice chased him, a cloud of furious sound. He was stumbling through bushes now, branches scraping his shoulders. He was rolling off the chain link of the tennis courts while someone called out and asked if he was all right.

No, he wasn't all right. His head buzzed with too many senses. Worms nestled in the folds of his brain. The world spun as he ran.

All the while, Armando's voice hissed and hounded him.

"I gave you a gift and you squandered your task!"

He was racing now, really sprinting past cars and houses, past parks where kids threw frisbees and dogs chased at their heels. He could feel Armando's pups behind him, gnashing and howling, so ravenous they might just devour him whole.

He shoved his way through a neighbor's garden and threw open a gate. He was home, here in the safety of their cool house, where Randall's fish tank burbled and his mother's patterned drapes blew in the breeze.

He knew what he had to do and he begged for the strength.

His vision dimmed and his ankles wobbled on the basement stairs. He vomited on the landing. There, at the bottom, that poster stared up with calculating eyes.

Armando the Great.

"Fucking... leave... me... ALONE!"

Then Lloyd was upon it.

The first punch shattered the poster's glass. The second loosened the frame. He threw another half dozen furious punches, each one stronger than the last. Shards tumbled free and clattered on the floor, each piece a cut in his mind.

His wrists throbbed and his knuckles burned. He saw blood on the glass, blood dripping down the old frame.

And still Armando glared, that head floating among the old-timey swirls. Those penetrating eyes. And those lips curled in an enigmatic smirk.

He'd wipe that smirk off his face.

Lloyd brought the Ka-Bar knife down on the old paper, splitting Armando's smug smile. Another strike, and paper tore free from the backing. A third strike, a fourth, and then Lloyd was slashing wildly, cutting the poster apart.

It all faded. The nausea and the glinting cold light. The grinding of metal and teeth upon bone. The buzz of static that he somehow understood was the language of the cosmos itself.

Spent and sweaty, Lloyd collapsed before these ruins of his making.

The poster was simply obliterated.

A few pieces still clung to the wood backing and broken frame. With a grunt, he grabbed that frame and twisted. A pop as the last shards of glass fell free and the edges buckled from their brackets. The whole thing collapsed.

In the welcome silence, the remains of that vintage poster fluttered and fell, torn scraps of paper, printed back when the world was smaller and people still believed in mystics and fortunes.

Lloyd sat before the mess, huffing and gasping. Every inch of his body quivered. And he felt... What did he feel?

Free. Yes, he felt free.

But only for a moment.

The voice returned, yawning from the depths of the house. *"Mmm, Lloyd... Oh, we have much to discuss."*

"No, no, no," he muttered. "I killed you. You're dead."

"Dead? No. Death is a word of no meaning to a god. Mmm... Be my emissary and we will bridge death together."

Lloyd wiped his eyes and stared at the ruined poster. "Please," he whispered. "Please, Armando, just leave me alone."

"Why do you keep calling me that? My name is not Armando."

Then it stirred. Not the poster, Lloyd realized, but the crawlspace *behind* it. That tunnel of shadows and dust leading into the very foundation of the house. Boards and beams crossed each other. Beyond, a small window looked out from ground level at the garden his mother loved.

The dust in the crawlspace sparkled like stars.

The wood beams, they grew fingers.

And from the distant glass, dark eyes opened, endless and seething.

A tired laugh fled from Lloyd's mouth. He understood it now. He had never been talking with an old poster and that face upon it.

He had been communing with something from the deep bowels of this house. Something in its fibers and stone. Something now stretching out from an undulating void and turning her unblinking eyes upon him.

CHAPTER FIFTY

It was an odd kind of day. First, the emergency alert for Zelda's missing friend put Mark in a weird mood. Then came the message from Steve Barker that Zelda had skipped out of his class at attendance. Perhaps it was a female thing. If so, he wanted to give her some space. Still, he'd need to know why so he could write up an excuse.

Now, an incoming call at a quarter past noon. The caller ID read *Greywood Bay Police.* He told his sophomore Spanish class to spend five minutes in free talk.

Then he answered the phone in the hall. He listened. His heart began racing.

Twenty minutes later, it hadn't stopped. He pulled up to the Greywood Bay police station, a two-floor building all concrete and glass. He ended his phone call with Ms. Phong, her advice still ringing in his ear: "Whatever you do, don't let Zelda make any statements until we all talk."

He took a deep breath and squeezed his shaking hands. There had to be more to the story.

In the station, he checked in with a surly attendant who nodded and knew who he was. "Just wait here a moment, sir.

We'll have the detective in charge come get you when he's ready."

Detective in charge, Mark thought. Christ, this wasn't good.

After ten long minutes, there was a clunk at the lobby door, and a fashionable husband and wife entered. The man's suit screamed bespoke, and the woman wore a colorful sundress with a vintage Louis Vuitton purse. The husband gave the attendant an earful as the wife waved at Mark.

"Zelda's uncle?" she asked. "Matt, is it?"

"Mark Fitzsimmons. Maura's mom?"

"Ruth. Ruth Goodman-Kerns." She gave a flick of a diamond-studded hand. "My husband, Dr. Henry Kerns. Heavens, what a mess. What have they told you?"

Mark swallowed. "Something about an incident with a man at a house. It's all pretty vague."

"Yes, vague. That's our police department for you. As transparent as a rock. You know, they actually refused to join the parade this year? Threw a tantrum because the town wouldn't buy them one of those armored cars. Tanks, really. Who needs a tank in Greywood Bay?"

Mark wasn't sure what this had to do with their kids, but he listened to Ruth's complaints. There was a gravity to this couple. They seemed to pull weight in this town.

At the reception window, Dr. Kerns raised his voice and leaned closer. The attendant nodded apologetically while some cop in the room beyond looked on, trying to figure out if she should join. She decided not to.

"Oh, he lives for this." Ruth gave a nod toward her husband. "One of the perks of marrying a professor of criminal law. Forgive me, we should have introduced ourselves sooner."

"No, I've been meaning to stop by. Especially with Ali missing, I figured we should know who our kids are playing with."

"Yes, of course." She leaned in, so close he could smell her perfume. She'd laid it on heavily. "But he's no longer missing. I spoke with Pavarti Khan on the drive over. She was playing doubles at the courts when this all happened. They found Ali. Poor boy got stuck in a shipping container. Can you believe that?"

"Is he okay?"

"As far as I've heard. Goodness, it's like one of those after-school specials. They really need to do something about that eyesore."

Dr. Kerns waved him over. "Mark, it looks like the squeaky wheel gets the grease. The detective wants to speak with you first."

Ruth gently touched Mark's hand. "If you don't have a lawyer, we can certainly recommend one. I hope it won't come to that."

"Me too."

Nerves tingling, Mark followed the attendant down a maze of corridors and rooms. He'd never been in a police station before. He realized now that it was just like any other government office, a place of bad lighting and bland decoration, the occasional accountant at their desk or a bored cop handling paperwork.

Detective Debra Brown was a broad-shouldered woman with sharp eyes and a smile that never rose above a flat line. She wore a dark blazer and her breath was redolent of coffee. Mark wasn't sure whether they should shake hands so he waited for her cue, which never came. Instead, she gestured into her office.

"First and foremost, your niece is fine. She's a little rattled, all things considered, but she's safe. Sit, please." She motioned to a chair across from her messy desk. "We've been having an interesting chat all morning, Zelda and I. Let me bring you up to speed."

"She's been talking?" Mark's stomach roiled.

"She's a firecracker, that one. I mean that as a compliment. I was a firecracker too. Some days we burn bright. But today, I'm afraid, will be one of the rough ones. How much have you heard about what happened?"

He told her what he'd gleamed from the conversation on the

phone and in the lobby. She nodded occasionally. Then she filled in the rest.

When she finished, his thoughts spun and his left foot jittered on the linoleum.

Trespassing.

Breaking and entering.

Assaulting a senior citizen in his own home.

"The whole situation is a mess," Detective Brown continued. "I know Zelda thought she was doing the right thing, looking for their friend Ali. But what I've also gathered is this wasn't their first run-in with Mr. Halgrove."

"Mr. Halgrove?"

"Chester, the gentleman currently hospitalized. See, the kids have long built him up to be some kind of boogeyman. From what I understand, he's an eccentric, a hoarder with untreated mental illness. That, plus the fact that he was in possession of the missing boy's phone, well, your niece and her friend put this together, took things into their own hands, and now here we are."

Mark leaned forward. "I don't understand. Why did he have Ali's phone?"

She sighed. "We're still looking into that. It seems that Mr. Halgrove found it in his junkyard last night. Found it right outside the container Ali was inside."

"But why didn't he check?"

"Unclear. Maybe he didn't hear him. It sounds like he wanted to return it. He also had some sort of model airplane the kids left behind. That was what he was reaching for at the door when Zelda assaulted him."

Mark scoffed. "Assaulted? A thirteen-year-old girl that weighs eighty pounds."

"A girl who broke into his house." She steepled her fingers. "Look, Mr. Fitzsimmons, I understand this is a tough time for your niece. Her parents, a new town, the disappearance of her friend, I get it."

"This has nothing to do with her parents."

"My point is this incident could be spun one of two ways. An accident, a misunderstanding, and a pair of girls who showed tremendously poor judgment and, more importantly, contrition. If you're religious, I'd put Mr. Halgrove in your prayers."

No, Mark wasn't religious. But he thought he might start clasping his hands and taking a knee if it got Zelda out of this mess.

"The other way this can go, Mr. Fitzsimmons, is that the prosecutor files charges. Section 240: assault. Section 459: burglary. And 602: trespassing. I could even see them push 368. That's crimes against the elderly."

This was insane. His fingers tingled and his mouth had gone dry. The moment the Ruizes heard of this, Ms. Chou would push for an emergency hearing. They'd paint him as incompetent, a bad guardian. And just when things were getting settled. He'd need to have Ms. Phong get in front of this immediately. He shuddered at the cost.

Something softened on Detective Brown's face. "My point is, I saw Dr. Kerns and his wife sharpening their knives in the lobby. I'm bracing for an earful. But they grew up here. They're dug in. As one outsider to another, perhaps a more subtle approach will improve Zelda's situation."

"I don't even know where to begin," he said, more to himself than the detective.

"Begin with a sincere letter of apology to Mr. Halgrove," she said. "And a long talk with your niece. We don't always know what our kids are up to. Sometimes, we can do everything right and it's still not enough."

CHAPTER FIFTY-ONE

She had never seen Uncle Mark so angry. He didn't shout or yell or raise his voice. He didn't lecture like her mom used to. Or ask questions and come up with plans like her dad. He simply withdrew into himself, brooding and silent while his eyes darted about.

The Subaru never felt as small as it did now, driving away from the police station. She wished he would yell or call her stupid. Anything was better than this silence. He didn't even say he was disappointed, which seemed worst of all.

Who wouldn't be disappointed in her?

They were on the crosstown expressway when her phone vibrated. A text message from Ali lit up the screen.

Hey Zelda-bo-belda, heard ur looking 4 me?

She typed:

WTF. Where are you? What happened? You okay?

@Hospital 4 observation. Dehydrated. Bored. What's⬆?

Big trouble.

Bummer. Me 2. We can b trouble buddies 2gether 4ever.

The little bubbles indicated Ali was typing something else.

But seriously. We need 2 talk.

Zelda took a deep breath and studied Uncle Mark, his knuckles clutching the wheel and his jaw tight. She could hear him grinding his teeth.

"Uncle Mark?"

He didn't say anything for a moment. Just waited until the light turned green, then continued driving. "Yes, Zelda?"

"I know I screwed up. I'm really sorry."

He tilted his head as if the words "no shit" teetered on the edge of his lips. Then he bit them and said nothing.

"Ali just texted me," she said. "He's at the hospital. I guess, well… I was wondering if we could stop by?"

His nostrils flared. "I just spent the past half hour listening to a detective describe you as a potential felon. I had to leave my class in the care of Ms. Layne, who was on the hiring committee. Your actions put an elderly man in intensive care. The only way we're going by the hospital is to drop off a letter of apology. So, you'd better get started—"

"I already did." She reached inside her jacket and pulled out several pieces of folded paper.

He gave them a sidelong glance. "When did you do that?"

"While you were talking to Detective Brown. I asked one of the cops. It's a draft, so…"

Something softened on his face.

"Will you read it?"

"No," he said. "Not while I'm driving. But read it to me."

So she did.

It wasn't much, just a page and a half, and she didn't know how to end it. But she meant every word. When she finished, she folded it and looked at her shoes. There was still dirt on them from this morning, and a few reeds clung to her laces.

For a moment, Uncle Mark said nothing. Then he glanced up at the street signs, and he put the left turn signal on.

THE HOSPITAL GIFT SHOP SOLD BALLOONS AND STUFFED animals, bouquets of flowers, and more. While Uncle Mark got a coffee, Zelda found some fancy stationery and asked the florist to pick out a nice arrangement. She paid with her own debit card, even though Uncle Mark gave her his. It wasn't fair to take his money.

For the next ten minutes, he sipped his coffee and talked with an attorney while pacing through the statue garden outside. She waited in the lobby, transferring her letter from the lined paper to the nice stationery.

She wasn't sure how to close it out, but once she got there, she found her ending.

People often say kids' opinions don't matter and our actions aren't very important. I guess I kind of believed that. But today I learned I was wrong.

Our opinions can hurt others if they're false. Our actions can cause a bunch of pain. Mr. Halgrove, I'm so sorry that my actions hurt you. I'll try to be better.

I wish you a super swift recovery.

Zelda Ruiz

Mark read the letter and nodded, passing it back to Zelda. "That's good. I think he'll like it."

SHE FOUND THE PEDIATRIC WARD ON THE FIRST FLOOR, its walls a colorful explosion of murals and clouds. There were toy bins and some life-sized statues of cartoon characters. The whole thing felt like a discount Disneyland.

Ali winced as he sat up in the hospital bed. "What's the haps, Z-bear?"

Zelda wasn't sure what she expected. She knew he'd been stuck in a shipping container for over half a day. He'd been rescued and fed and was now soaking up a vitamin IV drip. She knew he was probably still in shock.

And yet, there was something different about him. Perhaps it was the bandages on his fingers. Perhaps it was his eyes and how they blinked a little more than usual.

No, she realized as she drew close to his bed. A shadow clung to him now. A black-violet aura clung to his skin in tendrils and wisps, only visible at an angle.

"Ali, what happened?" she asked. "You're, like... smoking."

He grinned. "Yeah, smoking hot for a dude who went missing. You know they had an actual bloodhound out on the hunt?"

"No, it's your skin." She waved her hand over his bandaged fingers, brushing the smokey tendrils. With each pass, they faded. "You don't see that?"

He wiggled up a hand. "C'mon, stop messing with me. What's next? I'm a ghost and I was dead the whole time? Yeah, spoiler alert."

It unsettled her, this dark aura leaving his skin. Like water steaming off in a sunbeam. A sunbeam of shadows.

And yet he ignored it.

"So, what happened?" she asked.

Ali shrugged. "It's weird. Like, I remember little pieces. At first, I think I was trying to find something. But then it was like something was really trying to find me. Doctor thinks I'm concussed, but..."

"But what?"

He glanced at his relatives outside in the waiting room. Uncle Mark talked to Yanar while Ali's big sister helped their grandma to a chair. There were a dozen at least.

"Ali, what is it?"

He reached for a ginger ale on the table and sucked a long drink from the straw. The black-violet shadow left faint traces of his motions. This was going to drive her mad. Why couldn't he see it?

"What happened to your fingers?"

Ali turned his hand over and wiggled his fingers, plastic tape crinkling in the quiet. "Rats," he said.

"There were rats in the container?"

He nodded. "That's what they said."

And perhaps they had, but Zelda wasn't buying it because Ali wasn't selling it. She'd only known him for the summer, but that was long enough to know he was lying.

"Ali?" She sat at the edge of his bed and lowered her voice. "What really happened?"

He reclined in his bed and closed his eyes. For a moment, she thought he might be falling asleep or ignoring her altogether. Then his face twitched and his body tensed.

"I wasn't alone," he whispered. "In the container, I wasn't... Something *else* was in there, with me."

"What was it?"

Eyes still clenched shut, he drew in a deep breath and shivered. Had this room always been so cold and so dim?

"I don't know," he said. "I don't want to know. It was like being some tiny bug on a slide under a microscope and just getting... inspected, you know? Like something was poking and prodding and finding out how to hurt me."

He opened his eyes. They were wet and red and filled with latent fear.

"I think you were right," he said. "There's something wrong with this place, isn't there?"

Zelda hesitated. Yes, there was, but putting it into words was like catching smoke in her hands. Even her dreams felt cryptic and dreadful.

She was about to answer when Uncle Mark tapped on the door. He carried the vase filled with flowers.

"Zelda," he said. "He's out of surgery."

REVASCULARIZATION—ALSO KNOWN AS CORONARY artery bypass grafting—Zelda learned, was a process of harvesting arteries from other parts of the body, then attaching them to the outermost tissue of the heart.

Until an hour ago, Chester Halgrove's arteries had been so thick with plaque that the heart muscles were starved for oxygen.

Each breath had been a slow death sentence, nearing culmination. The good thing, the day nurse explained as he walked them through the ICU, was that they'd caught it now. Fortunate, really.

They turned a corner, memories of her father's final hours tightening her spine.

The machines that had clicked and wheezed to keep him alive, but only just.

The scent of medicated ointments, his ruined skin, his dying body.

The way his purple lips twitched as he groaned from the depths of a chemical haze. Because if he was to awaken, he would have pulled the tube from his throat.

"You okay?" Uncle Mark asked. He must have sensed her discomfort.

"Yeah. Fine." She picked her fingers with their chipped polish.

They came to a stop at the nurses' station, where the day nurse informed them Mr. Halgrove was still asleep and wouldn't be awake for several hours. "I'll place it by his bed," she said. "Follow me."

Zelda watched from the door as the nurse entered the room.

The man sleeping in bed hardly looked like that raggedy thing that had found them in his scrapyard. Nor did he resemble that wiry man who had chased her out of his house this very morning. His cheeks had been shaven, his face cleaned of those bizarre symbols. His bushy mane of gray hair was combed back to the side. There was a broken dignity to him. Someone not just physically sick but consumed from within.

But it was the shadows that Zelda noticed most of all.

Arms of oil and smoke stretched and clawed their way up the walls. Tentacles twisted and curled. Chester Halgrove's room was suffused in living darkness, an undulating tangle worming out from his slumbering body. Only a single, warm beam of light cleaved its way from the window and down through the shade.

The nurse placed the flowers and the card near the bed. She closed the door and stepped back into the hall. The shadows slid right off her and faded.

She didn't see it.

None of them did.

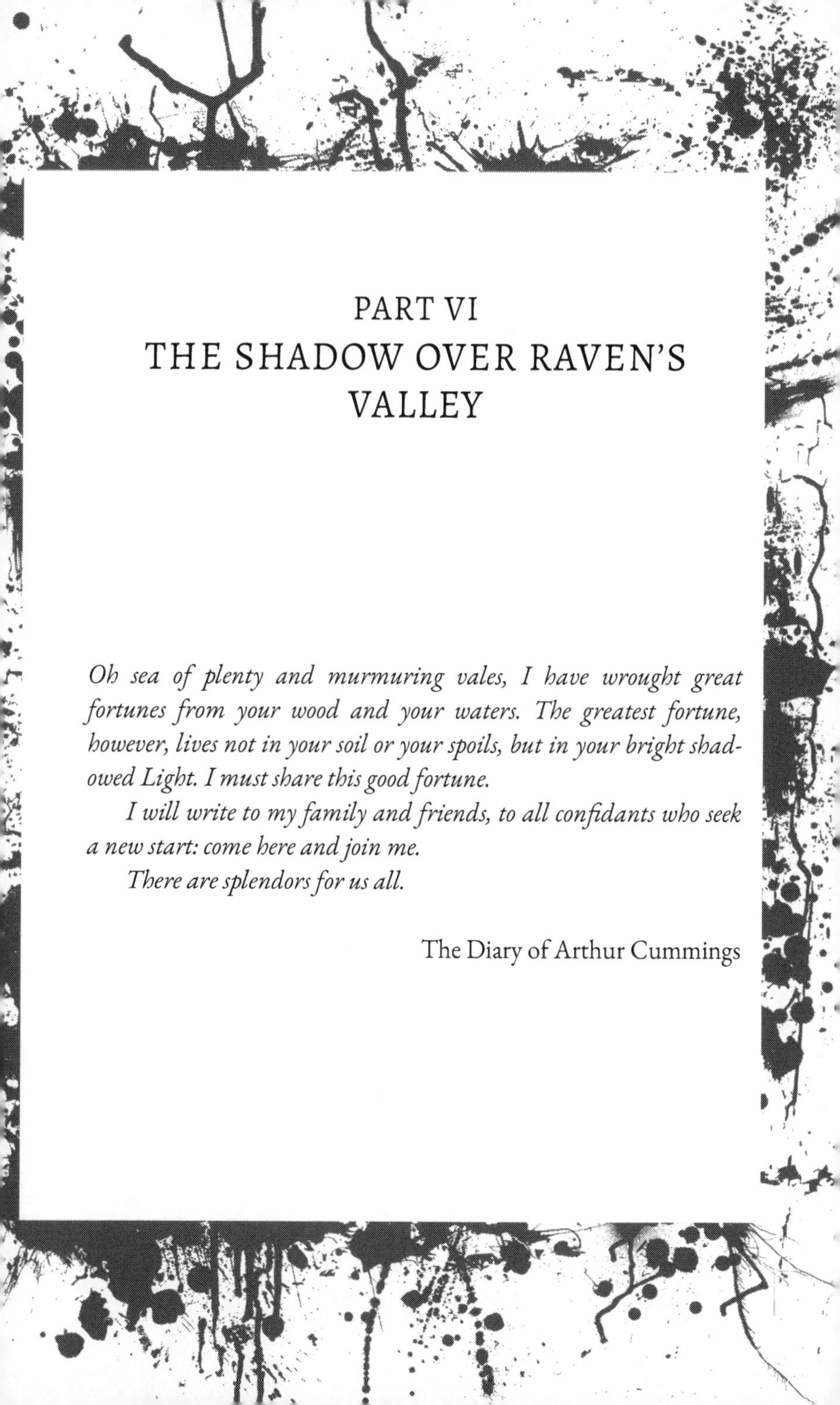

PART VI
THE SHADOW OVER RAVEN'S VALLEY

Oh sea of plenty and murmuring vales, I have wrought great fortunes from your wood and your waters. The greatest fortune, however, lives not in your soil or your spoils, but in your bright shadowed Light. I must share this good fortune.

I will write to my family and friends, to all confidants who seek a new start: come here and join me.

There are splendors for us all.

The Diary of Arthur Cummings

CHAPTER FIFTY-TWO

It was official. By the first week of August, the drought was now a statewide emergency. The governor ordered water rationing across all fifty-eight counties. Climate change and years of mismanagement had reduced the lakes to dry cavities. Green lawns gave way to amber. Even the foothills around Raven's Valley took on a scrappy appearance, the thirsty trees with their leaves browning at the edges, the summer reeds brittle and tall.

But at the Greywood Estates Country Club, its fairways were still vibrant and green, the grass trimmed twice a week. Healthy oaks offered leafy shade from the sun. This pleased Edward Strathmore IV, who was on the eleventh hole and on track to beat his best score.

"It's like my dad used to say," he said, lining up his drive from the tee box. "Eddie, my boy, you may be a late-blooming idiot, but you eventually shoot straight."

With a smooth pivot from the waist, he swung and connected, sending the golf ball deep down the fairway, much to the groan of his companions.

"Yep, your dad sure had a way with his words, didn't he?" That was Councilman Brand, a meaty man in his sixties and one of the

Strathmore family's friends. When the ball finally landed on the green, he said, "Jesus, Ed, leave some for the rest of us, okay?"

"Sorry, Don, just trying to put an old dog out of their misery quick."

"An old dog." The councilman chuckled.

While Councilman Brand teed up his ball, Edward gave a quick nod to Larry Larchmont, the third player in today's game. Larry wasn't a golfer, but he could swing a club and shoot the shit.

More importantly, he could make the councilman feel like he wasn't getting his teeth kicked in all afternoon. It wasn't exercise Edward and Larry were here for today, but opportunity. It wasn't often one got eighteen holes to honey the ear of the chairman of the city's zoning commission.

While Councilman Brand fished out his driver, Larry asked, "So, Councilman, I was hoping you'd had a chance to look over our proposal. If there're any questions—"

The councilman raised his hand. "One moment, son. You're gumming up my focus."

Backing away, Larry shot a nervous glance toward his partner.

Dammit, Edward thought, why did Larry always have to go straight for the close? Couldn't he try a little foreplay?

The councilman swung and hit a respectable drive. Larry teed up and followed through with a real doozy. He cursed under his breath and the councilman laughed. And that was why Edward brought him along, their two scores sandwiching Councilman Brand in the middle. Making him feel comfortable yet still on the back foot.

As they walked the fairway, Edward said, "What my partner was getting at—rather clumsily, I'm afraid—is that we're sitting on a ticking clock here, Don. We need to know if there's a play to be made."

"You mean if you've got my vote on Hawk's Hollow?"

Edward passed the councilman a bottle of water. "The development would bring a lot of good to our town."

"I thought you didn't like that word. 'Development.'"

"I don't like the word 'Karen,' but that doesn't stop my daughter from using it on my ex-wife."

The councilman chuckled. "Yeah, maybe you're right about the good it'd bring. But five hundred houses? That's a lot of mouths as well. A lot of parking spots and desks in the schools. People are worried about growth."

"Yeah, and people are worried that wind farms steal oxygen or cell towers scan our brainwaves," Edward said. "Just 'cause someone's afraid of something doesn't mean it's bad. Slow, sustained growth, that's our goal."

"Slow growth, huh?"

They were halfway to the green now. The councilman waved to Larry to take his swing so they could regroup. Edward winced as Larry chipped it into the bunker.

"The state's changing, Don," Edward said. "Cities are losing their luster. People want nature and fresh air. But they want to be near Costco, a Whole Foods, and get Amazon Prime in two days. Quality schools *and* quality of life. Greywood Bay ticks all the boxes. But if we don't act fast, West Pine or Fort Darrow or any of these other small towns'll wise up. They're already calling my office, asking what else we're planning."

"Are they now?" Don pierced him with his droopy stare. "Be that as it may, I've still got a duty to my constituents not to roll over."

"We've all got duties. I've got a fiduciary duty to my investors. I grew up here. My family goes back four generations—"

"As does mine, son."

"And that's my point. I'd rather build here, where my heart is, and not up in West Pine or Fort Darrow."

They strolled beneath the leafy canopy, the willows swaying in the warm breeze and the ducks resting in on the lake's shore.

"Maybe West Pine is a better match for a few hundred

McMansions," the councilman said. "I've heard they're courting Walmart as well."

Edward felt his toes clenching. He waited while the councilman took his pathetic shot and Larry ambled back. When they were all close to the green, he said, "These are quality homes, Don. Clean energy, green-certified, recycled and built to last. Each one as unique as the families inside."

"Yeah, I've read the brochure."

"If you had, then you wouldn't call them McMansions," he said, realizing too late how curt his tone was. Sure, he and the councilman's families went back a hundred-some years, but they swam in different currents, only overlapping when their interests aligned.

The councilman switched to a medium iron. "I've offended you. Apologies. It must be the heat."

Edward sipped his water to keep himself from talking while the councilman lined up his putt. The nerve of the man.

"What I think Ed was trying to get at," Larry said, "is that whether we like it or not, the town is growing. Raven's Valley is proof there's demand. I've sourced the materials and Eddie's already taken deposit on twenty percent of the units. It's a good deal, sir. And we want what's best for our community."

The councilman raised an eyebrow. "Twenty percent?"

Edward nodded. In truth, it was a little under. There were regulations on where the money had to sit and how much could be moved around. The last time he'd checked, there was over fifteen million on deposit. He'd used that to entice investors, who were already champing at the bit. Then came the gap financing, the grants, the tax incentives. The whole thing was a house of cards that spun his head and put him in a cold sweat. Sometimes he wished he'd just gone into philanthropy instead of carrying on the Strathmore business.

"Ed, I like you and your family," the councilman said. "But bureaucracy's a big ship and slow to turn. Like one of those ol' aircraft carriers. You folks in the private sector are like little speedboats buzzing about." He sank his putt and retrieved his ball. "We're moving at different speeds here. Unless, of course, we can figure out a way to sail together."

And there it was. Just the slightest of smirks lifting the councilman's lips and a gleam to his gaze. The man truly looked like a fox in a henhouse.

While Larry continued to chip away at his ball, Edward lowered his voice. "I understand your daughter's in the market for her first house."

"And my peckerwood son-in-law, some kind of writer of god-knows-what."

He retrieved his cigar from the golf cart and gave it a quick puff under the torch lighter. Sure, the country club had a no-smoking rule on the fairway, but the councilman knew the rules were looser for men like them.

Which was why Edward's company always kept a few housing units on reserve.

"We could set her up with one of the early investor homes," he said. "It'd be at cost of materials. The rest of it, well, we'll consider it an investment in our community."

The councilman took another puff on his cigar. His eyes met Edward's through the smoke and sunlight. They understood each other.

He gently tamped the cigar out on his nine iron.

"That's thoughtful of you. I'm fairly confident the zoning commission will be able to expedite your application. Of course, you've still got that problem with the junkyard and that old coot Halgrove. He's dug in deeper than a summer tick."

It was Edward's turn to smile now. "Actually, I think that tick has lost its bite."

He didn't keep up with all the gossip in Raven's Valley—and there was lots of gossip—but something last week had caught his attention. An altercation that led to a home inspection. An emergency mental health hold that was ordered. And now the word "conservatorship" was being discussed. But the real gift had come from the kid who got stuck in a container. He hadn't died, thank God. The stars sure were aligning for Edward.

He said, "Have you heard of the attractive nuisance doctrine?"

"Illuminate me."

Edward lined up his putt. He was going to sink this in three, his personal best for the eleventh hole. "It goes like this: you can't put a trampoline in a front yard with no fence and then act surprised when kids try to use it. An attractive nuisance creates a legal obligation to minimize harm. That house, that scrapyard, that whole crazy plot of land is one big magnet. With a little nudge, the city could get involved."

"And you're looking for someone to tip the scales?"

With a gentle but firm tap, Edward sent the ball straight ahead. It dropped into the hole with a satisfying *thunk*. "I'm looking for someone who isn't afraid of progress."

"Progress, huh? You sure like that word."

Edward retrieved his ball. "If we're not moving toward the future, we're getting left behind. That's a fact. And here's another. That property has been a blight for decades. Halgrove may've been dug in like a tick, but even ticks eventually come loose. That land could be the foundation of something better." He took his own cigar out and lit it with the councilman's lighter. He savored the peppery spice and the hint of coffee. "Yeah, I like the word 'progress,' sure, but you know what word I like even better? 'Eminent domain.'"

CHAPTER FIFTY-THREE

Mark tried to ignore the sweat inching down his back and pooling near his belt. He'd worn his favorite suit today, the gray three-piece he'd bought at Gieves & Hawkes on Saville Row nearly a decade ago. His messenger bag sat in his lap, thick with his CV, his teaching philosophy, and several lesson plans. He'd prepared for it all.

What he hadn't prepared for was the air-conditioning going out in the administrative office. Even the secretary was fanning herself.

"Sorry, folks." Stacey poked her head out of the conference room. "I know this isn't ideal, but it is what it is. Facilities is bringing over another fan."

"Not a problem, ma'am," said an affable man in his mid-thirties two seats down. "I'm from Dallas, so this heat's rather pleasant."

Stacey nodded, giving Mark a quick glance before returning to the conference room, where the first candidate was being interviewed. The other two, the affable man from Texas and the woman with piercing eyes, returned to their laptops and continued typing. One was a doctoral candidate, Mark had learned. The other spent a decade teaching at international schools in Central and South America.

And here he sat, his resume reading like a greatest hit of professional failures, his outfit too formal for the summer, his brow glistening. Shit, why did he always feel like a kid playing dress-up? Was that how everyone felt?

He tried not to think of what would happen if he didn't get the job. Sure, Stacey had been friendly, but that was before he'd left his class in her care to retrieve his niece from the police. Word which had, of course, made its way back to Neumann Prep.

A niece.

A car in his name.

A home loan and a half dozen financial entanglements.

Christ, he'd never wanted any of this. It was August. He should be on a beach at Costa Brava, or Tenerife, or out on Ibiza with a bellyful of *hierbas ibicencas* and a fire in his veins. He should be waking up hungover while Rosalía cooked eggs.

Rosy. His Spanish apartment. Madrid. It was all so distant now, like he'd stepped into someone else's life.

Then his phone rang.

Zelda.

He hadn't grounded her after the incident, but he'd come pretty damn close. She'd been tiptoeing around him for weeks, eating dinner in her room and doing her best to be invisible. Sometimes he wondered if she was on drugs. Not weed—because that wasn't a drug—but those synthetic ones with names like Sparkle or Brain Wreck or NeoDMT.

God, he was becoming his mother. Was this how it happened?

He answered the phone in a whisper. "What's up?"

"Hey, Uncle Mark," Zelda said. "Sorry to bother you, but... there's something wrong with the bathtub."

"What do you mean?"

"It's weird. Like, it won't shut off."

"Yeah, that happens." He rubbed his temples. There truly was nothing smart about the smart home they owned. It was just a gimmick with expensive sensors and chips. "There's a panel in the wall, near the shower. Shut it off there if the sensor doesn't work."

"I tried that."

"You tried the valve? With the red handle?"

"Yeah, it's horizontal. Horizontal means off, right?"

He visualized it in his head. The pipe running up and down the red handle. "Yeah, it should be facing away. Perpendicular, not parallel."

"It is."

"And there's still water coming out?"

"Yeah."

"That's not possible."

"Well, it's happening. And it's really cold and murky."

Damn. He was going to find that real estate agent Diana and that shady Edward Strathmore. He was going to sic his lawyers on them for selling him a lemon. Or he would if they weren't already focused on mitigating Zelda's legal fallout.

"Mr. Fitzsimmons?"

A pudgy man in a bowtie stood at the door of the conference room. The academic coordinator, shit. He was flanked by the assistant headmaster and Stacey, while the other candidate exited through the back.

"Yes, right here." He realized he was so tense he was hunching over.

"Join us inside when you're ready," the assistant headmaster said.

"Right away." He cupped the phone and closed his eyes, visualizing the house. "Okay, there's a main valve in the basement. If that doesn't work, call a plumber."

"A plumber?"

"I'm sorry, I have to go. I'll be home after the interview."

He ended the call and stood up, his back sticking to the plastic chair. He wiped a damp hand on his pants before offering a handshake to the hiring committee.

Stacey closed the door behind him and gestured to the conference table. "So how's Zelda doing?"

"Oh, she's a teenager, so she's always up to something." He chuckled, perhaps a little too loud. Stacey smiled.

The others did not.

"But she's doing well; thanks for asking," Mark said, adding, "Yep, everything's fine."

CHAPTER FIFTY-FOUR

Zelda was not fine.

She googled the top plumbing service and called them in a panic. The dispatcher assured her they'd have a plumber there within the hour. And yet, the pipes rumbled and the water poured from the showerhead above.

She hurried to the basement, turning the master water valve on and off, on and off. The little light on the digital readout blinked amber. The flow state read *NONE.*

And still it persisted. The rumbling pipes. The distant splash from the shower above.

She returned to the upstairs bathroom, where water gushed from the showerhead and the drain burbled. All she'd wanted to do was rinse off after class. But this water was cold, the occasional muddy lumps drooling from the holes.

The tub was almost full.

Stop it, she told herself. *This isn't your fault.*

She tried not to freak out, but she was making a mess of the house. The murky water couldn't drain fast enough for the flow. It rose higher, higher. Uncle Mark would be furious. Just one more thing on her long list of mistakes.

He'd probably had enough.

He'd probably just leave.

And she probably deserved to end up with her grandparents and their greedy questions. Or in foster care. Or alone.

As the muddy bathwater reached the three-quarter mark, her mind scrambled for answers. *Think. Think...*

Then it came to her, a science experiment in sixth grade. What had they studied? Siphons, right. She couldn't stop the flow, she realized.

But she could redirect it.

Zelda found the garden hose in the yard, curled by the summer squash she'd planted with Uncle Mark. She disconnected the nozzle, dragged the hose upstairs, and found the tub nearly full.

She placed one end into the bathwater.

She jammed the other end into the toilet.

But nothing happened. The shower still poured and the murky water still rose, dripping over the rim in thin, muddy fingers.

"No, c'mon, get in there." Perhaps she needed to straighten the hose, or squeeze it, or somehow—

Suction.

That was it. The siphon needed suction to start. Like those old movies where people sucked gasoline from a car.

"Uck." She pulled the end from the toilet bowl and wiped the hose fitting with a towel. She put her lips on the metal. She sucked in until bubbles rose from the tub. She sucked again, and again, and then a great spray of water burst forth.

Coughing, gagging, she stuffed the hose back into the toilet. For a moment, the bowl's level rose. A flash of that toilet and those red, bloody bubbles. She thought the murky water might keep rising forever.

But it didn't.

The plumbing, the pipes, and gravity all did their work. The water level stabilized as the bathtub drained, down, down...

Zelda took a few deep breaths to congratulate herself. She'd solved a problem, a problem with the house; she had *adulted*. Maybe Uncle Mark would be proud of the solution.

She raised her phone for a selfie. The pouring shower and the brackish tub, the hose and her grimace of disgust. She snapped the photo and added some text: *#homeimprovement.*

A droplet of water landed on the screen.

She wiped it off and swiped to her text messages. Ali and Maura would get a kick out of this.

Another droplet hit her screen.

Odd. She wasn't near the running shower or the tub. She looked up as a third droplet struck her eye.

Her heart sank at what she saw. A ribbon of brackish water traced its way along the ceiling, turning the paint into swollen, dripping blisters. There was some sort of leak from above, growing larger and larger.

"No," she muttered. "No, no, no."

This wasn't her fault; she knew that. But that didn't mean she couldn't get in trouble. Her mind raced for a solution. A bucket? Several? Did they even have any in the house?

The wet ribbon squirmed; the blisters shifted.

Bulge by bulge, they retracted back into the ceiling. The paint flattened as others grew and distended near the door. Button-like, they traced a path into the jamb over the door.

She followed underneath, waiting for the paint blisters to pop and rain filthy water. But they didn't. Instead, they tracked a straight path through the wall, out into the hall ceiling, then turned a sharp right.

As the blisters faded, new ones dotted the way down the hall.

Like they were leading her somewhere.

She hesitated, Ali's words from the hospital scratching at her thoughts. He didn't remember everything that happened, just what he felt. That he thought he'd been hunting for something. But really, something was hunting for him.

Was that what this was?

Maybe. Probably. Yet curiosity gripped her. She followed the blisters to the end of the hall, where the ceiling met the wall. The wet ribbon descended from the high ceiling to eye level and then to the floor. A framed picture of her parents tilted. The blisters stretched and quivered before leaving only a vague dampness behind.

The last blister protruded above the floor and retracted.

And just like that, they were gone.

What the hell was wrong with this house?

Another thought: maybe the blisters weren't done yet. Maybe they were—

She hurried downstairs, taking a left in the kitchen, visualizing where the blisters would travel if they weren't bound by the floor.

She was in the living room when she found it: a single, massive bubble pushing its way out from behind the sweating creme paint.

It was twice the size of her head.

The blister pulsed and descended, settling above the reclaimed wood mantle. Droplets glinted on its surface, dozens of wet beads.

The bulge grew and stretched, pressing against vases and photos, trinkets and mementos. With a clink, a silver picture frame toppled over. A photo of her mother and father, young and in love, long before they became parents and when their smiles seemed impossibly wide. All that she had saved from the old house and set up here now teetered and shifted. She caught the urn as it wobbled and fell from the mantle.

She clutched the photo and the urn, but there was too much else to save. A vase her mom bought in Mexico crashed to the floor. A cube with their pictures laser-etched in 3D fell and cracked on the tiles.

"No, stop it," she said. "Stop it!"

But the wet blister grew, larger and larger, paint thinning as bizarre writing formed in the surface, *scritch, scritch, scritch.*

She recognized the shapes and lines. They were the symbols

etched across Chester's sculptures. Scribbled in mad arcs across newspaper-covered windows. Drawn upon his very skin.

Scritch, scritch, scritch, went the lines on the swelling paint.

Clank, crash, crunch, went the objects falling from the mantle.

Photos and mementos and little figurines. All these treasures she'd saved from her old life—from *before*—they tumbled and fell as the great wet blister pushed its way out from the wall.

"Stop it. Stop it! STOP IT!"

And it stopped. The quivering paint and the bizarre writing inside it. It all stopped for the space of one breath.

There was a face within the blister.

A face pressing itself out from inside the wall.

Its eyes opened, and it saw her.

With a low, wet rumble, the blister finally popped.

In a shudder of collapsing wallboard, dark lumps tumbled from the hole. Frayed paint dripped in ribbons. For a blink, she thought she was watching something like the house purging itself.

Like it was sick.

But it was just dirt, she realized. Mud drooled between studs and rotted insulation. Mud slid down the mantel. And mud fell away from a wooden beam that ran vertical behind the mantel and up into the ceiling.

It reminded her of a bone. The very backbone of the house.

The beam...

There was a similar beam in her bedroom, running up the wall by her bed. And like that beam, there was something here, nearly a half dozen dark letters branded into the wood.

CHIATRIC H SP

She traced those letters as it all clicked into place. She raised her phone and snapped a picture. Then she ran.

Upstairs, she pushed her bed back from the wall, running a

hand along the wooden beam that bisected the wall. Her fingers found the letters.

ITAL FLO R 2

"No," she muttered to herself. It had to be wrong. She snapped another picture.

She thought of the other beams in the house. The old bricks and the windows. All those delightful reclaimed accents the real estate agent had pointed out and her uncle had marveled at.

She found a third beam in his bedroom.

A fourth that crossed the ceiling of the office.

And three wood beams that formed that gorgeous, rustic doorframe between the hallway and the kitchen.

There, at the left side of that frame, faint beneath the topcoat, eleven letters were branded into the wood.

WEST PINE PSY

She snapped a third picture and arranged them on her phone. She only had to fill in two faded letters, both O's, but she already knew what it spelled. Yes, she had sensed it for months. There was something wrong with this house, something wrong with this entire valley.

The words read:

WEST PINE PSYCHIATRIC HOSPITAL FLOOR 2

CHAPTER FIFTY-FIVE

After years of noise at Greywood Bay General Hospital, Samantha Lee enjoyed every quiet minute here at Harbor Home Convalescent. The nurses' station was hers to manage. Although her shift was twelve hours, time went by fast after lunch. Most of the patients had settled in for their naps.

Sure, there were still the occasional frustrations to contend with.

Ms. Thomlinson in room 402 was getting snarky now that her Vicodin was being reduced.

Mrs. Smith in 408 had taken to complaining about the food.

And Mr. Wilson, the burly boomer in 421, was a loud and proud racist. When she changed his catheter, he asked how she could see with squinty eyes. She batted those eyes and smiled and told him it wasn't hard. He didn't have much of anything to look at down there.

He shut up after that.

So here she sat at the nurses' station, listening to the distant soundtrack of cleaning equipment in the long halls. Getting lost in another Adam Nevill book on her Kindle.

She glanced at the monitoring display, a vertical screen that showed the patients' statuses. Their room number and next round, their fall risk and pain medication. And their out-of-bed status. A green horizontal man in bed meant the patient was sleeping. A yellow man meant the patient was up and probably using the restroom.

She noticed a blinking red man on the board now.

Mr. Halgrove in room 444.

Damn. And she was just getting to a good part in the book. She put her Kindle down and walked the quiet hall.

She knew Mr. Halgrove. Or rather, she knew *of* him, like most who grew up in Greywood Bay.

An old creep who lived in the collapsing mansion.

An eccentric sculptor who came from a rich family and never had children.

There were rumors that on nights with no moon, you could hear screams from his house. And that on Halloween, the kids who knocked on his door were never heard from again.

They were just stories, of course.

And yet, when he'd been transferred in, she'd made sure her rounds brought her by his room. She hoped to see the man behind the myths on so many mouths.

What she saw broke her heart.

Chester Halgrove was withered, weak, and in poor mental health. A feral light flickered in his eyes when they were open. When he slept, his lungs rattled. They'd found so much cancer inside him she could hardly believe the X-rays. His chest was like a tired sack of popcorn.

Mostly, he was just another senior who had fallen through the cracks in what America called a healthcare system. The whole thing was a mess.

Stopping outside room 444, she felt a compulsion to apologize to Mr. Halgrove. No man should be made into a monster by the town's cruel rumors.

"Mr. Halgrove? Chester?"

His bed was empty. The bathroom door stood open. She switched the lights on and scanned the four corners. The room was vacant.

Then she saw the flowers and the broken vase on the floor.

She spotted the IV pole on its side in the hall, one of the wheels still spinning. Nearby, she saw the blood.

Hurrying back to the nurses' station, she called Todd at security, who met her outside Mr. Halgrove's room.

"Shit." He eyed the droplets of blood leading down the hall. "Guess the old man went for a stroll."

They put on nitrile gloves, Todd following the trail while Samantha tried not to worry about her job. She'd be in trouble, no doubt. At the very least, she'd have to report it to her supervisor, who'd ask why she never noticed a geriatric leaving his room.

The trail of blood led to the stairs. Todd opened the door and called out, "Mr. Halgrove? Sir? Is that you?"

The droplets gleamed in the stairs and led out the service exit.

There, under the dim lights of the garage, a man shuffled toward the foggy exit ramp. Blood mottled his gown over legs so skinny they hardly looked capable of bearing weight. A foot dragged against the concrete, going *swish, swish, swish*. His left arm swayed and drooped.

But it was what he held in his right hand that caught their attention. Todd and Samantha both saw it at the same time.

"Mr. Halgrove, sir, you need to put that down," Todd said. He raised his walkie-talkie and whispered, "We've got a code gray in the garage. Patient is armed. Repeat, a code gray in the garage."

Samantha froze. For decades, her mind had built this old man up to be the boogeyman himself. But he wasn't. She had to do something.

"Chester? Sir?" she asked. "We don't want to hurt you or anything. We just want to help. Could you... could you please put that down?"

His shuffle slowed. The shard of vase fell from his fingers and clattered to the ground, startling Todd.

But not Samantha. Slowly, she stepped forward. She could see the blood on his collar, his wrist. "Sir, I just want to help."

"Help?" he wheezed. "How can you help? The door's unguarded and her eyes are on us."

Her heart sank when he turned. His face, she thought. What had he done to his face?

"God almighty," Todd muttered.

A sweaty, red mask looked back at them. Chester had carved bizarre symbols into the skin of his forehead, his cheeks, and his chin. Blood dripped down his neck.

"I tried to help," he muttered. "But I can't hold back her storm anymore."

Eyes, she thought. His eyes were no longer feral and fearsome. Instead, they glimmered with sorrow and exhaustion. It was as if two people existed here in the dark garage. One, a man cloaked in decades of madness. And another, someone so sane and aware that his gaze pierced her, and knew her, and shattered her heart.

"You want to help?" he asked. "Then help yourself. You run. Run far away and don't ever look back."

CHAPTER FIFTY-SIX

Driving home, Mark loosened his collar and pulled off his tie. He needed a stiff drink after the interview. The whole thing was a mess.

He'd shown up prepared with lesson plans and ready to discuss his teaching philosophy. He didn't like to lecture. He wasn't a "sage on the stage" or a "mentor in the center." His style of instruction was to be a "guide on the side." This summer's Spanish program was proof that it worked.

Over eight weeks, he'd set his students to tasks in groups and rotated among them, assisting where necessary, offering encouragement and strategy. His results? Not a single failing student in three classes and the best scores of the year. He was proud of his metrics.

But he hadn't been prepared for the committee's critique of his credentials.

No, he didn't have a degree in linguistics or in Spanish or in education.

Yes, he'd been teaching ESL for fifteen years abroad on the back of a master's in business.

But this was Neumann Prep, they said, and the faculty were

held to a higher standard. What had he done to upgrade his skills, his certificates, his publications?

Nothing.

And that was also the chance he gave himself to get this job. A fat fucking zero.

But of course, they were happy to consider his niece for late enrollment if she passed her math class. They were happy to take his money for tuition.

He squeezed the bridge of his nose. He had no idea how any of this was going to work out.

Zelda, shit. He was almost at the liquor store when he remembered her call about the shower that didn't shut off. Would there ever be a day without a crisis? He abandoned the idea of scotch whiskey for now and took a right on Mayacamas Way, skirting the western edge of Raven's Valley. There was the usual bottleneck of traffic at the gate.

A few blocks later, he saw the plumber's van in his driveway.

"Hell of a thing," the man said as he walked Mark through the house's problems. "I'd say the leak's been happening for years, but I know that ain't so. This house was probably just foundation and studs back in January."

"Something like that," Mark said.

When he saw the hole in the living room wall, he simply locked up. His mind had to assemble the damage in pieces. It was like someone had gouged a massive chunk from the wall.

"As for why the valves didn't work, that's a head-scratcher. I even shut it off at the street, but no dice. My guess? There's some second connection that's off the books. Maybe they've got you sharing water with your neighbor. I'd check into that."

Unbelievable, Mark thought. The mantle was covered in filth. The wall ruined. Yeah, insurance would probably cover it, but they'd still have to live with the mess.

And the smell...

He pointed at the brown lumps on the ground. "Is that mud?"

The plumber nudged it with his work boot. “Looks like it.”

“How did mud get inside the wall?”

“Beats me. They put this whole place together in record time, so… it wouldn’t surprise me if a few corners were cut.”

That wasn’t an answer, but Mark sensed it was as good as he would get from the plumber. The man handed him a tablet with the bill totaled up. Emergency call out. Two hours of service. Gratuity. When he saw the amount, he realized he really was in the wrong profession.

“Anytime you need a follow-up, give us a shout.”

Mark signed and tapped his credit card.

“Oh, and that thing your daughter rigged up in the bathroom? That was pretty clever. You got a smart girl on your hands.”

Mark wasn’t sure where Zelda had gone off to. If it was a study group at the library, like her text said, or somewhere else. He wasn’t even sure how much more time they had together. Another hearing loomed in a few weeks. He doubted Judge Fulghum would look favorably on his shaky employment starting this fall.

He spent the next half hour scooping mud into garbage bags, wiping down the mantle, and cleaning the bathroom. With a tired swipe, he removed the last of the dirt from the bathtub.

The dirt.

It catapulted him back to that spring night in Madrid, when he’d returned to his cozy apartment. When he’d found his sister sitting in the ashen waters. What had she said?

“Don’t let them grow maggots in her heart.”

No, he thought.

No, she hadn’t said anything. She’d been a hallucination, a series of misfiring synapses and memories. A coincidence and a coping mechanism he’d imbued with false meaning.

“Stupid, stupid, stupid,” he hissed. “What are you doing, Mark? What the fuck are you actually doing? You can’t do this. You can’t do any of this.”

He buried his head in his hands and squeezed his temples. And then, something happened.

He felt it first in his chest, a deep unraveling, as if he'd been underwater, holding his breath for all of these months and could now surface. His lungs heaved and a deep moan left his throat.

He hadn't cried at the funeral.

He hadn't cried for his lost relationship with Rosalía or the life he'd left back in Spain.

He hadn't even cried for his poor niece and all the wounds and scars that probably mottled her heart.

Because he knew he needed to be strong, to at least appear strong for her. He needed to be a rock.

No, he thought. A lighthouse in her storm.

But he was crying now. And it felt good, this release, this moment he denied himself and pushed away to a dark room in his mind.

He wiped his eyes and sighed. For a moment, he thought he saw a flicker of wet tendrils upon the walls of the house.

As if they were weeping as well.

CHAPTER FIFTY-SEVEN

Google only answered a few of Zelda's questions and her history book on Alder Glen was forty years old. So she sent a message to Maura and Ali, telling them to meet her at the library when they could. She spent the first hour alone, roaming the stacks and digging up books, the smell of mud still in her nose.

At first, she thought she'd made another mistake, come to another hasty conclusion. There wasn't much on West Pine Psychiatric Hospital. All she found were old architectural plans from county records. Or the occasional medical journal referencing some form of treatment. Otherwise, it was like the place didn't exist.

"Well, it did exist," the librarian said, walking Zelda toward the back of the local history section. "Much as the Larchmonts would like to forget everything, that hospital existed."

"Larchmonts?" Zelda tried to keep up. Despite the librarian's age, she moved quickly and with focus.

"You're not from here, are you?"

Zelda shook her head.

"Larchmonts. Strathmores. Cummings. A lot of old timber

and land in this area. Next time you take the crosstown expressway, ask yourself, why's it named after our councilman's family? Or just take a look at the donor list at the front desk."

She stopped at the shelf, fingers dancing across the spines of old books. She pulled two out and continued walking.

"Larchmont's trust probably pays a chunk of my salary. They can bury some of the news out there, but they can't bury the past. Here." She found a third book and handed them over to Zelda. "Good luck on your report."

Ten minutes later, Zelda found it on page 185 of a book dryly titled, *The Kirkbride Plan: Architecture and Mental Health*. Here it was, a black-and-white photo of a sprawling four-floor brick building with steeples: the West Pine Psychiatric Hospital.

It almost looked like a castle.

According to the book, the hospital was built in 1882, one of the last examples of Thomas Story Kirkbride's ambitious design. The ceilings were high and the airflow ample. There was plenty of light and access to nature. The hospital loomed at the end of a long drive beneath the shadow of Lone Pine Mountain, one of the very hills they'd passed on their drive into Greywood Bay.

But she hadn't seen that hospital, had she? No, she remembered every valley and hollow. There was nothing but vineyards and yoga retreats and plenty of farms.

When she opened the second book, she found out why.

And the floor fell out from under her.

"ZELDA, YOU KNOW YOU'RE MY FAVORITE PERSON, right?" Ali slumped into the chair at the reading room's desk. "But I am seriously missing out on some prime Netflix time."

"I thought you were out hunting cyborg werewolves." Maura pulled up a chair. "Trying to grind to level 1000 or whatever."

"I'm kind of done with that game." He glanced at Zelda. "No offense."

"None taken." She turned her phone toward them and swiped through the photos. "So, I found this written on the beams in my house. 'West Pine Psychiatric Hospital Floor 2.'"

Ali and Maura leaned in and squinted.

"Whoa," Maura said. "That's a huge frickin' hole."

"Yeah, and you'd never believe me if I told you what made it." She zoomed in on the beam with the letters inside the wall. "Have either of you found anything like this in your house? Anything at all?"

Maura shook her head but Ali wasn't so certain. His eyes darted about.

"We have a wood countertop in the kitchen," he said. "Last month, I was under the sink getting the trash. It said something, like, 'load-bearing beam, east wing, women's.' Do you think that's the same thing?"

"East wing, women's." Zelda flipped through one of the books. "You mean like this?"

She turned it toward Ali and Maura. Here was a blueprint of the psychiatric hospital, the old brick walls and ample gardens. And there, on one of the hospital's twin wings, was a section labeled *Patient's Quarters - Women*. It was on the east side of the building.

"Hold up," Maura said. "You're saying a piece of this creepy-ass hospital is in Ali's kitchen? Like the sink?"

"It's not the sink; it's the countertop," Ali said. "Oh man, my mom's going to freak. She loves those vintage accents. She polishes them like once a month."

"I don't think it's just the wood," Zelda said. "Look at the windows."

She turned the page to another article, this one from the 1950s. The headline: *Sanitarium Saved; Larchmont Donation Ensures Hospital's Survival.*

Beneath it, a photo showed a wing of the sprawling brick facility. Doctors and staff smiled as they filled the garden, blazers and white jackets gleaming in the light.

"No way." It was Maura's turn to mutter and peer at the picture. "That's the window over our front door. It's just turned sideways."

"Okay, guys, this is seriously messed up," Ali said. "We've got, like, crazy people's wood all up in our houses."

"It's an illness, and they couldn't help it," Zelda said. "Besides, I don't think that explains what I've been seeing."

"Whatever they are, could they just go away?" Ali asked. "Find another place or something."

"I don't think they can find anything," Zelda said. "Because most of them are dead."

Maura scoffed and Ali simply blinked. Zelda knew that reaction. She had the same one thirty minutes earlier, when the librarian took her through the microfilm from the late eighties.

She passed them the first printout, a page from *The Coastal Tribune*, the local paper Uncle Mark sometimes read in the morning.

There, in a bold headline: *Tragedy at West Pine Psych; Mudslide Claims 39 Lives.*

Maura pulled the page toward her and started reading. "In a month, when record rainfalls have turned parched rivers into raging torrents and softened the soil, patients, residents, and workers at West Pine Psychiatric Hospital found themselves awoken on Monday to a fresh horror: the once-steady mountain collapsing and crashing through their very walls."

The mud in the wall, Zelda thought. And the water in the pipes that came from nowhere.

"Okay, is anyone else getting goosebumps?" Ali asked.

"I thought you didn't believe in ghosts," Maura said.

"Psh. Of course not. But seriously, keep reading."

Maura eyed Zelda. "Should I?"

"Turn to the next page and tell me I'm not nuts."

Maura turned the page. Beneath an advertisement for Microsoft Windows 3.1, the headline read, *Trial Turns from Negligence to Homicide; Orderly's Actions Scrutinized; Former Patient Makes Statement.*

Maura cleared her throat. "On Tuesday, a packed courtroom was left stunned when the prosecution laid homicide claims at the foot of Grant Larchmont, twenty-nine, a deceased orderly at West Pine Psychiatric Hospital and grandson of timber magnate Victor Larchmont. Despite the threat of mudslides and an evacuation order, the prosecutors maintain magnetic key logs and computer security records prove Larchmont intentionally led patients to the basement, where he locked and chained the door. Several relatives of the deceased became visibly upset and excused themselves when Larchmont's diary was read to the court. 'Tonight is the night,' he wrote on January 27. 'I will finally do my part and she will do hers. I will..." Maura paused. "I don't like this."

"Dude, keep reading," Ali hissed.

"I will feed her with suffering and fatten her pups, and she will grant me ascension. I will soon shed the frailty of flesh. Together, we will fray the veil between realms. First, the mongrels and fools of wake minds. From their screams I will take new and glorious form."

Ali held out his phone. "That's Larchmont's staff photo. Third hit on image search. Tell me those aren't crazy eyes."

They studied the photo on Ali's screen. A man so ordinary it was like he could have been anyone. A simple buzz cut, a white collared shirt, and a flat smile. But Ali was right about the eyes. Something cruel and broken burned within them.

"I don't know if I want to read any more," Maura said.

"We need to," Zelda said. "We owe it to them."

Maura took a deep breath. "You're right." She scanned down the page to where Zelda tapped. There was a courtroom sketch of a man on the witness stand. He looked oddly familiar. Maura read,

"The prosecution ended their day by calling former patient—*holy shit*—former patient Chester Halgrove to testify."

"Wait, Chester the Molester?" Ali asked. "Our Chester? Crazy old dude?"

"He's not crazy." Zelda gave Ali's leg a kick beneath the table. "Keep reading."

Maura swallowed. "Mr. Halgrove claimed he had warned the staff of an impending disaster. He had raised concerns about Larchmont on multiple occasions. On cross-examination, the defense pointed out that Mr. Halgrove was a patient with a known history of psychosis and substance abuse. Prior to self-admission at West Pine, he ran a psychic and spiritual retreat center with his twin sister, Mabel."

"Whoa, Chester has a twin sister," Ali said. "So here's the plan: we get in contact with her, she comes and waves some incense and does her ghost busting. We're golden, right?"

"That's what I thought," Zelda said. "But she died almost fourteen years ago."

"Get this." Maura ran her index finger down the page. "Two weeks after the tragedy at West Pine Hospital," she read, "a body was discovered along Eel River. Authorities struggled to identify the deceased due to its condition and absence of teeth, until an autopsy found them in his stomach. Using dental impressions, the corpse was confirmed to be that of Grant Larchmont. The wounds were determined to be self-inflicted."

Ali shuddered at the mention of teeth.

"Something bad is going to happen," Zelda said. "I think that's what they're warning me about. Something we need to stop."

"How?" Ali asked. "We can't just, like, move out. My parents'll never believe me. And besides, they love that house."

Zelda blinked. "No, not without proof."

CHAPTER FIFTY-EIGHT

So much to do and so little time, Lloyd thought as he turned up the stereo. Kenny Rogers's husky voice filled the car, singing "She Believes in Me." Lloyd sang along.

And it was true: she believed in him, too. Believed deeply and would reward the deeds done in her name. But first, he needed to help her gather strength.

He guided the pickup off the freeway and checked the dashboard GPS. Darling Gardens, California, just another cow town off the interstate. There wasn't much here but car dealerships and stockyards and the stench of manure for miles.

But Darling Gardens was home to a state university, his former. Although Lloyd had only attended for a semester and a half, he liked to think that in another life, in another timeline, there was a version of him who had taken a different path.

A version that hadn't pledged a fraternity just to make a few friends.

A version that hadn't walked upon Lake Shauvason in the winter.

A version that hadn't plunged through the ice.

But Lloyd was glad he wasn't that version. His descent had

given him a glimpse of ascension. His fall had been an opportunity to meet *her*. And yeah, she believed in him. It was good that someone finally did.

Cruising past the university gate and the fountain, he wondered about the fraternity.

Had T.J. become a full brother?

Had Tyron made it through hell week?

Perhaps in that other life they were all sharing beers now, sitting on the porch of Omega Epsilon. Lloyd closed his eyes and imagined that moment.

Then the pickup hit the rumble strips and his eyes jolted open.

No, this was his life, an end to the old one and soon a new beginning. He had so much to do.

The Altadena Gardens were easy to find. The bland apartments were a decompression chamber between college and careers, a waystation for recent graduates and young professionals. Several of the Omega Epsilon brothers moved there after leaving the house. A quick internet search revealed his pledge trainer was no different.

Heart beating and hands clammy, Lloyd walked through the complex. The sun was low, the dappled light through the palms burning his eyes. He found the unit.

He knocked three times on the door and waited. He knocked again.

When the door opened, Lloyd's mind seized and sputtered. Wordlessly, he stared at someone whom he last saw in the hospital. A young man begging Lloyd not to press charges for a prank that had gone wrong.

"Holy shit," Sir Mister Dawson Sir said as the beer bottle nearly fell from his fingers. "Lloyd... Come on in."

As pledges, Lloyd and his brothers had never been allowed to look Sir Mister Dawson Sir in the eyes. He had been a form living at the edge of perception, always yelling instructions or quizzing them on the Greek alphabet and the brotherhood's rules. In the months since, Lloyd's imagination had turned their pledge trainer into a foggy golem, huge and vaporous.

But Nick Dawson was just a regular young man, twenty-three with a slight paunch from years of keggers. He looked like he was trying to grow out a mustache and failing. Lloyd almost felt bad for the guy.

He almost lost his nerve.

"Please, come in." Nick gestured to the warm apartment. There was a TV on and a ratty couch. A bong stood on a coffee table beside an Xbox controller and a bowl of pretzels.

"I would, but... Well, I don't have much time. I just needed to stop by."

"Yeah, no worries. Man, listen, Lloyd..." Nick scratched his cheek. It was weird how different he sounded when he wasn't yelling through a bullhorn. "I'm sorry about what happened. Really. I mean, we pushed it. I pushed you all way too far. Sometimes... Well, sometimes people get sucked into things they don't know how to get out of. The older bros gave me shit, saying I was too light on y'all. That they had it hard, so... Well, that explains it, but it doesn't excuse it. Lloyd, I am truly sorry for what I put you through."

Lloyd was studying his own shoes when a droplet of rain hit the pavement. No, he realized. It was a tear. He was crying.

Because he'd needed to hear this for too long.

"Hey, you sure you can't come in?" His former pledge trainer put a hand on Lloyd's shoulder. "Do you have somewhere you need to be?"

"Yeah," Lloyd said. "We both do."

It was remarkable how easily the knife slid in beneath Nick's jaw. Seven inches of 1095 carbon steel did its job in less than a second, piercing skin and soft palate, tongue and bone. The guard clacked against his chin as the blade buried itself behind his nasal cavity. With a crunch, Lloyd twisted the handle. One of Nick's disbelieving eyes bulged as pink foam drooled from his mouth.

Lloyd lashed out a hand and clamped his pledge trainer's lips shut. No more orders to carry eggs over icy lakes would ever be shouted. No more insults would leave these heaving lungs.

With a shove, his pledge trainer's legs simply folded, and they both spilled into the apartment. Rosy tears filled his blinking eyes. His hand clamped Lloyd's wrist and squeezed.

And yet, it was soon over, just like she had promised. It amazed Lloyd how much blood an artery could produce and how bright it all was. No one would have believed it.

He wiped the knife on Nick's shirt, leaving his former pledge trainer to the encroaching shadows, just as he'd once left Lloyd to the cold depths of a lake.

But not alone.

Lloyd sensed her pups scratching their way through the veil, hungry and grateful. Black tendrils descended. Ravenous forms danced at the edge of his vision.

He closed the door.

He was in the parking lot when the shakes overtook him. He gripped the pickup's hood as his body convulsed. He'd done it, yes. He'd struck true, just like she'd asked.

And he felt... What did he feel in this moment?

Alive. Yes, for the first time, he was alive and in charge. If he could take justice into his hands, what else could he do? What else could he become?

Her emissary.

Ascension.

Yes, so much to do and such little time.

He took out Randall's keyring and found the one for the storage locker. He tucked it into his shirt pocket, close to his heart. This was it, his final drive.

But he still needed to make a few stops on his way home.

CHAPTER FIFTY-NINE

Edward Strathmore IV should have been on his second course and third cocktail to celebrate the closing of another deal for Strathmore & Daniels. It was six o'clock, and the maître d' at Chalamar always held his table until eight. They should all be toasting to an incredible new year.

But here he was, elbow deep in the paperwork to get Hawk's Hollow on the books before the close of the fiscal year. Accountants always had such frustrating demands.

He studied his computer screen and scrolled through the spreadsheet. If he moved a few deposits here and wrote off some losses there, he could sweeten the books. And to think some people claimed business wasn't creative. With a click, he moved another house from the *Open* column to the *Reserved*, remembering that he owed the councilman's daughter a favor.

He was about to call Jeanette in to order some takeout when he saw the kids through the glass wall of his office. They were talking to his assistant.

And now she was walking them to his door. What the hell was going on?

Jeanette entered and tried to shut the door, but the three kids pushed in behind her. He recognized them, especially the skinny girl with the hoodie and ripped sleeves. Yes, he'd been there when Diana sold them the last house in Raven's Valley.

"Mr. Strathmore, sir… They insist on talking to you about something urgent."

Edward glanced from Jeanette to the teenagers at the door. He liked kids. But he didn't like being barged in on and put on the spot. "Okay, so what's this about?"

Jeanette leaned in and whispered, "West Pine Hospital. They *know*."

Something loosened in his gut. He was no longer hungry and his corner office no longer felt large. He forced his best salesman's smile to his lips and studied the trio. "Jeanette, would you bring our guests something to drink? You kids like sodas?"

The girl with broad shoulders crossed her arms. "What did you build our houses with?"

Jeanette lingered by the door, but Edward waved her off. With a twist of the rod, he closed the blinds. "Maura, is it? Your dad teaches at the university. We had a luncheon together in the winter. Sharp guy. I'm glad to see his daughter's just as smart."

"That didn't answer the question," the boy said.

"And Ali, I remember the day your family toured that house. You were one of our first clients. I'm glad we were able to help your parents find a forever home, even if they didn't quite have the credit. I don't think I've seen anyone happier than your mom when we gave her the keys. I heard about the incident in the junkyard. I'm glad that you're safe; that must've been quite a trauma. What a brave kid. All of you, three smart, brave kids."

"Threaten him again," Zelda said, "and this'll be on the internet in minutes."

She held out her phone. It took his mind a moment to assemble the three photos on the screen. She'd cropped them, zoomed in on the wood beams, and there were the words:

WEST PINE PSYCHIATRIC HOSPITAL FLOOR 2

Christ, this was worse than he'd thought. It wasn't just a rumor or an accusation; they had actual proof. Fucking Larry Larchmont. He'd told the idiot to sand down every board, brick, and beam.

Game face, Eddie.

"I know what this probably looks like, but trust me, it's all perfectly normal. That lumber has been tested and passed rigorous structural certification. Besides, it's gorgeous. You know how hard it is to source century redwood?"

"Normal?" Zelda asked. "There's nothing normal about what happened at that hospital."

Edward wiped a scuff off his desk. "You read about that, huh?"

"Read about it. Heard it. I've seen it with my eyes. The walls are leaking mud and something's scratching to get out. You sold haunted houses to people."

Edward blinked and tried to keep it in, but the chuckle exploded from his throat. "Hold on. First off, less than fifteen percent of the materials even came from that hospital. And second, haunted? Seriously? Don't be silly. This isn't Scooby Doo—"

"It's not silly," Ali said. "There's something wrong and you know it."

Edward took a breath. Damn, his stomach had turned sour. "I admit, there are still bugs in the systems. Smart homes aren't always that smart."

Zelda said, "He wasn't talking about the stupid app to dim the lights. He's talking about what's inside the walls."

"It's just wood and brick, okay? Upcycled and green-certified."

"Oh? Then you won't mind if we show everyone."

"Wait, hold on." These kids, they really had him on defense. If this got out, it could ruin things. Hell, he could kiss Hawk's Hollow goodbye. He squeezed his chair's armrest to steady his thoughts. "Okay, look, what do you want? Some video games or bitcoin or..." He opened his drawer and searched through the envelopes. "I've got some Apple gift cards somewhere. Just... give me a moment."

Zelda scooted her chair up to his desk. "You're seriously trying to bribe us?"

"Bribe? Nobody *bribes*. We're doing business. Negotiating. Coming to an arrangement. One second..." He pressed the intercom on his phone. "Jeanette, do we have any more of those movie passes?"

"Umm—"

Maura reached across his desk and hung up his phone.

"Hey, c'mon..."

"Why?" she asked.

"Everyone likes movies, right? You won't ever have to pay again. I can get you—"

"No. Why did you do it?" she asked. "Are you trying to kill us or what?"

Again, Edward found laughter flying past his lips. "You... You're serious. Why would I want to do that?"

Zelda said, "Grant Larchmont."

Edward blinked. "What about him?"

"He locked the patients in the basement before the mudslide. He knew it was coming. Thirty-nine people died because of him."

A brief flash of Larry's cousin Grant, from the papers. Edward had been a teenager, probably their age when it all happened. "Yeah, right, he went crazy. I'm sorry, but you're losing me. What does he have to do with any of this?"

Ali stared at him. "You're picking up where he left off, aren't you?"

Total silence. Edward wasn't even sure he'd heard it right. But judging by their flat expressions and serious glares, he had.

The laughter burst forth from deep inside his chest. He couldn't help it. The idea was so totally insane it split his ribs and put a stitch in his side. He held a hand out, begging them for a moment to catch his breath.

"Hold on... Hold on.... That's really something. H'okay. You... You kids think I... what? I reassembled pieces of the hospital to carry out some dead nutjob's work? Seriously?"

Their expressions told him that's exactly what they thought. And their nervous glances to each other told him they were having doubts.

Maybe that's what this really was. Not a rouse for cash or a shakedown for favors. Not some way to hold sway over him for years down the line. Jesus, he'd been swimming with sharks for too long. This wasn't blackmail. These were just kids with time on their hands and more imagination than sense.

A fucking Scooby Doo adventure indeed.

"Guys, I'm a businessman, okay? The last thing I want to do is piss off my clients: your parents."

"But... then, why'd you do it?" Zelda asked. "Why use all the stuff from the hospital?"

Edward tilted his head. He had to reach far back to remember a time when he'd been so naïve. In a way, he pitied these kids. "Houses need to be built with something, right? Most of all, I could get it for cheap. It's really that simple."

CHAPTER SIXTY

When Randall's car-tracking app pinged his phone for the first time, he was curious. There it was, his Ford F150, about twenty miles away from where he'd told Lloyd to deliver the rugs. So, the kid really was taking his sweet time.

An hour later, it pinged him again. Lloyd was on the interstate now, heading west out of Darling Gardens, fifty miles to the east. The guys at the auto shop had been right: this tracker worked well. He couldn't wait to hear the little shit's excuses when he got home.

"See? I fuckin' knew it," he told Diana, who was unloading the dishwasher. "That your son's taking my car for a joyride."

The glasses clinked as she shelved them. "I thought it was the company's car."

"Yeah, well, it's my name on the insurance. My responsibility."

"Then why is he delivering your rugs?"

Randall blinked. "Because he's earning his keep. There's no free rides in life; he needs to learn that."

She placed the last of the bowls on the shelf and closed the cupboard door, hard. "Is that what your parents taught you, Randy?"

"Those're the facts, Diana. I'm trying to help the boy, toughen him up. You're just making him soft."

"Sometimes it seems like you're trying to drive him away."

Randy's tongue circled his teeth. Yeah, she was right, in a way, but he'd never admit it. The happiest he'd ever been was the six months Lloyd was off at school. He'd had the house to himself. And Diana as well.

"Maybe if you didn't feather his nest, he'd be able to fly on his own."

"He's kind and he helps out around the house." She tossed the sponge in the sink. "Besides, I like having him around."

"You like having him around," Randy repeated. He poured himself some water, giving the fridge an extra nudge when it rumbled. "More than you like being around me?"

"It's not a competition."

Yeah, maybe it wasn't to her or to Lloyd, Randy thought. But to him it sure was. Attention could only be split so many ways.

She checked her watch. "Anyhow, I'm going to be late for my meeting. I'll take the Chevy."

Sighing, she fetched the keys from the table by the door. For a moment, she lingered there in the evening light. Her hair all done up for the Woman's Club. Her coral-pink blazer and that fancy purse he'd bought her on the cruise they'd taken last spring. She looked both beautiful and exhausted.

Hell, was he the one wearing the whole family out?

"What?" she asked.

"Nothing," he said. "It's just... You sure look pretty. That's all."

She blushed and gave a dismissive wave of her hand.

Then she left.

Maybe she was right, Randy supposed. He'd been wound up something fierce since that Taser incident and his suspension. Sure, the preliminary investigation had cleared him, but it still stung. All those screaming housewives at the tennis court calling his use of force "excessive."

Perhaps he should cut the kid some slack. Perhaps that might bring a little cohesion to the house. He wasn't a bad kid, his stepson. Just different in a way Randy didn't know how to connect with.

And he thought about this for thirty minutes.

Until he found the dead bird.

It was the smell that tipped Randy off. A sweet and sour reek, just like the streets of Ramadi, where old dogs lay dead in the dust and the heat. There was no heat down here in the basement, but there was plenty of dust. He was looking for that bottle of wine he'd hidden for a special occasion, tucked away in the crawlspace between the floorboards and the foundation. He thought he might just surprise Diana when she returned from her meeting.

His elbow bumped the cooler, the first whiff filled his nose, and he gagged. Leaning closer, he smelled death seeping from inside the box. The zip tie sealing the latch piqued his curiosity.

He found scissors, clipped the zip tie, and opened the cooler. He choked back his vomit.

The first thing he saw was the black feathers. A crow stared back through thin plastic with dry, milky eyes. Using a pair of barbecue tongs, he lifted the bag.

His horrors multiplied.

Dozens of clear bags sat stacked, like meat in some freezer. A cat. An opossum. A group of small feeder mice all huddled together. Brittle spiders and flies, dried worms and fish, they all lay in little plastic prisons. His mind reeled as the full depths of Lloyd's collection became clear.

And there, near the bottom, was that marble starfish.

Randy knew it. He *fucking* knew it.

Balling his fists, he closed the cooler and slid it back into the crawlspace. He needed a drink—or several. He reached for the wine bottle, surprised to find it'd slid further in. Funny, he didn't remember hearing it clink. But he was so wrapped up in his psychopathic stepson's box of horrors that he could've missed the end of the world. He stretched his hand into the shadows.

For a moment, the crawlspace seemed to glisten. Had something just dripped down from the floorboards? Were those teeth protruding from the concrete?

No. Don't be silly, Randy. *They're just shadows.*

And yet, the harder he stretched, the narrower the crawlspace seemed to get. Like it was compressing and darkening and... moistening. He could see the wine bottle on its side, resting beside what he had thought was a stack of flat cardboard.

But now, it almost looked like a tongue.

And the smell... God, the reek his stepson had made. He'd show this cooler to Diana the minute she was home. He'd make sure they had Lloyd committed. He'd sign him over himself.

"Fine." Randy retracted his arm.

Then he saw the piece of torn paper.

It jutted from between a stack of boxes, a torn chunk of some old poster as long as his hand. The cut face of a man peered back, some old-timey magician with a turban and a dark eye that seemed to track Randy as he moved. He lifted that piece of poster up to the light.

The magician's eye gave him a wink.

Randy felt the blade enter his back just below the shoulder and puncture something deep inside. His breath hissed and caught in his chest.

He felt the second and the third stab, but then nothing beyond. Searing light flashed, and the basement collapsed and rushed up to his face.

No, he realized numbly. He'd fallen onto the floor. Cold concrete pressed against his cheek while his arms twitched and flapped.

But his legs... His fucking *legs*. Why couldn't he feel them?

"Oh wow," said a voice above him that he distantly recognized as his stepson. "I think I just cut your spinal cord."

Lloyd bent down until his face took up Randy's field of view. He tried to push himself off the ground, but his arms weren't obeying. And each breath... Had it always been so hard to get air?

"Sorry, but it looks like your days of walking are over," Lloyd said. He held the Ka-Bar knife that Randy recognized. Was that his own blood darkening the blade?

"You motherfucker," Randy spat, but it came out as, "*You... mumma... fugga.*"

Lloyd wiped the blade on his jeans. "Technically, you are. Or you *were*, since those days are over, too."

Randy willed his arms to grab his stepson, to throttle him and really ring his bell. Instead, Lloyd swatted them away. There was a dark strength to him now, like he had two sets of eyes.

Lloyd reached into Randy's pocket and pulled out his phone. "I need your passcode. And the password to that stupid security alert thing."

"Fuck... you," Randy rasped. Again, he tried pushing himself off the ground, but his limbs were like wet noodles. That little fuck really had broken his back.

He felt the panic rising now, each breath burning worse than the last. His heart drummed deep in his tight ribs.

"Randall, I'm going to ask again. What's your passcode? What's the password to send a security alert?"

"Call... ambulance... Can't... breathe."

Lloyd sighed. "Very well."

He bent down and dug his hands under Randy's armpits. Grunting, he hoisted him up against the wall. Sweat bloomed on Lloyd's face. There was such strength to him, Randy realized. Not of muscle or might, but of some dark will to do such terrible deeds.

When Randy realized what was happening, his raspy gasps turned to pleas. "No... No no no, don't put me in there."

Lloyd slid him toward the crawlspace.

"Please... Please call... ambulance."

"Your phone passcode. Your security password."

Randy was on his back now, staring upside down as Lloyd shoved him further into the crawlspace and the thickening shadows.

And that *stench*. It was all over him now. A rot so pungent his eyes watered and he coughed with each biting breath.

"Okay... Okay..."

He told Lloyd everything. That he was sorry for being such a prick. He gave him the passcode to his phone and the password to the security app. He would tell him his darkest secrets just to make it all stop.

"Ambulance," Randy muttered. "I can't feel... anything."

"First, I want to tell you something. I want to tell you about the bombing of Dresden in World War Two. Did you know the Allied planes targeted specific locations to maximize the spread of their incendiary bombs? The wind patterns, the wood structures, even the topography. It's quite remarkable how they planned the fire. They even—"

Randy couldn't stand it any longer. The kid's mad rambling, the hitch in his throat. "Help... please... Help me."

"I'm trying to." Lloyd closed his eyes and ran a hand through his oily hair. "Ah, forget it. You wouldn't understand. The important thing is, I'm making myself useful, Randall; I'm helping you out."

With a final push, he hoisted Randy's limp legs into the crawlspace, entombing him here among the darkness of the house's foundation.

"Well, I guess this is it. I'm going to get going now—"

"Wait... wait..." Randy grunted. "Please... Please don't leave me... alone."

Lloyd smiled. And when he did, it seemed like something else was smiling through him, behind him, beyond. "But you're not."

Lloyd was no longer touching him. And yet somehow, Randy

was moving. He willed his neck to bend and look down past unfeeling legs.

A muddy hand gripped his numb ankle. A second muddy arm stretched out from the deep bowels of the house, teeth glistening on its fingers.

With a *scroosh* of dust beneath his back, they tugged Randy deeper into the crawlspace, deeper into the devouring shadows. Eyes of black violet opened amongst the woodwork and brick.

He screamed husky screams until his lungs could no longer hold breath. Until his heart slowed in his chest. *Lub dub. Lub... dub... Lub...*

There were worse things than a lazy stepson, he realized as the crawlspace stretched out, unbearably vast. Worse things indeed.

There were beasts of six legs, their mouths a cavern of knives. Drooling and gnashing, waiting as...

Lub... dub... lub...

And then it came, his last breath, and with it, the beasts pounced.

CHAPTER SIXTY-ONE

Visiting hours were over, the nurse informed them. And besides, Mr. Halgrove was in no shape to meet with three kids who weren't immediate family or friends. She pointed them to the exit, where a lonely patient in a wheelchair smoked a cigarette in the foggy evening.

But Zelda wasn't taking no for an answer.

"I can't believe we're doing this," Ali muttered as they convened near the vending machines. "I'm going to get grounded for life."

"It's physics," Maura said. "And you're the fastest. Just make one lap around the floor."

"Then drop it by the door and keep running," Zelda added.

Ali took a deep breath. "You sure we need to do this?"

Zelda and Maura studied each other. No, they weren't sure. In fact, Zelda wasn't sure about anything lately. The dreams half remembered that felt more like warnings. The shadows that lurked in the corners of her eyes. The whispering fear in the back of her thoughts: something terrible was coming for them all.

And yeah, maybe she was going totally crazy. But Mrs. Saperstein's words still echoed in her mind. "There are two forces in motion... One, who will bring suffering... And one, who can bring souls to the light."

Zelda had thought Chester Halgrove was the former. But maybe she was wrong about him. Maybe they all were.

"Okay," Ali said. "Showtime."

They waited in the alcove at the end of the hall. Across the way, the recreation room's TV buzzed out the evening news. Ali walked past with his hands in his pockets. Around the corner, he came to the nurses' station, whistling to himself like he was out for a stroll.

The nurse raised her eyes from the charts. "I thought I told you—"

In one quick gesture, Ali grabbed a clipboard from a drop box above the counter. Then he was off, a mad dash of swinging arms, scrambling legs, and shoes squeaking on the shiny floor.

"Hey! Hey! Get back here!"

The nurse raced out from the station, around the corner, and down the hall. She moved shockingly quick. Ali was in trouble.

"Here we go," Maura said.

Keeping low, they crept past the nurses' station, past quiet rooms. They could hear Ali and the nurse far off, followed by the sound of someone cheering and clapping.

Room 444 loomed in a dim corner. Dark, not because of the lighting or windows, but because of the waves of black violet pulsing out from the center. And from the old man in bed.

"Is it just me, or is the room cold?" Maura asked.

Zelda didn't answer. Her friend couldn't see what they were truly entering: a cave where warmth and light slowly died.

There in the center, like the silent eye of a midnight tempest, lay Mr. Halgrove. His face was a pathway of red wounds and stitches. Velcro restraints bound his wrists to the bed. With a low sigh, his head turned toward them and his gaze settled on Zelda. A tear rolled down his cheek.

"You got my message," he muttered. "I'm afraid... I owe you an apology."

"Me?" She wasn't even sure how he knew her name until she remembered the letter. "No, sir, you really don't. I'm sorry that I put you here."

"Here?" He gave his restraints a weak tap against the bedrails. "I'm safe here. Protected." He gestured with his thumbs to his face and the symbols still raw in his skin. "It's the end of my watch, I'm afraid. For decades, I've stood under her glare. You can see it, can't you? This dark scar it leaves upon us."

He raised bound hands, palm gesturing to the black-violet shadows blooming upon every inch of the room. The sheets and the blinds, the walls and the floor. Even their skin leaked tendrils of darkness. She envied Maura, who saw none of it. Ignorance really was bliss.

"Yeah," Zelda said. "I can see it."

He coughed. "It weighs... so much."

"Mr. Halgrove, sir," Maura said. "We know about the hospital in West Pine. You tried to warn them, didn't you? And nobody listened."

Zelda felt stronger to have her friend here by her side. She found Maura's hand and squeezed it.

"West Pine." He closed his eyes. "I think I died on that night and this broken mind is my penance. I couldn't stop it then. I can't stop her now."

"Stop what?"

"Her harvest of sorrow."

Zelda swallowed. "Who is she?"

He gave a weak tilt of his chin toward the table, where a bottle of water sat next to a straw. She unscrewed the cap, put the straw in, and brought it to his dry, grateful lips. He took several weak sips and coughed, so wet and raspy she worried he might choke.

"Sorry," he said. "Getting old is easy. It's being old that's hard. Time has a way of... slipping around, and I forget where I am."

"You're here, Mr. Halgrove. You're safe. You were going to tell us—"

"Her name, right." His lips stretched and his jaw loosened. "She's taken many faces and names, none that our tongues can do justice. J'harr. The Dead Star. Xooloocotiq'r. She-Who-Consumes."

"Damn," Maura said. "So, what is she? Like a ghost, or…?"

He coughed and shook his head at the question. Because she wasn't a ghost or a ghoul or something that went bump in the night. Zelda understood this. She was an entity, a thing no more comprehensible to a human mind than the stars were to a flea.

"Unending hunger and unquenchable thirst." His tired eyes settled upon Zelda. "She is spite for all sentient life. You can feel her dark glare upon us."

Zelda nodded. "Why me? Why can we see these things?"

He smiled the saddest smile she'd ever seen. It was the smile of bad news being broken. "Because we stood in her way. Somehow, somewhere, you've made a stand."

"That's not fair. It's not…" Zelda hesitated. "I don't even know her."

"Fair? No. Not for us. For us, time is linear. But for her, it's an infinite sea. And she senses your presence, like a body senses infection. She's scouring, and that's all that matters. When your mind collapses and your heart's filled with maggots, then, and only then, will you understand 'fair' isn't a word that she knows."

Something squeaked and clattered down the hall. Maura whispered, "We should leave."

But Zelda wasn't going anywhere, not until she had more answers. She drew closer to Mr. Halgrove. "How do we stop her?"

Again, that sad light glistened in his eyes and wrinkled his ruined cheeks. "I was afraid that's what you'd ask."

His right hand shot out and latched onto her thin wrist. Scabby fingers dug in. She pulled back on reflex but his grip was impossibly tight.

"Her new emissary is nearly ascended and their plans are in motion. He'll take form, not in rain or in mud, but something new and… warm. We're too weak without—"

Bright light filled the room. The door opened and the scowling nurse entered, a wiry security guard looming behind her.

"Well, now it makes sense," the nurse said. "You two can join your friend. I'm sure the cops will love to hear your excuse."

"Wait." Zelda leaned close to Mr. Halgrove. "How? How can we help?"

"All right, let's go, ladies." The security guard put a hand on Zelda's shoulder. But only for a second.

Zelda had seen Maura practice her wrestling moves and jiujitsu locks on Ali all summer. She had always wondered, would they work on an adult?

It turned out they really did.

With a quick pivot, Maura stepped inside the guard's grab. She twisted his wrist and gave an upward shove of her arm. Just simple physics. Suddenly, the security guard was down on his knees and groaning, his right arm raised like he was asking a question. His left hand swatted across his body, trying to free it from the girl latched to his wrist.

Zelda pulled her jaw from the floor. While the nurse and the security guard shouted at Maura, Mr. Halgrove gestured Zelda closer. He stretched his neck and whispered into her ears.

What he said made little sense.

"I've set it all up, but they need a connection. I'll reach into the Nether and call them from death, but they need the warm touch of life. Honor them…"

Then the guard broke free from Maura's grip. The nurse was on Zelda, tugging her away from the bed, away from that room full of shadows and the man at the center. "Honor their memories," he shouted. "And ask for their help."

CHAPTER SIXTY-TWO

Mark had a lot of respect for Stacey Layne. She was a hard worker and ran a hell of a summer program. The students all liked her. Most of all, she was a straight shooter; she knew how to break the bad news.

Which was why they were having dinner at Tamagasi, the new fusion sushi place downtown. As their plates arrived, he separated his chopsticks while she mixed soy sauce and wasabi. He braced for the worst.

"So, the interview," she said. "How'd you think it went?"

"Not bad for a public execution." He dipped his tuna roll in the soy sauce and savored the taste. At least the sushi was good.

"Yeah, that's James for you," she said. "I've met sledgehammers with a softer touch."

For a moment, they just ate in silence, Mark with his sushi rolls, Stacey with her sashimi and edamame.

He said, "Look, I really appreciate you pulling for me. I do. I just... I can read the writing on the wall. That guy from Texas has like three books to his name."

Stacey nodded. "I know you worked hard on your lesson plans."

"It would have been nice to go over them for more than two minutes." He regretted the words the moment they left his lips; he hadn't meant to sound so bitter. While Stacey added ginger to her salmon, he studied the cocktail pamphlet. "Anyway, I need a stiff drink. What can I get you?"

"Nothing." For a moment, she stiffened and her eyes flicked down past her plate. Then, "Actually, would you mind holding off on that drink?"

Mark blinked. He wasn't sure what she meant.

"I'm in recovery," she said. "Nine months, knock on wood." She rapped her knuckles on the table. "And today's been a tough one."

"Oh." He didn't know what to say to that. Congratulations? My condolences? He was flattered that she trusted him enough to bring it up. "Yeah, no worries."

"I mean, if you want a drink, go ahead—"

"Actually, green tea would do me some good," he said. "I'm fine."

But he wasn't fine. He'd had the shakes all afternoon. He didn't just *want* to get drunk; he *needed* it. He needed to feel warm. He needed to forget.

Forget his responsibility to his sister and his niece.

Forget the interview that he'd bombed.

Most of all, he wanted to forget himself. This suit that he wore and these ambitions he held, they weren't him. He was a professional faker, a fraud. Who the hell was he fooling?

Stacey sipped her miso soup and wiped her lips. "So, I was thinking... There may be another play we could make. I could—"

His phone buzzed. He went to silence it, but the caller ID stopped his hand.

Greywood Bay Police.

His world tilted. "I'm sorry," he said, and raised the phone to his ear. "I need to take this call."

FORTY-FIVE MINUTES LATER, HE STORMED ACROSS THE underground parking lot, heading back to the car as Zelda quietly followed. They were getting to know the police station by now: the parking spots closest to the stairs, which elevator to take up, which exit to use to avoid the curious eyes in the lobby. He could feel his teeth grinding.

"It's not fair," Zelda said. "They made it seem worse than it was."

"Worse?" His blood boiled. "This is the second time in a month I've had to pick you up from this place. They know you. If that prosecutor presses charges, you'll have a criminal record. Think about that."

"I'm just trying to help—"

"Stop! Just..." His voice echoed in the cavernous quiet. "Stop trying to help, okay? Stop trying to do anything other than just staying out of trouble and finishing your class. Can you do that? Yes or no?"

Beneath the lights of the parking garage, her eyes glimmered like wet marbles. She whispered, "Something bad is going to happen."

"No, something bad *is* happening. It's called juvie. It's called a judge and some lawyers choosing where you grow up. Is that what you want, Zelda? Huh?"

"It's what you want."

For a moment, he didn't quite know how to respond. The words died somewhere between his mind and his mouth. He swallowed the lump in his throat and asked, "Is that seriously what you think?"

"I'm not stupid, Uncle Mark. I heard you talking on the phone. Saying, like, that you missed your girlfriend Rosalita. That you wanted to get back. And that things were, like, so much harder in America."

"Rosalía," he corrected. "And she's not my girlfriend."

A car cruised by. For a moment, neither of them said anything. She just stared at her shoes while he searched for the right words.

"That was the other night, wasn't it?" he asked. "I was in the backyard and you heard it."

"I wasn't snooping. You just talk loud when you drink."

He winced. Of course, he remembered the call. Rosy had told him to find someone else to manage renting out his apartment. So he had. He'd hired them within a day. Then she'd called back later to call him all sorts of words, none of them nice.

"Yeah, things are different here," he said, "and I'm learning that. And yeah, sometimes I miss my friends in Spain. I won't lie to you, Zelda. This wasn't how I saw my forties panning out—"

"Then leave. Just get it over with and go."

Her eyes hardened, yet her lip quivered. She crossed her arms, shrinking inside that ratty hoodie with its thumbholes. Maybe she was trying to appear strong, but all it did was highlight how awkward she was in her own skin. God, he'd really forgotten those days.

"Seriously?" Silence passed for a moment. He asked, "Do you want me to leave?"

She said nothing.

He repeated, "Do you want me to leave?"

"Everyone always leaves," she muttered.

"What are you talking about?"

"That's what people do." Another beat of silence. Then, "Even my parents... They were leaving each other."

There it was. She knew. Mark felt something shift deep inside him and wondered if it was another part of his heart breaking for his niece. Divorce wasn't the end of the world; he knew this and lived through it. And yet, for a kid at her age with a near-perfect family, it must have felt like the end of hers.

"I'm sorry, Zelda. That sucks, I know. But it doesn't mean they were going to leave you."

"Yeah, but they still did."

He put his hand on her shoulder. Outside of a few high-fives and some playful teasing, this was one of the few times they'd touched since the funeral. He worried she might recoil. "Listen: I won't leave you. Not if you don't want me to. Not ever, okay?"

He sensed her locking up and retreating deep inside. Then a tear streamed down her cheek and her posture softened. She did something that surprised him.

She leaned in and hugged him.

Wrapped those skinny arms around him and pressed that baggy hoodie against him. Pushed her forehead against his shoulder. And squeezed while trying to hide her sobs.

"Why are you still here?" she whispered.

Because I made an impossible promise to your mother the night that she died.

Because you'd never believe that I saw her.

But he said, "Because you're worth it, kiddo."

They stood there, in the basement of that parking lot, just an uncle and his niece, two humans, both awkward and broken in their own ways.

Then it was over and she wiped her eyes. "Sorry."

"There's nothing to be sorry about," he said. "You've got a heart. C'mon."

He chirped the remote and unlocked the car. They climbed in.

As he backed out of the spot, she asked, "So, I'm still in deep shit, aren't I?"

"Oh yeah. Knee high at least. But we'll deal with that tomorrow. For now, let's just get home."

CHAPTER SIXTY-THREE

Years ago, when the COVID-19 pandemic was in its fearful beginnings and toilet paper was hoarded, Randall proudly announced over dinner that he'd bought ten fifty-five-gallon drums of hand sanitizer from a contact in China. He was going to make a killing, he promised.

A week after they arrived, two agents from the state's Department of Justice showed up on the doorstep. Lloyd had listened in, amused as Randall tried to explain that, yes, it was perfectly normal for his business to make such a purchase and, no, he wasn't trying to take advantage of the public during a crisis.

The agents hadn't bought it.

California had strict anti-price-gouging laws, they said. Especially during public health emergencies. If his business was legitimate, it wouldn't be a problem, they said. If not, well, they suggested he send the drums back for a refund.

His contact in China never returned his calls.

And so they sat in a storage locker, ten plastic drums of CDC- and FDA-compliant fragrance-free ethanol, eighty percent with an added glycerin moisturizer, all gathering dust.

Until today.

Sweat beading his brow in the evening light, Lloyd offloaded the final two drums from the pickup. He pressed the plastic key into the drum's bunghole (yes, that was what it was called, he had learned) and then twisted, unscrewing the cap.

Liquid sanitizer spurted as it tumbled onto its side. He placed a bucket beneath the bunghole and filled it. Then he gave the drum a kick. Sloshing and burping gooey gel, it rolled down the slope and into a dry gully.

Lloyd wiped his face and took a moment to admire the view.

From Raven's Peak, he could see the whole wretched valley. The rolling brown hills giving way to the tree-lined streets of Raven's Valley. The homes with their lawns and pools, their laughter and activities. There was a small concert in Fairchild Park to the east. To the south, he could see the little dots of a softball game in full swing. To the west, near the lake, a group sat around benches while someone manned a grill.

Yes, there would be a barbecue soon. One the community would never forget.

Near the end of World War Two, the allies dropped nearly 3400 tons of explosives upon Dresden, targeting precise locations to turn the medieval city into a tempest of flames. Lloyd knew this because he was a student of military history.

But his ambitions were more modest.

He raised the binoculars and scanned the dry hills. The other fires were burning already. Fanned by the coastal wind, they were growing from small flickers to veins of shimmering gold among the fog-swaddled peaks. He watched the embers rising.

He unlocked Randall's cell phone, thumbed his way to the community security app, and entered the password. Here it was, the Raven's Valley resident directory. He tapped *Select All* and scrolled to the bottom: *Compose Alert*.

Words had always come difficult to him, so he took a moment to consider his message. Then it came, divine inspiration. Something he knew would get their attention. He typed it out, hit *send*, and waited.

Randall's phone shrieked when the emergency alert arrived. Soon, other phones would shriek across the valley.

Now for the fun part.

Lloyd lit a match and tossed it into the gulley by the plastic drums. He had never suspected that hand sanitizer could ignite and even doubted her plan. Yet when he saw the plastic drums, there it was, a red warning: *FLAMMABLE.*

The trick, he had learned, was to be patient and wait. Ethanol burned with invisible flames.

The first drum had simply exploded, knocking him onto his ass from thirty feet back and peppering the SUV with rocks and twigs. After that, he knew to stand back.

A *whoosh,* and then the shimmer of shadows and the rush of warm wind. The gulley ignited as the drums bubbled and blackened. Twigs sparked, bushes shrank, and smoke rose from the ground. Then the drums detonated, spattering the landscape with sightless fire and smoldering debris.

It was really quite beautiful, Lloyd thought. Now the fun part was over.

What came next knotted his gut.

J'harr, he thought, *please grant me the strength.*

"A moment of pain for a lifetime of freedom," she whispered. *"Your ascension's at hand. Be my emissary."*

Lloyd raised the bucket and poured the sanitizer over his head. His skin stung as the liquid found wounds and scratches he didn't know he had. His eyes reflexively blinked.

Eyes...

Soon, he would never blink again. Soon, he would never flinch or feel pain or shame.

But first...

With wet hands, he raised the matchbook. *Do it*, he told himself. *Leave Lloyd Betancourt behind. Ascend.*

He struck the match on the third try.

The fumes ignited in a warping of air and breathtaking warmth. The hairs on his arm curled and vanished. In a boiling embrace, his shirt shrunk to his chest and his hair tightened against his scalp, a sizzling cap.

The heat grew, and grew, and soon Lloyd was dancing and twirling, singing and shrieking and crashing through bushes. He slapped his blackening skin as the world turned to shadows.

My eyes, he thought as pain chewed into his nerves. *I've cooked out my eyes.*

It was his last coherent thought.

And then, from a well of deep darkness, the shadows parted and he rose. He realized he could see something now, something new. A world in beautiful black-violet hues. He could see *all*. In all directions. Everything, all at once.

Yes, she had been right. He no longer had skin or bones or a body. That molted husk lay on the charred ground underneath him.

But he did have fingers and hands.

And they were formed out of flames.

CHAPTER SIXTY-FOUR

It was just after sundown when the emergency alert hit the cloud servers and passed it off to every registered cell phone in the Raven's Valley Homeowners Association directory. Mothers and fathers, grandparents and grandchildren alike. Eight hundred and twelve phones chimed at nearly the same time.

In downtown Greywood Bay, Edward Strathmore had finally gotten his table at Chalamar and was shooting the shit with Melissa Daniels, the granddaughter of their firm's namesake. They were trying not to talk business, but as usual, business quickly crept in. Neither of them really had much else going on in their lives.

When his phone chirped, he gave it a cursory glance. He didn't quite understand what he saw.

Two tables away, a couple he recognized from a home showing in March both stood up. With a clatter of silverware and a tipping chair, they rushed from the restaurant.

THREE MILES WEST, AT COOGAN'S WHARF, STACEY Layne walked along the foggy pier, sipping her mango boba tea and reviewing her evening. She felt bad for Mark. Like maybe she hadn't fought hard enough for him in the interview. Like maybe she'd led him on about the potential for a job in the fall. Like she could have done more.

And yet, she was proud of herself, too. She hadn't given in to the urge to knock back some sake.

Tozai Nigori.

Shichida Junmai.

Or perhaps a fruity Yuki No Bosha.

Yeah, the drink list had beckoned, but she'd resisted. It really was true what they said in her weekly meeting: one day at a time.

Her phone chirped and her walk ended as she read the alert. Her heels pivoted on their own.

She didn't have any children and didn't really want any. Still, what she read traced a shiver down her spine and quickened her heart. The walk back to her Mini Cooper turned into a brisk jog.

She needed to get back to Raven's Valley.

TWO MILES SOUTHEAST, WHERE THE UNIVERSITY'S soccer fields gave way to quiet, leafy streets, Ali's mom was speaking so fast he struggled to keep up. His father, a thin man with a lazy eye—a wound from a Shia militant group in Iraq—simply focused on the road and kept quiet. He'd seen true terror in his forty-seven years, and yet nothing scared him more than his wife when she was angry.

"Okay, okay, Mom, geez," Ali said. "I'm sorry."

"Don't dare you 'okay okay, Mom' to me after what you do. I'm not understand this, not one bit. Is like you become wild man. No. No more. No more video games, no more TV, none! You are taking in badly influence."

"Bad influence, Mom." She reached back and gave him a smack on his arm. "Oww."

"And no back-talking."

Ali grumbled. "Worst summer ever."

Three phones chirped all at once in the car. He waited for his mom to answer before sneaking a glimpse at his own. He squinted as he read it a second time.

A gasp left his mother's lips, and she spoke quickly to his father. Not in English but the Arabic they often shared. Ali recognized the fear in her voice as she repeated her command.

"Go. Drive faster. We need to get home."

In the middle of Raven's Valley, at the community center, Maura sighed and took a seat between her parents. They were still furious. Her dad had lectured her the entire drive home. Her mom was giving her the silent treatment, something she assumed Maura didn't like, but she was mistaken.

Mostly, Maura's arm had her attention. It ached with the same deep pain that had lingered in the weeks after the break.

She'd applied the armlock to the hospital guard without thinking. Yes, her coach always told her that in jiujitsu, technique trumped size nine times out of ten. Still, she was amazed it had worked.

She rubbed her sore arm and studied the auditorium. There were at least fifty people in here, more pouring in every minute. And yet, no one had shown up to explain the message. She watched Mr. Fox, the head of security, pacing the perimeter with a walkie-talkie to his mouth. Every now and then, concerned parents cornered him and he shrugged.

Why was he shrugging?

Because he didn't know what this was about, Maura thought. Because that wasn't the walk of a man taking attendance. Or a man with something to say. That was the expression of a man who was just as confused as everyone else.

Which meant...

"So, do we even know who sent the alert?" Maura asked.

Her mom gave a derisive snort: a flaring of the nostrils and a narrowing of her eyes.

Creases formed on her father's forehead. He glanced down at his phone and asked, "What do you mean?"

"I mean, like... Do you think that maybe it's a prank?"

"If it's a prank," her mother said, "it's in terrible taste. I mean, really, who would do such a thing?"

CHAPTER SIXTY-FIVE

By the time the Uber made it to the south gate of Raven's Valley, Diana was flustered and short-tempered. Too many things were happening at once.

First, the internet-connected smoke alarms had pinged her phone. Then the community alert squealed out its warning.

Emergency Alert
MISSING CHILD // ABDUCTOR & KNOWN VIOLENT PREDATOR SIGHTED IN RAVEN'S VALLEY // EMERGENCY MEETING @ COMMUNITY CENTER NOW // PLEASE HURRY // THIS IS NOT A TEST

And now, with the cars and nervous residents jamming the streets, she sensed she'd be better off walking.

"I'll get out here, thank you," she told the driver. Her house was only a block from the gate.

On Maywood Place, Pavarti Khan gave her a nervous wave from her Mercedes. "Evening, Diana. You ever seen anything like this?" She gestured to the traffic.

"No, sorry," she said. "I have to head home. Something's..."

Something is what? she wondered. Something was *wrong*. Yes, she sensed it in her gut. A charge in the foggy air and the scent of distant wildfire. That she hadn't heard from Randall all afternoon put speed in her steps.

"I'll see you at the meeting and save you a seat," Pavarti said. The car in front of her moved a few feet before stopping.

Entering her house, Diana wasn't quite sure what loomed before her. There, in the middle of her living room, sat some sort of plastic barrel. A dozen holes punctured it, and Randall's drill lay nearby.

The holes burbled clear liquid onto her precious rug. The air reeked of alcohol.

"Smoke alert, zone two," the fire alarm chirped. "Seek safety. Smoke alert, zone two. Seek safety."

It was the candles that brought a cry to her lips.

Dozens of little votive candles lay on the floor, flickering in the darkness among the glistening liquid. Dozens of flames in the bitter shadows.

Diana cleared the entryway and crossed the living room so quick she forgot she was wearing platform shoes. Gel liquid sloshed beneath her feet.

Crouching on all fours, she blew out the nearest candle. A quick breath. She blew two more and three after that. She crawled and blew, the wet rug scraping her knees, the liquid stinging. With each breath, the candles flickered and smokey tendrils curled in the air. This was insane. Who would do such a thing? And just when they'd finally settled into the house.

With a panicked breath, she blew out the last candle and scooted back. Her rug-burned knees shivered. Above, the fire alarm still chirped and warbled.

"Smoke alert, zone two. Seek safety. Smoke alert, zone two..."

But that was it. She was breathless and angry now. Because she knew. She had always known.

Lloyd.

Her son, whose problems she had pushed off and denied, promising herself that he would get better. That he just needed time. He just needed space.

But no, she realized. What he'd needed most had been her love and guidance, not her silence.

A flicker in the darkness. One by one, the delicate ember at the tip of each candlewick grew. A flame rekindled itself. Then another, and another.

It was the strangest thing, she thought. How with each smoldering wick, a thin finger of fire stretched out and reignited the next candle.

Impossible.

And yet, within several seconds, every votive was aflame once again, bright and angry. Wax dripped low to the wet rug. The candles were nearly burned to their base. Within the fumes that rose from the golden-lit floor, something unfolded.

Two eyes of fire crackled over a smile of dripping cinders.

Diana knew that smile in her body and bones. She had carried the boy who bore that sick grin into this world. And for so long, she told herself that nothing was wrong.

Then came the heat, and she ran.

Feet sloshing, hands scraping against the wet rug, she scrambled away from the living room, through the front door, and burst out into the foggy evening. The air reeked of smoke and cars packed the street. She could see the Montroses and the Patels, the Kims and the Rutherfords. Mr. Weiland jogged past with his Labrador on a leash, giving Diana a friendly wave.

She choked out a dry scream and turned to her house. Through that gorgeous wide window, the flames rose. The couches and the curtains, the doilies and wicker baskets. Shadows gave way to bright ribbons of fire.

And within them, she saw her son, his veins threaded with

sparks and his eyes two whirlpools of smoke. He tilted his ashy head and stretched his arms out as if reaching for a hug.

Diana didn't hear the explosion that blew out the windows. Nor did she feel the heat of the shock wave. She felt only the bite of the glass, a wall of glistening shards that shredded her ambitions and dreams, reducing her to a shrieking red mist blown outward by the arms of a young man reborn in flames.

CHAPTER SIXTY-SIX

Zelda was in her bedroom when the flash lit up the horizon a few blocks to the east. She wasn't even sure she had seen it.

Then the shock wave arrived.

The house shuddered and the window rattled. Dust curled from the trees. Something like pebbles clattered down the roof, onto the sidewalk, and across the street.

She peered through the window where the glass felt oddly warm. Outside, black curls of plastic fluttered through the fog while fragments of wood spattered the dry lawn.

What the hell was going on?

With a clang, a smoldering shape fell to the driveway, wobbled, and came to a rest. She recognized the shape of the number and the curl of the font. It was part of an address, the same metal numbers that adorned every house in Raven's Valley.

"Zelda, you okay?" Uncle Mark banged on her door. There was something hurried in his voice, so she opened it quick. "You heard that, right?"

She nodded. "Yeah."

"And you got the alert?"

She nodded again. "Something's happening down the street."

First, a distant siren. Next, the wail of honking horns. Then the squeal of wheels struggling for traction against asphalt. A loud pop and a crackling that Zelda recognized echoed out. That was a fender breaking, a hood crumpling perhaps. That was the sound of an accident.

"I'm going to check it out," Uncle Mark said. "Stay inside, okay?"

She followed him downstairs, where he grabbed his jacket and stepped out into the fog, immediately coughing. The air was tangy and sour. Something like snow fluttered down. The wildfire smelled so much closer.

No, not just wildfire smoke, she realized. That was the stench of burning plastic and metal. She touched the white flake as it came to a rest on her palm.

Ash.

A few blocks away, where the boom had come from, an amber flicker spewed a plume of dark smoke into the air. Someone's house was on fire.

And yet, she sensed there was more.

"Uncle Mark?" she shouted. "We need to go."

Another crunch boomed out closer, then the clink of glass and the squeal of rubber against asphalt. Uncle Mark hurried out onto the sidewalk, pulling his shirt up over his nose and cupping a hand to his eyes.

Down the street, at the intersection of Manzanita and Elm, two cars had T-boned each other. White smoke belched from the hood of a Mini Cooper while an SUV spun its tires on a lawn. The man behind the wheel shouted, "Move! Move!"

But his car wasn't going anywhere. The more the tires spun, the more dry lawn and dirt it kicked up. Neighbors approached, confused and annoyed.

"George, what's the matter with you?" asked a retiree Zelda

had seen playing bocci ball at the park. "You got somewhere to go?"

George ignored him, exiting the wrecked SUV through the passenger door. Dumbfounded, people watched him run off down the street.

"Is he drunk?"

"Did he seriously just flee the scene?"

Another group helped open the door of the Mini Cooper. There was a woman inside, blood trickling down from a wound on her forehead. Shit, Zelda recognized her.

Uncle Mark hoisted Stacey Layne out of the car, tucked his head under her arm, and helped her walk to the porch. "Zelda! Call 911. Do it now."

"On it."

She rushed inside and upstairs for her phone. She dialed 911 when a third crack of an accident echoed down the street. Someone screamed while a car horn wailed and wailed and kept on wailing.

Scanning the street, Zelda waited for 911 to pick up. Instead, it just rang and rang. A beep and a pleasant voice finally answered. "All circuits are busy."

Then it hung up. She couldn't believe it: 911, it hung on her.

She opened her window, searching for Uncle Mark. There he was, by the driveway, tearing a strip from his shirt and wrapping it around Stacey's forehead. More neighbors gathered, a dozen at least.

Then someone sprinted past them.

Running from something.

Running from what?

Her fears murmured in the back of her mind. *It's happening. It's happening again.*

She needed to see it. She needed to be sure.

Squeezing out of the window, she climbed onto the garage. She found her foothold against the chimney and kicked off the shutter. A quick scramble, a hoist, and she pulled herself up onto the roof, where she had watched the stars between the fog and felt so small beneath it all.

Tonight, there were no stars above. A coppery hue tinged the fog.

She looked to the south, where flames poured from a house and its shattered windows. Like it was reaching for the trees and the bushes.

Like it was living.

"Zelda, get down from there!" Uncle Mark shouted. "Where's the ambulance?"

"The lines are busy!" she shouted.

Someone on a motorcycle blew past Uncle Mark, driving reckless and fast. No, she realized. He was fleeing.

"Zelda!" Uncle Mark shouted. "Get down, now!"

She held a hand—*wait*—and scrambled up the last of the roof, clinging to the solar panels. She came to the top and stood.

A gasp flew past her lips.

Smoke thickened the fog, filling the air with falling embers. Yet even through the haze, she could see the hills lining Raven's Valley.

The hills were ablaze.

Fiery tendrils wormed their way down from the eastern ridges to the low trails. In the west, flames traced the hilly contours. Driven by the evening winds, a vortex of sparks swirled and danced and rained fiery ash. To the north, luminous veins converged in a channel of molten gold. For a moment, it staggered Zelda how swiftly it moved. It didn't seem right that fire could travel at such speed.

She hurried back to the edge of the roof and waved at Uncle Mark. "Hey! There's a really big fire in the hills. It's headed our way."

Disbelief froze his face. Then he swallowed and nodded. "Okay. Get down here. We're leaving."

That was when she realized her uncle looked different.

Smoke curled from his skin and wafted out from his eyes. For the space of one breath, his entire body was black.

"Zelda, grab the car keys. C'mon!"

No, she realized. It wasn't just Uncle Mark.

It was everyone down below. Stacey in his arms. The people racing down the street. The family in the van and the frustrated dad stuck in the traffic and now honking his horn.

They were all smoldering black-violet mist.

They just didn't know it.

CHAPTER SIXTY-SEVEN

Mark choked down his fear and gave himself one breath to come up with a plan. The air… how had it thickened so quickly? Yes, there was a wildfire coming down from the hills. Yes, Stacey Layne was in his arms, concussed or possibly worse. Yes, people around him were panicking.

He exhaled.

Right, the plan. Get Zelda and drive to the south gate. Take Stacey to the hospital. The house didn't matter. It was just walls and windows. What mattered were the people.

Zelda met him on the lawn with the car keys. She helped slide Stacey into the back seat. "I think… we're late for… meeting," Stacey mumbled.

Inside, Mark pressed the ignition when a piece of burning frond landed on the Subaru's hood. Jesus, this was really happening.

"Buckle up. We might have to hop the curb."

They didn't make it out of the driveway.

The Rivian was near silent and riding the sidewalk the wrong way. It plowed into the rear of Mark's Subaru, shattered the back window, and sent them fishtailing onto the lawn. His teeth rattled and his back instantly locked up.

They were lucky they'd only been going in reverse.

The woman driving the Rivian had been speeding.

With a squeal of brakes, the electric SUV swerved and hit a lamppost, bending it at the base and riding it up at an angle. For a moment, the Rivian teetered, front wheels off the ground and still spinning. Then it tipped and came to a rolling stop on its side, windows shattering.

Numbly, Mark climbed out of the Subaru and hurried to the passenger side. Zelda stumbled out, clutching her cheek where the seat belt left a red welt from her ear to her throat.

"I'm okay," she said. "You?"

He nodded. But he wasn't sure it would be okay. People were abandoning their cars in the street. The falling ash intermixed with embers now, glowing orange and red and starting small fires on the dry lawns. Nearby, the Rivian whined on its side, and no one bothered to help. As Mark hoisted Stacey from the back seat, someone shoved them aside and fled.

This was some kind of hell.

"Ali and Maura," Zelda said. "We can't leave them."

"One thing at a time," he said.

Limping together, they made it two blocks and turned right at Oak Way. The chaos was even worse than their own street.

A van and an SUV were engaged in a battle of push-pull, trying to squeeze their way between a fence and a driveway.

Hedges smoldered in the hazy wind.

A crying girl chased a scared Labrador, its leash dragging on the sidewalk behind it, *thock, thock, thock.*

Worst of all, orange tendrils crossed the street a few blocks away, a curling wave of flames moving with a mind of its own.

"It's no good, Mark." Pavarti hurried up the hazy street, her dark hair streaked with gray ash and a desperate gleam in her eyes. "That's a dead end."

"You've been there?"

"Total inferno. Diana's house and a few others just went up. Here, let me help."

She grabbed Stacey's other arm when a series of distant pops echoed out, followed by something like a low whistle. Mark looked up in time to see a spinning shape in the haze.

The propane tank skidded across the street and crashed into the garage of a bungalow unit, buckling the wood and setting off the home's alarm. Down the street, flames licked their way up a power line.

"What about the west gate?" Pavarti asked. "Has anyone tried that?"

He turned to Zelda. "You were on the roof. You sure there was a fire to the west?"

She nodded. "It was everywhere."

Another pop, only this time it came from a power line. Sparks drooled from the transformer as flames engulfed the pole and the cables.

With a buzz and a flash, the streetlights winked off as true darkness blanketed the street. Starlike cinders rained through the shadows. It might just have been beautiful if the very air wasn't choking them.

"We need to go somewhere," Pavarti coughed. "This whole place is going to be ashes any minute."

Panic gripped the crowd as loose shadows sprinted this way and that. Within the distant flames, Mark swore he saw something move behind a shattered window. Something that crawled down the wall of a house.

Something that—impossibly—had more than four limbs.

No. It was just the darkness playing tricks on his eyes. Just his oxygen-starved mind.

And yet...

Eyes narrowing, Zelda looked in that direction as well. She'd been looking funny at him for the past fifteen minutes. But now, it was like she was looking through all of them.

"Ashes." She repeated Pavarti's words. "Ashes. Honor them. Remember their names."

Something changed in his niece's face. It was that same hardening he'd seen countless times as she retreated inward. He wasn't going to like what she had to say.

"I'm sorry, Uncle Mark. But I need to go."

Then she took off running.

CHAPTER SIXTY-EIGHT

Zelda forced herself to ignore her uncle's shouts to get back here, to listen to him. She told herself not to look back. She ran as fast as her legs could take her.

Past a young willow fully engulfed in flames.

Past a house where fiery hands scratched at the glass.

Past three cars collided in an intersection, panicked families arguing and punches about to be thrown.

Her sprint brought her back to the door of her house. She hardly recognized the interior when she entered.

Smoldering ash coated the walls and windows. Inside, water dripped from the walls as muddy blisters bulged from the ceiling. And that hole above the living room mantle, it had become a wet orifice. It shivered as she drew closer, closer…

But she wasn't here for the hole or the beam behind it, nor the words written in the old wood.

She was here for the ceramic vase that once sat on this mantle.

The urn she had ignored.

Slowly, reverently, she gripped her parents' urn and unscrewed the lid. She looked inside. That two people she loved and who had formed the warm core of her life could be reduced to such indiscriminate matter and placed inside a cold vessel was a violation of all that was good in the world.

Her parents, they were gone. In their emptiness, Chester's words echoed through her mind.

"Remember them."

"Honor their memories."

"Ask them for help."

Turning in a circle, she dumped the urn out and closed her eyes as the ashes swirled around her and filled the room.

"Please," she whispered. "I need your help."

In the darkness behind her eyelids, there were no sounds or sights, nothing for her senses to latch onto. Only a void that stretched on endlessly into the cold oblivion of death.

"Please. We all need your help."

And then it came to her.

First, a sensation on her finger. The paper curl of a book. Then a scent filled her nose. Bacon. And a sound, the sizzle of fat and grease in a pan.

She tasted it now, that breakfast they'd had on their last morning at the lake. The aroma of pine and juniper in through the window. The spring air, crisp and dewy from the night before.

Her mother sipped fresh coffee while her father turned the bacon. Zelda closed the old graphic novel she'd found at the cabin. She said, "I still don't get it. Of all the names, you chose a stupid video game princess."

"It was better than Mario," her dad said.

Her mom gave him a playful nudge and stole a slice of bacon from the plate.

"Plus, she's, like, not even the main character," Zelda continued. "That's Link. All she does is get rescued, which is kind of lame and borderline sexist."

"Borderline sexist, huh?" Her dad gestured toward the book with his tongs. "Read it again."

But she was done with the graphic novel. The phone had her

attention now, the latest school gossip scrolling past with each swipe. At some point, she'd tuned out her father altogether.

Listen to him, she thought. *He was trying to connect, but you blew him off. Listen to him.*

"We named you Zelda," her father said, "because she's what matters most in those games. Without her, there's no adventure, nothing worth fighting for or saving. And yeah, sweetie, you're right: it's not her story. But you know what she is? She's the center, the heart, what holds it all together. Zelda's the protector. And that'll always be you."

In a cloud of smoke and ash, it all faded. The salty scent of bacon. The cool breeze through the dewy pines. The morning light off the lake and in through the window.

And her parents, frozen for one perfect moment on their last vacation together.

Alone, Zelda stood in the dark living room, tears wetting her cheeks as the last of their ash fell from the urn.

It drifted and swirled in impossible currents. It rose and it flowed through the house, chasing itself over the banisters and stairs. Sometimes it sparkled, and sometimes it burned. And within those errant wisps, she saw it all: thirteen years of laughter and love, of pain and regret, all the kind words and smiles they'd given each other. All they'd built and all they'd lost. With a puff and a curl, the ash played against old bricks and beams, touched windows and boards, danced against the very fabric of this home, a place pulsing not with life or death but something imbued with meaning.

Memory.

Yes, her parents were gone; she accepted that now. She would carry the love and carry the loss.

But that didn't mean she was alone.

Dozens of figures crowded her, black eyes weeping rain as their muddy skin quivered. Memories, yes. Not from her or her parents but from thirty-nine broken souls. They stretched damp fingers out.

And she almost laughed. She understood it. She had been wrong about Chester Halgrove, but her dad had been right about her. This wasn't Zelda's story to finish.

It was Chester's.

She closed her eyes and let the dead embrace her.

CHAPTER SIXTY-NINE

Samantha Lee and a handful of the convalescent hospital staff huddled around the computer. The news was coming in fast. From the ringing phones that warned them to be ready for overflow from the general hospital. From the calls to friends or colleagues in Raven's Valley. From social media. Todd even set up a radio to listen in on police chatter.

In the rec room, several patients stared slack-jawed at the nine-o'clock news. She had to shut the windows to keep out the smoke. She knew what she was really smelling in the air: death.

Back at the nurses' station, she spotted the blinking icon on the monitoring display. A red empty bed in room 444. Mr. Halgrove again.

But that didn't make sense. Per protocol, he was still in his restraints.

Unless someone had undone them.

She called Todd, and together, they hurried down the hall. She wasn't sure what to expect. Perhaps those kids, back again. Or perhaps Mr. Halgrove on another confused walk. It always broke her heart to see sundowning patients.

What she didn't expect was the dampness.

It hit her like a cold slap as she opened the door. Moisture charged the dark room and dirt danced on her tongue. Even the lights were dim and distant, the ceiling impossibly high.

At the bed, Mr. Halgrove's restraints hung loose, the Velcro and nylon marred by muddy fingerprints. Someone had unbuckled him.

He stood at the window, his left hand pressed to the glass while the fingers on his right traced curious symbols.

No, she didn't need this, not tonight. Two of her colleagues had families in Raven's Valley. She should be listening to the news. She should be preparing to help.

"Mr. Halgrove, I don't know how you got out but..."

Three paces into the room, Todd came to a stop. So did she.

Because it was no longer just the three of them here, in room 444. She sensed there were others as well. Shapes brushing against her. Shoulders sliding past hers. Damp hands gently pushing her aside. She thought of the crowded city subways from her medical school.

A tunnel of souls.

"Michael Andover..." Mr. Halgrove muttered. "Gretchen Swann... Jerry Jenkins..."

As he listed off these names, a gasp left Todd's lips. "Look. The window..."

And she saw them.

In the reflection, dozens of bodies streamed past her. Eyes of dark sorrow and mud-spattered skin. They converged upon Mr. Halgrove, swarming him. And yet even his reflection was no longer his own.

A second shape swam beneath it, a girl with smooth skin and eyes that sparkled with youth. A young woman Samantha knew. She had—impossibly—been here some hours ago at the start of her shift.

"I don't care if I get fired," Todd said, "but I ain't touching him."

Samantha realized she'd taken several steps backward as well. Back to the door and the hall. Back toward the warm light and its promise of sanity and security. Back to a place where phantoms didn't drift past like the errant winds of her darkest dreams.

"But... We need to do something," she whispered.

"Yeah, good luck."

Another three steps back. An icy breath bloomed upon her neck as it passed, and she screamed.

Mr. Halgrove turned from the window, spearing her with a twinkling gaze. "Robert Benson..." he continued. "James Cleary... Reggie Black..."

Yes, she was backing out through the door now, Todd behind her. Because she knew Mr. Halgrove's eye color. She'd looked into those tired brown eyes while she fed him dinner just two hours ago.

But these eyes looking back were youthful and blue.

Then the patient's door closed. Samantha wasn't sure if it was by her hand or another's. The past five minutes swam behind a shroud of confusion, locked in some liminal space of the mind. She told herself not to open it, never. There was more within this room than Mr. Halgrove and his misfiring neurons.

All her charts and medicine, her faith in anatomy and science, they all ended here, at the threshold of room 444, where an old man pressed his palm against a window and dozens of hands reached back.

CHAPTER SEVENTY

Maura was trying not to freak out. When the fire appeared beyond the hedges of the community center, she knew the meeting was over. When her dad insisted they abandon the car due to traffic, her doubts took jagged form. And when they came to a stop three blocks from the west gate and saw the wall of flames, that's when her fears finally took hold.

They were going to die here.

Acrid smoke clung to her throat and dried out her tongue as cinders rained the streets. Flames sprouted from parched lawns and gardens and crawled up from smoldering trees. An empty Jeep rolled down Sycamore Street, its hood belching black smoke. It passed a man sitting on the curb, rocking back and forth and making the sign of the cross.

Adults weren't supposed to be acting like this. They were supposed to have all the answers. They were supposed to know what to do.

Yet even her father stuttered and scanned the ashen streets, confusion infecting his eyes. "I don't... I don't know," he said. "There has to be another way out, right? Right?"

Then she saw someone running the opposite way.

Someone shouting and waving.

Zelda.

"Hey! I need your help."

"Zelda, where's your uncle?" Maura's mother asked. "We need to get you to safety. Come!"

"That's what I'm doing." She turned to Maura. "Call Ali. Have him use his drone to find us a path."

"A path where?"

"We're going to Chester's house."

"No, she's not," her father said. "We're going to the west gate—"

"Then that's where you'll die," Zelda said. "There's no other way out."

It was a curious thing, the strength of Zelda's words and the piercing will of her stare. Like someone else was speaking through her. Adding their voice to hers.

Again, that indecisive blink in her father's eye and the stutter on his lips. "I don't think—"

"You don't get it, do you?" Zelda said. "This isn't an accident; someone did this. We need to go. Now."

Maura swallowed. "Okay."

Zelda led the way among a tempest of cinders and ash. The haze reduced every street to an identical nightmare. Fingers shaking, Maura dialed Ali. "C'mon... C'mon..."

On the first try, the network was busy.

On the second try, it went straight to his voicemail.

On the third ring, he finally picked up.

"Holy shit, tell me you're safe," Ali said. "I'm at the south gate and there's, like, every fireman in town trying to get in."

"I'm with Zelda," she said. "We're stuck inside Raven's Valley. It's bad, Ali. I'm really scared and—"

"Okay, okay. So what can I do?"

That simple question brought a smile to her cheeks and a tear to her eye. It was probably the smoke, she told herself. No, she wasn't catching feelings for Ali.

"We need your drone," she said. "We can't figure out where we are—"

"Yeah, got it. Okay, I'm remote starting it right now. Give me... just a few... seconds and... Damn, password expired. Okay... logging in... now."

She put Ali on speakerphone while the jog brought them to the intersection of Cherry and Magnolia. She gave him their location and waited.

As a burning house crackled and glowed, something moved among the embers. Something skittered and rose.

Just a trick of the light, Maura thought. How the smoke curled and parted. How the flames came together like legs in motion. Numbly, she watched the fire reach out, touching the curtains and drapes, the furniture and bookshelves. Arms spreading flames like a mad dancer.

And the eyes...

Two smoldering eyes turned and glared out from behind the window.

"Run," Zelda said.

Every window in the house shattered at once. Glass peppered the street and the trees as they raced away.

"Okay... I'm about a hundred feet up and climbing," Ali shouted from the phone. "Oh geez, this is... this is really bad. I'm over the climbing wall now and the park's just... *gone*."

"Find us a path," Zelda said. "We're coming up on Cherry and Spruce."

"Okay, good news is, you're like three blocks away. Bad news: you'll have to circle back and go through the tennis courts. Make a U-turn."

Beneath the wail of distant sirens and the screams, the crackling of wood and the popping of glass, a high-pitched buzz grew closer and closer. The drone shot over them and made a quick figure-eight turn.

"Oh, I see you," Ali said. "Wave to the camera."

"Ali, directions."

"Right! Right! Take a right through the cul-de-sac. There's a bike path at the end. See it?"

Maura spotted the path between a chain-link fence and the wall. She waved her parents toward it. They'd picked up a few stragglers, a family she recognized from the park, Mr. Merrick and his daughter, as well as a scared Labrador just looking for someone to follow.

Using Ali's directions, they cut between the tennis courts and the duck ponds, where smoldering reeds lined a lake glimmering with falling embers.

"Straight," Ali said. "Keep going past the water fountain."

The drone zoomed ahead, low at first and then pulling up and banking.

"This is so bad," Ali said. "I can see my house from here. There goes my computer."

"I'm sorry, Ali," Maura said.

Coughing and panting, they followed a wall bordering the scrapyard, its hedges lit like oil derricks. They emerged at the end of Ponderosa Court, the smooth asphalt of Raven's Valley giving way to the shoddy street and Chester's leaning fence. Red tape crisscrossed the gate above a black sign proclaiming:

CITY OF GREYWOOD BAY
WARNING! NO TRESPASSING!
PROPERTY NOT FIT FOR HABITATION!
VIOLATORS WILL BE CITED!

It amused Maura to see her father, a man who studied laws and regulations, tearing that sign off and kicking the gate open. And then they were here, Chester's property, where rumors lived and madness slept.

At first, she didn't notice anything different. There were the empty fountains and the ivy-swallowed fences. The birdbath leaned on its side. Zelda hurried up the creaking porch, where another sign warned that the building was condemned.

The fire, Maura realized. The weedy lawn was unburnt. The dry hedges had yet to ignite. Even the falling cinders disintegrated before reaching the ground.

The flames hadn't touched an inch of Chester's house.

"There's a basement inside," Zelda said. "Get everyone down there and you'll be safe."

"How do you know this?" Maura's mom asked.

"Because Chester does. He's been preparing for decades."

Inside, it wasn't so much of a house but the husk of a once-gorgeous structure now gutted and splayed. Maze-like beams and half-shattered walls wound their way inward. Even the papered windows with their insane symbols seemed to glow. And yet, the confusion of doors and ruined halls all led back to a gutted hole and a stairwell descending into the cool depths.

Maura was three steps down the stairs when she realized Zelda wasn't coming.

"Wait!" She hurried back, but her mom grabbed her. "Zelda, what are you doing?"

It was the oddest thing, Maura thought. Zelda, this summer school friend that she'd known for only two months. This skinny girl of thirteen who looked like she might blow over in the breeze. And yet, in these shadows, she appeared older and wiser, both exhausted and energized. When she spoke, there was an echo of Chester's locution to her words.

"I'm going to finish what he started."

"Let me help."

Zelda smiled with teeth no longer white but old and brown. For a moment, wrinkles stretched across her smooth cheeks.

She said, "I've got all the help that we need."

CHAPTER SEVENTY-ONE

Zelda knew she was changing. Emerging from Chester's refuge to the fiery streets of Raven's Valley, she could see more than her eyes had ever been capable of seeing.

She could see *beyond*.

This wasn't just a fire, but a doorway tearing itself open. A feeding frenzy. An orgy of destruction and torment.

Dark creatures skittered and stalked the smoke, canine forms only mere suggestions of twisted physics. Beasts of six legs and slathering mouths and unblinking eyes, each movement contradicting the last.

Pups, Zelda realized. The dogs of J'harr.

And they were hungry.

A car crashed through the tennis courts, struck a roundabout, and exploded. The man who emerged was already engulfed. He ran for a dozen steps until the flames fully consumed him. A part of Zelda's mind retreated inward, telling herself this was all a performance. Yes, he was just singing and dancing.

But she knew he was shrieking.

Like a pack of feral dogs, the pups cornered him as he collapsed. Their teeth didn't break the burned flesh when they pounced. And yet Zelda knew that what they were devouring was something deeper than skin and bone, something that lived in the core of every creature.

Something like a soul.

As they feasted, black-violet tendrils glistened into existence, umbilical cords stretching skyward, where—

No. It was too much. Her mind recoiled and walled it all off.

When she opened her eyes, the pups were glaring at her.

"Mmm... You're a curious one." A dark feminine voice rained down from the sky. *"How'd you slip past my gaze? Ah, an outsider, yes. No matter. Crawl back into that house and hide among the madman's burrows. Count your days henceforth as blessed."*

Another skyward glance, and her body simply took over. She backed up onto the porch, faster and faster. The wood creaked beneath her feet.

"Go, little girl. This has always been my hunting ground. And out here... you're alone."

Then her foot stopped.

Alone.

No, she thought. She had Uncle Mark, and he was still out there, lost and scared and trying to help Stacey. She could sense his presence.

And she had others as well. Ali and Maura. A room full of classmates she had laughed with. She had a teacher, Mr. Barker, with his silly mustache and affable smile. She had a town she was just beginning to discover. And a home they were building.

Alone?

No, she wasn't alone.

Step by creaking step, her feet found their way back down the porch until she stood in the garden, the fiery streets before her.

And someone *behind* her.

It began as a whisper in her mind and a damp hand on her shoulder, one after the other. It began as a wind in her lungs and a hum in her throat.

Names.

A storm of names danced on the tip of her tongue and came to her lips. Yet her voice wasn't alone, but a duet. It came from a man who had chased her through the scrapyard. She wasn't speaking. She just let the names flow through her, neither sounds nor syllables but the sum total of their memories. Their births and their deaths. The lives they lived in between.

The lives ended too soon.

Honor their memories and ask for their help.

"Michael Andover... Gretchen Swann... Jerry Jenkins..."

Yes, she had read their names in the articles, just text on a page. But to Chester, they had been more. They had been fellow patients and friends, broken souls he'd tried to save.

"Michael Andover... Gretchen Swann... Jerry Jenkins..."

Zelda, who had flattened her smile and rolled her eyes often. Who armored herself in cynical detachment. She felt it now, the weight of each name and the memories behind it. They flowed through her heart. She couldn't stop it any more than she could hold back the ocean.

"Jerry Jenkins..." She caught the dry warble of the old man's voice in her throat. "Jerry Jenkins," she repeated.

A hand lifted from her shoulder. There was a *whoosh* from behind her. Then a moment of impossible quiet.

The shuddering began from the corner of her vision, with something languorous and vine-choked in the garden. That surreal human sculpture she had passed three times now.

It was *moving*.

With a creak of metal, a crunch of springs, and the grinding of gears, seven feet of welded scrap metal took a hesitant step forward. Ivy stretched and snapped. The sculpture made another lurching step—and another. Its head turned to her, regarding her with an eyeless gaze, and yet she knew it saw her.

"Jerry Jenkins," she said.

With a low moan, it charged from the property and onto the ashen streets.

The pups raised their scabrous heads and arched their backs as the sculpture crashed into them. With an impossibly fast backhand, it sent one pup rolling. The others circled and snarled, shaking barbed tails in warning.

"Robert Benson..." Zelda continued. "James Cleary... Reggie Black."

Another release of a hand on her shoulder and a *whoosh* as someone rushed past. Metal clattered and clanged by the dry birdbath. The sculpture of a three-armed man pushed itself up from the dirt. Like it was just rising from a long afternoon nap.

"Reggie Black," she repeated.

With two shields, the sculpture primed a rusty leg. It charged the snarling pups and hit them like a freight train, decades of fury called back into this world.

Because that was what she was doing, she realized. This battle, it wasn't hers; it was Chester's. He had spent every ounce of his sanity building to this moment. This wasn't her fight.

But she could help him see it through.

She was Zelda, after all.

She was a protector.

CHAPTER SEVENTY-TWO

Ali blinked and wiped his eyes, not quite sure what he was seeing on his phone's screen. After the car exploded, the drone lost Zelda through a plume of black smoke. It took him a minute to reposition. If he flew too high, he might lose his signal. If he flew too low, he could hit a tree or get lost in the haze.

Banking around the duck pond, he spotted Zelda running through the brambles along the side yard of Chester's property. He had read that most people didn't die because of the flames but of oxygen starvation. Was she lost or confused?

And her voice... It was like there were two voices intermixed on the phone. Zelda's and something older, something tired. They spoke together. "Jason Freeman... Lee Schwartz... Angie Retcliff."

A thin shadow moved in the side yard.

It was a statue, Ali realized. One of Chester's creepy sculptures. From the drone's view high above, Ali watched it twitch and take off in a running sprint.

He blinked and scoffed. No, that simply wasn't possible.

"Zelda... Uh, what am I looking at?"

"I'm not really sure," she panted. "But whatever it is, I think it's working. I need you to find my uncle, okay? I left him by the playground at Magnolia and Vine."

On-screen, her run came to a stop beneath an old tree. Odd, Ali thought, how Chester's property wasn't completely ablaze.

Like the fire was afraid of it.

She began rattling off those names again in that bizarre voice. "Matt Sparks... Johnny Berrong... Sam Evansworth..."

And again, something moved below. Yes, it didn't make sense, but there it was: another sculpture took off, tearing through the fencing and bushes and dragging a loose gate like a weapon.

"Ali, please find my uncle."

"Y-y-yeah, sorry. On it."

He wiped his eyes. Nearby, his parents had parked as close to Raven's Valley as they could, which was four blocks from the east gate. Onlookers packed the streets, the police and first responders begging them to clear the road and step back. No one listened. Now and then, a scuffle broke out as someone tried to break through a barricade and enter Raven's Valley. To rescue a family member, a friend, or a pet.

Sliding his thumb on the screen's control pad, Ali guided the drone over flaming neighborhoods. The ruined streets were unrecognizable in the haze, so he marked GPS waypoints on the map.

Below, trees burned like candles.

Cars tilted upon melting tires.

Windows winked amber as roofs collapsed into hot pits.

And among the smoke and the fire, Ali was certain he saw figures moving. Things of rusty metal wrestling with hound-like shapes. Arms grabbing at tails. Walls of fire being shepherded away from the streets.

A battle waged in the shadows and smoke.

Ali brought the drone lower until he could identify the streets. Manzanita. Sequoia. Pine. There was the playground, the plastic slide dripping as swings smoldered. He circled at the intersection of what the GPS said was Magnolia and Vine.

But no one was there.

Charred cars clogged the street and the sidewalks. Lawns had become blankets of embers and ash. Blackened trees dripped cinders over a maze of fallen branches.

"Zelda, I don't see your uncle. I don't see anyone."

The line hissed as two voices overlapped. "—Stevenson... Raymond King."

"Zelda? There's no one here."

"I'm thinking... I'm thinking..."

He thumbed the altitude control, hoping to get a higher view of the neighborhood, but the haze was impenetrable. He had to descend.

He banked over the ruined backyards of the largest houses, what Raven's Valley called the Pinnacle units. Five bedrooms, three garages, and a pool on a third of an acre. It all burned the same as the rest.

A crash boomed out below as a fence fell inward. Something like a mechanical man clomped through splintering wood. Its right arm glowed orange, super-heated metal dripping.

Its left arm was on fire.

No, Ali realized. It was dragging someone. A person formed out of flames.

He thought of his grandmother's superstitious tales of spirits and ghosts. Of an *ifrit*, a demon of heat that stalked desert ruins at night. Was that what this was?

In a furious turn, they pivoted and twisted around each other, the metal sculpture slow but strong and precise. It grabbed the *ifrit* and pulled it into its embrace.

And yet the fire was nimble, flames shifting and collapsing, dissolving in a spray of sparks and reforming.

As the two shapes traded blows, Ali noticed the cindering bushes and hot coals were cooling. Flames that had been ten feet high now barely licked the fence.

He had to get this on video.

He brought the drone down, skimming left to get a better angle. Too close, he realized.

With a fiery snap, the *ifrit* whipped out a molten tendril. The drone shook and plummeted, collision alarms blinking on-screen. Then came the noise every drone pilot dreaded: the unmistakable crunch of rotors against earth.

"No, no, no," Ali said. "Something hit the drone. It's... *shit*."

He tried mashing the auto-stabilizer, the return-to-home command, anything to get it off the ground. But it was over. From an upside perspective, he watched the fight rage on at the edge of the lens. The sculpture and the *ifrit* thrashed each other, metal and fire spilling.

"Sorry, Z-dog," Ali said. "I think I'm down for the count."

The last thing Ali saw before the feed ended was a furious face wreathed in flames. A young man he remembered from a store several weeks ago. A young man with tired eyes and a smile that screamed of infection.

CHAPTER SEVENTY-THREE

Coughing, Mark came to a stop among the ashen ruins of Pickford Park. This was it, he realized. Nowhere else to go. He helped Stacey rest against a stone bench, her head lolling to the side. Pavarti brought a handful of warm water from the drinking fountain. Dozens of people lingered with them, catching their breath and wiping their eyes. Neighbors or strangers, they all shared the same desperate look as they scanned the park for a way out.

Exhaustion.

Disbelief.

And despair.

Because a hellscape of heat and cinders lay before them.

Flames licked the baseball backstop and burped up from the dugout.

Fiery umbrellas and melting chairs surrounded the community pools.

A bed of embers beneath sheets of ash was all that remained of the park's grassy expanse.

"No, no, no no no," Mr. Parson shouted. "There has to be another way out. There has to be."

"You led us here to die," Mrs. Hammond hissed. "We trusted you."

"Oh, like you could do better, Cindy," Don Roberts snapped. "Ten minutes ago, you were running in circles."

"At least I had somewhere to run."

Mark tuned them all out, his world narrowing. He dialed Zelda's number again and again. Twice it went straight to voicemail, and three times the call never went through. He thought of those 9/11 tapes he'd heard in college, all the goodbye calls from the passengers of hijacked planes. Would that be what they made of his last moments? Some phantom voice on the news?

No. To hell with all that.

His gaze fixated on something at the edge of the community gardens: a tangled hose snaking its way to a spigot. There were more hoses and spigots near the smoldering tomato bushes and piles of compost.

"Jose, Kevin, I need your help," Mark said. He knew some of them from the monthly homeowners meet-and-greet. "And you, you're Quong, right?"

"Yeah, you're Mike," Quong said.

"Close enough. Listen, we're not dying here, okay? We are going to spray the fence with those hoses, just past the garden. See them?"

Two of the men nodded. "That fire's like thirty feet tall," Jose said. "We can't put it all out."

"We don't need to put it out," Mark said. "We just need to make a hole in it. Here we go."

They hurried across the community garden, stumbling through blackened shrubs and tripping over warm tomato cages. Mark found a spigot and a hose first, passing it off to Quong. The water was warm, the pressure low.

"Cover it with your thumb," he said. "Like this."

It was an improvement, but not much. The spray only made it ten feet.

Kevin found a hose coiled by a shed and connected it. Jose tore out the drip irrigation, uncrimping the end and opening the valve to full. Mark dragged another hose over.

Between the four of them, it was a decent spray.

The burning fence and the ivy hissed. Steam mixed with the smoke in sizzling white plumes. Slowly, the flames flickered and fell.

"*Dios mio*, we're fuckin' doing this, eh?" Jose said.

Then the flames redoubled. It was as if two terrible hands grew from the fire, cresting as waves and clawing at the wood.

Impossible, Mark thought. Fire shouldn't move like that.

Like it was moving *into* the wind.

A clang boomed out beyond the fence, metal grinding against metal. A shadow bobbed beyond the hedges. Mark blinked as something like a gaunt iron figure charged through the smoke and the flames.

The fire along the fence receded.

"There, spray there." He aimed his stream where the fire was weakest. The others followed. Soon, the flames lowered, lowered, and vanished.

"Keep on it."

Mark aimed his shoulder square at the center of the charred wood. A memory of high school football and his coach's words: head down, drive through, push off with your feet before impact.

So that's what he did.

The fence didn't break on the first try, nor the second. On his third charge, something snapped in his shoulder and knives slid down his left arm. His fingers stung as every breath became painful.

But Kevin and Jose were at the fence now beside him, kicking and battering while Quong sprayed them all. Wet ash dripped into Mark's eyes, his dry tongue lapping at the water.

"On three," Kevin said. "One, two, and—"

With a final kick, the fence fell inward, scattering sparks across a dark yard. Clutching his shoulder, Mark surveyed the fire-gutted house. His stomach twisted when he realized where they were.

This was their home, 33 Manzanita Way.

Just the blackened bones of a frame and the barest suggestion of walls.

They'd gone full circle.

And yet, between the stinging water in his eyes and the smoke in the air, Mark saw someone standing among the fallen bricks of the chimney and the smoldering beams of the mantle. A woman he'd seen two Christmases ago in the States and then in his apartment the night that she died.

"Maya?"

Coughing, he limped into the ruins of his house. He stood so close to her now he could count the freckles on her face and see the curls of her dark hair. He could see the seven-year-old child he had played video games with as a kid. The ten-year-old-girl who'd watched scary movies by his side in their basement. The nervous young woman he'd driven across three states to help her settle into college. The brave woman he'd picked up from the county lockup after she'd been pepper sprayed and arrested at another protest, something about voting rights or endangered wolves.

And then they'd drifted apart. The weeks between phone calls became months, then yearly chats on their birthdays. A vacation that overlapped. An email long overdue.

Yet here she stood, Maya, as clear to his eyes as she'd ever been.

Mark clutched his tingling arm. "I'm sorry, sis. I don't know how to do this."

"No one ever does."

"I can't find her. I can't save her."

"No." She smiled. "But you've saved each other."

"Hey, Mark." That was Quong, the floor groaning as he stepped lightly through the burned house. "Be careful. This whole thing's about to come down."

Mark turned back to Maya. He had so much to say and so much to ask. So many words he'd never expressed.

But she was gone. Only a glimmering shard of the ceramic urn remained there among the blackened ruins at the heart of this house.

"Hey, you okay?" Quong shined his phone's flashlight in Mark's eyes.

"Yeah, I think that I am."

Quong nodded. "The fire's dying down on the street. Looks like a way out. We should bring the others."

In groups of eight or ten, they led the survivors through the side yard and out onto streets clogged with burned cars. There was only one way to go, a path clear of the flames yet still hazy and warm. Mark's shoes stuck to the ground. He wasn't sure which had melted, his soles or the asphalt.

Every now and then, something rushed through the haze and the distant blaze. He swore he saw arms or legs, twisted bodies of metal. Other times, shadows crawled and skittered, always at the corner of his eyes.

A trick of the eye, he told himself. His oxygen-starved brain was probably hallucinating now.

Probably.

Oddly, the word "pup" came to mind.

They found another group at an intersection, residents so blackened by ash that their eyes and teeth seemed to emerge from a void. Someone shouted that there was shelter just up the road. That there was a basement and safe passage out of Raven's Valley. Something about a girl who had found it.

Zelda.

Mark's walk quickened. Helping Stacey, they passed charred tennis courts and a cul-de-sac. Then it came into view: that ramshackle house.

The fire had barely touched it.

Dozens and dozens of people all streamed toward the old structure with its wild lawn and its garden of weeds. Some stood on the porch, waving others toward them. Mark passed Stacey off to Jose, who said, "C'mon. We need to get going."

"Not without my niece."

And that's when the hand tugged at his shirt. He recognized that hoodie and those thumbholes cut into the sleeves. Zelda pushed her way through the crowd.

He hugged her faster and harder than he had hugged anyone. He stroked the ash from her hair and wiped a smear from her cheek.

"Your eyes," he said. "Zelda, are you okay?"

For a blink, it was like looking into the face of an old man.

She nodded. "Yeah. We're almost done."

"Let's get you in there." He took her hand, leading her toward the porch and the wide-open doors. He could see people descending stairs deep inside.

But Zelda shook her head. "We have to be sure."

"We?" He didn't understand. "Be sure of what?"

"That we've saved them all."

Someone else tugged on him now. Stacey. Even with her head wound and Jose's help, she had limped her way back to him. "Thank you, Mark," she muttered. "I... Thank you."

And then she was gone, just another person in the river of bodies streaming into this forlorn house just past the edge of Raven's Valley.

An eyesore.

A blight.

And now a sanctuary fast-filling with life.

CHAPTER SEVENTY-FOUR

It was an odd sensation, this division inside Zelda's mind. At an instinctual level, she understood she was more than just a thirteen-year-old girl. She was a vessel, a conduit, a link in a chain that stretched back thirty-odd years.

There were no more invisible hands on her shoulder as she stood on this porch, watching the last survivors hurry into the house. But there was her uncle beside her. "We really need to go. We did everything we could."

Yes, she thought. We did.

Flames danced and rose among the smoldering trees. Cinders rained down on the bushes and brambles, igniting little fires at the edge of the dry garden. Daring to come closer, closer...

And yet she knew it would all eventually burn itself out.

"In we go," Uncle Mark said.

Something released deep inside her. She looked at her hands. They no longer bore the shadows of wrinkles. Her voice no longer carried Chester's echo. Relief. Sweet relief.

But it only lasted a moment.

"Mmm, there you are, little girl," whispered that dark feminine

voice. *"I warned you, yes, I did. But you stood in the way. Turn around now and show me your face."*

She didn't think she had any choice. She turned around.

Distantly, she knew Uncle Mark had paused by the door, his mute voice a thousand miles away.

Her eyes traced the black-violet strands rising from the smoke and the ash and the community's suffering. The tendrils thinned and narrowed, mere filaments among the night sky.

And then they withered and frayed altogether.

The howls of the pups filled the air and faded. They would go hungry tonight.

The wind shifted. The smoke parted. For an instant, every cinder hung as time came to a halt.

There, behind the clouds and beyond the cold void of space, a dead star bloomed in bright darkness, pouring cold murmurs into her mind.

"You could have run. Mmm... You could have grown old and cozy, bore many children and died warm in your bed. But you've gone and scratched your name in my eye. Zelda. Zelda Ruiz of my Greywood Bay. I... see... you."

The world fell away beneath her. All the fires and swirling ashes. All the air choked with smoke. She stood at the edge of Chester's porch, yes, but that porch teetered upon the threshold of a great cosmic maelstrom. Gaseous clouds spewed plumes of green fire while red lightning scratched its way across the lifeless vacuum of space.

And there, at the center, her mind could receive only glimpses.

Waves of black violet crashing over an ocean of flesh.

Valleys of dark muscle and gnashing teeth.

Canyons of wormy lips beneath towering mountains of eyes that devoured the very light and warmth of existence itself.

With horror, Zelda looked upon a thing so terrible her mind trembled and went blank. She was simple. Scoured of language and logic.

"You are no conqueror, little girl," the lips spoke. *"Mmm... Your deeds earned no victory tonight, only a delay. And I have all the time in your world. You have won... nothing."*

And yet, from that void of numb thoughts, Zelda found a warm ember of strength.

Her mother, linking arms with her fellow protestors as the police marched in with batons.

Her father, telling his parents it didn't matter what they thought about nail polish; Zelda could wear black if she wanted.

Maura, taking a chance and asking if she wanted to go check out the park.

Ali, encouraging her to climb higher.

And Uncle Mark, putting his life aside to help her build something new.

From that ember of strength, she found her voice faint and quivering, so small in the face of the hungry cosmos that the words almost died in her throat.

Almost.

And she said, "If we haven't won, then why are you retreating?"

The dead star heard her words and shuddered.

J'harr. The Last Refugee. She-Who-Consumes. Chester was right. All those names were abstractions. They did nothing to seed her mind as the eye opened and turned its glare toward her.

The darkness of space fell to a pinprick. Chester's porch rose behind her. She was falling, falling through the infinite cold cosmos and then into the warm arms of her uncle.

Her mind simply shut down as flashes rolled past.

Stairs leading into a basement.

A basement becoming a tunnel.

A tunnel winding its way through excavated earth and brick, through concrete and metal.

"J'harr. The Last Refugee. She-Who-Consumes." Zelda's lips moved and her lungs gave breath to the names. She could only repeat them, like a mantra, while her uncle carried her through the dark depths. “J’harr… The Last Refugee… She-Who-Consumes… J’harr… J’harr… J’harr…”

PART VII
BY THE LIGHT OF DEAD STARS

Yes, tell mother to sell the cutlery and the cattle and to hem your sturdiest dresses for the journey west. Or stay, perhaps, and scratch my name from our tree of ancestry; these conventions are of no further burden to me.

I have found it here, my ascension beyond these sheltered groves and lost coasts, above these valleys rich and teaming. This Light of Lights, forever shining upon my Greywood Bay.

Our Greywood Bay.

Her Greywood Bay.

The Diary of Arthur Cummings

CHAPTER SEVENTY-FIVE

The rumors were right about old Chester Halgrove: he had been digging for years. He wasn't burying bodies or the bones of dead trick-or-treaters. He had carved out a series of tunnels in his basement that wormed their way beneath the scrapyard and connected to a storm outlet at the edge of the dry Eel River.

When the first survivors reached the rusty gate, they found crowbars and hammers, enough tools to break the lock and make their escape. Within thirty minutes, rescue workers made their way back through, stringing lights and helping the elderly, the infirm, and the wounded.

There were so many wounded.

The last to evacuate through the tunnel was a man carrying an unconscious teenage girl, both of whom were treated for smoke inhalation. As the paramedics loaded them into the ambulance and the lights began flashing, the survivors of Raven's Valley lined up and clapped.

The firemen didn't quite understand why, not until someone told them as the ambulance drove off.

The girl, it turned out, was some sort of hero.

Of the 222 homes in Raven's Valley, 174 were burned to the foundation. Another twenty-two suffered partial damage. Twenty-six homes remained untouched by the fire, yet all were declared uninhabitable due to smoke damage that seeped into the walls and beams, stained the glass and blackened the bricks.

After forty-eight hours, the Raven's Valley Inferno death toll stood at fifteen lives forever lost.

Two days later, they revised it down to eleven.

Most called it a tragedy.

Some called it a miracle.

A few even whispered of strange things running through the smoke and the fire. Gaunt shapes of metal embracing the flames. When asked what they meant, most simply shook their head and claimed they couldn't remember. It was foggy and smoggy; it all happened so fast.

It took weeks for a clear picture of the chain of events to emerge. The fire had destroyed most of the evidence, and what forensics and digital reconstruction uncovered often conflicted. The university dispatched experts to analyze how a fire could rage so fast down the hills. Wind patterns and a confluence of drought conditions were blamed. Computer simulations were run.

They reached no agreements.

Eyes turned toward Strathmore & Daniels for the development's location and design: its high walls and exclusive, gated entrances; the narrow streets that had become traps during the inferno. Auditors pored over the spreadsheets, uncovering cut corners, dubious permits, and kickbacks. By mid-week, gavels banged at the city hall and hearings were promised.

IT LEAKED ON A WEDNESDAY NIGHT, AND THE LOCAL paper ran the story in the morning: *Homes Built from Horror? Raven's Valley Materials Sourced from Rubble of State Hospital.*

Families grew furious when they learned their eco-friendly green-certified houses and reclaimed lumber had once formed the walls and windows and ceilings of a psychiatric hospital where tragedy claimed the thirty-nine lives.

The lawyers, however, were elated and their litigation was swift. The words "class action" came up often.

In the end, it was an empty storage locker, a white pickup truck, and a murdered fraternity kid seventy miles east of Greywood Bay that connected it all: the story of Lloyd, a troubled young man in the midst of a mental health crisis who took his anger out on a community that hardly knew who he was. Most people didn't understand it.

So they chose to ignore it.

Like with Grant Larchmont before him, the town was good at forgetting.

And yet, when Zelda saw the face of Lloyd Betancourt on the front page of the newspaper, she felt pity and regret. She remembered that young man from the model store and how the shadows clung to his skin.

She should have said something, she told herself. Maybe that would have made a difference. Maybe.

Or perhaps the sickness was already too deep.

Maggots. Something grew maggots in his heart.

Zelda wasn't sure why she thought that.

Or why it had been spoken in her mother's voice.

CHAPTER SEVENTY-SIX

The custody hearing took place in a small conference room in the east wing of the Santa Clara County Superior Court. Mark winced as he squeezed into the chair, the shoulder brace bulging under his blazer. He'd broken his collarbone in two places on the night of the fire. First on the fence. Then carrying Zelda through the tunnels beneath Chester Halgrove's house.

"Thanks for driving down, Mark," Mr. Hoffman said. "It always helps to show the judge a friendly face in person."

"And remember: keep your answers brief," Ms. Phong added. "No rambling."

Mark nodded, trying to ignore his racing heart.

They stood as Judge Fulghum entered. As always, her face was unreadable and her demeanor brief. She spent a few moments thumbing through the files before her.

"I understand there were a few incidents recently." She peered over her glasses and drilled Mark with a curious gaze.

Jesus, this was it.

"Several incidents, your honor," Ms. Chou said. "The Ruizes wanted to call your attention to—"

"Yes, I've read your brief, Counselor," Judge Fulghum said. "Mr. Fitzsimmons, it's your perspective I'm most curious about. Under your guardianship, Zelda's had quite the summer."

"Your honor, if you're referring to the run-ins with the police," Mr. Hoffman said, "no charges were filed. In fact, Zelda's set to receive a commendation for her bravery—"

Judge Fulghum folded her hands. "Why is everyone talking except the gentleman I've addressed?"

Mr. Hoffman cleared his throat and gave Mark a nervous nod.

"Your honor?" Mark asked. Goodness, his voice was so small.

She tilted her head so her glasses inched down her nose. "Mr. Fitzsimmons, why do you believe you're the best person to care for Zelda?"

He considered it. "I'm not sure that I am."

Ms. Phong closed her eyes and sighed. A smirk tugged on the corners of Ms. Chou's lips.

"I don't know the first thing about raising a kid," he continued. "Let alone a teenager. My dad wasn't around. My mom worked two jobs. My sister and I pretty much raised each other on video games and microwave dinners. I probably shouldn't be trusted with a plant."

The judge curled a bushy eyebrow.

"Four months ago, all I could think about was getting back to Spain. To sleepwalking through my job and pretty much everything else. Maybe getting drunk in the evening. That was my life and all that I wanted. It was easy. But now there's a girl sitting out in the hall, a girl that I love. Yeah, she makes mistakes, and yeah, so do I. We talk about them. We try to learn from them. Sometimes we laugh and sometimes we cry. She's taught me to be a better person, to become involved in her life and not just sleepwalk past it. It's difficult. The truth is, on most days, I have no clue what I'm doing. That scares me. But maybe that's a good thing, right? If you'd told me four months ago that I'd actually look forward to the first parent-teacher conference of high school, I'd have called you crazy. But it's next Tuesday at 2:15 in the afternoon with Mr. Barker. You can damn well believe that I'll be there."

Hands shaking, he reached for his water.

"I'm sorry, your honor, but what was the question?"

He found Zelda's chair empty and no sign of her in the hall. He was about to call her when his phone vibrated and an alert popped up on the screen: *Rare Spawn Detected! Battle Underway.*

It had been a month since he'd played *Critical Mass*, and his character had de-leveled. Some of his items were in need of repair. He launched the game, swiped through the map, and was pleased to see a Cyber Minotaur had spawned outside the courthouse.

It wasn't hard to find Zelda. He just looked for the crowd of young professionals, high schoolers, and a few legal types playing the game on the sly. They all held their phones at eye level. Fingers swiped across screens, firing off rockets and lasers, flinging bladed boomerangs and bolts of plasma.

"I need a heal," said a girl in her twenties with bubblegum hair.

"My armor's getting thrashed," a college kid shouted. "Anyone got a repair bot?"

"I just used my last one," said a guy with a nose ring. "Shit, this fight is taking forever." Nose ring guy glanced at Mark and Zelda. "Sorry about the language."

With her phone held loose, Zelda took in the game's chaos and the odd fellowship forming near the courthouse. "Let me guess: I'm on the next plane to Texas."

"It's your call. Is that what you want?"

"I thought I didn't get to choose."

"No, it doesn't always work that way." He watched with amusement as two more players hurried over, raised their phones, and joined the assault. "But it turns out you wrote a fairly convincing email to the judge. I can read it if you'd like—"

"No no no, please don't." Her cheeks turned scarlet.

"I won't torture you." A beat passed, and he said, "They want us to attend therapy. Sit on a couch and pour our feelings out to a stranger."

"Like, together?"

"Oh, God no. I enjoy torturing you, but that would be cruel."

There was something about the way she nodded that seemed like relief. She had her secrets too, he supposed. And whatever they were, he'd respect them. If she wanted to talk, he was always ready to listen.

The crowd swelled with new players, their phones raised and their screens flickering as they waged an unseen battle against a foe that wasn't giving up.

"So, what do you think, kiddo?" Mark asked. "You want to do this? It's going to be hard. To be honest, I'm not sure I'm good enough. I'll need your help, okay?"

Her eyes sparkled as they met his. He could see a shadow of his sister. And his mother. And Juan Carlos as well. He could see so much else within: softness and strength, certainty and fear.

"You're a good uncle," she said. "I don't want to be with anyone else."

The smile stretched across his face and creased his eyes. The world got a little brighter.

"Aww, look at that: a compliment. Thanks, Zelda." Then he winked and raised his phone. "But I was talking about this rare spawn. Think we can take it?"

She pursed her lips and hid her grin. "Yeah, I think we can."

CHAPTER SEVENTY-SEVEN

On a cool and breezy Thursday, Edward Strathmore IV stepped out of his Jaguar, ducked under the barricade tape, and walked among the ashes of Raven's Valley. After a few hundred paces, he was lost. The street signs had been melted into mounds of dark steel. Blackened sticks stood where trees once lined the sidewalks. And the houses—all those beautiful homes he'd pre-sold—were simply smudged out of existence. A wasteland of charred foundations stretched out for a mile.

He was in a lot of trouble.

Soot crunching underfoot, he tried not to think of the lawyers working late into the night. Or the mountain of subpoenas. Or his country club pals and how they had stopped returning his calls. Or this morning, when someone stuffed a bag of dog shit into his mailbox.

This was it. What his father had feared was now coming to pass: the Strathmore legacy was in full collapse. Like the Larchmonts or the Cummings, or all the other fallen families of Greywood Bay.

And he deserved it, he supposed, as he followed a dark scar

through the ruins of the community park. Whatever punishment came, he would accept it.

But until then, what should he do?

He wasn't sure.

So he roamed the dusty sidewalks and cindered streets. Here was the sunken amphitheater where summer concerts had rung out, now a black hole. There was the skatepark, a concrete bowl of gray dust.

God, what a mess.

But a miracle, too, that so many survived. One he didn't quite understand but was grateful for. Something about a basement or a catacomb. Rumors of those young kids who came to his office. And that crazy old man who owned the junkyard he'd wanted for so long.

An old man who was finally willing to sell his plot of land.

If only Edward's assets hadn't been frozen.

Ash swirled in the wind, a dust devil just for him. He watched it dance westward in the morning sun, moving with grace.

And then the dust devil died at the feet of a curious object. From a distance, he had thought it another charred tree or a lamppost half melted and bent. But no.

It was a sculpture.

Seven feet of fire-scarred metal loomed, melted in mid-step. It retained a vague human shape, left arm outstretched, lumpy fingers pointing. It held something like a rectangle in its drooping right arm.

A shield, he realized. One of that crazy old man's sculptures. Had Edward wandered all the way past the edge of Raven's Valley?

But no, he was mid-valley. Here was the shadow of the children's playground. He could see the remains of the community gardens just south of the duck pond.

And something else.

Another sculpture stood near collapsed fences. A twisted thing with three arms and two faceless heads, it slumped to one side, as if it had come to rest in the shade of the fence.

He spotted a third sculpture too, far off. And then a fourth, melted in the middle of a tarry road. A fifth even further.

Had the inferno somehow scattered them about? It must have. He even heard fire tornados had formed, and the flames moved like water. Someone claimed to have seen the face of the devil in the smoke.

None of it made any damn sense.

He ran a finger along the half-melted sculpture, surprised to find it damp to the touch. And the detail, he'd never quite noticed it before. There were strange symbols scratched into the metal.

And a name.

"Frank Westerfield," he said, and wiped the wet metal.

A ribbon of dust slid from the sculpture's fingers, drawing his eyes to its feet. Then he saw it, a vibrant yellow against the sooty earth. Bending down, he brushed the ash away. A smile creased his face.

Life was emerging at the edge of this metal foot. An emerald wisp and yellow petals stretched for the sun. Carefully, he dug his fingers into the soil and scooped the flower out. Perhaps this was it, what he needed to do. Perhaps he could replant, starting with this seedling right here.

Something moved among the black foundation of a house. Mounds of dirt shifted and slid. He could see the pit forming the basement, the rightward turn of the stairs. A concrete crawlspace, once topped with floorboards and crossbeams, now open like a pillaged grave.

Two hundred and twenty-two homes in Raven's Valley. Two hundred and twenty-two unique configurations. And yet somehow, he knew this very house.

Randall Larson. Diana Betancourt. And that kid of theirs, the one who set this whole mess in motion.

What the hell was his name?

Lloyd, he thought. Yes, Lloyd was his name.

The wind picked up, sending a whorl of ash skittering from the foundation and out toward Edward. For a blink, he swore he saw footprints moving from the crawlspace, up the concrete steps, and across the debris. He swore he saw embers forming under the ash.

Then came a groan of metal behind him. A thunderous crash drove his heart into his throat as a cry left his lips.

The sculpture tilted. Its great metal shield lowered, its shoulders slumped and twisted. Whatever internal structure had kept it erect was collapsing. With a final creak, its left arm fell from a brittle socket and swung downward. Pendulum-like, it swayed in the breeze. The whorl abated and fled east, back to the shadowed ruins and charred basement.

Seedling in hand, Edward decided it was time to get going. He didn't believe in haunted valleys and cursed lumber. He didn't run all the way back to his car.

But he didn't walk either.

CHAPTER SEVENTY-EIGHT

Chester Halgrove celebrated his eighty-first birthday in the Sequoia Room of the Pacific Manor, an assisted living facility on the south side of Greywood Bay. With trembling hands, he slid the knife into the red velvet cake, his favorite flavor. Zelda, he had learned, put in a sneaky call to the care worker and her uncle Mark had the cake custom-made.

Now, Chester savored the cream cheese frosting and the mixture of buttermilk, vanilla, and cocoa. He ignored his aching teeth. It had been a long time since he'd tasted something so rich and delicious.

"Dig in, please." He pointed a fork at the girl's plate. She ate. He enjoyed being around someone so young, so full of energy. He took another bite and closed his eyes for a moment.

He could see it: the dark glare of J'harr marring her like a spotlight of shadows.

It was a pity what would happen.

And yet, he wasn't sure he could have borne it any longer. Thirty-some years he'd held it all back, alone, while the maggots chewed at his mind. Yeah, he knew the town's rumors, and sometimes he fed them.

Because if people feared him, they would stay far away.

Because if they stayed away, they couldn't get hurt.

"It's a nice place." Mark's eyes traced the room and the window with its view of the ocean. "We saw some humpback whales when we were parking."

Chester grunted. Yeah, it was a nice enough place to spend his remaining days. He was tired now, like a battery nearing empty. He could listen to the foghorn at night.

God, when had he gotten so old?

He took another bite, then another. Zelda smiled. It seemed to make her happy that he was eating, and that warmed his heart.

Zelda, poor girl.

It was her burden now, her flame to enkindle and keep bright. He supposed he'd have to teach her some things before the glare scarred her heart and darkened her mind.

As it always would.

He chewed and swallowed, suppressing a cough. He could feel the cancer inside, the roots and nodules dug in deep and still growing. Yeah, they'd have to get started soon with her training.

But first, there was still cake to be eaten.

"Uncle Mark," Zelda said. "Would you grab me a soda from the machine?"

He wiped his mouth. "What do you want?"

"A Diet Coke, please."

Chester could tell she was lying by the spikes in her aura and the curls of smoke from her eyes. Lies always flickered violet.

"Can I get you anything, sir?" Mark asked.

Chester shook his head.

She waited until her uncle was down the hall and out of earshot. "Mr. Halgrove, I had—"

"Chester," he said. "I already told you: call me Chester."

"You did?"

He considered it. After decades of time misbehaving, it was unsettling to have things so linear again. Hours progressed one after the other. Night followed day. "No, you're probably right. I s'pose I didn't tell you... yet." He pointed his fork at her and grinned. "But consider yourself warned."

She took a deep breath and looked down. "I don't really remember everything that happened. It's like I get flashes and... then it's a blank."

"You'll find it," he said. "Or it'll find you. Eventually, it all comes together. The hard part is keeping yourself together."

"Keeping myself together?"

He pointed his fork skyward and whispered, "Surviving."

She swallowed and blinked those bright eyes. Thirteen years old, gods have mercy. He couldn't imagine being under the dark glare at that age. He didn't envy her.

But he didn't envy her enemies, either. There was resiliency within her, a light sometimes too blinding to behold. She'd probably give anyone who crossed her ten kinds of hell.

If she could learn how to focus it, to live with it, and not let it consume her.

"I remember something," she said. "That night, I think you were helping me, weren't you? Like... guiding me."

He forked the last piece of cake into his mouth and savored it. Yes, he was fairly certain this was the last time he'd ever taste such flavors. "We always help each other," he said. "That's how it works out. We're like links in a chain, each of us."

"We?" Her eyes sparkled. "There are others?"

"Some, sure. Sometimes too many. But never enough of the good ones."

"And these symbols." With her fork, she traced a chocolate spiral on the plate. "I can't get them out of my head."

She started to cross it with a triangle and two parallel lines. When he understood what she was composing, he shot out a hand and stopped her. "Careful!"

The sparkle left her eyes and something wounded flickered. He'd been too rough.

"Sorry," he said. "It's just... There're other layers, other realms all around us. Some doors try to open themselves."

She was about to ask him another question, but her uncle returned. He could almost see the words retreating down her throat. Yeah, there were hard roads ahead for her. People wouldn't understand. They wouldn't believe her. And the things she would learn would make them uncomfortable. She might insist or persist, but eventually, they would leave her.

People didn't like to know what lurked beyond the frayed veil.

And how hungry the cosmos truly was.

"One Diet Coke." Mark placed the can on the table. Chester liked him. There was a flicker in him, too. Not as bright as the girl, but a spark nonetheless. Maybe she'd be in good hands, after all. Maybe it wasn't an accident they'd come together.

Yeah, no accident indeed.

Then Mark's aura flickered green. He was hiding something. What was it?

"So, I think it's time," Mark said, looking at Zelda. Something nervous settled over her face.

"Mr. Hal—Chester." Her hands disappeared into her baggy sleeves. "I'm sorry that your house burned down. I'm sorry about everything that happened. But you should know that we're grateful. All of us. And there's something you should see."

She walked over to the window and twisted the blind rod. The bright afternoon light stung his eyes. She gestured beyond and Mark offered him a hand, but Chester wanted to walk on his own.

Or shuffle.

Or whatever it was a man did at eighty-one.

God, when had he gotten so old?

You already thought that, his mind grumbled. *Try to keep track of your time.*

At first, he wasn't sure what he was looking at. The blue sky loomed over the trees and the courtyard and...

People. There were so many people down there he had to blink to bring them into focus.

With a tug, Mark raised the blinds so he could see it all clearly.

There were a hundred people at least. Young men and women, young brothers and sisters. There were old folks too, though not many his age. He recognized a few among the crowd. He'd seen them moving into Raven's Valley over the past six months, trucks packed with furniture and houses growing warm with their dreams.

These were his neighbors.

"They wanted to thank you," Zelda said.

"Of course, the facility would only let two people visit at once," Mark added. "Bureaucracy, right?"

The applause thundered across the courtyard, hundreds of hands clapping and waving and a few voices cheering. Although his vision wasn't good anymore, Chester was certain a few were even holding up signs.

What was this odd feeling that fluttered in his chest? Was he dying?

No. Perhaps this was the opposite. Perhaps this was what it felt like to be alive, to be a part of something once again. It was strange, this happiness now crowding his heart.

Still, there was work to be done.

He didn't like being the focus of so many eyes. And yet he forced himself to scan that crowd again and again, seeing every face, every neighbor they'd saved.

They.

There, at the far-left edge, separate from the residents of Raven's Valley, stood a group that had haunted his years. His breath hitched in his throat and his vision grew misty.

There were thirty-nine of them.

Thirty-nine names that he knew as well as his own.

His fellow patients. His failures and greatest regrets. His

friends. As he named each of them, they gave him a slight nod, then turned and walked off, fading among the bright afternoon haze.

"Michael Andover..." he said. "Gretchen Swann... Jerry Jenkins."

CHAPTER SEVENTY-NINE

On the last Tuesday of August, Zelda grabbed her skateboard and her new backpack, then rushed for the door of their apartment. It was a cozy place, two bedrooms, two bathrooms, and a balcony that looked out on the long stretches of beach. It even had a swimming pool that was open until eight.

The best part was that Ali's family lived a few units over, and Maura's family was two blocks down the street. Zelda didn't understand why they couldn't build new houses quickly. Uncle Mark had tried to explain that it had something to do with mortgages and money, lawyers and lawsuits. It confused her so she tuned it all out.

She did that a lot these days.

"Z to the E-L-D-A. What's that spell?" Ali slid down the banister and stumbled into the apartment's courtyard. "Zebra."

She brushed her hair from her eyes. "Morning, Ali."

He unlocked his bike from the rack and pointed to her Chuck Taylor All-Stars. "So, just FYI, but your shoes are mismatched."

She gave him a flat smile. Yeah, she knew.

"Right, fashion. That's important now that we're in high school. Gotta look peng, right?"

"Peng?"

"That's an adjective for, like, appealing or attractive or fresh. I looked it up last night."

"I bet you did."

"I memorized, like, thirty words for girlfriend. You want to hear them? Datemate. Partner-in-crime. The Big Squeeze. My bub. My bubbalicious. My bubbly booty—"

"Zelda?" Uncle Mark hurried down the stairs with an envelope in hand. "You forgot your permission slip." He tapped the envelope. "You sure you want to do this?"

She nodded.

"Take care of that brain of yours, okay? It's the only one you've got." He gave her a friendly smack on the head with the envelope. She'd been forgetting things as well. Sometimes it felt like time skipped around.

"Hey, sir, that's abuse," Ali said. "I'll have you know that at Neumann Prep, we don't tolerate such yobbishness."

Mark blinked. "Yobbishness?"

Zelda said, "He's been into the dictionary again."

"Thesaurus, technically." Ali snapped his fingers.

"All right, get out of here, you two," Mark said. "Go. Begone. Scram. See you at school. I'll be down the hall if you need anything."

She liked the thought of Uncle Mark on the faculty at Neumann, even if it was only part-time. He wasn't teaching Spanish; that appointment had gone to some serious young man from Texas who insisted his students call him "doctor." Still, Ms. Layne had worked a bit of magic with some grant money and created a new elective for the juniors and seniors: entrepreneurship.

She'd been stopping by a lot lately. It seemed like the fire had brought them closer. And Uncle Mark had joined some sort of group meeting with her on Wednesdays. Afterward, they went out for coffee and ice cream.

Now that she thought of it, he hadn't been drinking in a few weeks.

Ali and Zelda crossed the street, skating and biking toward Maura's executive residence, which looked like a cross between a luxury hotel and an apartment.

Ali asked, "What's the permission slip for?"

Zelda said nothing for a moment. The idea still scared her, but she liked the thought of doing something new. "I'm going to try out for the wrestling team."

"Aww, man. You sure you won't join the drone club? We've got, like, a thousand open spots."

"Yeah, 'cause you're the only one in the club," Maura said, hurrying down the steps to the sidewalk.

She showed them her new backpack and the ultra-lite cast wrapping her arm. Her hospital room jiujitsu had cost her half the football season at least.

"So I'm gonna dump all my knowledge into you," she told Zelda, and sat on the back of Ali's bike. "Seriously, you're going to love wrestling."

Ali grunted as the suspension bottomed out. "Oh man, what'd you have for breakfast, a handful of bricks?"

"Less talk, more peddling."

Thirty minutes later, Maura said goodbye and ducked into her homeroom. Ali and Zelda dodged the hall traffic: the wandering freshman, the quiet sophomores, the juniors and seniors taller and confident. She wondered if she'd ever feel like that. Less awkward in her walk and more comfortable in her skin.

Perhaps.

In the homeroom, she found a seat near the window and Ali took the desk beside her. She waited as the conversations drew to a close in that no-man's-land between first bell and second. Her teacher, Mrs. Hayleman, already had the morning's slides on the smart board and the attendance sheet open. Zelda heard she was a stickler for being on time.

As the second bell rang and attendance began, Zelda's attention drifted to the window. From the third floor, she could just see the dark scars in the hills and the edge of the charred walls being bulldozed.

Sometimes, she had to remind herself Raven's Valley no longer existed.

"Michael Abernathy?" Mrs. Hayleman asked. "There we go. Brianna Alvarez? Hi, Brianna. Lucy Chang?"

Zelda looked closer, where a figure emerged from the ruined walls at the edge of the road. A man of blackened skin and smoldering embers inside sad, hollow eyes. Another man joined him, the smoke wafting from seared nostrils. And then a woman.

And a child by her side.

"Zelda Ruiz?"

And a dog. And a father clutching an infant that silently hiccupped curls of smoke.

"Zelda Ruiz."

Eleven. Eleven dead sets of eyes stared back at her, envious and as black as the far depths of space.

"Zelda Ruiz..."

Her eyes rose to the sky, where the daylight furled and darkness bled through, inky and consuming and eternally hungry. An eye, a single covetous eye, looked back upon her. One eye among thousands that swam among the maddening folds and fissures of that dead star, glaring across the cosmos and now fixated on her.

"Mmm... There you are, Zelda Ruiz. Now, do I have your attention?"

AFTERWORD

It's a curious thing, how stories come together. I've wanted to write a haunting story for awhile. Not just a house but a community. Some place menaced by a Thing Out of Space. I tried my hand at a few different beginnings, always stumbling around and grasping blindly for plot threads and coming out empty handed. I saw the story in fragments but never a cohesive whole. I raged against the abandoned pages as evidence of my incompetence. Us scribes are quite dramatic, aren't we?

And then two things happened almost at once.

First, my wife and I returned to the United States after a decade abroad, bringing with us a deep sense of reverse culture shock and confusion. We felt like strangers in a place we should know. Sometimes we shook hands and sometimes we bowed. We didn't know how to stand in lines the right way. We met old friends, many who were starting families, and many more who had changed. Sometimes, we felt like aliens wearing human skin.

Second, the Tubbs Fire roared through Santa Rosa, California, erasing entire communities, destroying nearly 37,000 acres, and claiming nearly 22 lives. For days the sky turned a sickly amber gray as confused crickets sang out at noon. If you've ever had the dark fortune of seeing a fire sweep over dry hills you'll agree with one thing: it moves like it's living.

The third, and most important thing happened years later, when Zelda rolled into my life. She didn't come from a dream or after hours of character building exercises. She simply skateboarded past me on a warm summer day while I was walking my dog. Her hoodie was baggy, a bit ratty, and her legs a little too long. She teetered between childhood and adolescence with a few scabs on her knees. She didn't even say anything, this girl on the skateboard. She stopped by the park and helped one of her friends up into a tree. There, they sat playing on their phones, back to back, and talking about school and video games and all those things that are so important at thirteen. I don't even remember what that girl looked like because from that moment on I only saw Zelda Ruiz.

And that was it. A group of new teenage friends, a recovering expat struggling with sudden responsibility, a community haunted by its past, and the impending threat of an ancient evil both from outside and within. It all came together.

I couldn't stop writing if I wanted to.

My editor often leaves me brief notes in the Track Changes section of my manuscript. It's how we talk. One of his read: *I can just imagine you wandering through the tampon section, snapping pictures and taking note*s. Yes. Yes I did. Another read: *Your Google search history must be wild*. This was after reading the hand sanitizer firestorm sequence. Indeed, my search history is a place of great darkness. I like to think I'm keeping the FBI cyber monitors employed. Your tax dollars at work.

I'm excited for this series and these characters. It will not be easy for them, but life never is. In many ways, this is my most personal novel yet. Some moments and places have come directly from my life. Yes, there's a stairway in Madrid that I fell in love with. Yes, I was in a fraternity. No, I didn't fall through a frozen lake nor heed the call of an Eldritch abomination.

But there was that one time I found that book made of skin...

Thanks as always to my editor Bodie for wrangling my errant commas and continuing to help me refine my prose. Someday I'll remember the difference between lay and lie. Thanks to the design team at Damonza who did a wonderful job on this cover. It's truly a stunner.

The following people have offered great help, advice, suggestions, or simply listened to me vomit out ideas and nodded along. Taddy and Will Pepper. Tom & Sarah Rey. Mike Keane offered some great writerly advice at a time I needed it most. My discord writing group, Author Focus, always keeps me in line. Thank you, all of you.

And thanks to my Beta Readers and my wonderful Street Team who share my words with the world. I'm the worst marketeer imaginable and they truly help out. Y'all rock!

My wife often catches me staring off blankly, like a shell-shocked vet after two tours of duty. She's learned that look means one thing: I'm working. Thanks honey, for knowing when to rescue me from my daydreams, and when to let me stare off into the Nether.

And thank you, dear reader, for making it this far. This isn't the end of Mark and Zelda's journey.

It's not even the end of the beginning.

ABOUT THE AUTHOR

A child of the eighties, Andrew Van Wey was born in Palo Alto, California, came of age in New England, and lived as an expatriate abroad for nearly a decade. He currently resides in Northern California with his wife and their Old English Sheepdog, Daeny.

When he's not writing Andrew can probably be found mountain biking, hunting for rare fountain pens, or geeking out about D&D and new technology.

For special offers, new releases, and a free starter book, please visit andrewvanwey.com

instagram.com/heydrew
facebook.com/andrewvanwey
goodreads.com/andrewvanwey
bookbub.com/authors/andrew-van-wey
amazon.com/author/andrewvanwey

ALSO BY ANDREW VAN WEY

Novels

Forsaken: A Novel of Art, Evil, and Insanity

Head Like a Hole: A Novel of Horror

Beyond The Lost Coast

By the Light of Dead Stars

Tides of Darkness

The Clearwater Conspiracies

Blind Site

Refraction

The Last Shadow

Collections

Grim Horizons: Tales of Dark Fiction

Made in the USA
Middletown, DE
25 May 2024

54846947R00253